# CHASING ZERO

## (AN AGENT ZERO SPY THRILLER—BOOK 9)

## JACK MARS

## Jack Mars

Jack Mars is the USA Today bestselling author of the LUKE STONE thriller series, which includes seven books. He is also the author of the new FORGING OF LUKE STONE prequel series, comprising six books; and of the AGENT ZERO spy thriller series, comprising ten books (and counting).

Jack loves to hear from you, so please feel free to visit www.Jackmarsauthor.com to join the email list, receive a free book, receive free giveaways, connect on Facebook and Twitter, and stay in touch!

# Agent Zero - Book 8 Recap

*Immediately following the first test of a high-tech and top-secret railgun, the weapon is stolen by unknown aggressors intent on using it for destructive means. In a mad race against time, Agent Zero must use all of his skills to track down an indefensible weapon and figure out the intended targets before it's too late. Yet at the same time, Zero learns of a shocking development that could help with his failing mental condition—if he is not first sidelined for good.*

Agent Zero: Lapses in his memory continue to plague him in new ways, including putting others' lives at risk in the line of duty. Despite his condition, Zero agreed to become part of a new division in the CIA, along with his teammates and at the behest of the president, that will work autonomously and answer only to the Oval Office. He has still not told those close to him about his failing deteriorating memory, though he asked for his daughters' blessing to propose to Maria.

Maria Johansson: Having spent months secretly visiting Mischa, the twelve-year-old girl who had been a part of the ultrasonic weapon plot and is being kept in a sublevel holding cell by the CIA, Maria confronted her superiors and demanded the release of the girl into her care.

Maya Lawson: After striking out on her own and finding a former CIA agent who had a prototype memory suppressor implanted in his head, Maya now suspects that her father was also a victim of a wiped memory, though she doesn't know the extent or even if it's true. As a result of being caught with classified information, Maya was ordered to return to West Point to complete her education, suggesting she's being groomed for something bigger than she knows.

Sara Lawson: Having successfully confronted her own demon of addiction, Sara helped her friend Camilla by defending her against an abusive drug dealer and checking her friend into rehab. Sara then decided to join a support group for abused women, though the ordeal has planted a new idea in her head—that she is capable of doing more than just supporting.

President Jonathan Rutledge: After a successful treaty with the Ayatollah of Iran and the king of Saudi Arabia backing down from threats, Rutledge has nearly accomplished his goal of securing peace in the Middle East. He plans to establish a small new division of the CIA, an ultra-clandestine arm headed by Agent Zero and his team.

John Watson/Oliver Brown: Former Agent John Watson, real name Oliver Brown and the murderer of the late Kate Lawson, was revealed to be working as a CIA assassin when he killed the sheikh responsible for the railgun's theft.

# PROLOGUE

"This," said the Israeli man, who called himself Uri Dahan. He smacked his lips as he scooped another spoonful of the dish before him. "I quite like this." He spoke Arabic for the sake of his dining companion, a language that he was fluent in but not native to, Hebrew being the tongue of his ancestors. "What is it called?"

Palestinian President Ashraf Dawoud smiled. "*Maqluba.* It is a West Bank favorite." And a personal favorite of his as well, one that his own mother had made frequently in his childhood.

Uri frowned. "Upside-down?" he asked, translating the dish's name literally.

"Mm." President Dawoud nodded. "Fried tomatoes, potatoes, eggplant, and cauliflower, layered carefully with minced lamb and then flipped upside-down when served. Hence—*maqluba.*"

"I see." Uri Dahan, the diplomat from Israel, sent on behalf of the prime minister, raised an eyebrow slightly. "Kosher?"

"…Halal."

"Close enough." Uri smiled jovially. He had insisted upon being called such, and not Mr. Dahan or any such formality. "You know, almost half of Israeli Jews do not observe *kashrut*. Something of an antiquated notion, is it not? Much like, say, religious ideology getting in the way of peace between nations."

"Indeed," Dawoud agreed. The restaurant was quiet but for their two voices. It was a small place, only eight tables and currently only one occupied. By no means upscale, which made it the perfect place for such a meeting. The food was simple but authentic and delicious. Ashraf Dawoud had enjoyed this establishment frequently in his younger days, before his political rise through parliament, long before he became the president of Palestine. They were three blocks from the Mövenpick Hotel in Ramallah, center of the Palestinian National Authority, and approximately ten kilometers north of the holy city of Jerusalem.

Dawoud had paid the owner handsomely to close for the evening so that this meeting could take place. A phone call may have sufficed but

1

the prime minister had insisted on a face-to-face; not with himself, of course, not yet, but with Uri Dahan, a mustached member of the *Knesset*, Israel's legislative body. Uri had an auspicious outlook from the start—quite the opposite of what Dawoud had expected, which, if he was being honest, was more of a suspicious outlook.

But now Uri's joviality faded into solemnity as he stared at the remnants of the *maqluba* before him. "I am confident I speak for the prime minister when I say that we have all long waited for this day." He looked up at Dawoud. "But we must understand there will be resistance. This sort of change is… difficult, for some."

Dawoud nodded. "And impossible for others." There already was resistance, particularly in Gaza—but when was there not? The more rumors of approaching peace between Israel and Palestine ran rampant, the greater the efforts of dissenters became.

"But… I understand you have some help." Uri's smile returned.

"You may speak plainly," Dawoud assured him. "Everyone present has been fully vetted." Besides the two heads of state, there were only six others in the restaurant: two Muslim guards that Dawoud trusted with his life and more, thick-necked members of the Presidential Guard with perpetual scowls who clung to the wall not five yards from the table; two Israeli guards posted near the door, one of which, curiously, was a woman with short black hair and a seemingly discerning eye that occasionally drifted the president's way; the cook, who had not once been seen but had prepared the sumptuous meal; and their waiter, a young man with large ears who could not be a day over twenty-five, and who also happened to be a trained member of the Palestinian Interior Security. Just as a precaution. Dawoud had been accused of many things in his day; the truest one was sincerity, with paranoia a close runner-up.

"The American president," Uri said, pausing to wipe the corner of his mouth. "What do you make of him? You believe his efforts genuine?"

Dawoud stroked his chin. "I do." President Jonathan Rutledge was not a man that anyone would have assumed to become a legend of the office at the start of his tumultuous term. The former Speaker of the House, Rutledge had found himself propelled to the presidency by way of scandal and impeachment of his predecessors. Yet he had formed a plan and, so far, had seen it through—to foster peace not only between the United States and the Middle East, but between all Middle Eastern

2

nations. The young King Basheer of Saudi Arabia had, not three weeks ago, signed Rutledge's accord, as had the Ayatollah of Iran, undoubtedly the feather in the US president's cap—until now.

Rutledge and Dawoud had spoken multiple times, at length, in the past few months. Dawoud had even begun to look at the American statesman as a friend.

When Rutledge put forth the idea of brokering a peace deal between Palestine and Israel, it had seemed laughable. Overly optimistic. A reach exceeding a grasp. But now, with a member of the *Knesset* and proxy to the Israeli PM dining across from him, Dawoud could see what Rutledge had already seen, those months ago when he first proposed the treaty: that it was not only possible, but necessarily inevitable.

"Gaza?" Uri asked, an eyebrow arching precipitously.

He did not need to elaborate. Dawoud knew he was referring to the dissenting cells in the Strip, pockets of fanatical factions who would under no circumstances accept the peace and would fight at every opportunity, would kill others and themselves for an ideology that transcended any politics or even reason beyond their beliefs.

"As your intelligence suggests... I have help." Dawoud straightened his tie and opted for candor. "A small unit, but very elite. On loan from the American CIA."

At this the female Israeli posted at the door glanced over again, for only a moment, her dark eyes searching for something that Dawoud could not determine. But in a flash she stared forward once more.

Uri nodded, seemingly satisfied. "This has been a most productive meeting, President Dawoud. I believe our business is concluded. If there's nothing else...?"

"Nothing else, no." Dawoud stood as Uri did, both men buttoning the topmost button of their suit jacket before clasping hands across the round table. "Thank you for coming, Uri Dahan, and please tell the prime minister that I eagerly await his call."

"I shall. I have no doubt it will be a most favorable conversation." Uri flashed his pleasant smile once more. "And please—give my compliments to the chef. Good night, Mr. President." Uri and his pair of guards pushed out the door and into the night.

Dawoud's heart swelled. How strange, he thought, an integral step of making history occurring in a hole-in-the-wall over a childhood dish. He was certain that this meeting had been a test, one issued by Prime

Minister Nitzani to closely inspect the validity of Dawoud's intentions. And if he was right, he was sure he'd passed. Uri had been charmingly disarming, yet Dawoud could not help but notice the furtive glances from the female Israeli.

*Mossad, no doubt*, Dawoud guessed. He wondered if she was the one actually conducting the test. Either way, he was not concerned with his success; he had been genuine.

Ashraf Dawoud's heart may have swelled, but his bladder protested. It was only a fifteen-minute drive from here to his home, quicker if he demanded it, but an unnecessary delay when there were perfectly adequate facilities here.

"One moment," he told his guards as he headed toward the restroom in the rear.

One of them, a turbaned man called Marwan, stepped forward to accompany him, but Dawoud stopped him with a chuckle and a gently raised hand. "I think I can handle this fine on my own, my friend."

Marwan nodded once and retreated to his position against the wall. Dawoud would not admit it, not openly, but lately his prostate had been less than kind to him, and attempting to urinate in proximity to others left him red in the face.

He pushed open the door to the restroom, took two steps inside, and halted suddenly at the sight of a gray-uniformed man mopping a toilet stall. Dawoud blinked at him—there was not supposed to be anyone else in the restaurant this evening, even if he was only cleaning the toilets—and the man blinked back at him, likely because he had not expected the president of his country to come barging into the men's room.

"I... I'm sorry, sir," the man stammered, staring at the floor. He was thin, his head shaved, with an unruly black beard. "They said I should stay out of sight, I didn't think you would... I mean..."

"It's fine," Dawoud assured him. "You're just doing your job."

"I'll go, sir, I'll go." The janitor stuffed his mop into a bucket affixed to his cleaning trolley, a wheeled cart laden with cleaning supplies, a trash bin, and other custodial paraphernalia.

"Sir, please." Dawoud stepped forward and put a hand on the frantic man's shoulder. "Think nothing of it. Go about your duty."

"Y-yes. Thank you. Sir. I shall." The janitor hesitated once more, but retrieved his mop from the trolley and turned his attention back to the stall.

4

Dawoud went to the sink and splashed cool water on his face. He was only fifty-three, yet the creases around his eyes had deepened lately. His beard had been flecked with gray for years and now threatened to go entirely white. The bald spot on his pate had, in the span of only one year, gone from the size of a five-*agorot* coin to that of a plum.

He had never been a drinker—he was a faithful Muslim in at least that regard—but he couldn't help but wonder why he had given up smoking when politics took so many more years off his life.

Dawoud dried his hands and headed to the second stall, the only one not occupied by a janitor and his mop. He pushed the door open and froze instantly.

It was, for a moment, as if Dawoud's brain had short-circuited. His first and only thought in the moment was to wonder why there was a full-length mirror in a toilet stall, because staring back at him was... himself. The precise same height. The same gray-white beard. The same creases around the eyes. The same gray jacket over a white shirt and blue tie.

Except that the mirror image of him did not hold the same perplexed, bemused expression he knew to be on his own face. His image smirked back at him.

Like a computer rebooting, Dawoud's brain registered what this was. His surprise was replaced by a blend of curiosity and a small amount of anger.

"You," he said. "What are you doing h—"

He felt a hand on the back of his head. Another grasped his chin. Someone, behind him. But before Dawoud could turn, the hands jerked smoothly in opposite directions.

There was no pain, oddly, but there was the startling sensation of soft bones giving way and popping. Dawoud was looking backward now, sparks dancing in his failing vision as he now looked backward at the janitor's dark, cruel eyes, for Dawoud's head had turned completely but his body had not.

Then he was falling—collapsing. His muscles gave way; there was no feeling in his limbs. There was no sensation of hitting the ground. Only falling. Falling forever into darkness.

*

5

"Quickly now, grab his shoulders," the Double demanded as he bent and lifted Dawoud's legs. "Those idiot guards know he takes forever to piss, but they won't wait much longer."

The assassin, wearing the gray uniform of a janitor, was thin-framed but stronger than he looked. He hoisted Dawoud's top half and together they unceremoniously deposited the body of the Palestinian president into the trash bin of the custodial trolley, his eyes still wide in shock and head twisted around unnaturally.

The assassin folded in limbs, dumped the restroom trash atop the body, and then cinched the black garbage bag tightly. The Double checked himself in the mirror, adjusting the blue tie. Smoothing the jacket.

He couldn't believe that this had been the easy part.

The hard part had been the planning. Finding out where the meeting was going to take place. Discovering what the president was wearing and quickly procuring the necessary wardrobe. Planting the assassin as the janitor after the restaurant had closed. And, of course, stealing the president's medical report, the one that determined he would most definitely be visiting the bathroom before leaving.

The Double stared at himself for a long moment in the mirror. "Himself"—that concept was laughable. He no longer knew what he looked like. What he would have looked like, had he not taken on the role. Had he not had his hair and beard carefully colored. Had he not had the top of his head waxed to match the growing bald spot. New creases around his eyes surgically folded. Thousands of hours listening to tapes, to speeches and laughs and inflection and repeating it, over and over, until he was the perfect Double for a paranoid Middle Eastern president.

"I am President Ashraf Dawoud," he told his image.

Suddenly the door to the bathroom swung open, and a thick-necked guard took a large step inside, blocking the doorway with his bulk. The guard scowled deeply at the janitor and made a reach for the lump beneath his jacket.

"Marwan," the Double said, easing into a relaxed smile. "All is fine. Come now, let the man do his job. Let's go."

Marwan hesitated, but nodded tightly. "Yes sir." The guard led the way out of the bathroom, across the restaurant floor, and out to the car.

Not even Dawoud's closest Presidential Guard, up close, could tell. Not even Dawoud's wife would be able to tell. The Double had years

6

of experience being someone else, and that someone was a president who was so paranoid of attack on foreign soil that he was blind to the threat directly in front of him, trusting his life to a man he should not have.

The janitor would dispose of the body and make sure no one ever found it. And in the meantime, the Double would work toward their end.

*I am President Ashraf Dawoud. And Israel will know peace only in death.*

# CHAPTER ONE

"You know," Maria whispered, her lips nearly brushing Zero's ear, "this isn't exactly what I meant when I said I hoped we'd get closer."

Agent Zero would have laughed had he not been as equally troubled by the cramping in his limbs as he was the knowledge that this was not the first time he'd crammed himself into a small crate for the sake of an op.

*Might not be the last, either.*

Still, the company could have been worse. Hell, being stuck in a crate with Maria Johansson practically constituted a vacation these days. He could barely see, couldn't make out the details of her blonde hair, pulled back into a practical ponytail for the sake of their goal, or her slate gray eyes, or the lips that he kissed each night before bed and again before each op in lieu of saying a potential goodbye.

"I think it's rather cozy," he whispered back, slowly and painfully extricating an arm from behind Maria's back.

"I do not get paid enough to be privy to your pillow talk," came Penny's Camford-tinged accent in his earpiece. Dr. Penelope León was the twenty-seven-year-old wunderkind covert engineer of the CIA's Special Operations Group who had succeeded Zero's friend Bixby. She was currently six thousand seven hundred and eight miles away from their current position—but with them in more than just spirit.

"Where are you, Penny?" Zero asked.

"Me? I am currently in a La-Z-Boy I recently had installed in the lab. Suede, if you're wondering. I'm wearing a VR headset and there's a cup of Earl Grey at my left elbow—"

Zero scoffed. "No, Penny, where are you *here*?"

"Ah. Right. Drone is about an eighth of a mile northeast. I tell you, the optics on this are incredible. I can see the driver's eyes through the windshield."

"Terrific. Now tell us where *we* are?"

"You're coming up on the compound in about a half a mile."

Zero sighed. *Another compound, another day.*

Not three weeks earlier, President Jonathan Rutledge had created the Executive Operations Team, a subdivision of Special Operations Group in the CIA that consisted solely of Zero and his four-member team. It had seemed like a win-win at the time; Director Shaw didn't want to deal with them, and Rutledge did. The idea was that this team would work in absolute secrecy (nothing new to them) and answer only to the president or, in his absence, the Director of National Intelligence.

It had seemed like a great idea. None of them had expected to become the president's glorified errand runners.

"Glorified" might have even been overstating things; no one would ever know what they'd done. But in the interest of Rutledge's quest for peace in the Middle East, they had successfully dismantled two terrorist cells in the Gaza Strip so far, and today would make three.

*It's always a compound.* Each of these factions seemed to favor an isolated location, a collection of squat, nondescript, flat-roofed buildings surrounded by walls or sandbag-bolstered fencing topped with barbed wire.

*They might as well hang a sign. "Beware of Insurgents."*

The plan was simple enough. Alan Reidigger's extensive network of underground and underworld contacts had gifted them a munitions dealer that sold explosives to this particular Hamas-affiliated group. The deal of a wiped record yielded two crates in his most recent delivery that held a total of four CIA operatives. Zero and Maria were in one. In the other, the young agent and former Army Ranger Todd Strickland cozied up with their newest addition to the team, the Texan pilot Chip Foxworth. It was late at night, almost late enough to be considered early morning, and the hope was that the insurgents would drive their canvas-covered cargo truck into the compound and leave the crates until daybreak. At which point the agents would extricate themselves by way of a secret interior latch, locate the leader, and cut the head off the snake.

Penny would provide their eyes in the air via drone, scoping the layout and communicating any movement or vital intel. Reidigger was their wheel man, currently three miles due south in a Jeep waiting for the signal when they were ready to bug out.

Easy.

It was not at all lost on Zero that the desired effect could be obtained even easier with a drone strike, but the nature of this op was highly covert; no one below the DNI, not even the Secretary of

9

Defense, Colin Kressley, knew they were here. In fact, earlier that night a man bearing Reid Lawson's passport crossed the border to Canada to visit a friend. A woman named Maria Johansson had been pulled over for speeding. If Agents Zero or Marigold died on this op, it would be chalked up to an unfortunate accident and their ashes would be remitted to next-of-kin—in Zero's case, his teenage daughters, Maya and Sara, and in Maria's case, her father, Director of National Intelligence David Barren.

Zero did not want to know whose ashes they would actually be.

The rear wheel of the truck hit a rut and Zero bounced, grunting as his shoulder bumped roughly against the side of the crate. He was no stranger to pain, dull and insistent or sharp and fresh, but wondered how much longer he could keep doing this. He was in good shape for forty, healthy and strong—if no one was counting his deteriorating brain that would systematically destroy his memories before it eventually killed him...

"Rolling through the gates now," Penny told them through the wireless earpieces. Sure enough, the truck slowed. Zero could hear voices shouting in Arabic, but despite his being fluent the rumbling truck engine drowned out the words.

Zero reached for his hip, feeling for the familiar and comforting shape of the Glock 19 holstered there. Across his chest affixed to a nylon strap was a Heckler & Koch MP5, a 9x19mm Parabellum submachine gun outfitted with an eight-inch suppressor and a forty-round magazine.

His other hand fumbled in the darkness of the crate, feeling a shoulder, then an elbow, and sliding down until he could give Maria's tactical-gloved hand a squeeze. She squeezed back. Somehow, being in this tiny space with her, the scent of her hair filling his nostrils, warded off the usual pre-op butterflies. Maria's presence was more than reassuring; it was reinforcing. Despite the struggles in their tumultuous relationship—her going from a fellow agent, to being nothing when his memories of her were erased, to a cautious colleague again, to a lover, a girlfriend, a boss, an agent once more, his team leader, and then to a live-in girlfriend—there was no one he'd prefer to have by his side.

The truck engine's rumbling ceased and the voices became clearer, still muffled beyond the walls of the crate but clear enough for Zero to make out several distinct ones.

"Unload quickly!" commanded a sharp voice in Arabic. "Check the contents and stow them. Hassad has reason to believe we may be under satellite surveillance."

*Check the contents?* Zero felt a knot of uncertainty in his gut.

"Penny?" Maria whispered into the earpiece.

"I heard it too," said the engineer briskly. "Looks like they're going to unload and open them right now. So much for the plan... Looks like you may have to improvise. I've got eyes on seven hostiles on the ground, plus one more still in the truck. Let me get closer and see what else I can see."

"Strickland? Foxworth? Come in." Zero pressed a finger to his ear as if that would help the signal. "What's going on? Are they on another channel?"

"Might be interference from the electronics in these crates," Penny admitted. "I can't be sure—"

Zero lurched suddenly as the crate shifted, accompanied by the grunting of at least three men directly outside it. He braced himself against the crate walls with a forearm while Maria braced against him. Then there was a sudden acceleration. The crate quaked and clattered its way down a ramp of metal rollers. Zero gritted his teeth and held on—

And then the crate hit the bottom of the ramp, tipping precariously, and fell onto its side.

"Idiots!" cried a furious voice outside the crate. "Be more careful! Do you have any idea what is inside those? You could kill us all!"

Zero was on his back now, and Maria was on top of him. The latched side of the crate that should have been above them was now the side closest to their heads.

"Well, open it!" shouted the angry Arab voice. "We must make sure nothing is damaged."

"Shit." Maria grabbed her own MP5 and cocked it. Zero couldn't reach his; it was pinned between his body and hers. "We're going to have to make a move here..."

A sliver of light appeared overhead as the tip of a crowbar worked its way into the lip of the crate.

"I see seven total," Penny told them, her voice tight. "Release the latch and roll out facing due north. There'll be two on your twelve, two more at three and four, and—"

"I don't know where due north is right now!" Maria hissed. "Are they armed?"

The crowbar wrenched and wood groaned as a corner began to lift.

"Armed, yes," Penny confirmed. "But their guard is down. Go now!"

"You're going to have to go first," Zero whispered. "I'll be right behind you…"

The crowbar wrenched again. Bright light suddenly flooded the crate, practically blinding Zero as the top lifted away. *Floodlights*, he realized.

A face peered down. Shock registered.

At the same time, Maria reached for the interior latch and flipped it, shoving the side of the crate open like a door. She tucked into a roll and pushed out, coming up on one knee and bringing the MP5 to her shoulder.

Zero raised his own SMG and fired a three-shot burst.

Even with the suppressor, the gunshots easily drowned out the frantic shouts of the insurgents as their shocked comrade's head snapped back, bloody mist spraying in its wake.

Zero stood. The MP5 was tight against his shoulder as if it had always been there.

*Pop-pop-pop.*

Two shots to the chest and one to the head downed another man. Three yards to the right, one grabbed for an AK-47 dangling near his waist. Another short burst from Zero tore the man down before the assault rifle was in both hands.

He tracked to the right, his barrel swinging over Maria's head as she took out two more with expert precision. It might have been three; he merely saw falling bodies in his periphery.

A man dressed in beige was running, his back to Zero. Two shots later he tripped on his own feet, skidding face-first to a stop in the dirt.

And then there were none. The only sound besides Zero's own breathing was the buzz of four powerful floodlights, set up on poles around the truck. The silence reigned for several long seconds before Maria said, "Clear." An eerie silence, because even suppressed shots were loud enough to wake the dead in the otherwise quiet desert at night, and Zero did not for a moment believe that there were only eight men in this compound.

"If there are others," Maria said, as if reading his thoughts, "they're rousing and arming. We need to move quickly."

"I've got several heat signatures in the building to the northeast," said Penny in their ears. "Moving quickly. Eight or nine, possibly more—the stone walls could be blocking my view."

"Where the hell are Chip and Todd?" Maria asked suddenly.

Zero felt a blend of panic and shame. Shame, because he'd been so caught up in the mini-firefight that he hadn't even thought about them since the shooting started. And panic, because they hadn't sprung out to help. Radio issues were one thing, but this…

"Cover me." He sprang up into the bed of the canvas-covered truck. "Strickland? Foxworth?" He knocked frantically on each of the seven crates in the truck's rear, slapping the sides, hoping for a sign of life.

*Knock-knock.* It came from nearby. Zero dropped to his knees and knocked again.

*Knock-knock.* A muffled voice from within.

Of course—they couldn't get free because another crate was stacked on top of theirs. Zero groaned; one thing they hadn't planned for was these insurgents being negligent enough to stack volatile explosives in the bed of a rusty truck on rutted desert lanes.

"Hang on, guys." He let the MP5 hang as he pressed both palms against the top crate and pushed. It budged barely an inch. "Maria!" The crate was bottom-heavy and weighed a few hundred pounds, easily.

"Busy!" she called back. She'd taken a kneeled position at the rear of the truck, aiming into the darkness beyond the floodlights as shouts floated to them. A muzzle flashed; Maria fired at it with pinpoint accuracy. A man yelped. She aimed upward and took out two of the floodlights to make their position less obvious.

Zero put his shoulder into it and heaved, teeth gritted, but the crate wouldn't move.

*Leverage. I need some leverage,* he thought. *No… I need inertia.*

A burst of automatic gunfire tore from somewhere in the darkness. Wooden splinters stung his face as a bullet struck the crate nearest to him. These men had no qualms about firing at a truck laden with explosives.

Zero leapt out of the truck. At the same moment Maria fired upward again, taking out the other two floodlights and plunging them into

13

murky blue darkness. He fumbled for the driver's side door and wrenched it open.

The keys were still in the ignition. *Finally, some luck.*

The engine roared to life and Zero slammed down on the accelerator. He lurched back in his seat, surprised at the power this old bucket had. He accelerated rapidly, heading straight for the nearest squat, sand-colored building without letting up on the gas. In the rearview, he caught a glimpse of Maria; she had leapt up onto the bed, gripping a canvas strap with one hand to keep from falling out while laying cover fire.

But their position was obvious, and the truck was a big target.

"Here goes nothing." Zero held his breath and yanked the wheel hard to the right, turning as tightly as he could. The back of the truck swung wildly. Tires kicked up a sandstorm of dust and gravel as rubber and steel groaned in protest. He felt the truck tilt slightly, the passenger-side wheels coming off the ground...

Behind him, the crate shifted with the sudden change in motion. It slid, teetered precariously for a moment, and then tumbled off the lower crate.

Zero winced as it fell. *Please don't explode.*

The crate clattered heavily to the bed of the truck, and he breathed a sigh of relief as he pounded the accelerator again. The truck ran parallel to the building now, passing it by. Zero made another turn, doubling back as more gunfire split the air. The passenger-side window exploded.

He reached for a knob at the side of the steering wheel and flicked on the lights. A half a dozen men shielded their eyes against the sudden brightness, caught in the path of the high beams.

Most had the sense to leap out of the way. Zero felt at least one caught under the massive tires. Maybe two; it was hard to tell.

He cut the lights and hit the brakes, slowing the truck but not stopping. He let the nearest building do that for him, the front end of the truck colliding with a one-story flat-roofed structure and taking out a significant portion of the wall. The engine sputtered and died before he could turn it off.

Zero ducked instinctively and covered his head as gunfire split the air directly behind him. But they weren't shooting at him. He hazarded a glance back to see the crate open, Chip Foxworth and Todd

Strickland in standing positions, firing on the still-standing assailants, their shots going right over the head of Maria's kneeling form.

And then, silence again.

Zero climbed out of the truck, his left knee aching in protest. Sore, cramped, aching—these were normal states of being for him. It was when he didn't feel those things that he'd start to worry.

"Nice driving, McQueen," said Penny's voice in his ear.

"Clear," Maria announced, though she didn't lower her gun yet. "Penny?"

"I'm showing two heat signatures in the two-story structure to your nine," she told them. "That's all I'm seeing. Must be him and someone guarding him."

Hassad. The leader of this faction. He was the reason they were here. The other—what was it, seventeen?—they'd taken out were lackeys. Men who would give their lives for Hassad's cause. Unless there was no Hassad and no cause. But now Hassad had only one.

But one was enough. One would still do whatever he could to protect him.

Chip Foxworth climbed out of the crate first, grinning from ear to ear. "Well," he said in his Texan drawl, "that went about as tits-up as it could have, huh?"

Foxworth was a former pilot who had proven his mettle by disobeying Director Shaw's direct orders and helping Zero and his team get to Addis Ababa last month, and then had refused to speak to authorities and gotten himself arrested on their behalf. After Foxworth's pardon, Zero recruited him for the Executive Operations Team and hadn't yet regretted it. Foxworth was Zero's age, but somehow made him feel old. The pilot was light on his feet, sprightly even; operations like these seemed to fill him with youthful exuberance.

"Radios conked out," Strickland announced as he hopped down from the back of the truck. "As you probably guessed." Todd was the youngest of their team by far, only thirty-one, a former Army Ranger who had once been tasked with hunting Zero—and did. It only made sense to make an ally of him.

"Maria," Zero said. "Call it."

"Todd, Chip, clear the building." She gestured toward the nearest structure, the one Zero had unceremoniously crashed into. "Move clockwise. Zero, you're with me. Let's finish it."

15

They parted wordlessly, staying low and moving quickly across the dirt to the two-story structure ahead. There was a light on in the upper level.

Only two left. One was the target. *What's the worst that could happen?*

# CHAPTER TWO

"Penny?" Zero asked quietly as he and Maria took positions outside the wooden door.

"Second level. Neither is moving."

Zero felt uneasy. He didn't care for standoffs, despite how many he'd been a part of. It usually meant that the other party had, or at least thought they had, an upper hand by letting them come. But there wasn't much choice in the matter now.

He reared back and kicked the door, just above the handle, and it flew open. Maria was inside in an instant, tracking her barrel left and then right before nodding him in.

It was dark in there, darker than outside without the moonlight. Zero clicked on a flashlight and briefly swept the room before turning it off again. This place was storage, it seemed. Weapons, food, and...

"Medical supplies?" Maria asked.

"Mm-hmm. Let's head up. I'll lead." His mouth felt dry. The first stair creaked under his weight and a bead of sweat formed on his brow. There were the familiar butterflies, that near-nauseating blend of nervousness, fear, and adrenaline. No matter how many times he did something like this, they were always there eventually, fueled by the realization that at any moment gunfire could erupt from some unseen position and end him in a heartbeat.

But he reached the top of the stairs and there was none. Nothing. Silence.

A corridor emptied in a doorway at the far end, the door only slightly ajar, light from a single bulb spilling out.

Zero cleared his throat. "Hassad. We know you're in there," he called out in Arabic. "We know there is one other. Put down your weapons. Come to where we can see you. Put your hands in the air."

The only response was a dry, rattling cough from the lit room. Zero threw a confused glance over his shoulder. Maria shrugged slightly and motioned for him to proceed.

Of course they weren't going to just come out. They never just came out.

Zero stepped slowly, heel to toe, heel to toe, keeping the barrel of his MP5 perfectly perpendicular to his body, tracking at approximate center mass of a six-foot man. Head shots were more effective, of course, but a smaller target, especially if that target was moving.

He reached the door and put one shoulder against it. He could see nothing in the few-inch span that was open except for the foot of a bed.

Behind him, Maria knelt with the gun aloft, and nodded.

Zero took a breath. He shouldered the door open and swept the barrel from right to left.

He blinked. In his sights was a man, no more than forty, but facing partially away from Zero. There was no gun in his hands; instead, he held the hand of the much older man who lay in the bed at the far end of the room. It looked like a hospital bed; there were wheels on its frame and adjustable steel bars at its sides.

The old man sat upright, his beard white and his head entirely bald. The medical supplies they had seen downstairs suddenly made sense. Zero recognized the equipment at the bedside.

*Chemotherapy.* Hassad was already dying, it seemed.

"Hands up," Maria ordered. "Turn around slowly."

The younger man released his grip on Hassad's hand and turned slowly, raising his arms as he did.

*Shit.*

"I will not let you kill my father," the man told them quietly.

The man's shirt was open. Beneath it was a vest layered with C4. In his left hand was a small black rectangular device. The detonator.

Hassad erupted into another chest-rattling cough.

"Maria," Zero said in a whisper. "Back up. Get clear."

"Absolutely not," she replied tightly.

She was stubborn. It was one of the things he liked most about her. "Fine. Chest."

"Arm."

"Wait for it," he told her.

"Are you him?" Hassad's son asked, staring curiously at Zero. "My father knew you would come. We thought he was paranoid. He was right. But... you do not look like him. I was told he is a ghost."

"Sorry to disappoint," Zero muttered.

*Come on. Do it again.*

He waited, finger on the trigger. The man's finger twitched on the detonator's switch.

"I do not want to kill my father," the bomber said frankly.

"Your father is a murderer who orchestrated three bombings that claimed twenty-seven innocent lives," Maria said harshly. "Either way, he dies tonight."

Hassad's bony fingers reached for his son's arm. "Omar. I am ready, son. I will greet Allah with open arms, and I will know pe—" The old man lurched forward suddenly, launching into another coughing fit.

*Now.* Zero fired twice. Both shots struck Omar in the chest, above the vest and just below the collarbone.

In the same instant Maria fired one shot, striking Omar's forearm and nearly severing it. The man fell back. The detonator flew from his now-useless hand and clattered to the floor.

Zero ducked and covered. Not that it would have done any good against the bomb.

But for the second time in ten minutes, there was no explosion, and he could breathe.

He and Maria charged into the room. Omar gasped for breath, blood eking from his mouth, his body trembling.

Hassad stared up at them with pure avarice in his milky eyes. "You think this means you win," the old man croaked. "But we will be rewarded greatly in the next life for our service to Him."

Zero wanted to retort, but the words were lost. All he felt in the moment was a crushing sadness for this man. And for the others, these men who were so indoctrinated by belief and alleged purpose that they were willing to kill and to sacrifice their own lives for it.

It felt like a lifetime ago that he had been Reid Lawson, Professor of European History. So many lectures about so many wars fought for religious reasons. An ideological juxtaposition, one that could never be proven but could always be justified by the faithful.

He felt a hand on his shoulder. Maria gave him a small squeeze.

"I'll do it."

He stepped aside as she brought the MP5 to her shoulder. Hassad, to his credit, did not even blink.

Zero saw movement from the corner of his eye. He spun quickly. Omar had managed to flip himself onto his stomach. His good hand wrapped around the fallen detonator.

"No!" Zero wrapped both arms around Maria's waist and twisted, yanking her off her feet. He shoved forward with his full body weight, propelling them to the window.

Glass gave way. Shards tore at his tac vest, his shirt sleeves, his skin.

He didn't hear the explosion, but he felt it. The heat of it. The percussive blast shoving them forward even as they fell. Tumbling out over nothing.

And then—they hit something. It gave way beneath them. There was no sound as their bodies bounced in tandem, fell a little further, and then hit solid ground.

Stars danced in his vision. Maria was atop him. Beyond her the sky was ablaze. He tried to breathe but the air had been forced from his lungs.

The entire second floor of the building was destroyed, burning. Flaming debris fell around them. Maria was lifted away from him, and then strong hands were under his shoulders, lifting him easily, setting him on his feet as he coughed and sputtered.

"Zero!" The voice sounded far off. His ears were ringing. "Zero, you okay?" Todd Strickland shouted in his face.

"Yeah," he tried to say, though it came out as, "*Ugh.*"

"Anything broken?"

He took a couple of shaky steps. No, nothing seemed to be broken. He was tired, sore, cramped, aching—the usual. Tomorrow morning he would wake to all sorts of new aches and pains. Just more guests at the party.

Maria looked like she'd fared better than him. He'd taken the brunt of the window, and she'd landed on top of him. He glanced back; they'd fallen about twelve feet and bounced off the roof of a car parked behind the building. The ceiling was caved and the windows were blown out.

"We gotta get clear," said Foxworth. "Penny? Call Alan for extraction."

"Already did," came the voice in his ear. No sooner did she say it than a pair of round headlights swept over them. The Jeep screeched to a halt and the burly driver climbed out. He scratched his unruly beard and adjusted his trucker cap, the brim of it stained with sweat.

"Jesus." Alan Reidigger chuckled as he surveyed what remained of the compound. "You guys are about as covert as the goddamn Macy's Thanksgiving Day Parade."

*

Zero winced as Strickland applied a thick bead of superglue to a two-inch cut on his jaw line, a temporary measure until he could get it properly sutured. Whether it was from leaping through the window or falling on the car, he wasn't sure and didn't care. All he knew was that it stung. And that was a good thing, because he could still feel.

The sun was just rising as the five of them waited on a rocky bluff overlooking the sea, two miles outside of Ashkelon and a quarter mile from an old airstrip that served as their extraction point. Any moment now the plane was due to arrive. Until then, they sat and chatted idly and stared out over the placid Mediterranean as dawn broke behind them.

From here it was hard to believe that the still-smoldering compound was only a handful of miles to the southwest. If Zero ignored the pain and focused on the point where the orange-tinged horizon met the sea, he could almost believe this was a vacation, and he was somewhere more exotic, more desirable than the war-torn Israeli coast.

Maria sat on a large flat stone about eight yards from the Jeep, her knees drawn up as she stared out at the water. He made his way over to her and lowered himself beside her, accompanied by only a few groans of pain.

"How are you feeling?" he asked.

"Could be a lot worse." She smiled but didn't look over at him. "Glad to be feeling anything right now."

He nodded appreciably. "What are you thinking about?"

"Right now?"

"Right now. Right this second."

"I'm thinking… it's beautiful." She sighed heavily. "Kind of makes it all worth it."

"All of what?"

"What we're doing. Risking our lives to help bring about peace in a way that very few will ever know about. Rutledge's plan. All of it. Everything we do. Moments like this… makes it seem worth it. Not only worth it, but necessary."

Zero said nothing. If Maria had been grappling with some sort of inner turmoil over their assignments of late, she hadn't said anything. It was a thought that had crossed his own mind more than a few times as well, not just lately but over his entire career with the CIA. He had two teenage daughters who were mostly independent now, but would still need him from time to time. He had a future with Maria, however long his own future might be. Or hers, for that matter. Despite the atrophy in his brain, he could just as easily have caught a bullet tonight.

When the Swiss neurologist, Dr. Guyer, had told him that the damage caused by the memory suppressor would deteriorate his memories and eventually kill him, Zero had made a promise to himself. To live life to the fullest, to stay in the present. The past was the past; the future was uncertain. But now…?

*Now…*

*Now.*

*It's the right time. Now.*

He unzipped a small front pocket on his tac vest and reached in with two fingers, tugging out a small manila envelope the size of a dollar bill. He shook the contents, a single item, into his palm. It was by no means flashy; one-half carat, round cut, on a white-gold band. But the clarity was flawless and it sparkled in the morning light with the brilliance of a star.

"Zero…?" Maria murmured, watching him as he held up the ring.

He couldn't help the smile that crept across his face. He didn't get on one knee or wait for her to stand. He merely held the diamond up, pinched between a thumb and forefinger, seated beside her on a flat rock in Israel overlooking the Mediterranean Sea, and said, "Will you marry me?"

She smiled too. Then she snorted, attempting to hold back a laugh, and then she couldn't. "You're doing this here? Now?"

"Yeah. Here and now."

"And you… you carried this on the op?"

"Yeah. I did." Truth be told, he'd carried the ring with him everywhere for the last three weeks, ever since he got his daughters' blessing on Valentine's Day, ever since he bought the ring less than twenty-four hours later. He'd carried it with him on the last two ops they'd gone on. He'd carried it and waited for the perfect moment, and here it was. He had blood on his neck and dried around one ear and both their faces were streaked with soot. Maria's hair was a mess and they still wore tactical vests and MP5s slung over their shoulders by a strap, and it was perfect.

"Are you sure?" she asked suddenly, the smile giving way to concern. "I mean, have you thought about this? The girls, and Mischa, and the team, and the—"

"Yes," he told her simply. Yes, he had thought about it, had even lost sleep over it before he realized he was just torturing himself with the what-ifs. His girls loved her. They would handle Mischa together. They were a team, and there was one simple fact that he couldn't refute: "Everything about my life is easier when you're in it. I want you to always be in it."

"Then... yes." She nodded. "Yes, I will." She laughed again. "Of course I will." Maria put out her left hand before realizing she was still wearing the black Kevlar tactical glove. She hastily tugged it off and presented her hand again.

Zero slipped the ring on. A perfect fit.

And then she leaned in and she kissed him. He wished they could stay like that forever, right there on a warm rock in the morning sunlight on a foreign shore with no one else around—

"*Ahem.*"

Right. There were others around.

Zero and Maria both turned to see that Chip and Todd were blatantly pretending to have a conversation and looking anywhere else. But Reidigger stared directly at them, his thick arms folded over his chest, the corners of his beard tugged up in a broad grin.

"Well! It's about damn time," he announced. "*Mazel tov.* I suppose this will make you Mrs. Zero?"

Zero pinched the bridge of his nose, but still he couldn't help but laugh. "Thanks, Alan."

He climbed to his feet and held out both hands for Maria, helping her up and then wrapping her in a tight hug. Her hair smelled like shampoo and smoke and gunpowder. A roar from above signaled the incoming Learjet, their transportation back to the States.

They were going home. Home to the house they shared, where his girls would be ecstatic that he'd finally gone and asked the question, where they would soon welcome a new addition to their odd little family.

Nothing about it should have felt like the perfect moment, but everything about it did.

23

# CHAPTER THREE

Maya Lawson was carrying six books and a tablet when the Firstie bumped into her.

He didn't even try to make it look like an accident. The tall, sandy-haired teenager bee-lined for her, looking her right in the eye, and when she stepped to the left to avoid him he stepped with her. He didn't slow down, and he puffed out his chest as he collided with her.

The books scattered across the floor. Maya's nostrils flared as she stared up at the boy, Chad something-or-other, a fourth-year cadet (or Firstie) who was, of course, one of *them*.

"Ooh, sorry, Lawson," he chided. "Guess you should watch where I'm going." As he stepped around her he pretended to trip and kicked her physics textbook another fifteen feet down the West Point hall as onlookers snickered at her expense.

A fist balled by her side. The boy had seven inches and at least a thirty-five-pound advantage on her, but she knew she could take him apart easily if she wanted. But she couldn't. Not now. Instead she swallowed her pride and started retrieving the fallen books.

*Maybe it was a mistake to come back.*

None of this, the bullying and hazing, would be happening if it wasn't for her sort-of ex-boyfriend, a senior named Greg Calloway whom Maya had slighted and then made look foolish in front of many. Rumors ran rampant through the halls of West Point; depending on which cadet one asked, they might hear anything from Maya refusing to sleep with him (which wasn't true, their relationship had never even gotten to that point) to Maya leaving him abandoned on a trip to Maryland with no way to get back to school (which was true, because Greg was being a monumental ass and deserved it).

But Greg had friends. Greg was top of his class, one year ahead of Maya. Greg had influential and wealthy parents. And so others in the school came to his defense. Just a few at first, calling her names and writing profanity on her locker. Then stealing her things. Idle threats. Following her to the dorms. Escalating.

And then over Thanksgiving break the dam broke. Maya had opted to stay on campus because of a falling out with her father. After a shower in the girls' locker room she found herself cornered by three boys, locked in with no help in sight. She had only been wearing a towel at the time; the vulnerability and fear she'd felt in that moment would never fade, and still stung her from time to time.

She didn't know what they had planned to do, but they never got their chance. Maya blacked out. When she came around, there was blood on her hands, blood on the floor. Two of the boys were beaten badly. The third, within an inch of his life. He was hospitalized for three weeks.

That act of self-defense, of intense preservation, only made things worse. It was a line in the sand to these boys, that when push came to shove it was her versus them. It was utterly idiotic logic, the type that teenagers would dream up as truth but someone like Maya could never understand.

So she took some time off. A semester and a half spent with her dad and her sister and Maria. It was nice, until a few weeks ago when Dean Hunt called her personally and gave her an ultimatum: Maya would return to West Point, make up for lost time, and graduate on time, or she would never set foot in the academy again.

The choice was obvious. She had plans. She was going to be the youngest field agent in CIA history, and a West Point education would make that possible. She refused to rely on nepotism.

Maya trudged to the spot where her physics book had been kicked and reached for it. A hand fell on hers at the same moment and she pulled away briskly, her body tensing for a fight.

The boy put his hands up in a gesture of surrender. "Hey. Sorry. Just… trying to help."

He flashed a smile. It was a kind smile. Too kind to be genuine.

"It's Zane, right?" She stooped to pick up the book herself.

"Yeah. We had a history class together. I sat behind you—"

"I remember." Zane was a Cow—the West Point equivalent of a junior, same as her. She had an excellent memory but couldn't recall them ever speaking more than once. "You asked me to borrow a pen one time."

"I did…"

"I never got it back."

"Oh, uh…" He grinned sheepishly. Disingenuously. "Sorry about that. Guess if I find it, I'll have to get it back to you. Maybe over lunch sometime?"

She narrowed her eyes at him. One of Greg's cronies, probably. If he was, he was trying to lure her into a trap that would attempt to humiliate her. If he wasn't, she didn't care. She didn't need friends any more than she needed enemies here. She needed to focus, to catch up on her studies, and to keep her spot at the top of the class.

"Leave me alone, Zane." She turned and walked briskly away, enjoying the momentary flash of bemusement on his face as she spun.

She had to hand it to him. Most of the cadets avoided her these days. Those who felt they had something to prove, like Chad Whatever, would harass her openly because they knew they could get away with it. The only way that Dean Hunt could have Maya back and make it look good was to claim she was on academic probation. It wasn't true, at least not on paper—it seemed that Maya had a strong ally in the dean—but still, parents needed to be satisfied that their precious baby boys were safe from this monstrous girl, so Maya had to stay on the straight and narrow.

She missed her sister. Sara would understand. Sara would goad her big sister into punching out Chad's front teeth, and then stand over him and laugh.

Maya made a mental note to call her later as she headed toward the physics class. But as she neared the lecture hall, another body stepped into her path, and Maya tensed for another provocateur.

"Lawson," said the man crisply, his body rigid and dress uniform impeccable.

"Corporal. Sir." She straightened her spine quickly, ready to snap a salute when she realized both hands were laden with the stack of books she'd elected to carry to class. She fumbled with them, attempting to transfer the weight to one arm.

"At ease, cadet," Corporal Brighton told her. Just the hint of a smirk played on his face. He was young, early thirties at best, and well-liked by staff and cadets alike. He reminded Maya a little of the former Ranger Todd Strickland, disciplined yet good-natured and personable. "Dean Hunt wants to see you at your earliest convenience, Lawson."

Maya frowned, knowing full well that her "earliest convenience" meant *right now*. Hunt had been keeping pretty close tabs on her ever since she'd returned to the academy, but outside of one in-person meeting had maintained a distance.

*Did I do something wrong?* She wanted to ask but she knew that the corporal probably didn't know, and if he did he wouldn't tell her.

"Yes sir. Thank you, sir," she replied, and she headed toward the dean's office.

Behind her, a boy who had overheard the exchange called out snidely, "Maybe Hunt will do us all a favor and kick your ass out for good this time."

\*

An administrative assistant led Maya into Hunt's office wordlessly and closed the door behind her. Maya had left her books on the desk outside so her hand was free to salute this time. She stood at attention as she waited for the dean to address her.

At last Brigadier General Joanne Hunt looked up and set down her pen. "Have a seat, Lawson."

Maya did so, setting herself down into one of the comfortable padded chairs across from Hunt's desk, but not allowing herself to slouch or be at ease. She and Hunt had an easy relationship, one that occasionally marked Maya as a "dean's pet" in the eyes of some of her peers, but decorum was still a hallmark of West Point cadets.

Dean Hunt folded her hands atop the oak desk and inspected Maya for a long moment. The dean was a discerning woman, with hawkish eyes and a practical haircut and a pressed uniform. The knot in the black tie at her throat was perfect. There was a lot to admire about the dean, what she'd accomplished in her career. Still, a woman like Hunt was the furthest from what Maya wanted to become. Sitting behind a desk all day was about as appealing to her as drinking bleach.

"Settling back in, Lawson?"

"It's been three weeks, ma'am."

Hunt raised an eyebrow. "And?"

"I am fully settled and nearly caught up with my fellow second-class cadets."

"Good. You're a hard worker, Lawson. You're smart, and you have goals. Those three things are a powerful combination. Few things can stop someone like you."

27

Maya frowned at that. What should have sounded like a compliment sounded more like some sort of foreshadowing. Or perhaps even a warning. But her response was simply, "Thank you, ma'am."

"Lawson, I called you here because I need a favor." Dean Hunt leaned forward and hunched her shoulders. "It has recently come to light that a number of students on campus have obtained convincing forgeries of a number of documents. It first came to my attention via a recommendation letter. I read it myself and wouldn't have questioned it had it not claimed to come from the Director of National Intelligence, whom you are aware is an acquaintance of mine."

"Yes ma'am." She remembered all too well the day that DNI David Barren and Dean Hunt cornered her in this very office to ask if she knew the whereabouts of her then-MIA father. They were two of only a handful of people in the world who knew that Maya Lawson's father was the CIA operative designated Agent Zero.

"In another case," Hunt continued, "two senior cadets were caught with falsified military IDs that cited their age as twenty-one so they could procure alcohol. Another student had a fake driver's license, having never passed the exam, and ended up crashing his parents' car while on weekend leave."

Maya frowned. She'd heard nothing about forgeries on or around campus. But then again, few people spoke to her. Where was the dean going with this? Unless...

A knot of panic formed in Maya chest. "Ma'am," she blurted out, "I can assure you I have no prior knowledge of any of this, and am in no way involved in any—"

Hunt held up a hand. "Relax, Lawson. I know you're not. This isn't an interrogation. Like I said, I need a favor."

"Ma'am?"

"Find me the forger, Maya."

She blinked at the dean and forgot formalities. "Sorry, what?"

"I want you," the dean pointed at her, "to find me the person responsible. I don't know if they're a student, or if it's someone off-campus. If the latter, they must have a student liaison that is helping them, sending cadets their way. Regardless, find them for me."

"I..." Maya cleared her throat. Why would the dean ask this of her? More importantly, how could she say no? "Ma'am, don't you think this might be a job better suited for MPs? Or if it's off-campus, the local police?"

"Certainly," the dean agreed. "And I would be talking to them instead of you if I thought they could do a better job of it. I'd love to believe that any one of our cadets would be honest and forthcoming to authorities, but I think we both know that's simply not the case. I need someone out there, in the student population, someone who might hear or see something that a cop or an MP wouldn't."

Maya fidgeted in her seat. Everything about this request was bizarre. She was more than swamped catching up on what she'd missed and balancing it with her current workload. As it was, she was averaging five hours of sleep a night. Sometimes less.

"Ma'am," she said carefully. "I think you should know that the student population... well, most of them don't like me very much." It sounded lame when she heard the words aloud, but it was the truth. Something like this certainly wouldn't help her popularity—or utter lack thereof.

"Then I suggest you get creative, Lawson."

Maya's throat flexed. "This isn't the sort of thing I can say no to, is it?"

Dean Hunt breathed a long sigh, in through her nose and through her mouth before she said, "Is it something you want to say no to, Lawson?"

*Do I really want to be Hunt's narc?*

Strange. This was all so strange. There had to be a reason, a reason for the coyness and the excuses. She worked it over in her mind. Hunt had come to her. She'd mentioned the DNI, who Maya knew was aware who she was and what she wanted to do. The dean was probably equally aware of her less-than-stellar social standing. Which meant...

*This is a test.*

*No—this is a* mission.

To what end? To test her capability? To ensure her loyalty?

*Does it matter?*

"No ma'am," Maya said suddenly. "I accept the task. I'll find them for you."

"Good. That's all then, Lawson. You're dismissed."

"But wait," she said quickly. "You must have some information for me to go on. The students that were caught, they must have given something..."

"Those students have already been sent home. Expelled."

Maya blinked in surprise. Four students, maybe more, expelled quietly without a word or buzz of a rumor in the halls? Falsifying military identification was a felony. Did she really have nothing to give her?

"The forger, Maya." The dean's gaze bored into hers as if reading her thoughts. "That's who we care about. Not students with fake IDs."

"Yes ma'am." Maya rose, saluted, and headed for the door. Her mind immediately went into overdrive. Find the forger. To do that meant talking to people. Students. Gaining a lead. No one would do that. Not with her. Not unless…

She paused with her hand on the knob. "Ma'am. My academic probation might be a problem."

Dean Hunt seemed to think about this for a moment. "Perhaps you can use it your advantage," she remarked casually. "At the very least, try not to break any noses."

"I can't promise that, ma'am."

Hunt smiled for the first time since Maya had entered the office. "Good."

Maya retrieved her books and headed back into the halls, blind and deaf to the cadets who passed her by as her mind churned. She would need to change the perception of herself if she was going to get any answers out of anyone. Gain trust through guile.

*Step one.* She weighed the physics textbook in her hand. It was thick, probably near eight pounds. A hearty text and a formidable weapon, depending on intention. *Find Chad What's-his-name, and teach him a lesson in physics.*

# CHAPTER FOUR

President Jonathan Rutledge ran his fingertips along the edge of the Resolute desk in the Oval Office of the White House. It was his favorite piece of furniture in the entire complex, and the one thing about this office that never changed. The sofas, the guest chairs, the coffee tables, even the portraits on the walls seemed to be swapped out monthly, but this desk—it was always here.

Resolute. Like its namesake.

It was magnificent craftsmanship, to be sure, but his fondness for it stemmed from much more than that. Rutledge was a bit of a history buff, and this desk had an incredible history. It was named for the HMS *Resolute*, a British ship built for Arctic exploration that was abandoned when it became trapped in the ice in 1854. Two years later the ship was recovered by an American whaling vessel.

This desk, the one that every president since Jimmy Carter had sat behind, had been built from the timbers of that trapped Arctic vessel, and thusly named the Resolute desk. It had even been on display in the Smithsonian for a time, between the JFK assassination and Carter's reintegration of it into the White House.

*Resolute*. More than its artistry, more than its history, more than it being a constant in his office, it was a reminder to the president. Resolute. Rutledge had been the Speaker of the House when the enormous scandal involving former President Samuel Harris had erupted. History was made several times over in a dizzyingly short span: Harris's impeachment proceedings were the fastest the US had ever seen. His vice president was ousted alongside him for his involvement in the Russian betrayal. And the Speaker of the House suddenly found himself being asked to be the commander-in-chief.

His first months in office were met with something less than zeal. How many times had he questioned his ability to perform the role? How many times had he thought of stepping down? But then he had been delivered a saving grace.

"Sir."

Rutledge jumped a little in his seat. Then he chuckled at the sight of her, standing just beyond the double doors to the office, her hands folded neatly in front of her black pencil skirt.

"Joanna. Please come in. Have a seat. Are you that quiet, or is this old man just going deaf?"

"Perhaps a bit of both, sir." Joanna Barkley's expression did not change; for a moment Rutledge couldn't tell if she was joking dryly or being perfectly candid. And then she allowed herself a small smirk, and he shook his head at her.

Vice President Joanna Barkley had been the youngest female senator in US history at age thirty-two. Now at thirty-six, she was his second in command. The naming of her as his VP had come with as much applause and commendation as it had contention and derision, but Barkley let it slide from her back like she was waterproof in a thunderstorm. Nothing seemed to get under the woman's skin. Her attitude was so admirable and her mind so keen that Rutledge had, briefly, considered resigning immediately and handing her the keys to the kingdom.

But he had been inspired to remain. Not just by her, but also by a new friend. Agent Zero. His literal secret weapon in Gaza.

Barkley took a seat on one of the parallel sofas facing each other beyond the Resolute desk and Rutledge joined her on the other sofa. She sat with her knees together and slightly to the side, pointing toward the wide window, not crossing her legs. Rutledge sat heavily, his knees far apart—then he remembered his daughter telling him what "manspreading" was and how unbecoming of a president it looked, and he quickly closed his knees.

"Joanna," he told her. "It's happening. I wanted you to be the first to know, and a phone call would not have sufficed."

She nodded slowly, as if she had known this was coming. Maybe she did. Barkley had a remarkable mind; throughout her career thus far, one thing had remained consistent. She did not see problems, but rather saw a series of steps that were required to a solution. While others might look at an impossibly tangled ball of string, Barkley saw every knot, every loop, as a sequence that needed to be painstakingly worked at, one at a time. While others would throw it down in frustration and call it insurmountable, Barkley would patiently tug at each thread until she was left with a single string.

And so it had been here as well. When Rutledge told her that his goal for his presidency was peace between the Middle Eastern nations and the United States, she did not laugh at him. She did not call it impossible or a waste of time. She simply said, "Okay, Jon. But in order to do that we're also going to have to unify the Middle East."

It sounded impossible. Insurmountable.

But so far, every knot they'd encountered had come undone.

"Not forty minutes ago," he told her, "I had a call with Prime Minister Nitzani. He sent an ambassador to meet with President Dawoud and it went, and I quote, 'extremely favorably.' They are ready to do this, Joanna." He sighed and added, "I will be personally brokering a peace treaty between Israel and Palestine."

He felt a giddy, tingling sensation in his chest as he said it. Saying it aloud somehow made it so much more real.

Barkley smiled broadly. "That is incredibly great news, Jon. Saudi Arabia has agreed to our terms, as has Iran. With Israel and Palestine, there will be few more pieces of the puzzle remaining."

Rutledge returned the smile. "This is significant progress, to be sure."

"Just keep me in mind when you accept your Nobel Peace Prize—"

"When *we* accept it," he corrected her. "There will be no crediting me without your name in the same breath, Jo. This is as much yours as mine." She would be president one day, he had no doubt about that. But he did not say that aloud; he didn't want to come off as pandering. And she likely already knew it.

"When?" she asked.

"Soon. Very soon. Within the week. It's going to happen fast. Which means arranging an attaché and security team to Jerusalem..."

He trailed off as Joanna frowned and held up a hand. "I'm sorry," she said. "But Jerusalem? Why not here, on US soil? It's not atypical for such an accord to be signed here in Washington."

Rutledge nodded. He'd expected that she might have thoughts on this matter. "True. But this is anything but a typical situation. President Dawoud was insistent. He believes it will be symbolic, help unify the people, and to be frank, I'm of the same mind. The prime minister agrees. There's no other place for it."

Joanna said nothing further, but her troubled expression spoke volumes. Rutledge stood, his knees cracking a bit as he did, and took one of her hands in both of his. "It's perfectly safe, Jo. This is in the interest of peace and it will be peaceful. This is a huge and necessary win. The entire world will be watching, and with a little luck, others will follow this example." He chuckled slightly and added, "Besides, I have the very best security available. Trust me on that."

Barkley raised an eyebrow. "Your newly minted Executive Team?"

Rutledge nodded. Barkley was his biggest ally, to be sure. But he had another, and one that was just as crucial. If Joanna was the patient hands that worked at the tangle, Agent Zero and his team were the scissors, ready to cut at unruly knots that threatened to halt progress.

Zero would be in Jerusalem for the accord. Rutledge would see to that.

# CHAPTER FIVE

*Mrs. Zero.*

It was a joke. Maria knew it was just a joke and that Alan hadn't meant anything more by it. But still, with that simple comment came a plethora of thoughts, intrusive ones, uninvited ones.

What would it mean to be his team leader and his wife?

What would his girls think? They knew she had no intention of trying to replace their late mother, Kate. But they were as strong-willed as the man who raised them—maybe more so.

What would it mean for Mischa? Would it mean more stability, or more chaos?

She fidgeted in the hard-backed plastic chair outside Director Shaw's office. Her lower back was cramping; she'd been sitting there for thirty minutes now and was fairly certain that she was being made to wait on purpose.

So she sat, and she waited, and she tilted her hand left and right and admired the way the diamond caught the light in a thousand dazzling ways in its faceted façade, and instead of being elated she sat there half-terrified and had her intrusive thoughts.

*Mrs. Zero.*

What if things went wrong again between them, like they had before, more than once?

What if his memory issues came back? He claimed to have them under control, but she always felt like he'd been closely guarded about that part of him.

The ring itself was perfect. He'd told her, two days ago right after he proposed, that he'd chosen it because it reminded him of her: brilliant and beautiful without being ostentatious. That was the word he'd used—"ostentatious." She could take the professor out of the classroom, but...

But what if he decided he wanted to quit the agency again?

What if he came to despise her for being the one who forced him back in? When he had gone rogue and helped the interpreter, Karina Pavlo, Maria had no choice but to retroactively renew him as an agent

35

so he could avoid a lengthy jail sentence. Now *he* had no choice but to continue being Agent Zero. Was that even what he wanted?

What if she couldn't be Kate Lawson? Or Karina? Or the Israeli Mossad agent, Talia Mendel, who made no efforts to hide her obvious attraction to him—

"Johansson." CIA Director Edward Shaw looked down at her, his spine as straight as if it was made of wood, his mouth grimacing. She'd only ever seen the man smile once, and that was when he was certain he was about to fire her entire team and have charges brought against them.

She rose and wordlessly followed him into his office. He lowered himself into a high-backed leather chair; she remained standing.

"Your team is well?" he asked stiffly.

She knew he didn't care. Though they still technically worked for the CIA, it meant only that their paychecks were drawn from agency funding. They answered to Rutledge now, and there was no love lost between her and Shaw.

"Let's skip the pleasantries," she said plainly. "You took your time with this enough as it is."

Shaw's throat flexed but he held back whatever barb he might have prepared. "These things take time," he said instead, and he pushed a thick folder across the desk to her. "It's not terribly easy to invent a new citizen."

Three weeks prior, President Rutledge announced the formation of the Executive Operations Team. That same day—that same meeting, in fact—Maria issued a threat to the CIA director. He would release the girl into her care, or Maria would tell the president, and the press, that the agency was in the habit of illegally detaining minors without due process in secret subterranean holding cells of the George Bush Center for Intelligence in the unincorporated community of Langley, Virginia.

She'd given him a week. He had taken three. Her patience, needless to say, had run out.

"Go ahead," Shaw prodded. "Ensure it's all there."

Maria reached for the folder and opened it.

The first page was a birth certificate issued in the state of Virginia, from a Presbyterian hospital, citing the abandonment of an infant girl. Mother unknown. Name: typical for the child welfare system when dealing with unknown origins. "Foundling child."

The next few pages were documents from an orphanage that alleged to have harbored the girl until she was nine years old. There she had been given the name Mischa.

The Social Security card that had been issued bore the full name of Mischa Doe, since she had no known parent. She had been with three foster families between the ages of nine and twelve. There were report cards from schools. Immunization records. Even a passport, stamped with a single entry of a trip to Germany, likely the product of a vacation with a foster family.

The only word of it that was real was the name Mischa.

Otherwise, it was one hundred percent fabricated. Yet at the same time it was as real as Maria's own documentation. The CIA had seen to that. As Shaw had said, they had invented a citizen out of the girl.

The last sheaf of papers was the most important, at least to her. The adoption papers, from the Commonwealth of Virginia, releasing Mischa into the care of one Maria Johansson, making her the full legal guardian of the twelve-year-old. And, on the last page, an official change-of-name allowance.

Mischa Johansson.

Seeing that made it suddenly so real that Maria had to blink away a tear. There was no way in hell she was going to shed one in front of Shaw.

"Is everything to your satisfaction?" he asked.

She nodded. "It is." Despite herself, and despite how long he'd taken, she added, "Thank you."

"There's no going back on this," Shaw warned her. "Once she walks out of here, she's your problem entirely. We will disavow any knowledge whatsoever—"

"I know how it works," Maria interjected curtly. "I've been at this longer than you have."

"Then, if there's nothing else…"

"There's not." Maria turned on a heel and exited the office quickly, tucking the folder under one arm. There was no sense in delaying it further. She moved with purpose, entering the elevator as if Shaw might change his mind and come dashing after her. She swiped her CIA keycard through a vertical slot in the panel just below the floor buttons and pressed the sequence of 4-2-3. The code that would take her down, down below the basement, down even below the Research &

Development level where Penny would be hard at work on some new weapon or gadget.

As a former deputy director, Maria knew there were at least four sublevels beneath Langley—at least four, because she was certain there were others that she had not been cleared to know about. There was a saying among them, a joke, that for every secret you learn there are ten more you don't. Maria knew a lot of secrets. But after today there would be one fewer.

The elevator doors opened on a cinder-blocked corridor painted blindingly white, bright fluorescent bulbs buzzing overhead. The clack of her shoes echoed as she marched to the third steel door on the right, once again swiping her keycard and waiting for the heavy electronic bolt to slide aside.

Ben, the gray-haired security guard, nodded to her. His job description seemed to be to sit behind a beige desk and read back issues of *Sports Illustrated*. "Ms. Johansson. Nice to see you again."

She showed him the folder. "Last time in a while, I imagine."

"You don't mean...?" He grinned broadly as he shuffled his feet off the desk. "Well, I'll be damned. Let me get my keys."

"Hang on. I want to talk to her first. Just for a minute."

Ben nodded. "Go ahead. Just give a holler when you need me."

"Thanks." Maria passed his desk, through another steel door with a security-glassed window that led to a corridor lined on both sides with cells. Each cell was twelve foot by twelve foot, with a floor and ceiling of concrete. Instead of bars, the walls were comprised of two-inch reinforced glass with a grid of half-inch holes in the side facing the corridor. There were no windows—they were, after all, underground—but even worse was that there did not appear to be any door in the cell. It was a psychological maneuver, intended to make a prisoner believe there was absolutely no way out. No one could even attempt to escape if they didn't see a means by which to do so.

Maria knew that the cells were accessible by a hidden panel in one of the glass facades, carefully hidden by optical illusion and clever engineering. Prisoners here were brought in sedated and woke up in an inescapable glass cage.

The thought made her heart break all over again, as it did every time she was down here. It had only been three days since her last visit—she tried to come at least once a week, twice if she could, because the girl had no other visitors. Hell, there were less than a dozen people on the planet that even knew she was down there.

Maria stopped in front of the final cell on the left side of the corridor, the terminus of which was merely another concrete wall. The cell contained a small cot with blanket and pillow; a tiny, open bathroom area of sink, toilet, and shower head, with a metal grate in the floor below; a single steel chair, bolted to the floor; and in that chair, a twelve-year-old girl, blonde, green-eyed, her expression as flat and passive as ever as she thumbed through a well-worn paperback copy of Dostoyevsky's *Notes from the Underground*.

She must have read it a dozen times since Maria had brought it to her. On every visit, the girl's thumb was keeping a different place.

"I could have brought you another book, you know." Maria's voice sounded louder than it should have in the empty space, the corridor, the vacant cell block.

"I like this book." Mischa looked up. Her expression did not change from its blank, passive slate, but she nodded once. "*Privyet*, Maria."

*Hi.* All things considered, it was a small victory that the girl chose to use such an informal greeting. Mischa spoke fluent English, Russian, Chinese, and Ukrainian—the ones Maria knew of—and could not only switch between them flawlessly but could affect an equally appropriate accent when needed. Her language skills were so convincing it was impossible to tell where she actually came from, what language she might have learned first.

Considering she had been a sparrow-in-training by a Russian expatriate and spy, it was not only entirely possible but likely that she had been brought up learning all of them.

Mischa had been an unwitting terrorist. Maria knew that, by virtue of the fact that the girl had tried to kill both her and Zero. She had been a part of the Chinese/Russian squad that initiated attacks on US soil with an ultrasonic weapon. But Maria and her team had agreed not to breathe a word about it in their briefing. The CIA had nothing on her but speculation. They could prove nothing. Mischa was equally silent, not out of solidarity but from indoctrination and training. As far as anyone else was concerned, this was an innocent twelve-year-old girl who had been held in the bowels of Langley for the past four months.

Mischa was deadly. She could fight. She could kill. She could load a gun one-handed and drive a car with the other. But she was just a child, one who never got the chance to know any other sort of life.

"Mischa," she said, "you're getting out of here today."

The girl's eyebrows twitched. It was almost imperceptible, but as far as Mischa's expressions went, the girl may as well have dropped her jaw.

"Will you be able to visit me where they send me?" she asked.

The response stunned Maria. She had expected the first question to be where she was going, what would happen to her. It was as if the girl had consigned herself to this glass-walled fate.

"I... no. I mean, yes. I mean—I'm sorry. You don't understand."

*God, why is this so hard?*

Maria had been careful to avoid any mention on past visits about Mischa being released into her care. She didn't want to jinx it, to get any hopes up only to encounter some bureaucratic stymie. Still, she had dreamed so many times of this moment, what she would say, and now the words seemed to fail her.

She cleared her throat and tried again. "What I mean is, you're coming home. With me. To my home. Our home."

Maria didn't know what she had expected. It wasn't as if the girl was going to jump for joy or weep or even thank her. But the last thing she had expected was a deep frown to appear on her young face.

"Why?"

And with that, Maria realized her fatal mistake. She'd had the CIA jump through numerous hoops to do this and hadn't once considered asking Mischa if that's what she wanted. She had just assumed that anything was better than this.

"Because... I want you to," Maria said plainly. "I want you to get out of this place and come live with me and..." This was not going as well as she'd hoped. "Mischa, do you remember the game that we played? 'Never Have I Ever'?"

The girl nodded.

"You told me, then, that you wanted to play soccer. And have friends. Right?"

"Yes. And you want to see the Bahamas and raise a garden."

Maria smiled. "That's right. I can do those things, and so can you. If... if you really want to." She paused to give the girl a moment to respond. But when she didn't, Maria added, "So do you? Want to?"

Mischa glanced around at her glass walls. She closed her book and held it in both hands.

"Yes. I will go to your home."

Maria let out a sigh of relief that she didn't realize she'd been holding. "Good," she said. "I promise… this will be good for you. For us both." And she called for Ben and his keys.

*

Twenty minutes later,Maria and Mischa walked out of Langley through the front doors. No one looked twice at them. No one tried to stop them. Mischa had been allowed to have back the clothes she'd been wearing when she arrived, a green sweater and jeans and black sneakers. It was cold out, but the sun was shining and Mischa paused on the front steps, tilting her head upward to let the rays shine on her face for a moment.

They climbed into Maria's blue sedan and Mischa dutifully clicked her seatbelt. It wasn't a far drive; the small craftsman bungalow she and Zero had bought together was in the suburbs of Langley, in Fairfax County.

It was real. This was real. Mischa was sitting beside her, in her car, no longer in a glass cell and paper clothes and barefoot.

And Maria was terrified all over again.

*What the hell do I do now?*

"Um… so we'll go home first," she said, trying to sound like she had it all planned out, "and let you get settled in. See the place. We'll have to get you some clothes. Figure out what food you like. Oh! Speaking of. Do you have any allergies?"

"Yes. Strawberries."

Maria couldn't help but chuckle. "Really? Strawberries?"

"Yes."

"Okay. Good to know. Um… it's already March, so we'll wait to enroll you in school until the fall semester. I'm guessing your reading and comprehension level is much higher than seventh grade anyway…" She trailed off, noticing that Mischa was staring directly at her. "What is it?"

"I will go to an American school?"

"Well… yes. An education is important."

"I have been educated."

"No, you've been——" She stopped herself short.

*Indoctrinated.* That's what she was about to say. *You've been indoctrinated.* "There are other things you need to know," she said

41

instead. "Forget it for now. We'll cross that bridge when we come to it."

"What bridge?"

Maria held back a short laugh. "It's an idiom. It means, we'll deal with that later when the time comes."

"Ah. We will cross the bridge when we come to it." Mischa said it as if she was trying on a new shirt, and then nodded, seemingly satisfied.

They drove in silence for a few minutes more. Maria desperately hoped that Sara wouldn't be home when they arrived. Maya was off at West Point, and she'd asked Zero to get lost for a while… but it seemed like Sara was always coming and going, and Maria would much rather introduce the girl to her new home while it was just her and Mischa.

*Her new home.* It sounded so strange, even in her head.

"What is this?"

Maria looked over. Mischa had opened the folder from Shaw, and was pointing at a line on the adoption paperwork.

"Oh… that's my last name. Johansson. Well—it's your last name now, too. It's what you'll need to call yourself now."

"Johansson. This is Swedish?"

This time Maria did laugh. The girl was not only sharp, but suddenly far more inquisitive, and even talkative, now that she was out of the cell. "Yes. It's Swedish."

A few minutes later she pulled into the driveway of the Craftsman bungalow—that's what the Realtor had called it—home that she, Zero, and Sara shared. It was one story but spacious, with white shutters and dark brown siding made to look like wood. They had finally, after some months, finished the basement and Sara had moved down there, leaving the spare bedroom open for their new arrival.

"This is where you live?" Mischa asked. She leaned forward slightly. Outside of the day that Maria had brought her the Dostoyevsky book, this was the first time she'd ever seen the girl look genuinely interested in anything.

"Yes. It's where *you* live now too." She paused a moment. "Do you like it?"

"It is…" Mischa seemed to struggle to find the word. "Nice."

"Well. Glad you think so. Come on, I'll show you inside." Maria led the way, unlocking the three locks on the door and punching in the six-digit security code to disarm the alarm. Living with Zero required extra security, as well as a basement panic room and seven hidden, loaded firearms throughout the house.

"So this is it. Pretty basic. Foyer, den, kitchen, dining room, and bathroom are back there, living room… my room is that way, and…"

Maria stopped herself. Mischa took two careful steps into the foyer, looking around disconcertedly—or at least in a way that she thought was disconcertedly, but quickly realized was something else, something entirely foreign to the girl.

Mischa simply did not know how to look at something in wonder.

"I… am to live here now?"

"That's right. And, uh, if you come this way…" Maria led her down the foyer, through the kitchen, and around to another room. "This is your bedroom."

"My bedroom." Mischa seemed hesitant to cross the threshold. "*My* bedroom?"

"I know it's not much," Maria said quickly, "but it's your space, to do what you want. Uh, the walls are green, because Sara painted them, but we can repaint if you like, it's no problem—"

"I like green," said Mischa softly. "Who is Sara?"

"Oh. Right. Uh… other people live here too."

*Dammit, Maria, you are really dropping the ball on this one.*

"How many?" Mischa raised an eyebrow. Before Maria could respond, she quickly asked, "What are their ages? Genders? Relation to you?"

"Whoa." Maria held up a hand. "Remember what I said about crossing bridges?"

"When we arrive at them. Yes. All right."

"Good. Um…" Maria felt drained already. What did she know about raising twelve-year-olds, much less ones that had been raised as spies by former Russians and Chinese nationals?

*Get out of your own way*, she told herself. *Just talk to her like you would anyone.*

"So, there are fresh sheets on the bed. There's some clothes in the dresser, some older stuff of Sara's that she outgrew. Should fit you until we get you some of your own. What else? Oh! I have something for you." Maria hurried to the closet.

"This is more than enough. I do not need anything more."

"I know," Maria said, pulling open the closet door. "This is a gift."

Mischa frowned. "Like the book?"

43

"Yeah. Something like that." There it was—the soccer ball she'd bought yesterday. "Here. For you. To, you know. Play soccer, if you want."

Mischa set her book and the folder down on the bed and reached for the ball with both hands, taking it gingerly as if it was a balloon that might pop. "This is mine?"

"That's right."

"Hm." The noise the girl made was not an inquisitive one, or a confused one, but a lilting one. If anything, it sounded like she had held back a laugh, however short it might have been.

It was leagues beyond any sort of reaction that Maria would have hoped for. She bit the inside of her cheek to keep from shedding a tear.

"Okay then!" Maria said suddenly, more enthusiastically than necessary. "Bathroom is right around the corner, towels are in there. I bet after all that time, you'd like to at least freshen up, maybe shower or bathe with some privacy, huh? Take all the time you need. I'll be in the, uh, kitchen."

She retreated quickly, giving the girl some privacy and space for herself, something she hadn't had in months, if she'd ever been allowed it. Once she was alone in the kitchen Maria let herself heave one sob, just one, and then quickly wiped her eyes and laughed at herself.

This was going to be a long, uphill road. To acclimate this girl to any sort of normal American life was going to require as much effort as teaching a Cro-Magnon man to use indoor plumbing. But her reaction to the soccer ball was real, and more visceral than anything she'd gotten out of Mischa in the months of visits to the cell at Langley.

This was real. It was happening. Maria had no misconceptions about her chances of having a baby at thirty-eight, but the instincts were there. And now Mischa was there.

How she would handle the job and the girl at the same time, she wasn't yet sure. Hell, she didn't even know how she was going to introduce Sara and Zero to her.

*But we'll cross that bridge when we come to it.*

# CHAPTER SIX

Zero sat behind the wheel of his SUV, parked only three minutes from his house.

"*Just get lost for a little while.*" That's what Maria had said. "*I just don't want to intimidate her.*"

Zero had respected her decision to retrieve Mischa from Langley herself. He had no problem with that at all, and in fact agreed that it was a good idea.

*But how am I intimidating?*

He'd asked her that. She hadn't answered. She only laughed at him, kissed his cheek, and said, "Just get lost for a while."

"Penny?" he said into the phone. "You got anything?"

"You cannot rush genius, Agent Zero," Penny replied. "You said his name was Connors?"

"Connors, yes. Seth Connors."

Get lost for a while. Sure, that was easy enough. Usually that might have involved hitting up Third Street Garage, where Alan Reidigger had set up shop, for a couple of beers and a chat about the "good old days." Or maybe he would have hit up the gun range. Or just cruise around for a while.

But he had not, in fact, gotten lost for a while. Instead he had driven a short distance, parked, and pulled out the secure and cloaked satellite phone that Penny had given him if he needed discreet and untraceable communication.

According to his friend and scorned CIA engineer Bixby, Seth Connors had been the only other agent, besides Zero, to have a memory suppressor installed in his head. There was, however, one key difference: Connors had volunteered for the procedure and the early prototype suppressor was still in his head. Zero's best friend, Alan Reidigger, had stolen the suppressor chip, small as a grain of rice, and hired the Swiss neurologist Dr. Guyer to install it. And Zero's chip had been unceremoniously torn from his head by an Iraqi member of the now-defunct terrorist organization Amun.

"Bloody hell," Penny murmured. "We spend billions on security and I can back-door this system in under two minutes…"

Zero wanted to urge her, but he held his tongue. He'd waited this long; there was no rush.

Last month, while he and Maria and the team were chasing Saudi insurgents around the globe, his eldest daughter, Maya, had taken it upon herself to find Connors. All she knew was that her dad was looking for him and she had one single lead on his whereabouts. She'd done it, she later admitted, out of some need to prove herself, or to prove something *to* herself.

She didn't have to say it. He knew exactly what she had been feeling: she needed to prove to herself that she was just as good as her dad. That she could be every bit the agent he could be.

And he'd be damned if she hadn't gone and tracked the guy to a CIA safe house in Columbus.

He sighed. *Why couldn't she have wanted to be a doctor?*

"Bingo!" Penny exclaimed. "Connors, Seth. Formerly Agent Condor. Condor? Not exactly a far cry…"

"Penny."

"Right. Let's see. Looks like they moved him to another safe house, this one in D.C. About… twenty-five minutes from your location. I'll ping you the address."

"Appreciate it."

"Yeah, you owe me a pint." She hung up. A moment later the phone chimed and the address came through, and Zero started the car.

*Get lost for a while.*

He took his time getting there. He didn't speed up through any yellow lights or even attempt to pass anyone on multi-lane roads.

Truth be told, he wasn't in a huge rush to see for himself what fate he might have succumbed to had the suppressor not been removed. On the one hand, the violent extraction was the most likely culprit to the havoc being wreaked on his limbic system. Losing memories, occasional blackouts, and—if Guyer's assessment was to be believed—inevitable death. Would it be two years from now? Twenty? There was no telling without regular monitoring of his brain function and rate of deterioration.

But Connors, on the other hand, his suppressor was still in his skull. And according to what Maya had seen, it was failing. Just as Bixby had assumed it would after five to six years.

What was worse? Regaining everything only to lose it a little at a time? Or regaining memories of a life you never knew you had and thinking you've lost your mind?

Zero made a mental note to check in with Guyer. Despite the doctor being a few thousand miles away, he had colleagues, trusted ones in the States that could scan Zero's brain and send the results to Zurich. In his mind he was already making excuses about why he'd waited this long.

*Gee, Doc, I would've gotten my head checked sooner, but I've been so busy.*

He hadn't had an episode in two weeks. In past episodes, he'd forgotten his late wife's name for about six minutes. Once he had forgotten Sara's face. He'd very nearly bungled an op when he'd forgotten how to reload a Glock in the middle of a firefight. But that last one, from two weeks ago—recalling it sent a shiver down his spine.

Sara had been at an art class. Maria, on a visit to Mischa. And he had been at home, chopping an onion for chili. Whistling a tune. Knife in hand. When as suddenly as a blink, he didn't recognize his own home. He had no idea where he was or how he had gotten there. But he was armed; he had a knife.

He'd gone from room to room, stalking silently, knife at the ready, heart pounding as he threw open doors and thrust the blade into closets. He'd cleared the basement last. It wasn't until he entered his daughter's domain, smelling strongly of her perfume and her acrylic paints and chalky makeup and unknown teenage scents, that he had snapped out of it.

Then, when he realized what had happened to him, he simply... went back to making chili. And he never spoke of it to anyone.

God only knew what might have happened if anyone had been home.

The phone dinged and told him that his destination was two hundred feet ahead on the right. Zero shook out of his thoughts; he was there already, following the GPS directions on some sort of mental autopilot. He glanced around; he didn't know this neighborhood, but it looked rather plain. A quiet suburb of the nation's capital, a nicely paved road of two-story colonials that ended in a cul-de-sac.

This wasn't a place like any safe house he'd ever seen. Maybe someone at the agency had suddenly grown a conscience and realized Connors deserved better after what they'd done to him.

He parked right in front of a white house bearing the street number Penny had given him. There was no use hiding; if Connors was guarded, they were already watching. If he wasn't, there was no use hiding or sneaking about.

*So why are you just sitting here?*

He found it difficult to move. To get out of the car and do the logical thing—walk up to the door and ring the bell. He wanted answers.

Didn't he?

Then why were his hands wrapped so tightly around the steering wheel that his knuckles were white?

*Come on.* He forced himself to release the wheel. To take the keys out of the ignition. To open the car door. One thing at a time. Then his feet were moving, up the pavement.

He paused. The front door of the house faced him.

*What if there's no going back after I hear what this man has to say?*

He couldn't do this. He shouldn't be here. He turned to leave, to hurry back to his car...

The front door opened behind him.

"Can I help you?" a man's voice called out.

Zero stopped and turned, forcing a smile onto his face.

A sandy-haired man was standing in the open doorway, squinting out at him. He was barefoot, wearing jeans and a T-shirt. His file said that he was a few years younger than Zero, but the bags beneath his eyes were deeper, and he carried a little extra weight in his midsection.

"Hi. Um... are you Seth Connors?"

The man hesitated. Then his gaze flitted left and right quickly, as if he was looking for others. "They... tell me I am. Yes. Did the agency send you?"

"No, sir," Zero said quickly. "My name is Reid Lawson. Last month, my daughter Maya found you in Columbus. They brought her, and you, back here. Do you remember her?"

He nodded, though his expression was hesitant. "I do."

"I just want to—*need* to—talk to you. Just a few minutes. If that's all right."

Seth Connors thought for a moment. "I think you should come in." He stepped aside for Zero to enter, and then glanced left and right once more before closing the door.

48

Zero glanced around. The house was very nice, modern, no more than twenty years old. The furniture all looked new, albeit a bit bland, in beige and brown. The walls were mostly white. The décor was spartan, not lending anything to a particular personality or taste.

It wasn't like any safe house Zero had ever seen.

*Because it's not a safe house*, he realized heavily. *This is a convalescence home.*

"Can I get you something to drink?" Connors called from the kitchen. "Water? A beer?"

"I'm fine. Thank you. But can we speak somewhere more… private?" He had no doubts this place was bugged to high hell.

"Sure. This way." Connors pulled open a sliding glass door and they stepped out onto a patio, where the younger man lowered himself into an Adirondack chair before popping the tab on a beer.

Zero pulled out his phone. Penny had installed an app for him, one of her own design that scanned for specific radio frequencies transmitting a signal—a quick-and-dirty bug finder. A thirty-second sweep of the patio told him there were no discernible devices out there, so he lowered himself into a chair opposite Connors.

"I imagine this is all very difficult for you," he began.

Seth Connors rolled his eyes. "You sound like a therapist. Is that what you are?"

"No." Zero sighed. "Seth, no one can know what I'm about to tell you. Do I have your word?"

Connors narrowed his eyes slightly, but he nodded. "Okay, Mr. Lawson. You have my word."

Zero tilted his head to the side and put one finger to his neck, behind his ear and just below the hairline. He couldn't see it, but he knew exactly where it was. Slowly, he traced the thin, jagged white scar there, where his spine met his brain stem. Where Amun had cut him open to tear out the suppressor.

Connors leaned forward, his face a blank mask as two fingers instinctively touched the same spot on his own neck. He had no scar. But he knew.

"Jesus," he whispered. "You too?"

Zero nodded.

"And it's… out?"

"Yes. Not by choice, trust me." He quickly held up a hand and elaborated, "And not by them, either. This was… someone else."

Connors stroked his chin. "Did you get them back?"

The memories. "Yes. Not all at first. But eventually. And now I'm losing them again."

"I'm sorry." Connors took a long pull on his beer. "I didn't know there had been anyone else like me. Hell, I didn't know that *I* had been like me until recently. I thought I was losing my mind. These memories... they come back to me, a little at a time. Like just a few frames of a movie. A couple of seconds." Connors stared ahead at nothing. "It's like a flashback, except not one I'd ever seen before. But it was me. I can feel it. Feel what I was feeling in that moment. It was me." He looked up. "So you were an agent too?"

Zero nodded. "Yeah."

"They tell me I volunteered for this. Did you?"

"In a way."

"Shit." Connors shook his head. "Look, man, I appreciate the visit—I don't see a lot of people these days. But I don't know what I can do to help you. I don't know who I am, let alone who you are. So if you came looking for answers, believe me, this is the very last place you're going to find them."

Zero nodded as if he understood, or even accepted that, but that's not what he came to hear. "Seth, what I'm about to tell you is going to be rough. Maybe hard to accept. I'm sorry."

Connors frowned. "What is it?"

"Okay." Zero took a deep breath. "The CIA probably told you that they kept you around in that safe house because you volunteered for this and wanted to live a quiet life—and that part is true. They might have also told you that part of their experiment was to see how long the suppressor would last, if it would fail and when."

"They did," Connors confirmed.

"And that's also true. But there's something more that I'm betting they didn't tell you. I have it on good authority that the other reason they kept you around is to see if this process could be reversed. They figured out how to do it; they needed to then know how to undo it."

Connors shook his head. "What are you saying?"

"I'm saying that I think they did experiments on you. Ones they kept you from remembering. But now they don't get to say what you remember or what you don't..."

"That's enough," Connors said quietly.

But Zero pressed on. The man needed to hear this. "They were worried that the tech could fall into the wrong hands, and they were right. Someone stole a more advanced suppressor." Alan Reidigger had stolen it—for him. But the CIA didn't know that. As far as the agency was concerned, it could have been Russians, North Koreans, the Chinese. "They were afraid that it could be replicated and used against them, and you were their only test subject to find a way to combat it—"

"Enough!" Connors stood suddenly and flung the beer can. It hit the wall and sprayed white foam up the window. "Stop. Please. If it's true then I'm glad I don't remember it."

Zero gave him a moment to calm down. He had tried the direct approach; what he needed now was an emotional punch. "Seth. I didn't mean to upset you. I'm sorry. But I need you to understand. I know the man who created it. He was there when they put it in your head. He's gone now, on the run from them for what he's done. But he told me why you volunteered. He also told me they took so much more from you than they were supposed to. Not just her; they took your entire career away. Your friends, your family. Everything that made you, you."

Connors faced away from him, watching the foamy beer slide down the window. Suddenly his shoulders heaved and a heavy sob erupted from within. He stood like that for a full minute, sobbing into his hands, and Zero let him.

At long last he wiped the back of his hand across his eyes and slowly lowered himself into the chair again. "I hear her, you know. At night. She speaks to me. Or sings, sometimes." He smiled sadly, staring into a middle distance. "I remember her name too. Alison." He shook his head. "That was a bad day, when that one came back. A bad day."

There was nothing Zero could say that would console this man. Zero had loved and lost as well, and that was why he knew this better than most. Words of consolation or even empathy tended to feel empty at times like this. It was best just to let him talk.

Connors had volunteered for this, Zero knew, shortly after the death of his young daughter in a car accident. Zero had agreed to it after the murder of his wife, Kate Lawson, at the hands of another CIA agent that he thought was a friend.

"You're right," Connors admitted. His voice was barely above a whisper. "They did things to me. To my head. I'm sure of it. I get those little… flashbacks, brief memories of it, them poking and prodding in

51

my skull. But I don't have any details. I don't have any information for you. I'm sorry."

The man's hands trembled in his lap. To Zero it looked like Connors was on the edge of a breakdown, and there was nothing he could do for him. He couldn't take him away from here without alerting the agency and sending them after his own scent. The least he could do was the most he could do: exactly this, sitting here, helplessly, and listening.

"More surfaces all the time. And each one time it does, it only leads to more questions. No answers. Never answers. At least, not ones I want to hear." Connors looked up, and his gaze met Zero's. "I think I was a bad person. I think I killed people."

"Yeah," Zero agreed quietly. "Most likely. We all have blood on our hands."

Connors breathed a long sigh, a little ragged, but mostly in control again. "I'm sorry I don't have anything for you. But if I do, if anything at all comes back, how can I reach you?"

"You don't," said Zero. "I'll come to you. If that's okay. I'll stop by every now and then, as often as I'm able." He felt a relationship to this man; not kinship, per se, but more of an odd sense of duty, especially given his obviously fragile state.

Connors nodded. "I'd appreciate that. It'd be nice to have someone around who can relate. Who can understand."

Zero smirked. "A friend, Seth. You're describing a friend."

"Guess I am. Well, all right, Reid." Connors stood and shook Zero's hand. Then he chuckled a little to himself. "I'll remember you."

# CHAPTER SEVEN

"I did everything I was supposed to do," the young woman said. "I did what my family told me I should do. What the cops said I should do."

Sara leaned forward in her folding metal chair, her elbows on her knees, and she watched the young woman's face. The speaker was twenty-four, her brown hair tied back in a ponytail. Almost no makeup, as if she'd just swished her cheeks with a brush and called it a day. Her hands fidgeted in her lap as she spoke. She had a habit of involuntarily smiling, just a little, when she said something she was ashamed of.

Most of the women here, all seated in a wide circle in the same scuffed folding chairs, they didn't look the person in the eye when they were speaking. They'd look down at their hands, or at the floor, or maybe even at the speaker's shirt. But never their eyes.

Sara did. It was the only way to feel what they felt.

"He found me anyway." The young woman telling her story, her name was Lisa. "I don't know how. I moved. I changed jobs. I started going by Ellie. But he found me anyway. Last week. And he made sure I saw him. I was in the grocery store, getting eggs, and... there he was. Right there in the dairy aisle. He didn't say anything to me. He just looked at me, and when I looked back, he walked away." Then came the small, sad smile. "I dropped the carton of eggs. I felt really bad for the boy who had to come clean it up."

Lisa fell silent for a long moment. There weren't many rules here, in this support group. Common Bonds, it was called. *Sharing trauma, sharing hope.* That was the slogan. It was a support group, a place for any woman who had been through the wringer. Domestic abuse. Emotional or mental abuse. Drug addiction. PTSD. Depression. They shared their experiences, and through each other found... well, common bonds.

And rule number one was that you didn't interrupt. Sometimes someone would break down in the middle of their story. Or they'd have to pause and pull themselves together. But you didn't interrupt.

That was hard for Sara, because she had a lot of questions.

Like now. *Why didn't you walk up and give him a swift kick to the nads?*

"I've seen him twice more since," Lisa continued at last. "And I know what you're thinking. 'Why don't you call the cops, Lisa?' I tried that. They said that even with the restraining order, they can only arrest him if they catch him too close to me, or if I can prove he was there. He's sneaky. He just makes sure I see him, that I know he's there, and then he leaves. He's messing with me…"

"He's stalking you." She couldn't help it; she just blurted it out.

"Sara." The leader and organizer of the support group, Maddie, issued a soft reprimand and a slightly raised hand. "We don't interrupt."

"Right. Sorry."

It was hard to believe that Maddie had ever been through any sort of trauma. Her skin was flawless and healthy, unlike the rest of them. Unlike Sara's, even. Her blonde hair was always set perfectly on her head. It was even harder to believe she had two kids, and downright impossible to tell her age. Maddie looked like the Queen Bee of the Suburban Soccer Mom Elite. Sara had long wondered why she was slumming it in a classroom-style room of a community center twice a week with the likes of them, a place of melamine tables and uncomfortable folding chairs and its constant scent of cedar chips.

But every now and then, she'd get a glimpse. That's why Sara always looked them in the eye. Every now and then, a shadow would flicker across Maddie's face, something beyond sympathy or commiseration—it was understanding.

"Yeah." Lisa nodded Sara's way. "Stalking me. And I know it's him, because of that stupid car." She let out a short, bitter laugh. "He has this 'baby' of his. A red Mustang, but not like a nice one. It's one of those five-point-oh's from the nineties. He keeps it running. There's nothing he cares about more in the world." She shook her head. "No one else drives that car. But I've seen it, more than once. Two nights ago, it was parked across the street from my building."

Lisa sighed. She opened her clasped hands. Between them was a seashell, just a simple one, an orange and white scallop shell. She stood and handed it back to Maddie to signal that she was done talking.

"Thank you, Lisa. Thank you for sharing," Maddie said in her gentle, matronly voice.

"Thank you, Lisa," the group echoed.

54

"This is a unique situation," Maddie continued. "Most of the traumas that are shared here are past traumas, but what you're experiencing is here, now, in the present. If the police aren't being as helpful as you'd like, I would suggest you reach out to a local women's shelter. They have resources that can help someone in your position. They can help keep you safe, and stay vigilant if he comes around again. I'll give you the contact information for a couple of them in the area."

Lisa nodded. "Thank you."

Sara felt uncomfortable again. She fidgeted in the metal seat, but that wasn't the problem. No, the problem was rule number two: members did not get personally involved in each other's trauma. They could share. They could talk, and be friendly, and even exchange information, but they did not get directly involved.

And what that meant for Lisa was that she got to say her piece, but she was still leaving here alone and going out into the world undefended against this stalker ex of hers. It didn't sit right with Sara. It made her fidget.

She had her fair share of her own trauma, and she'd shared in others'. She'd been abducted twice. Had seen people get killed in front of her. Abandoned her dad and turned to drugs. She'd gone back to him, though—or, more appropriately, he had come for her. She'd slipped up again. Maya was there that time. And Sara had been there for her former roommate Camilla when she'd needed it.

If people couldn't get involved in each other's trauma, how the hell were they supposed to get over it?

"That's all the time we have for today," Maddie announced. "Thank you all for coming. See you next week."

The group rose, and they dutifully folded their chairs and replaced them on the rack at the rear of the linoleum-floored room. Sara hefted her backpack. It was heavier than usual today.

"Sara?" Maddie called to her.

She paused. "Yeah."

Maddie lowered her voice as the other women left the room. "You've been coming here for three weeks now, right?" The smile never left her lips. "But you haven't shared yet." She quickly held up a hand and added, "Of course there's no rush. You share when you're ready. All I'm asking is if you've thought about anything you'd like to say."

Sara returned the woman's smile with the biggest, fakest one she could muster. "Maddie, trust me, there is *tons* I'd like to say."

"Oh. That's great! Maybe next week then?"

"Sure." Sara waved a hand dismissively as she left. She had to hurry.

Out in the hall, she half-jogged to the glass double doors of the community center and out into the brisk March day. Her bicycle was chained to the rack; despite how cold it had been this winter, she still preferred to bike whenever possible.

But that's not where she was headed.

"Hey," she called out as she hurried to catch up to Lisa. The brunette was halfway across the parking lot, walking toward a hatchback that might have been as old as Sara. "Hey, Lisa."

"Yes?" The young woman paused and turned.

"Listen, I… I'm sorry that all that's happening to you. All that stuff with your ex. You know?"

Lisa shifted from one foot to the other. "Yeah. Thanks." The two of them had never talked before. And Sara was certain it wasn't lost on the older woman that Sara was only seventeen, and (as far as most adults assumed) had little idea of the horrors of the world.

*If they only knew.*

"So, like, do you think that guy moved here to follow you?" She twirled a lock of her blonde hair around one finger. *Let them think you're just a dumb kid.*

Lisa shook her head. "I don't know. I mean, I don't think so. He's got a buddy, out in Columbia Heights. Probably staying with him, if I had to guess. But I'm not going anywhere near there."

"Yeah. Totally. Anyway, sorry. Guess I'll see you next week, yeah?"

"Yeah." Lisa frowned a little, probably perplexed by this odd teenager, and hurried to her car.

Sara gave her a little wave and then headed back toward her bike. She adjusted the backpack on her shoulders.

It was heavier than usual today.

\*

56

It took forty-five minutes for her to pedal to Columbia Heights from the community center. By the time she got there her fingers were chilled to the bone and her nose was bright red, but she didn't care.

This was not a good neighborhood, even by D.C. standards. But she had spent more than a year in one of the worst parts of Jacksonville and survived. Every now and then she'd catch a scowl, and she would scowl right back.

*Look them right in the eye. Never look away or down or pretend they're not there. That shows your fear.*

She weaved up and down streets. After twenty minutes of hasty riding, she began to get discouraged. Maybe Lisa had been wrong, and the guy wasn't staying in the Heights. Maybe he was, but he wasn't here right now. Maybe she was even wrong about the car...

Sara skidded to a stop. There it was. A boxy, cherry-red Mustang parked in the narrow gravel drive alongside a shoddy, green, one-story house. She almost laughed; it looked like the car from that ancient music video "Ice Ice Baby," but red instead of white.

*Now or never. You're here. No going back.*

She swallowed the lump in her throat as she put the kickstand up and slung her backpack from her shoulders. Inside, among sketchbooks and pens and brushes and pencils and used makeup containers, was a claw hammer.

It was daylight. She was in full view of the neighbors and the house and anyone who happened to drive by, but she didn't care.

In four strides, she was alongside the car. And on that fourth stride, she reared back, and she smashed the rear driver's side window in with the hammer.

The feeling of glass giving way under steel sent an electric thrill up her spine.

She reared back again and smashed in the driver's side window, glass raining down on the seats. She thought of Jersey, the Latina girl who had been trafficked alongside her and Maya, years earlier. Sara had watched her get gunned down in the dirt.

She hadn't even known her real name.

The hammer crashed through the passenger-side window with ease as Sara thought of her sister, and the permanent scars on her leg where she had carved a message to their dad just before those same traffickers drugged her.

As the rear window gave way, she thought of Camilla, who was currently in rehab at Sara's insistence, and the lunatic boyfriend who had tracked her from Florida all the way to Maryland and attempted to hold her and Sara hostage.

Then she saw the windshield, and cold fury ran through her. It was so clean, so spotless. The hammer wouldn't do. She glanced around and spotted a large, flat rock in the front yard.

It was heavier than it looked. She hefted it with both hands, raising it above her head, ready to bring down the wrath of those scorned and abused everywhere—

"What the *fuck* are you doing to my car?!" a voice screeched. A man practically fell through the screen door of the house. He was skinny, wearing only socks, basketball shorts, and a white tank. He started toward her, but stopped dead in his tracks when he saw the rock. "Don't. Don't... don't you fuckin' do it..."

Sara flashed him a grin, and then she heaved the rock downward as hard as she could. The sound was so satisfying it gave her chills. It didn't smash through, but spider-webbed the entire windshield in white cracks and stuck there, leaving an impressive dent.

"You crazy bitch!" The man started toward her quickly, fists balled and gaze hard with fury.

Sara's heart pounded as she snatched up her hammer. When he was only an arm's length away she swung. He leapt back, his eyes suddenly wide with fear. She swung again, missing him by barely an inch as he jumped. She wasn't trying to hit him, not really... but if she did, it was his fault for not getting out of the way.

On the third swing he tripped over his own feet and fell backward onto the dirt lawn. He cowered there, covering his head and waiting for the hammer to fall.

"Lisa!" Sara shouted.

The man dared to look up at her through his fingers. "Wh-what?"

"Lisa. You know her?"

"Y-yes?"

"You're going to leave her be. You're going to pack your shit and go back to wherever you came from. Got that?"

"You're crazy!" the man shouted.

Sara flipped the hammer around so that the claw side was facing him and reared back. "Got it?!"

"Yes!"

She didn't wait around. She retreated quickly, stepping backward, still holding the hammer aloft until she reached her bike. She rode one-handed, the other still holding her weapon as the man rose to his feet and stared after her. When she was a block away he shouted a profanity-laced diatribe that didn't stop until he was out of earshot.

She pedaled faster, fearful that the man would somehow find a way to come after her even though every window on his beloved car was destroyed. She wasn't just fearful; she was *terrified*. Her heart was pounding and adrenaline coursed through her veins.

But she couldn't help the smile that came to her lips and persisted there. The fear, the thrill, the payback, the look in his eye… it was a cocktail, and she felt a high unlike anything she'd felt before.

# CHAPTER EIGHT

Zero took the long way home, meandering down back roads and through suburban developments. He kept the radio off and his phone on silent so he could think.

He thought about what Seth Connors had told him. He thought about what Seth Connors had showed him. But more than that, he thought about what Seth Connors *didn't* show him. The man had broken down in front of him. Men like Connors and Zero, they didn't reveal whole truths. Memories or not, that behavior was ingrained, subconscious. Connors was in a lot more pain and anguish than he'd let on.

Zero had vowed to return, and he would; not just for any information that might find its way to the forefront of Connors's memory, but to check in on the man. He needed support, and there was no one who could relate but Zero.

As he neared the small home he and Maria shared in Fairfax, he found himself suddenly eager to talk about it, to tell her where he'd gone and what had happened. Maria had a way of elucidating scenarios like this in ways he couldn't. She would either confirm or assuage his concerns. She would tell him he'd done the right thing and what the next right thing would be.

But when he spotted her car in the driveway, he suddenly remembered why he had been asked to get lost for a while in the first place, and a whole new wave of troubling thoughts came.

He was here. There was no delaying it.

Zero got out of the car and let himself into the house quietly. The alarm was disarmed, thankfully, so they wouldn't hear the telltale beeps that signaled someone entering. Soft voices floated to him from the kitchen, with the aromatic scent of garlic.

"So I'll simmer the garlic for just a minute or two," he heard Maria saying, "before I add in the tomatoes and paste…"

He slipped out of his shoes before heading down the foyer, wondering at the same time what exactly he thought he was doing.

*Sneaking in on them? Why?*

60

Still he padded softly down the foyer and found Maria at the stove, an array of ingredients for her homemade pasta sauce laid out on the counter and a tall pot of water boiling.

And there *she* was, her back to him, watching Maria carefully. Before Zero could say a word she spun suddenly, her small, wiry body tense but her face an impassive mask.

Zero took a step back, unnerved. She looked the same as she had the last time he'd seen her. When she had been on the other side of the fight, trying to kill him and helping the Russian double-agent Samara cause a meltdown at the Culvert Cliffs reactor. But that's not what was unnerving. She wore a pink T-shirt and corduroy pants—Sara's old clothes. With her blonde hair and green eyes, she almost could have passed for his younger daughter, several years earlier, except that there was no joy or mirth in her expression.

"Hi," Zero said cautiously, for lack of anything better to say. He knew this was coming, and yet now it was here. She was here, in their house. Here to stay.

"Hello," Mischa said back. The tension in her shoulders slackened a bit, but not entirely.

"Hey, welcome back." Maria strode to him quickly and kissed his cheek, likely more of a tactic to diffuse the situation than a display of affection. "We're making pasta."

"Yes. I see that. Smells great." Zero cleared his throat. The girl watched him as he hung his keys on a hook and shrugged out of his jacket. "So you, you're here. That's good. Have you settled in okay?"

He wanted to smack himself in the forehead. He'd raised two girls, both of whom were independent and strong if not stubborn as hell. Why was this so hard all of a sudden?

"Yes," the girl said. She looked him over, from his socks to his hairline. "You look the same."

"Oh. Do I?"

Behind her, Maria mouthed, *I think that's a compliment.*

"Um, thank you. You do too. Looks like the clothes fit okay."

"Yes." Mischa looked down at herself. "I do not like pink very much. But if I am to be an American girl now, I suppose I should learn to like it." She looked up at Maria. "Is that right? American girls enjoy pink?"

Maria smiled. "American girls can like whatever colors they want."

61

*Jesus, I need a drink.* Zero pulled open the fridge and retrieved a beer. He popped the cap and took a long swig.

"Tell me, are you still employed as a CIA operative?"

Zero coughed, nearly choking on the mouthful of beer. He rushed to the sink and spat it out, coughing for several moments.

Maria patted him on the back and whispered, "Yeah, it's been a day." While Zero coughed, she turned to Mischa and said, "Yes, he is. As am I. But you understand, much like your own history, that's not something we discuss openly."

"Of course," Mischa replied. "I assumed we were speaking in confidence. I will be discreet."

When he turned back, the girl was still watching him. It was eerie; she was like a little automaton. Like she wasn't even human.

He felt a pang of shame at that thought. It wasn't fair to her. She was a girl, and deserved a chance at a life. It was just going to take some effort. Besides, she knew the secret about him and Maria—one of the secrets, anyway—so having her here and in their trust was better than her being anywhere else.

The front door opened, and a moment later slammed shut again. Zero silently thanked all of the gods for the much-needed interruption.

"I'm home!" Sara called out. And then: "Is the little psycho here yet?"

Maria winced. Zero just shook his head as his youngest rounded the corner and stopped dead in her tracks.

"Oh. Hi," she said sheepishly. "I guess that's a yes…"

"I am not a psycho," Mischa said quietly.

"Yeah, no, of course not," Sara backpedaled. "That's just something teenagers say. Like 'lit' or 'sick.' You know, 'psycho.'"

"Jesus, Sara," Zero muttered.

"Okay. So if anyone needs me, I'll just be in the other room, putting my foot in my mouth—"

"*Sara,*" Zero scolded.

"Fine." She turned to Mischa. "I'm sorry. I didn't mean that. Let's start over. Hi, I'm Sara." She put out a hand.

Mischa looked at it for a moment, and then took it carefully. "I am Mischa." Then she glanced over her shoulder at Maria and said, "Mischa Johansson."

"Nice to meet you." Sara shot Zero a wide-eyed glance, and then set her backpack down on the floor. It clanked as if something heavy was inside—art supplies, most likely.

"Where you been?" Zero asked her.

"Art class at the community center." Sara slid onto a stool at the counter. "And then took a bike ride."

Zero was about to question it further—it was freezing out there—but Sara quickly asked, "So, Mischa, what do you like to do for fun?"

For the most part, Zero believed in being honest with his daughters. But there were just some things that he couldn't tell them. So as far as Sara knew, Mischa had been in a psychiatric hospital and had been recently cleared for release. She had no known family, and Maria had decided to adopt her. Of course there had been a lot of follow-up questions, but Zero had ducked them with the age-old go-to that there were just some things she was better off not knowing.

"Fun," Mischa said thoughtfully. "I don't quite know yet. I would like to try soccer."

"And she likes reading," Maria added.

"Huh. You and Maya should get along well," Sara said.

"Who is Maya?" the girl asked.

Sara shot Zero a look. "My older sister," she explained. "She's off at school right now. Kicking ass at West Point."

"Sara," Zero muttered, "language, please."

"West Point," Mischa repeated. "The American military academy in New York."

"That would be the one, yup." Sara ran her hands through her hair, and something tiny fell out of it, making a sound—*tink!*—against the tile. Ceramics, Zero told himself. Most likely. "Anyway, so I guess when these two get hitched, you and I will be stepsisters."

Mischa frowned slightly. "There is much about that statement I don't understand."

"Well, 'hitched' means married. See, my dad and your new mommy are engaged—"

"Sara!" Zero put up his hands in exasperation. "Could you at least *try* to exercise a little bit of couth?"

At the stove, Maria pursed her lips to hold back a laugh as she spooned tomato paste into the pan.

"Then we will be... sisters?" Mischa asked.

"Yeah. Through marriage," Sara told her. "Crazy, right? Just when I thought this family couldn't get any weirder, here we are."

"Why? Is this not normal?"

Maria turned to the girl. "Yes, it's perfectly normal. People get married all the time, and sometimes those people have children from other relationships. That's how new families are made. Just like adoption."

Mischa nodded. "So what do *you* do for fun?" she asked Sara.

"Oh, the usual teen girl stuff. I go to a support group for my PTSD, smash car windows for catharsis..."

"Sara Jane Lawson," Zero scolded firmly, leaning across the counter toward his smirking daughter. "Do you and I need to have a talk? Do not mess with her, you got it?"

"Sara is an artist," Maria said. "She paints."

"Oh." Mischa thought about this for a moment. "I would like to see."

"Really?" Sara seemed taken aback. "Uh... okay then. Come on." She slid off the stool and motioned for Mischa to follow as she pulled open the door to the basement. "My room's down here."

Zero waited until the sound of footsteps retreated down the stairs before he sighed the heaviest sigh he'd heaved in a year. "I'm so sorry about her," he said to Maria. "I don't know what's going on in her head sometimes."

"It's fine." Maria smiled and waved it off with a sauce-stained spoon. "To be honest, that's probably the most normal conversation we've had all day."

Zero grinned too. "This is crazy, right?"

"Oh, absolutely crazy."

"And how are you holding up?"

"Me?" Maria let out a short laugh. "I'm in so far over my head I don't know which way is up."

Zero wrapped his arms around her as she stirred the pan. "It'll be okay. It'll be great. We'll get through it together. This was the right call and you know it."

"Yeah." Maria sighed into his shoulder. "So, where'd you go today?"

Zero just shrugged. He wanted to tell her, but it was far from the right time. "Nowhere important. Just... got lost for a little while."

His phone buzzed in his pocket. It was a text message from Todd Strickland. *Check the news.*

Zero frowned as he opened the phone's browser and navigated to CNN. It didn't take long to determine what Todd was referring to; it was the top headline: PRESIDENT RUTLEDGE TO BROKER HISTORIC TREATY BETWEEN ISRAEL AND PALESTINE.

"Huh," he said softly.

Maria glanced over his shoulder. "Oh my god," she breathed. "He actually did it. That's incredible!"

"Yeah," Zero agreed in a murmur. "Sure is."

"Is it? Then why do you look so concerned?"

He shook his head. He knew all about Rutledge's goals in the Middle East, and that their work in Gaza had been blazing a trail toward this sort of end, but... but it seemed too easy. Too convenient. He was well-versed in the history of the region; Israel and Palestine had been at often-violent odds since the Arab-Israeli conflict of 1948. Multiple attempts at peace had been tried over the last seventy years, none to an even semi-permanent avail. The peace that was being offered couldn't even speak for a unified Palestine; it would be between the Israeli government and the Palestinian National Authority, under President Ashraf Dawoud. There would be dissenters. There would be more violence.

And the speed with which this was happening... he hadn't expected to see real results of their efforts for months. Was this to suggest that Rutledge had asked nicely, taken out a couple of troublemakers, and the two nations' leaders were so satisfied they were ready to shake hands and sign on the line?

Not to mention that behind the scenes, Rutledge had famously bad luck dealing with volatile foreign powers. The Saudis, the Russians, the Chinese... any one of them would stick a knife in his back given the chance, and it was only through concerted efforts that there hadn't been an attempt since the plasma railgun had been stolen from South Korea.

"Hey." Maria took his arm gently, shaking him from his thoughts. "You have the president's ear now. If you have concerns, he would listen to you."

Zero nodded, but he couldn't help but wonder if it was his own experiences and cynicism causing him such doubts. This was a win, to be sure. But something about it struck a chord of distrust within him.

"Call," Maria prodded. "At least leave a message with his people. I'm sure he'll hear you out…"

Zero's phone buzzed. An incoming call. At the same time, Maria's phone buzzed too, from inside her purse on the counter. His screen read "Private Number."

She looked from him to the open basement door. They both knew what this meant. Zero didn't have to call. They were being called in.

# CHAPTER NINE

Zero had always found the Secret Service to be a little amusing. In general they were pretty ordinary guys—family men, many of them veterans, just sharper and in better shape than most. But when on duty, they were all business, spines straight, solemn and silent as three of them escorted Maria and Zero into the West Wing of the White House.

Funny, most people thought that the sole duty of the Secret Service was protective assignments, specifically of the president and vice president, but their agency was much farther reaching than that, including fieldwork, foreign liaisons, investigating financial and technological fraud, and much more.

Of course, the "faces" of the operation tended to be the stoic Men in Black who stood near the president in dark suits and sunglasses and transparent earpieces.

"Are you *sure* they'll be okay?" Maria asked quietly and for the fourth time.

"Yes," Zero assured her once again. "They'll be fine. Sara may be a wiseass, but she's responsible enough to feed and watch a twelve-year-old for an hour."

Maria let out a sharp sigh. She didn't say anything further but he knew she wanted to; that was no ordinary twelve-year-old, and Sara had no idea who Mischa really was or what she was capable of.

*But it won't come to that*, Zero assured himself.

The private caller had been an aide to the Oval Office with a simple message: a car was en route to collect him and Maria and they should be prepared for pickup in ten minutes. They'd left immediately in the clothes they were wearing; for Zero, that meant jeans, a striped button-down, and a brown leather jacket. Certainly not his top wardrobe choice for visiting the White House, but this was far from his first time. He'd been there more times than he could remember—literally—and in the last two years of tumultuous American history, had shaken hands with three presidents in these halls: Eli Pierson, Samuel Harris, and Jonathan Rutledge.

"This way, please," said one of the Secret Service agents as they led them down a corridor and toward an elevator.

"Oh," said Maria resignedly. "Of course."

Zero had already guessed that they were not there for a visit to the Oval Office, but for something a little… deeper.

The basement of the West Wing was called such, but was not like any basement the term typically brought to mind. It was more of a complex, comprised of conference rooms, waiting areas, a bowling alley, the president's barber and dentist, and the John F. Kennedy Conference Room, a five-thousand-square-foot command center known by most as the Situation Room.

And since neither of them needed a root canal, he could guess where they were headed.

They stepped off the elevator and were led down two more corridors before they came to the wide double doors that granted entry to the command center where the president and his staff took their most important meetings. It was in this room where declarations of war were made, where operations were discussed, where the most sensitive information in America was given to the highest office in the land.

They were ushered inside and the Secret Service agents closed the doors after them, no doubt posting themselves just on the other side. Zero had been in this room before as well, at least three times on previous occasions of national security. Usually it entailed revealing to him some new or sinister threat, but he already had the feeling he knew why they were there—and what they were about to be asked to do.

President Rutledge rose as Zero and Maria entered the room. He was seated at the farthest end of the long table, at its head. There were two people to his left, Vice President Joanna Barkley and the White House Chief of Staff, Tabitha Halpern.

To his right was a single man, his brown hair going gray, his midsection going soft with age but his eyes just as discerning as ever. The Director of National Intelligence, David Barren, was the only boss to CIA Director Shaw besides Rutledge, and the only other boss that Zero and his team answered to in the event of the president's absence.

He also happened to be Maria's father.

"Mr. President," Zero greeted, shaking Rutledge's hand. "Ms. Vice President. Ms. Halpern. Director Barren."

"Zero, Ms. Johansson, thank you for coming on such short notice," said Rutledge, more cheerfully than Zero would have imagined for the Situation Room.

Maria nodded to the DNI. "Director."

"Ms. Johansson."

It was a very strange exchange for a third party like Zero to witness; very few people in the hierarchy were aware of the relation and both Maria and the DNI liked to keep it that way. Zero was well aware that their relationship had been strained ever since Maria's mother died several years earlier, but it was made all the stranger by the fact that she had been born Clara Barren, named for her grandmother on her father's side. During her brief tenure as a CIA deputy director, she had legally changed her name to her CIA alias of Maria Johansson, claiming it was easier since more people in her life knew her by that name than by Clara.

It was difficult for Zero to even see her as a Clara, much in the same way that he couldn't imagine most people who knew him only as Zero would ever think of him Reid. And funny, despite her new namesake being Swedish and Maria fitting that bill physically, she was actually Ukrainian and German by heritage.

"Please have a seat," said Rutledge as he lowered himself back into the chair. "I don't want to take a lot of your time. We're keeping this small and on a need-to-know. I'm sure by now you've heard the news."

"Yes sir." Zero nodded. He was right; he knew why they were there, and it only came with a sinking feeling as he took a seat beside the DNI. Maria sat on the opposite side, next to Tabby Halpern.

"Good. Now, before we get into details, you should know that after the debacle with the Ayatollah last month, we're in the process of fully re-vetting every Secret Service agent and all members of White House personnel."

*Debacle.* That was an interesting way to put it. The loyalty of a single Secret Service agent had been bought for eight figures by the Saudis to assassinate the Ayatollah of Iran. Maria had stopped him with a single, well-placed shot. But the "debacle" had called into question every person who could get close to not only the president, but any foreign dignitaries during Rutledge's tireless campaign to unite the Middle East.

"That being said," the president continued, "I want you and your team there as additional security. You'll be undercover, in plainclothes, in the crowd for the signing of the treaty."

And there it was. Precisely as Zero had thought and feared. Under Special Operations Group, they had their fair share of freedom and often did things on their own terms, so long as they got the job done. They never would have been asked to do something like act as security guards.

Under the Executive Operations Team, they did what the president told them to do. Period. And judging by the subtle flare of Maria's nostrils, she was thinking the same: that this was well below their pay grade.

"And where is this to take place, sir?" Maria asked. "The Oval Office? The White House lawn?"

Rutledge smiled, though he shook his head. "No, Ms. Johansson. This is taking place in Jerusalem."

Maria was a master at hiding her reactions when she needed to. The slight twitch of her left eye might as well have been outward balking to Zero. "Sir," she said carefully, "with all due respect to you and the leaders of these two countries, I would personally advise as the lead of the Executive Operations Team that the treaty be signed on US soil."

Across the table from him, Vice President Barkley gave Rutledge a pointed look that suggested she had said the same.

"Your input is appreciated and valued," Rutledge told her—giving her the brush-off. "But it's already decided. To sign the treaty between Israel and Palestine in Jerusalem would be symbolic. Many people on both sides still scorn the United States. We want to make it as clear as possible that this accord is between two governments, with me simply acting as mediator. I believe it will send the right message, and put us in better favor with both countries and their leaders."

Barkley spoke up. "And I believe that given recent events, this is not the best time for the leader of the free world to be publicly present in a politically fragile city so close to a region of such civil unrest."

"Seconded," Tabby Halpern admitted.

"And your concerns are acknowledged," Rutledge told them. He turned to his right. "Zero? You're awfully silent. Any thoughts on the matter?"

"Yes sir." He didn't much like being at the president's beck and call like this, though he wasn't going to say that. He agreed with the vice president's admittedly accurate assessment, but he wasn't going to say that either. Because ultimately, he knew Rutledge was right. "These two nations are divided enough as it is. To sign the treaty in Jerusalem makes sense."

He could feel Maria's eyes on him, burning a hole in his head, but he did not return her gaze. He knew precisely what she was thinking. She had brought Mischa home not three hours ago, and now they were going to be expected to jet off to Jerusalem. Even if it was only a day or two away, she wouldn't want to leave so soon.

"Sir," she spoke up, addressing the president. "The other four members of my team are fully capable of carrying out this operation without me. With your permission, I would like to excuse myself on the basis of a very important personal matter."

Rutledge frowned at that. But before he could answer, David Barren cut in. "Ms. Johansson, you are the leader of the Executive Operations Team, are you not?"

"I am. But in my absence, Agent Zero is fully able to lead—"

"Are you willing to divulge the nature of this personal matter?" the DNI pressed.

"I am not, sir."

Zero glanced over at Director Barren, but his attention was directed elsewhere—at the diamond ring on Maria's left hand.

She hadn't told her father about the engagement. She certainly hadn't told him about adopting a twelve-year-old, and she *absolutely* did not tell him the nature of that girl's background, if she ever would.

"I'm sorry," said DNI Barren, without sounding the least bit remorseful. "If you're unable to provide a reason that we can deem valid, then we cannot excuse you from such an important task."

Maria didn't argue it. Her jaw flexed and she nodded tightly.

"Right then," said Rutledge. "I'll turn it over to Tabby then for the details."

The Chief of Staff opened a folder in front of her. "You'll be expected to prep your team tonight for a departure at oh-eight-hundred tomorrow morning. There will be a Gulfstream waiting on the usual runway at Dulles. There will be one stopover to refuel. With the time difference, that should put you at Ben Gurion Airport in Tel Aviv around six in the morning, local time. The treaty will be signed at ten a.m. You'll be in plainclothes, no CIA credentials, and no weapons. Especially not firearms—"

71

"Excuse me," Zero interjected. The thought of going in unarmed was ludicrous. "We're supposed to be presidential security with no weapons?"

"You are expected to be eyes and ears in the crowd," Halpern explained. "Security will be extremely tight. There will be Israeli police, Secret Service, and an extensive detail of Presidential Guard provided by President Dawoud and the Palestinian National Authority. Think of your presence merely as hedging our bets. Chances are better than not that intervention on your part will be wholly unnecessary. However..." She glanced over at Rutledge, who nodded to her to continue. "Our Secret Service agents will be informed that there will be undercover American security in the audience. They'll each be carrying an additional sidearm. If you feel that security is threatened—and we expect you to exercise your *utmost* discretion—you can approach a Secret Service agent and tell them the codeword."

"Which is?" Maria asked.

Rutledge could not help but grin. "Rhubarb."

"Rhubarb," Maria repeated flatly.

"Chose it myself," said the president. Clearly he was enjoying being so close to the cloak-and-dagger aspects of their job.

*But this isn't a movie*, Zero thought. Those who treated it like it was often found themselves sorely disappointed at best and dead at worst.

"We'd like to get a look at the venue before the event," he said.

"I'm afraid that won't be possible," Halpern replied. "It's already strictly off-limits to civilians until the signing of the treaty, and you'll be going in as such. We have schematics for you, a three-D rendering of the layout, and a list of official personnel who will be in attendance. They'll be waiting on the plane for you."

*I don't like this*, he wanted to say. But he said nothing.

Zero glanced across the table and met Maria's gaze. He couldn't read anything behind her slate-gray eyes. Whatever was going on in her head, she wasn't giving it away. Not here and now, anyway.

"Any questions?" DNI Barren asked.

"No sir," said Zero.

"No," Maria agreed.

"All right then." Rutledge rose again and buttoned the top button of his suit jacket. "Dismissed. You'll see me in Jerusalem. Hopefully, I won't need to see you."

"Thank you, Mr. President." Zero rose as well, and he and Maria strode to the door without another look back.

The constant assurances that their presence would most likely not be needed were not at all reassuring. As the two of them were escorted back to the waiting SUV, he had only one thought running through his head.

*I don't like this at all.*

# CHAPTER TEN

"I don't like this at all," Maria said.

The ride back to the house had been a silent one, neither wanting to speak in the black SUV that carried them home. But as soon as they were deposited on their own front lawn and the car disappeared around the corner, Maria spoke her mind—and Zero couldn't help but agree.

"Neither do I," he said. "But maybe we should just chalk it up to them being overly cautious. They're probably thinking the same thing that we are and don't want to admit it—"

"Are you sure?" Maria interrupted. "Because you agreed with the president pretty quickly back there."

Zero scoffed. "Only that it made sense to me. I didn't say I liked it or wanted it." He paused a moment before asking, "Why didn't you tell your father about the engagement?"

Maria shook her head. "Please. He knows we live together. I'm sure he put two and two together."

"And what about Mischa? Are you going to let surveillance be the way he finds out about her too?"

"Mischa is none of his concern," Maria shot back. "Just like my relationship with him is none of yours. And while we're on the subject, what am I supposed to tell that little girl in there? 'Hey, I know you're probably scared and not at all used to any of this, but I have to run off to another country now'?"

"Mischa is intelligent and independent," Zero assured her. "And Sara will be here. I have every faith..." He trailed off as Maria scoffed aloud. A heat rose in his face. "What? You don't think Sara can act responsibly?"

"Of course she can. Sara's a great kid, but..."

"But what?" Zero forced himself to stay calm. "By all means, say what's on your mind."

"Fine." Maria folded her arms defiantly. "Sara is gone half the time. She's always away at 'art classes,' and I think you and I both know she's *not* always away at art classes."

Zero narrowed his eyes. "Just what are you suggesting?"

74

"I'm not suggesting anything. I'm saying it. I don't want to leave Mischa alone. Sara's constantly gone. And we can't forget that she is a former drug addict."

Zero threw his hands up at that. "There it is. There's the elephant in the room. That girl will never get out from under that, will she? She went to rehab—"

"She *fled* from rehab—"

"She's been clean," he argued.

"We don't know that!" Maria practically shouted. She bit her lip then, and took a small step backward on the dark lawn. "I'm sorry," she said quickly. "But we don't."

Zero sighed. One way or another, they were getting on a plane come morning. "Then we better find out." He started for the door.

"Wait, what are you going to do?"

"I'm going to ask her myself. With you in the room. You're better at reading faces than I am."

"Jesus, Zero, don't put her on the spot like that. She's only going to get pissed off…"

But it was too late for that. Maria had thrown down a gauntlet and there was only one way to pick it up. Zero unlocked the three locks on the front door, forcefully punched in the security code, and strode down the foyer—

"Oh. Hey, Dad."

Zero froze in his tracks. Maria did too. Sara sat cross-legged on the sofa facing Mischa. Something played on the TV at low volume as she painted the younger girl's fingernails a sparkly green.

"Hope this is okay," Sara said without looking up from her work. "It is *creepy* how still this girl can sit."

"What is 'creepy'?" Mischa asked.

"Uh, it means it's scary how good you are at it."

"Oh. Yes. This makes sense," Mischa replied. "When I was younger I often had to balance full glasses of water in each hand without spilling for several hours."

The tiny brush paused mid-stroke as Sara's eyes went wide at that.

Mischa frowned and looked over at Maria. "Is that okay to say?"

"I…" Maria was not often at a loss for words, but now she just shook her head at Zero. "I'll talk to the little one. You talk to the bigger one. And I'm *not* admitting you might have been right."

75

Zero stifled a satisfied smirk and took a tentative step into the living room. "Sara? Can we talk a minute?"

"Right now?"

"Yeah. Right now." He headed back to the dining room as Sara rose from the sofa.

"Don't touch anything," she told Mischa. As she joined her dad in the dining room she lowered her voice. "Don't freak out, it's just her fingernails—"

"We have to go," he said. "Maria and I. Tomorrow morning."

"Work thing?" Sara asked.

"Yeah. Can't get out of it. Including travel time, it should only be two days, tops."

"And you need me to watch the munchkin," his daughter said knowingly.

"We do. Yes. Please. Maria is telling her right now that we have to go."

She nodded. "Okay."

Zero was instantly suspicious. "Okay? That's it? No pushback, no attitude?"

"Of course not," she said sweetly. "But… you should know that my going rate is fifteen an hour."

Zero groaned.

"If you're gone for forty-eight hours, that'd be… you know, I might have had plans, so let's just round up to seven hundred and fifty." She picked idly at a cuticle. "Unless you have someone else in mind?"

"That's extortion."

"That's capitalism," Sara countered.

"You're a pain." He smiled despite himself.

"I was raised by the best of them."

His smile faded. "Fine, it's a deal. But you need to take this seriously, okay? She just got here. She's not used to any of this yet. You need to be here."

"I will. Can I use the car while you're gone?"

Zero raised an eyebrow. "For what?"

"Groceries?"

He pointed at his youngest. "Don't take her anywhere I wouldn't take you."

Sara held up a hand. "I swear it."

76

"Fine." He kissed her on the forehead. "Go finish up." But as Sara turned to go, he said, "Wait a sec." He didn't know how to ask it without, as Maria had said, pissing her off. "Um... are you good? You know, with everything else?"

*God, that sounded lame.*

Sara stared at him for a long moment. His daughters, both of them, had become almost as good as him at obscuring what they were really thinking. He couldn't tell if she was trying to discern his meaning or if she knew full well and was determining how to answer.

At last she smiled. "Yeah. I'm good." She headed back to the living room.

He believed her. At least he wanted to believe her. For the moment, he had little choice.

Zero entered the kitchen to find Sara hanging back as Maria, in the adjacent living room, knelt in front of Mischa. "...Just a couple of days," she was saying. "And in the meantime, you'll stay here with Sara and she'll make sure you have everything you need. No reason to worry."

"I am not worried," Mischa said. "I would often spend days at a time without adult supervision."

Sara shot her dad a flat look.

"Okay," Maria replied slowly. "But that isn't the sort of thing we do here. In fact, it's illegal."

"Why?" Mischa asked. "Can American children not take care of themselves?"

Sara snorted a little. Maria looked to Zero for help, and he held up both hands in the international gesture of, *I'm not touching this one.*

Then he retreated to the bedroom before she could recruit him. Besides, he had a phone call to make. He retrieved the secure satellite phone from his sock drawer.

"Agent Zero," Dr. León answered on the second ring. "To what do I owe this pleasure?"

"Penny, are you still in the office?"

She let out a small laugh. "I've had a cot installed in the back lab. I've actually forgotten what my apartment looks like."

"Good," he said. "I'll see you in thirty minutes."

*

77

Despite the hour, the gate guards at Langley let him through without any issue. It paid to have high clearance, though Zero knew his was still far from the top. He couldn't imagine what sort of secrets those above him were privy to, and frankly, he didn't want to know.

Once inside, he took the elevator down to the R&D sublevel and swiped his ID card at the heavy steel entrance to the lab. The CIA logged every swipe of a keycard, but he didn't care. They could know that he went to visit Penny in her lab. And the cameras would see him walking out again empty-handed.

The place never failed to impress him. The lab was a wide, cavernous room, high-ceilinged and big enough to park a plane in. The walls were pure white and powerful halogen bulbs reflected from them, probably to help simulate daylight. Warehouse-height shelving units were arranged lengthwise in the lab in the shape of a huge H, containing all manner of gadget, device, instrument of war, espionage equipment, carefully labeled and catalogued in a way that Zero could not begin to guess.

He felt a pang of remorse at the thought of his old friend, the former head of R&D. Every time he walked in here he thought, for just a moment, that Bixby might come around the corner in his horn-rimmed glasses and three-button vest. He still had a tendency to think of it as Bixby's lab, though it wasn't anymore. He had last seen Bixby in the Saskatchewan region after tracking him down at the beginning of February—and he knew it was more likely than not that he would never see him again. The brilliant engineer wouldn't let himself be found a second time.

Classical music floated to him from beyond the huge shelves. Though this was the main chamber of the underground lab, there were offshoots, halls and smaller labs, clean rooms, server banks, and who knew what else.

He found Penny at a workstation near the rear of the lab. She hummed along with the music—Wagner, if Zero wasn't mistaken—as she tinkered with a black object three feet in length, with four propellers on arms and a pair of curved wings.

"Is that the drone from the Gaza operation?" he asked.

"Indeed it is," she said without looking up. She appeared to be affixing something to its undercarriage.

"Are you... putting a gun on it?"

"Indeed I am." She looked up at last and flashed a grin. "Though that's putting it a bit simply. This is a miniature low-recoil cannon. Designed it myself. It uses an electronic firing mechanism rather than a mechanical one, which feeds from the drone's battery. No powder or incendiary necessary, which makes it a lot quieter as well. It fires these."

She tossed something small in an arc, and he caught it deftly. It was a perfectly round steel ball, a little smaller than a marble.

"Nonlethal?" he asked.

She shrugged. "Depends on how close it is. And where it hits, I suppose. So." She turned and gave him her full attention. Despite her immense intellect and upper-tier English education, she wore a studded belt and a purple Hard Rock Café T-shirt. "What can I do for you this evening?"

"We're leaving in the morning," he told her. "I could use a couple of things."

Penny frowned. "I wasn't informed of an operation."

"I know. It's last-minute and we're going in empty-handed."

She grinned. "You mean you're being expected to go in empty-handed. Let me guess: Jerusalem?"

"That's right."

Penny clucked her tongue. "Careful, Zero. Sounds like you're becoming a security blanket."

*No kidding.* What would be next—the president expecting his team to accompany him on every foreign outing? How long would it be until EOT was simply folded into the Secret Service?

"Details," Penny prodded.

"Right. High security. Metal detectors, I'm sure. Probably wands and frisking. So no guns, nothing overt. Nothing that would be picked up in a scan."

She frowned. "You're not making it easy on me." Penny rubbed her chin for a moment. "Well, there's the usual defensive gear—graphene-infused shirts and jackets. Won't be picked up on metal detectors. It'll stop a bullet as small as a nine millimeter and as powerful as an AR, as long as it's not point-blank. For offense… ah! Come with me."

Penny scurried across the lab floor with Zero trailing, to another workstation with a stainless steel table. "What size shoe are you?"

"Eleven and a half? Why?"

She pulled a black footlocker from underneath the workstation table and dug through it. "I've got a twelve. Try these on." She pulled out a pair of brown boots and held them out for him.

He didn't even bother asking what was so special about these seemingly ordinary brown boots. He slipped out of his sneakers and pulled them on. They were a little loose, but just enough for him to wiggle his toes freely. "Okay, they're on. What are they, rocket boots or something?"

Penny grinned. "You wish, Zero."

"Hang on." He teetered from one foot to the other. Something was uneven about them. "Is the left boot a little heavier?"

"Maybe. Go ahead and punch the left heel."

He stared at her for a moment. "Sorry? Punch it?"

"Like this." She brought her own left heel up, her leg behind her and bent at the knee, and at the same time brought her fist down in the act of miming a punch to one hot-pink Chuck Taylor.

"Sure," he muttered. "Punch it." He did the same, bringing the boot up and his fist down, hammering once solidly on the heel.

A five-inch blade sprang from the toe, glimmering steel sharpened to a deadly point.

He chuckled. "Boot knife. How very Bond of you."

"It gets better. Now slam the heel down with your toes aimed upward."

"Okay…" He kept his toes up at an angle and stomped down. The heel gave way slightly under the pressure—and the blade shot forward at a staggering velocity, embedding itself two inches deep into the wall.

"Ballistic knife," he said appreciably. "Now we're talking."

"The blade won't retract, so once it's out, you have to fire it. But there are three blades in there," she told him. "I'll reload that one for you. If you have to go through a metal detector, take the boots off and tell them they're steel-toed. Which they are."

Zero brought up his right leg and smacked at the opposite heel. But no blade sprang out.

"What are you doing?" Penny frowned. "Blades are only in the left boot. That's why it's heavier." She shook her head. "I thought you used to be a professor."

He ignored the jab. "Why only the left?"

"Because they were designed for a right-handed person," she said, as if it should be perfectly obvious.

80

"Um... okay." He slipped the boots off. "Thank you, Penny. With any luck I won't need any of this, but still."

"But still," she parroted. "If there's any trait you share with our illustrious president, it's just a dash of paranoia." Penny winked. "Just wish I could help more. Oh! You can take the drone."

"The one with the cannon?" Zero shook his head. "I don't think I'm going to sneak that thing past security..."

"No, you dunce. Once you're in Jerusalem, deploy it somewhere open and hidden. Ideally a rooftop somewhere. If things go sideways, I can connect via satellite and be your eyes in the sky."

"Uh-huh," he said flatly. "And also you want to test it..."

"And also I want to test it, yes."

He couldn't help but laugh a little. Penny's mentor, Bixby, had been the same way. *Here, take this highly experimental piece of tech that's never been field-tested and see if it saves your life.* And on more than one occasion, it had.

"One more thing," he told her. "This needs to look like a social call..."

"Say no more. Departure time?"

"Eight a.m."

"It'll all be there waiting for you at the jet," she promised. "Good luck, Zero."

"Thanks, Penny. Good night." He headed out of the lab. Now to go home and pack a bag. He didn't think he was going to get much sleep that night. But come morning, they'd be setting off for Jerusalem, one way or another.

# CHAPTER ELEVEN

"If nothing else," Maria murmured, "I never get tired of seeing that jet."

Zero and Maria arrived at the government runway of Dulles International Airport at seven thirty the next morning to find the familiar Gulfstream G650 waiting for them, all white and shining in the early sunlight, its windows black and polished. It was a sixty-five-million-dollar private plane that the CIA had purchased and outfitted for international operations. And its seats were *really* comfortable.

Zero was right about not getting enough sleep. His night had been restless, brief catnaps interrupted by seemingly interminable periods of him fidgeting and tossing, unable to get out of his own head. He didn't know why he felt so uneasy about this trip; it wasn't like they were the first line of defense on this. Hell, they weren't even the *third* line of defense. They were a worst-case scenario.

Maybe it was because someone had considered that scenario, the one in which they'd be necessary, that had him on edge.

Come sunup he'd finally given up and risen, only to find Sara and Mischa both already awake, the former making eggs. He was suspicious, of course, but decided not to look a gift horse in the mouth. It was likely just Sara trying to prove a point. She was headstrong, like Maya, and having her believe that she wasn't capable of something only made her want to prove it more.

The ever-punctual Todd Strickland was already there, chatting with the young dark-haired pilot who stood dutifully near the entry ramp. He smiled as he saw them approach and rubbed his hands together excitedly.

"This is going to be great, I can tell," he said by way of greeting. Todd was smart, capable, and as all-American as they came; he'd been an Eagle Scout, a high school quarterback, and an Army Ranger. Getting to watch the president sign a historic peace treaty was probably like Christmas come early for him.

Zero approached the pilot with a nod. "Morning. Was there a delivery?"

The pilot returned the nod. "Yes sir. Already loaded."

"Good. Thank you." Penny had come through. Now all he could do was hope that she had been right, and suffer through some jabs later about his paranoia.

Chip Foxworth arrived five minutes later, in his usual uniform of a black bomber jacket and a five o'clock shadow. "Morning y'all," he announced. Foxworth had been a good addition to the team so far; he was a former Tomcat pilot that had applied for, and been summarily rejected from, Special Operations Group a few years earlier. Zero and Maria had fast-tracked him into EOT and hadn't had any reason to doubt the decision. He had good aim, better instincts, and a Texan drawl that added some charm to their little coterie.

"Hi again, baby," Chip cooed as he ran a hand over the Gulfstream's fuselage. "Did you miss me? I know you did."

Maria made a face. "When he's like this, he's *your* hire," she murmured to Zero.

Alan was, in true fashion, the last to arrive at five minutes before wheels-up. His rusting pickup rumbled right onto the runway, black smoke chugging out of the exhaust pipe and sounding as if the truck was giving a death rattle. To look at it would be to assume it was about to fall apart any moment, but in reality the pickup could outrun and outmaneuver a police Interceptor.

Alan Reidigger parked and climbed out of the cab, scratching idly at his beard. A few crumbs fell out. "Stopped for a danish," he admitted.

"Are you really just going to leave that there?" Maria asked.

He glanced back at the truck. "Mm," he said. "They want it moved, they can move it." Reidigger's disdain for the agency was well documented. Even in the face of a long jail sentence for helping Zero on an unsanctioned op, he had still resisted Maria's offer, and had only agreed to return to the CIA in the capacity of an "asset"—a vague term that basically meant he'd be called in as-needed. But when EOT was formed, Alan's choices were full-fledged field agent or bust. He'd chosen agent for Zero's sake, choosing to stick by his friend's side but using every opportunity to show how much he didn't like it.

Zero suspected that it wasn't just for him, but also for Maria, and even Todd. And maybe even because Alan missed it, at least a little. Though he'd never admit that.

He boarded the jet and sank into a cream-colored seat. There were eight in total, with wide armrests and pillow-top headrests. Another four seats could fold out from bench seats at the front and rear of the cabin to seat up to twelve if necessary. A stout black footlocker sat at the rear of the cabin, blocking those seats; no doubt Penny's delivery. Maria sat in the seat facing his, a fold-out tabletop between them and a brown leather portfolio atop it.

A minute later the entry ramp was up, the door secured. And ten minutes after that they were airborne, the Virginia coast falling away below them and giving way to the endless blue of the Atlantic.

It wasn't until they'd reached cruising altitude and a steady air speed of six hundred and fifty miles an hour that Maria addressed the team. Her seat swiveled with a release switch at its base so she could see everyone.

"This is straightforward," she told them as she opened the brown portfolio. "We're there in the capacity of extra eyes and ears. Security in the crowd. We'll be there under the guise of an American press crew. The passes are all here, along with IDs…"

"Christ," Alan muttered. Zero knew exactly what he was thinking; if they'd known they were going in as press, they could have prepared better. Possibly even hidden weapons in fake video cameras. They could have justified surveillance equipment, headphones, the whole nine.

"We had less than twenty-four hours to prepare," Maria countered. She knew what he was thinking as well. "Look, guys, this is as simple as it gets, okay? We go in. We watch, we listen, we leave." She powered up the tablet and opened a CAD program, placing two fingers on the screen and spreading them to enlarge the 3D schematic of a building. "This is the Generali Building in Jerusalem. An administrative building that holds government offices—"

"Not to be confused with the Generali Tower in Milan," Zero interjected.

Maria shot him a look and turned the tablet screen for all to see. "Here's the main atrium, where metal detectors and the first wave of security will be. Guards at the doors to the conference room they're using as an auditorium will be doing random stop-and-frisks. So don't try to smuggle anything in, all right? Israeli police will be posted at all points of egress." She pointed as she explained. "And Palestinian Presidential Guard, along with Secret Service, will be posted all along the stage they're erecting here. Press line is here, so we'll have front-row seats." She pointed to Todd. "But we're not there to watch the president. We're there to watch everyone *else*."

"Yes ma'am." He nodded.

"This is as old-school as it gets," she continued. "We'll have phones, but not radios. No guns. No weapons of any kind."

Zero felt a pang of something—shame, or something close to it—at the thought of the boots hidden in the footlocker.

"This is a classic 'if you see something, say something' situation. We'll daisy-chain each other in our peripheries. Todd, you'll keep an eye on Chip. Chip, on Alan. Alan on me, and me on Zero…"

"And me on Todd, got it," Zero said. If someone else on the team noticed something amiss, they wouldn't exactly be able to shout it out in the middle of a treaty-signing without causing chaos. Keeping an eye on each other would be paramount.

"Exactly," Maria agreed. "Alan—keep sharp. Todd, stay attentive. Chip, don't pull any rookie moves."

The three men exchanged a glance and a shrug as if such notions were entirely beyond them. Zero almost laughed; if anyone who put their trust in the Executive Operations Team could be privy to this meeting, they'd probably be rapidly losing faith. But when the hammer fell, they were a unit, and an effective one at that.

*Then why are the butterflies starting already?*

"One last thing," Maria told them. "If you're absolutely certain of a threat and you have need of a firearm, use the codeword on the nearest Secret Service agent."

"Right," Alan muttered. "Walk up to one of the president's meatheads and tell them 'rhubarb.' They definitely won't think you're batshit crazy."

"They've been briefed," Maria said dismissively. "Look, if we can't trust inter-agency cooperation then there's no point in us ever being involved in something like this…"

"I agree," Alan said with fake enthusiasm.

Maria ignored him. "So that's it. With that, I'll turn it over to Agent Zero to tell us what's in the box." She gestured with her chin toward the rear of the plane and the footlocker.

Of course they'd all spotted it. Of course Maria knew he'd visited Penny the night before and come home empty-handed.

He shrugged. "Contingencies."

"Contingencies," Maria repeated, with just the hint of a smile on her lips. "Sure. Let's hope it doesn't come to the box then, huh?"

He nodded, and even tried to return the smile, but it wouldn't come. Instead he looked away—and caught Alan's gaze. There was worry there, even beneath the beard and the shadow of his trucker's cap. He was sure that Alan was seeing it too in his own face, mirrored, and he wondered if Reidigger also wondered why he felt like that. No one had better instincts than Alan in a situation like this—except maybe Zero.

And that thought did not help the anxious feeling he felt in his gut as they hurtled eastward toward the Mediterranean.

# CHAPTER TWELVE

*Elbows are to remain off the table.*
*Proper posture: sit up straight, don't slouch.*
*Chew an appropriate sized portion with mouth closed.*

These were rules straight out of the cadet's handbook. Maya knew them by heart, and the myriad others—correct placement of utensils, bringing food to your mouth and not your face to the plate, et cetera, et cetera, on and on. Rules. Endless rules.

She leaned over her plate, one arm around it as if someone might take it from her and the other propped, with an elbow, as she tore a hunk of bread with her teeth.

For anyone outside of West Point to hear the rules of the Mess Hall would think it a sacred place—and for all intents and purposes, it was. Mealtime was important in the military academy. But more than that, this was also where assemblies, awards ceremonies, and other gatherings were held.

"Lawson!" The Table Commandant, seated at the head of the table, barked in her direction. "Elbow off the table. Sit up straight."

She slid her elbow from the table's edge but didn't improve her posture. The Commandant was a second lieutenant, name of Collins, no more than twenty-one or twenty-two. He was a recent Point graduate who should have been an officer in the Army now, ordering around grunts at Fort Drum had he not torn his meniscus while demonstrating a routine training exercise. Now he was here, babysitting teenage cadets in the Mess Hall, and his surliness illustrated the ignominy of such a relegation.

Simply put, Collins was not well liked by the cadet body, and Maya was no exception.

A sesame seed stuck in her teeth and she picked at it with a pinky.

"For God's sake, Lawson!" Collins growled. "What is with you? Show some decorum—"

Maya slammed a hand down on the table, palm flat, hard enough to make the cadets around her jump a little. "I'm having a rough day," she said through gritted teeth. "So maybe you can back off? *Sir?*"

Several of the students at her table went wide-eyed. Two of them grinned in anticipation of seeing Collins fly off the handle at her.

But instead he seethed and said quietly yet forcefully, "Stand. Now."

Maya made a show of glancing down at the brace on his knee. "You first."

"That's it!" Collins pushed himself up from the table, nearly toppling his chair. "Let's go. Or I'm calling the MPs…"

The sesame seed finally dislodged from her molar. So she stood, and she spat it in his face.

The collective gasp from those around her was almost as satisfying as watching the seed bounce off Collins's nose. His cheeks flushed red, and despite his youth Maya feared he might pop a blood vessel in his forehead.

He ignored the metal crutch propped against the table and lurched for her, hands outstretched. Maya made a quick sidestep an instant before his hands would have wrapped around her lapels, and he grasped at nothing. Collins wobbled uneasily for a moment before his injured knee gave out and he collapsed to the Mess Hall floor.

To their credit, most cadets maintained their composure. But a few snickered and sputtered, unable to suppress their laughter.

Maya grinned and turned back to her seat—and nearly bumped into the barrel chest of a very stern-looking Corporal Brighton.

"Dean's office," he said in a low voice. "Now. Do you need an escort?"

She waved off the suggestion. "I know where it is."

*

"This is not at all what I meant when I said to use your academic probation to your advantage." Dean Hunt sighed and shook her head across the desk at Maya.

"This will work," she insisted. "Look, no one trusts me. They think I'm a snitch. I needed to change things up a bit."

*To think like a spy,* Maya thought.

For the last two days she had pored over a cadet list for each class, tracking down the four offenders who had been dismissed from the academy for attempting to use forgeries. Once she had identified them, she looked into their social circles, common friends close enough to share such a secret like the whereabouts of the forger—and she had identified one, a fellow Cow named James Bradley. Jimmy to his friends.

But Bradley wouldn't even let Maya look his way if he thought she was up to something. So she needed a damn good reason to talk to him—and now she had one.

"What am I supposed to tell Collins? Or Corporal Brighton?" Hunt asked. "This sort of thing cannot go unpunished, and you're already supposed to be on probation."

"Tell them whatever you can," Maya insisted, before adding, "ma'am. Tell them… I'm spending nights in solitary. Just buy me a day or two, and I'll solve this."

Dean Hunt stared without blinking. "Am I going to regret asking you to do this, Lawson?"

*Probably.*

But she couldn't say that.

"You're friends with the DNI, right?" she asked instead. "And I'm sure he told you a story or two about my dad."

Hunt nodded, but did not elaborate. Maya didn't need to either; they both knew what she was referring to. Any story about her dad as an agent would involve a monumental mess—but the job would get done.

"Fine," the dean said at last. "I'll get you a day or two. Go. Find them."

"Thank you, ma'am." Maya rose quickly before Hunt could change her mind.

But as her hand reached the doorknob, the dean called out to her. "Who's your lead?"

"Sorry?"

"Your lead," Hunt repeated. "You wouldn't have acted so rashly if you didn't have a lead."

Maya smirked. Hunt was shrewd. "With all due respect, ma'am, I'm not going to tell you that. I can't have anything jeopardize the operation. When it's done, I assure you, you'll get everything I know. But not until it's done."

Hunt returned the smirk. "As you were, then, cadet."

Maya slipped out into the hall, doing her very best to look as if she had just been severely reprimanded. To her own surprise, she even managed to moisten her eyes a bit. Anyone passing by and glancing at her—and there were many—would probably think she was on her way out for good after the Mess Hall spectacle.

It was 1330. She'd memorized Jimmy Bradley's schedule and knew just where to find him. She pushed out through a pair of double doors and was met by a sudden and almost breathtaking chill. March in upstate New York was freezing—hell, *May* in upstate New York was still cold. But she gritted her teeth and bore it, walking up to the track in long sleeves but no jacket.

Several boys were on the track, jogging in gray sweatshirts and pants emblazoned with West Point insignia. She approached the track, arms folded over her chest, ignoring the glances from some of the boys as they ran past her.

Then she spotted him, coming around the final bend. Bradley. He had brown hair, shorn short as usual for cadets, which didn't suit his facial structure with his bony cheeks and hooked nose. He looked her way as he passed, a mixture of curiosity and amusement—he recognized her.

And she nodded, only slightly, as he passed.

Maya resisted the urge to shiver in the time it took him to come around again. A quarter mile at a minute forty-five. Not bad, though she could do better.

For a moment, she thought he would just keep going and ignore her a second time. But no; he slowed his pace as he approached the final bend, and by the time he reached her he was walking, chest heaving. Sweat ringed the neck of the gray sweatshirt, turning it a few shades darker.

"Lawson," he said with a slight nod.

"Jimmy."

"Only my friends call me Jimmy."

"Then let's be friends."

He chuckled. "You're not my type." He turned toward the track.

"Wait." She took a step toward him. "I need help. You heard what happened?"

Jimmy Bradley grinned. "Everyone heard what happened. What, did you snap or something?"

She shook her head. "Like I told Collins, I was having a bad day. He was getting on my case. I just did what everyone else wished they could do."

He nodded. "Sure. So what's it got to do with me?"

90

Jimmy wasn't pals with the Firsties that had aligned with Greg and liked to make Maya's life miserable—but that didn't mean he would be kind to her or do her any favors. She had to play it carefully.

"I was already on probation," she said. "I'm going to be gone if I can't do something about it. I need a signed letter from my doctor saying that I skipped my meds and wasn't in the right state of mind. Some insurance snafu kept me from refilling my scrips."

Jimmy shrugged. "Too bad I'm not your doctor." He turned again to leave.

"No, but you know him," she called after. "And I bet he's not cheap."

Jimmy stopped. He sighed. "Who talked?"

"No one talked. I figured it out."

"And how do I know you're not a narc?"

Maya scoffed. "I spat in Collins's face. I'm on probation. Jimmy, they're going to *expel* me. And then my dad is going to kill me. Three years here down the drain. My life as I know it is going to be over."

"Yeah. Guess you're right." Jimmy picked at a fingernail. "You know, there are a lot of cadets here that wouldn't mind seeing you gone. Why should I help you?"

"For one? I have money. Name a price. Two?" She stared him right in the eye, as somber as she could. "If you turn me down I'll go to Hunt with what I know and try to use it as leverage. It probably won't work, but you'll go down too."

Jimmy tried to keep his cool, but Maya definitely noticed a flicker of fear cross his face for a moment. "You've got nothing. No proof."

She shrugged. "No, I don't. But that won't stop them from looking deeper. At least talking to your expelled buddies. Maybe even opening an investigation. You really want them breathing down your neck?" She gave him a moment to process that. "But… if you help me out here, I'm implicit. If you go down, you can name me and I go down too."

"I do like that." Jimmy rubbed his chin. "All right, Lawson. Five hundred. You good for it?"

She nodded, trying to hide her surprise. She thought the price would be a lot higher. "Not a problem."

He grinned at her. "No, no. Five hundred is *my* cost to tell you where to go. The real thing will be a lot more than that."

91

*Should have figured.* She had already assumed that Jimmy wasn't the forger but the intermediary between them and cadets. Now she knew it. That was just one reason she hadn't given him up to Hunt; she didn't want the dean sending any dogs after his scent before she could get answers herself.

"Of course," she said. She reached for her bag for the money.

"Not here," he said quickly. "You know Graham? He does the radio station." She nodded. "Give it to him in the next twenty-four hours. He'll pass it on to me. Got a pen?"

She pulled one from her bag and held it out. He took the pen and then grabbed her left hand. She instinctively pulled away and balled it into a fist.

"Chill, Lawson. Give me your hand."

She scolded herself internally and held out her hand. He scribbled an address in blue ink on her skin. "Memorize it, and then wash it off right away. Got that? Go there. Tell him JB sent you. Don't tell a soul about the address or me."

"I won't—"

"I mean it," Jimmy said forcefully, his voice taking on an edge harder than Maya thought he could muster. "Anyone comes to me saying you sent them, I'll deny everything and give you up."

"I'm not interested in sending you referrals," she said coolly. "I'm just doing this to save my own ass. I don't see why we should ever have to talk again."

He smirked at that. "See you around, then." Jimmy took two steps back toward the track and paused. "Hey, is it true you broke Chad's nose with a textbook two days ago? Behind the gym?"

She nodded. "Yeah."

Jimmy laughed. "Good. That guy's an ass. Good luck, Lawson." He reached the track and broke into a jog.

Maya looked down at the address inked on her hand. For the briefest moment, her mind flashed back to the memory of the train. Losing consciousness as the drugs the traffickers forced into her took hold. Carving the letters into her own calf with a sharpened metal clip torn from a sandal. A message for her father, who she had only been half certain was coming...

She shook the thought from her head. That was a long time ago. Yet it had set the stage for where she stood now. After her rescue was when she had made the declaration for her future that she now stood by. The scars were still there, thin and white and almost illegible. But they were there.

She still avoided shorts whenever possible.

The address was one line in blue ink: *817 Butler St, PK.*

*PK?* Ah—Poughkeepsie, she realized. About thirty miles north of the academy.

It would have been a lot easier if Jimmy Bradley was the forger. But of course he wasn't. It would have been equally easy if he'd pointed her in the direction of another cadet, someone on campus—but of course he hadn't. No, the forger was off-campus. A civilian.

As she made her way back toward the building, shivering slightly in the chilly breeze, an idea came to her, one that could solve both her and Dean Hunt's dilemma. She needed to get off campus, and the dean needed to make it look like punitive measures had been taken.

Maya licked two fingers and rubbed the address off the back of her hand. She could have just given it to Hunt, along with Jimmy Bradley's name. But no. She'd been tasked with finding the forger, and that's what she was going to do.

Armed with a new direction and feeling like she was close, she headed toward the dean's office to ask Hunt to suspend her from the academy.

# CHAPTER THIRTEEN

Zero shrugged into the blue blazer and straightened the lapels, It was a little snug around the shoulders but otherwise fit well. Penny had been thorough, not only making sure that their graphene-laced attire was businesslike enough for their purpose, blazers and collared shirts, but getting the fit mostly right.

He had to say "mostly" because at that moment Alan was struggling to fasten even one button of a tweed sport coat over his fairly substantial midsection.

He grunted. "Bet she did this on purpose."

Zero grinned. "Consider it a subtle hint, maybe?"

The flight to Ben Gurion Airport in Tel Aviv had been grueling. Almost twelve hours total with a stop to refuel in Zurich. He'd thought of his friend Dr. Guyer and wondered if he might be at his office. But of course there was no time for a visit, social or medical.

With the time difference, they'd left Dulles in the morning just after sunrise and landed the next day just before sunrise. A waiting car took them to their hotel, an upscale and admittedly nice place eight blocks from the Generali Building, where the treaty would be signed. Their aliases had been checked in there for two days already; their room keys had accompanied the fake press badges in Maria's dossier.

Waiting for them in the hotel room was a video camera, two tape recorders, and a microphone, the instruments that would further verify their cover. Alan had taken one look at them and sighed.

"Could easily fit an LC9 in there," he said, gesturing to the digital camera.

"Sure," Maria retorted. "Could you imagine how every foreign press conference would be from here on out if supposed reporters started pulling guns out of cameras?"

Chip and Todd were in the next room over, adjoined to theirs with a connecting door. They came in, dressed in the smart garb Penny had provided them with and looking for all the world like they were about to attend a summit in Silicon Valley.

"Time?" Zero asked Strickland as he pulled on the brown boots, the three ballistic knives hidden in the left toe.

"Oh-nine-hundred," Todd responded. "Sixty minutes to curtain."

"What's with the boots?" Maria asked him as she pushed a small silver stud through her earlobe. She was dressed in a charcoal gray blazer with a white blouse. The way her blonde hair flowed around her shoulders made her look, at least to him, like she really could be a news anchor.

"Uh... they're very stylish?" he replied.

"Sure," she said flatly. "Anything you want to tell me?"

"Yes." He stood and kissed her gently on the forehead. "You look terrific in gray. Really makes your eyes shine."

"Let's save the foreplay until this is done," Alan grunted. He hefted the camera—no one had said it, but everyone there knew that his appearance lent the most credence to being the cameraman in their troupe.

"Let's go," Maria announced. The group of them moved toward the door. Except Zero, who lingered. "You coming?" she said over a shoulder.

"Yeah. Be right behind you. Just... need to hit the head." He rubbed his stomach and winced. "All that flying made me a little queasy."

"Uh-huh," she said in that way that meant she didn't believe him for a second. "We'll wait in the lobby. Make it quick."

"Of course." He waited for two full minutes after the door was closed, until he was certain they were at least on the elevator heading down, if not in the lobby. Then he hurried to the footlocker and pulled it open.

And for a moment, he just stared down at the object. He knew he should have known what it was, but its shape just confounded him. It was angular but smooth, with four propellers, and an odd little barrel on its underside...

"Not now, dammit!" He gripped his forehead as if he could squeeze the knowledge out like an orange. He had gone so long without an incident. And now? When he already felt so uncertain about what they were there to do? The last thing he needed to worry about was whether or not he'd forget where he was, or why he was there...

*Calm down. Just breathe a minute.*

He closed his eyes and took a deep breath, in through his nose and out through his mouth. And then again. Then a third.

95

He opened his eyes and breathed a fourth breath—this one a heavy sigh of relief.

"Drone," he said aloud. "You're a drone. I've got this." He scooped it up and hurried out of the room, heading for the elevator.

It was at least a silver lining that it hadn't happened with anyone else in the room. Alan knew something was amiss, ever since he'd witnessed Zero forgetting how to load a pistol in a firefight. Alan had told Maria about it—not to be a snitch, but out of genuine concern. And she, in turn, had told him that if she had reason to believe he could jeopardize an op, she'd pull him from it in a heartbeat.

Future wife or not, she was not above dealing with him bluntly when it came to his or any other team member's safety.

From the elevator he found the access stairs to the rooftop and headed up. The heavy steel door, thankfully, wasn't locked. It was surprisingly pleasant out, the temperature in the mid-sixties with clear skies. Or mostly clear—he heard the thrum of helicopter blades and saw at least two of them in the sky, no doubt circling near the Generali Building.

He found a spot in the corner of the roof where the drone was decently obscured from anyone who might come up there, behind n large square air conditioning vent. He shot Penny a quick text with the satellite phone—*Placed*, was all it said—and then hurried down to the lobby to meet with the team.

"All good?" Maria asked as he rejoined them.

He flashed her a thumbs-up.

The walk to the location was like a funeral procession. They went single-file to avoid passersby with the busy foot traffic. None of them spoke, and they kept their heads down. There was no need to, really, since no one knew who they were here. But, Zero mused, maybe the others were thinking the same as he was. That despite the clandestine nature of their visit to Jerusalem, this all seemed so... *normal*, compared to what they were usually asked to do. Dress nice, pretend to be press, and watch the signing a treaty. Even the city around them was, for lack of a better term, normal; culturally and architecturally there was no pretending they could have been walking down a busy American avenue, but it was certainly a far cry from the desert compound they had stormed a few days prior.

When they were within two blocks of the Generali Building, things began to look a lot less normal. The thrumming helicopters flying lazy perimeters around downtown Jerusalem only added to the scene in front of the building. Sawhorses had been set up at a distance from the front entrance, partially blocking the street and limiting it to one lane. Two officers directed the slow flow of traffic while other Israeli cops corralled the gathering crowd into an orderly line.

Zero and his team fell in place with this line. It seemed that most of the attendees were far better dressed than he was; dignitaries and members of the Palestinian and Israeli governments alike were present, along with attachés and entourages, but as far as the police and security were concerned they were just another body to get safely inside the building.

The first security point was an ID check. A stern-faced officer in a black tac vest and helmet checked Zero's press badge and American identification, holding it up as he glanced several times between his face and the ID. Finally he handed it back and waved him through.

The second checkpoint was just inside the bright atrium. Metal detectors. Zero took off his watch and belt, and from his pockets took the satellite phone and the wallet that contained his fake ID and some cash. Finally he slipped out of the boots and placed all of the items in a gray bin, along with the tape recorder in his pocket.

He stepped through the detector without incident. On the other side, a white guy in a black suit held up a hand to gesture for him to pause. A second agent peeked into the bin and gave it a once-over.

Zero held his breath as the agent picked up one of the boots. The left one. He bit the inside of his cheek as the agent ran a latex-gloved hand over the sole, around the contour of the underside, and over the toe of the boot.

*If that knife was to spring out right now…*

But it didn't. The agent set the boot down again and slid the gray tray over to Zero.

After pulling the boots back on, he headed toward the third checkpoint. Palestinian Presidential Guard by the looks of them, in black uniforms and black berets. They were posted by the door to the auditorium and kept a keen eye on the attendees as they filed past, occasionally pulling someone aside for a brief frisk, checking handbags and waving security wands.

Zero passed them without incident, and the rest of the team followed him inside.

97

The auditorium was not large. An elevated dais at the far end of the room held a podium bearing the seal of the President of the United States, and a table, the cloth covering of which displayed the flags of Israel and Palestine. Three chairs behind the table indicated where the men of honor would soon be seated for the signing.

Directly before the dais was a press pit, a standing-room-only span of open floor where already more than a dozen cameras were set up, facing the dais as reporters gave introductory reports and traded information with their counterparts back in whatever studio they hailed from. Behind the press pit were rows of seats for the guests of the signing, dignitaries and diplomats and military personnel, the chairs set upon curving elevated rows like an amphitheater.

The five of them filed into the press area and took positions in the order that Maria had dictated earlier. He checked his watch; less than ten minutes before the ceremony would begin. More press members pressed into the pit with them, forcing them nearly shoulder to shoulder. There were tons of media there, from a number of countries, each wanting a good vantage point, a clear shot, and some breathing room when there wasn't much.

Zero realized the flaw in their plan; as press, they'd have a front-row seat to ensure nothing happened to the president, but maneuvering out of there would be difficult.

"Like sardines in here," Alan said, his voice a low rumble. He had a knack of reading Zero's mind in moments like these. They often seemed to think alike. Alan's instincts in a situation like this were just as keen as his own, and he wondered what his friend was thinking in the moment. If he had the same butterflies in his stomach, congealing into a nervous cocoon of a knot.

Alan brought the digital camera up near his face and turned slowly, as if getting a panning shot of the crowd behind him, but likely scoping the crowd for anyone suspicious or looking anxious—besides Zero, that was.

*All the personnel has been carefully vetted*, he reminded himself. *Security is thorough and tight.* There were eight members of the Palestinian Presidential Guard flanking the dais, possibly more elsewhere that he couldn't see, spanned about eight feet from each other, hands clasped in front of them and eyes straight ahead, automatic pistols slung on straps over their shoulders…

Zero frowned. It seemed an odd choice of weapon for security in a situation like this. He struggled to remember the service weapons of the Palestinians.

"Alan," he said quietly. "Do you know what the—"

A speaker hummed before he could finish, and a male voice said solemnly over the PA system, "Ladies and gentlemen." A hush fell over the crowd instantly as the greeting was repeated in Arabic and Hebrew. "The President of the United States of America."

Applause broke out behind and around him, but Zero did not join them. His muscles were too tense for that.

*Here we go.*

# CHAPTER FOURTEEN

Stefan Krauss did not like to ask for help. He preferred to do as much as he could on his own, and did not share his ideas or plans with anyone. However, he recognized that sometimes help was necessary, and as he convalesced in a thatch-roofed hut on a white-sand beach at the edge of the world, he was thankful he had allowed himself a few minor concessions to his independent nature.

The thirty-six-year-old German-born assassin reclined on a white cot with steel bars along both sides, watching a small television that sat upon a table at the foot of the bed. Satellite TV—that was another thing for which he was thankful.

That, and being alive.

He still struggled to believe that the man he had fought with on the South Korean boat had been the real Agent Zero. The man just seemed so… austere, to him. Too much so to be the terrifying specter of so many hardened men's nightmares. Yet he had bested Krauss, had shot him in the back—the bullet had missed his spine by an inch and a half—and had blown up the boat, using its own charge, the plasma railgun, against it.

Sheikh Salman, Krauss's most recent employer, was dead by an alleged self-inflicted gunshot wound. The Ayatollah of Iran was alive. But so was Krauss.

Agent Zero would certainly not believe it possible. It would have taken a miracle for Krauss to have survived the gunshot, the explosion, the plunge into the icy Atlantic waters with no hope of rescue.

But Stefan Krauss had allowed himself those concessions, to put into place certain measures, contingencies, in the event of failure. He was not a stranger to failure, and was not so haughty or hubristic to believe that such things were impossible. That sort of arrogance was best left to cinematic villains and soon-to-be-dead men.

Krauss was *alive*.

Stefan Krauss was not his real name; he had abandoned that long ago, at age fourteen, when he was forced to flee his former life for murdering his rapist stepfather. His first kill. Sloppy, emotional, some

100

might even say inefficient. There had been a real Stefan Krauss, a German football player with the Dortmund club. The now-Krauss remembered him well from his boyhood, even if he had only played for one season before being killed in an automobile accident near Dusseldorf.

On the television, the American song played that cued the introduction of the US president. "Hail to the Chief," it was called. He smiled; they had an anthem for everything, the Americans.

The president spoke a few words, even quoted Einstein. A fellow German. Krauss supposed it was intended to inspire but he failed to relate. A peace treaty? Anyone who believed in treaties hadn't been paying attention. Did history not prove, again and again and again, that violence was a faster and far more effective path to peace? The Americans had every tool necessary to put a swift and crushing end to violence and infighting in their targeted regions, yet they chose diplomacy and peace talks. Such things were fleeting. Did they genuinely believe it would last? Or were they just pandering?

He flexed the fingers on his left hand and pain shot through them. He had sustained some nerve damage from being in the water for so long. Most likely permanent.

Krauss should have been dead, but he was alive. Thanks to his contingencies. Yes, three weeks earlier he had been shot, and he had been on the boat when the railgun was directed at its bow and fired. He'd been flung many meters, and thrown into the thirty-five-degree water of the Atlantic, a hundred and sixty miles from the American shore.

He had been wearing a neoprene dry suit under his clothes, polar grade. The sort of suit divers wore for dangerous underwater expeditions in the Arctic.

If he had lost consciousness when he hit the water, there was no doubt he would have drowned. But he did not lose consciousness, and clung to a curved fragment of hull, flipping it upside down, creating not only cover but a small, dark pocket from which he had managed to keep his face and hands just warm enough, by his breath and the heat from his own head.

The suit protected him enough from the freezing waters, but Agent Zero had shot a hole in it. Water was seeping in slowly; he could feel it, though he couldn't feel the bullet wound anymore as he huddled beneath the fragment of hull, slowly succumbing to hypothermia. Freezing to death.

The second molar on his upper right side was an implant. He reached for it, fingers shaking, twisting it slightly to pull it free, though not without some difficulty and several sharp pains. Eventually the fake tooth came loose. It was made not of enamel but of ceramic—he had to be vigilant not to chew hard foods on that side of his mouth—and he bit down on it, hard, with his left molars to activate the tiny device inside. A beacon, a GPS signal.

Stefan Krauss did not like to ask for help, but he recognized that sometimes help was necessary. Someday he would die, probably much sooner than he would like, but he refused to die for Salman's cause. So he shivered in his dark, watery, frigid little hull hovel and he counted. Minutes stretched like hours and he counted, for lack of anything better to do than shiver and bleed into the ocean. Eighty-four minutes and twenty-seven seconds went by before he heard the thrum of helicopter rotors. It could have been the Americans, come to survey the wreckage and take him prisoner. But no.

One thing that Stefan Krauss had learned early was that people would do almost anything if the price was right. He lived by that notion. He made contracts by that notion. He planned by that notion. And on that day, blue-lipped and bleeding and near-dead, he survived by that notion.

His rescue had been coordinated by a wealthy Belarusian benefactor, one whom Krauss had made immensely wealthier by eliminating two of his fiercest competitors in the cocaine trade. The benefactor owned a yacht with a helipad and had a pilot on standby two hundred and forty miles from the American coast, as Krauss had requested. He'd never fully believed that the railgun would make it to their target destination.

His neoprene suit was cut away on the helicopter, and he was treated for hypothermia and the bullet wound in his back as he was transported to his safe house, first by the helicopter and then by boat and eventually by seaplane.

The Maldives were a non-extradition archipelago, more than seven hundred miles from the Asian continent's mainland, but neither of those reasons were why he chose it. Less than five people in the world even knew he was there. No, the location was a matter of convenience; there were more than eleven hundred islands in the Maldives, some of them so tiny they could barely even constitute being called such or warrant being given a proper name. The owner of this island was another for whom Krauss had done a job; he'd killed the man's older brother so that he could inherit their family's fortune. And in lieu of payment, Krauss had set up a safe house here, a small thatch-roofed hut stocked with nonperishable food, medical supplies, the bed, a television, and satellite signal.

His caretaker was a retired nurse and native Maldivian from Malé he had flown in. People would do almost anything if the price was right, including being on-call for a man with a bullet hole in his back and nerve damage in his extremities, with no questions asked.

The hut was less than thirty meters from the stretch of white sand. He could hear the surf crashing just beyond it, a lullaby that put his mind at ease and helped him to sleep each night. The Maldivian nurse slept in the next room over and checked in on him every hour. She fed him his meals until he could manage it himself. She helped him out of bed to use the restroom when he was again able to walk, and she sponged him clean until he could bathe himself.

He felt no ignominy about his situation. It was necessary. To think it indignant to recuperate properly was best left to those soon-to-be-dead men.

On the live broadcast from Jerusalem, the American president introduced the Palestinian leader, Ashraf Dawoud. He was met by applause, and he too said some words. The camera angled, panning around the auditorium for reactions from the assorted dignitaries present.

Stefan Krauss leaned forward suddenly and with interest. He ignored the pain in his back, in his limbs.

Had he just glimpsed the face of Agent Zero?

No; it was a trick of his mind. It must have been. Although, it would not have been all that difficult to believe he might be there. But in plain sight? Among the press? Unlikely.

It was more likely his own fixation that had caused him to mistake a face. He believed in vendettas—most of his career had been based upon them, in fact, though usually they were those of his clients. What he did not believe in, however, was revenge. It was a silly idea, to pursue and retaliate based solely on the desire to inflict harm for a wrong suffered at their hands.

Besides. There was no money in it.

Krauss preferred the art of subtle manipulation. He had ways of getting information, and he brought that information to those who did not yet know they needed it. He let them believe that his conclusions were their own, and that the plan that was already evident to him had been theirs all along. Case in point: it was he who had discovered the South Koreans' development of the plasma railgun. It was he who had faked his way onto the research team as security. From there it was a matter of pinpointing the person who would pay the most for his efforts. When the Saudi Arabian king had died, it became perfectly evident who needed it most. The sheikh paid him handsomely, upfront, and the man's conceit was ample enough that making him believe it had been his work and his plan was simple. Now Salman was dead. And Krauss was *alive*.

No, Stefan Krauss did not believe in revenge. He had no need for it. Which was why, as soon as he was healthy enough, he would return to the world and find the person who would pay him to find and kill Agent Zero.

# CHAPTER FIFTEEN

"Ladies and gentleman," the voice said over the loudspeaker, "the President of the United States of America."

"Hail to the Chief" played then, to polite applause as President Jonathan Rutledge stepped out onto the dais from a curtain at the rear of the auditorium. A door, Zero realized, obscured behind the curtain.

Rutledge raised one hand in a slight wave as he approached the podium. He carried himself well, dignified, his suit perfectly pressed and affixed with a pin of the American flag. He had makeup on his cheeks, Zero noticed, and under the flattering soft lights he looked ten years younger.

"Good morning," said Rutledge into the microphone. "Ladies and gentlemen, it is my great and humble honor to witness this moment in history. Albert Einstein said, 'Peace cannot be made by force; it can only be achieved by understanding.' I say that understanding is just the first step. Understanding breeds compassion. Empathy. Camaraderie. Through mutual understanding we can transcend borders and beliefs; we can overcome our differences and realize that we are all one. Though this is but one step of many to achieving true understanding, it is a crucial one, a necessary one, and one that will be written in the annals of history and set a precedent for generations to come."

Zero winced a little, not only at the president's speech writers throwing in an Einstein quote, but getting it wrong—it was, "peace cannot be *kept* by force"—but he quickly reminded himself to stay alert.

"Without further ado," Rutledge continued, "it is my privilege and honor to introduce the president of the Palestinian National Authority, President Ashraf Dawoud."

The curtain moved again, and Dawoud emerged to appropriately restrained applause. Dawoud, Zero knew, was fifty-three, fairly fit for a man of his age but softening in his past few years. His neatly trimmed gray beard was flecked with white, and when he turned slightly to face the US president at the podium Zero caught a glimpse of a shining bald spot on his crown.

Dawoud smiled warmly as the two men reached to clasp hands.

An electric jolt surged through Zero's brain. There was no pain; it was more like a flash of lightning in his head, intense and sudden and bright. And with it, an uncovered memory broke the surface of the ocean that was his limbic system.

*You've met Dawoud before,* he realized. Years earlier, long before Ashraf Dawoud was president, when he was a representative in the Palestinian Legislative Council. Zero had been the CIA contact involved in a multinational covert operation to find and eliminate a Hamas-affiliated bomber, and Dawoud had been his parliamentary liaison.

He had met Dawoud before—had stood in front of him, had shaken his hand.

Zero watched as the two presidents shook hands now, on the dais, and he honed in on it. He recalled, as if it had only just happened, that Dawoud had a unique handshake. It was the only time in Zero's life (that he could recall) that a man had folded in his pinky finger. He remembered the odd feeling of a knuckle against his palm, and had restrained himself from showing any reaction.

Here, now, on the dais, Dawoud shook Rutledge's hand firmly, pumping it twice, all five of his fingers clasping the US president's.

*What does it mean?*

Nothing. He knew that. It was a tiny, meaningless idiosyncrasy from years prior. An unfolded pinky meant nothing.

At least that's what his brain told him. That damned logical wad of fat and tissue in his skull sending electrical impulses down his spine even while actively trying to kill him. It had, for the most part, served him well over a lifetime of parenting, teaching, and surviving.

But so had his heart, and it was pumping double-time.

*What does it mean?*

Dawoud smiled and spoke a few words at the podium, but they were lost on Zero as he inched closer. It meant something. His heart told him so.

There were too many people. He took the slightest of steps forward, shouldering into a man with a camera and eliciting a sharp scowl.

"Zero," Maria said in a hissing whisper behind him.

106

On the dais, Rutledge spoke again into the microphone. "Please join me in welcoming the Prime Minister of Israel, Jacob Nitzani."

More applause. Another ruffle of the curtain. Zero moved, or tried to. Too many people. He didn't take his eyes off the dais and bumped into someone. An object clattered to the floor. A woman swore at him under her breath. He crept closer. He heard his name hissed again behind him.

Nitzani was a slender man, wearing a brown suit and the owlish glasses that had become as much of a trademark of his appearance as the thin mustache he'd maintained throughout his political career. He flashed a gentle wave to the crowd of attendees before turning to Rutledge. He shook the president's hand and gave Rutledge's shoulder a squeeze with his left in a subtle gesture of appreciation.

Zero shoved forward. This was wrong, he *felt* it. He pushed between two reporters and both cried out. Eyes were directed his way, the type of attention he didn't want. Presidential Guard members. Two Secret Service agents scowled.

*Secret Service...*

Nitzani turned and shook Dawoud's hand.

The two men exchanged a few words between them. Smiles on their faces. Hope for the future.

The pinky did not fold.

Zero pushed again. A Secret Service agent positioned in front of the dais locked eyes with him and stepped forward, one hand reaching for the hidden holster beneath his jacket.

He had no choice.

"Rhubarb!" he shouted. It sounded utterly ridiculous. But he had no choice. "Rhubarb!"

The agent paused a moment, a quizzical expression on his face. Clearly he'd been briefed on the codeword, but when it came time for action he froze.

*But what did I expect? That he would throw me a gun?*

On the dais, Dawoud released Nitzani's hand. The smile never left his face as the Palestinian president's right hand reached for the inside of his suit jacket.

"Rhubarb!" he shouted once more.

"Zero!" Maria shouted behind him.

"Stop there!" the Secret Service agent bellowed at him.

Rutledge looked down. His gaze met Zero's, and an instant of confusion became panic. He could see it, that something was wrong. Nitzani looked too at the sudden outburst from below them.

President Dawoud, however, never took his eyes off of the Israeli prime minister. The hand came out of the jacket again gripping a small, silver pistol. He held it to Nitzani's forehead and pulled the trigger.

# CHAPTER SIXTEEN

Prime Minister Nitzani's body crumpled instantly. He was dead before he hit the ground. The gunshot did not get a single echo in the chamber before the screams began. Bodies surged suddenly against Zero, a sea of them, limbs in his face and shrieks in his ears.

The Palestinian president had just murdered the Israeli prime minister in front of the entire world. Right in front of...

*Rutledge.*

*Get to Rutledge.*

In movies there was what was commonly referred to as a "reaction shot," a moment after a big event that seems to freeze in time to give actors the chance to emote, to show their terror or shock or resolve. In reality, that moment rarely existed. Terror fueled adrenaline, and few things provoked genuine, knee-quaking terror like the impossibly loud sounds of a gun fired in close quarters. Like watching a man die in front of you.

The crowd surged against him, everyone trying to scramble backward, to the exits, as Zero struggled forward. A quick glance over his shoulder told him his team was following suit and having just as much trouble. Foxworth was knocked down. The people on the elevated rows were pushing, shoving each other out of the way, falling off the edges, undoubtedly being trampled under feet.

*Get to Rutledge.* That was all that mattered.

A burst of automatic gunfire tore the air. More screams followed it. Zero ducked and covered his head. He tried to look behind him, to find Maria or Strickland or Alan, but couldn't see anyone else. Only surging bodies.

When he dared to look up again, the Secret Service agent at the front of the dais was clutching his own chest as blood sprouted against his white shirt from several places.

Another burst of fire. The Presidential Guard members closed in around the dais, the automatic pistols in hand. They boxed in the Secret Service agents and executed them in seconds.

Zero shoved a man out of his way and caught a glimpse of Rutledge. His face was white as a sheet, his arms struggling against Dawoud, who held him from behind with one arm around the president's neck and the gun pressed to his temple.

*No...*

But he didn't shoot. Instead he pulled Rutledge backward, in small steps... toward the curtain. Toward the door through which they had emerged.

A black uniform suddenly blocked his view as a member of the Presidential Guard leveled his weapon directly at the media crowd.

"Down!" he shouted, to no one and everyone, as he crouched and covered his head.

Bullets tore through those around him. Bodies fell. More gunshots, this time from the back of the room. The security out in the atrium, trying to return fire. But Zero knew they would hit just as many innocents as insurgents.

He saw a path. The Presidential Guardsman popped the clip on the automatic pistol and reached for another. To him, Zero was the press. Not a threat.

He brought his left heel up and punched it. In two long strides he was there, close enough to kick up. The toe of the boot caught the man in the abdomen, just below the belly button. Five inches of steel tore into him as Zero wrenched the gun from his hands.

He spun, crouching as he did, and fired. Bullets tore through two more black-clad Palestinians. If they were even Palestinians.

Shots rang out behind him as the most severe pressure broke across his back. The shock of it forced him to the ground, forced the air from his lungs. It felt like he'd been shot—he *had* been shot—but the graphene held. He gritted his teeth against the pain and rolled over in time to see Alan grappling with the man, forcing the gun upward and kicking out a knee.

Another came from the left, raising a pistol. Zero kicked off the boot in one fluid motion, spun it in his hand, and hammer-fisted down on the sole.

The blade shot out and glanced off the man's neck. Blood erupted from the cut and his hands flew to the wound immediately. Zero punched the heel again and a new blade sprang out. he rolled, covering the distance between them rapidly, and punched the blade once into the guard's heart.

Alan looked down at him, breathing hard. The other man's neck was broken and his pistol was in Reidigger's hand. Zero's own hands had blood on them, and a boot with a knife protruding from the front.

"There were more," Alan panted. "Where'd they go?"

Zero's head whipped around. He saw Maria, helping injured press members up and out of the auditorium, ushering them toward the exits. Strickland hauled Chip to his feet. The former pilot had blood on his forehead.

*There were more.*

Alan was right; earlier he had counted at least eight Presidential Guardsmen in the room. Five of them lay dead. He and Alan had taken out three. Had the Secret Service gotten off a few shots? It hadn't seemed like they'd had time in the melee. Friendly fire, perhaps? Or...

*Or they weren't actually Presidential Guardsmen.*

The others were simply gone. The curtain still ruffled slightly.

*The door.* Dawoud was gone. Rutledge was gone. They'd vanished behind the curtain.

Zero vaulted to his feet and beelined for it. "Let's go—"

"Freeze!" a voice boomed.

He turned. Most of the attendees had fled, or at least made it to the back of the auditorium, while the Israeli cops and Secret Service agents in the atrium had made their way in. Guns were drawn—and directed at them.

Zero raised his hands. The bloody ones, still holding the boot and knife.

"CIA!" Zero shouted back.

"Drop your weapons!" the lead agent commanded.

Maria stepped forward and spoke quickly, despite being out of breath. "Executive Operations Team. You were given a codeword. 'Rhubarb.' We have to go after the president, he was taken hostage and—"

Suddenly the power went out. All at once, every light in the place flickered out, throwing them into near-total darkness. Guns fired, muzzle flashes lighting up the room for fractions of seconds at a time, like an intermittent strobe light.

Zero dropped the boot and hit the deck, leaping onto his stomach in case anyone was firing in his direction. He didn't know if it was the Israelis, or the Secret Service, or both, but he didn't want to be the victim of a friendly-fire incident.

He got to his hands and knees and crawled forward, toward the best approximation of where he had just seen Maria. It was the only thing that made sense in the moment, to find some sort of oasis amid all this chaos. Someone in the darkness yelped; a gun went off again and he winced.

His hand reached forward for the floor and instead landed on something soft and yielding. He yanked it back. The body was still warm but did not react to his touch.

*How many died today? And why?*

There was a shuffling to his right. Zero froze, and a moment later a man grunted as he ran right into him. It wasn't one of his teammates, he was sure of that much. The invisible man hit Zero's shoulder and arm at his own knees and stumbled forward, tripping, falling.

Zero reached in the darkness for the fallen man, grasping, and found an upper arm. Arms ended in hands, hands held guns, and guns could kill the wrong person in a moment like this one. He slid his own hand down the length of the arm until it found a fist closed around a pistol, and he forced it upward.

The agent fired two shots, the sound of it breathtakingly loud and the muzzle flashes leaving spots in Zero's vision. But still he held onto that fist, as he twisted his body around and brought the agent's hand to his own opposite hip in a throw. Once he heard the dull thud and the whoosh of breath leaving the lungs, he wrenched the gun from the man's hand and stood.

The lights blazed back on just as suddenly as they'd gone out. Zero winced… and then realized how this looked. He was standing, armed, pointing the gun at the ground. But on the floor before him was a Secret Service agent, unarmed and on his back, hands in front of his face as if that could stop a bullet.

Zero quickly dropped the gun and put his hands up. There were four guns trained on him from various angles. And others on his teammates.

"CIA!" Maria said again. "Executive Operations Team! Stand down!"

"ID?" the lead agent demanded.

"We're undercover," she explained quickly. "You've been briefed on a codeword, right? Rhubarb. The president chose it himself. He was taken that way, behind the curtain, by Dawoud…"

"And some of the Presidential Guard," Alan added. He was bleeding from one nostril from a scrap in the darkness, but the agent nearest to him was unconscious on the floor.

"We have to go after him," Zero added.

The lead agent held up a hand and scowled. "You five are going to stay right here, you understand me? We have protocols. Every exit of this building is being guarded by half a dozen men and we've got choppers in the air. There are armed men holding the president hostage somewhere in this building, and if we go running after them like some kind of derring-do we may give them cause to do something we'll all very much regret later."

"Derring-do?" Chip Foxworth scoffed.

Zero held back a far stronger rebuke. His instinct was to chase them down, kill every one of them, and get Rutledge to safety. But the agent was right. A single bullet could end Rutledge's life, and he had last seen the president with a gun held to his head by another president.

"Lock it down," the lead agent told his black-suited team. "No one gets in or out. And call it in: POTUS is a hostage of the Palestinian president."

"Not the Palestinian president," Zero muttered. He'd been thinking it ever since the handshake with the unfolded pinky. There were only two possible solutions: either President Ashraf Dawoud had gone completely insane, or whoever that was on the dais, whoever had killed the Israeli prime minister, was not President Ashraf Dawoud.

And while the former might have been more plausible to most, plausibility had never been a terribly strong concern in his line of work.

"You five," the lead agent barked. "Stay put. Consider yourselves locked down as well. You do not leave this room. Am I clear?"

"Clear," Maria told him, though her teeth were gritted.

"I want a thorough sweep of every floor," the lead agent commanded his team. "Starting at the top floor and working our way down. Do not engage." He led his fellow agents to the curtain, which they pushed aside to reveal a dark-stained wooden door that led to who-knew-what other part of the Generali Building. "Henderson, contact the embassy in Jerusalem for anyone they can spare. Then contact Air Force One and have the president's medical team on standby…" His voice trailed as they headed carefully through the door.

Zero kicked at a microphone near his foot. It rolled away until it came to rest against the body of the female reporter who had sworn at

113

him in the crowd. He shook his head. At least a dozen civilians were dead, maybe more, and not counting the Secret Service who had been inside at the time, and the Presidential Guardsmen that he and Alan had taken out—if they were really Presidential Guardsmen at all. Two Israeli officers took the tablecloth from the dais and carefully laid it over the body of Prime Minister Nitzani.

And here Zero was, with his team, stymied by protocol. Made impotent by hierarchy. He retrieved the boot he had dropped and pulled it on. The blade was still extended; he stomped down on the heel and it ejected, clearing the room and bouncing off the far wall of the auditorium.

"Just a boot, huh?" Maria said behind him.

"Just a failsafe," he said.

*A failsafe.* Right—he had deployed the drone as Penny had asked. He quickly pulled the satellite phone from his pocket and saw that he already had a message from her.

*Initiated,* was all it said. Good; at least they had eyes in the air.

"Everyone all right?" Maria asked the team.

"No," Strickland answered candidly. The young agent couldn't seem to take his gaze from the covered body of the prime minister. "We should be going after him."

"It's literally their job," Maria reminded him. "Not ours."

"We're *his* team," Strickland argued.

"For matters of executive orders," said Maria firmly. "Not to be his personal security detail—"

"That's why we were here," Foxworth interjected, joining the fray.

"They're right," Zero added.

Maria shot him a stern look. "Taking their side on this?"

"Not taking any side. Just saying—they're right. We're his team." *But he's not the only one we answer to.* Zero made a call and put the satellite phone to his ear.

"Zero!" Penny practically shouted at him through the phone. "My god, I saw the whole thing… what's going on right now?"

"I think you'd know more than I do," he replied. "What's the word?"

"Chaos is the word," Penny said flatly. "I've got the drone in the air. The Generali Building has been evacuated and locked down. General belief is that the president is being held hostage inside—"

"Yeah, we're still inside," Zero told her. "What else?"

114

"Jerusalem is being locked down as we speak. All exits, roadways, airports are being shut down temporarily and blocked. Police are establishing a two-block perimeter from your location and trying to empty it." She paused for a moment. "Jesus, the Palestinian president actually did it himself. Zero, that was awful—"

"Penny," he interrupted, "I need you to put me through to DNI Barren."

She heaved a short sigh. "I'm doubtful he's available at the moment."

"Make him available. I know you can."

She was silent for a moment. "You're asking me to hack the Director of National Intelligence's cell phone?"

Zero glanced up at Maria. "It's either that or I have his daughter call him, and I have the feeling your way will be faster."

"Yeah. All right. Give me a minute or two."

"On hold," he told the team. Not one of them there, not even the unenthusiastic Reidigger, was the type to stand around and wait for someone else to do the work for them. And if Rutledge wasn't available, they were to take their orders from elsewhere...

"Why did you say that?" Alan asked him.

Zero frowned. "Say what?"

"When the Secret Service suggested this was a hostage situation, you said, 'not the Palestinian president.'" Alan scrutinized him from beneath the shadow of the trucker hat's brim. "And you tried to get their attention just before Dawoud acted. Why?"

Zero nodded. "All right. Don't laugh. This is going to sound crazy..."

*But when did it not?*

So he told them about the handshake, about meeting Dawoud years prior, about the folded pinky, and noticing that this Dawoud didn't. Twice.

"I know how it sounds," he concluded, "but I don't think that was President Dawoud."

No one laughed. It wasn't exactly the occasion for mirth.

"Christ, Zero." Maria pinched the bridge of her nose. "You were going to interrupt an internationally televised treaty conference because of a *finger*?"

"Hey, he was right," Alan retorted.

"About something going down?" said Foxworth. "Yeah. But about that being an *extremely* convincing fake president? I don't know, y'all."

Zero shook his head. He didn't have to convince them. Not now, anyway. Because Dawoud or not, the man who had shot the prime minister was the target.

"Who is this?" came the sudden and gruff voice through the phone. "How did you get this line? Do you have any idea what's happening—"

"Sir, it's Zero."

"Zero! Christ Almighty. Is he alive?"

"…Unclear, sir."

"They say he's still in the building somewhere."

"Also unclear, sir."

"How the hell is it unclear?" Barren demanded. "There are dozens of cops and agents surrounding the place on all sides!"

Zero didn't answer immediately. His mind was turning over and over. Why had the power gone out like that? It couldn't have been more than a minute or so before it came back on. Clearly it wasn't the work of the Secret Service or the Israeli police, and there must have been a reason for it. A distraction…

*To get the president out somehow.* A disabled alarm, perhaps? Or to obscure their destination from anyone who might have followed?

"Sir," he said suddenly, "I have reason to believe that President Rutledge is no longer on the premises."

"The building, and the whole damn city, are locked down," Barren replied curtly.

"And so are we. Under orders from the Secret Service. You're the only one that can authorize us to act right now. Let us try. We won't step on any toes."

"The world is already reeling, Zero. As we speak, emergency executive power is being transferred to Vice President Barkley in the event that demands are made." Barren sighed. "But I can make a damn good educated guess of what he would want in this situation. Go find him, Zero. Bring him back. *Alive.* And if anyone gets in your way, you tell them to contact my office."

"Yes sir. Thank you, sir." He ended the call.

Not ten feet from him was a fallen Secret Service agent, one of the first gunned down when the Presidential Guard opened fire. He knelt, silently apologized to the man, and relieved him of both his sidearms. One was the dependable Glock 19. The other, a black Walther PPK.

116

"Well?" Maria asked.

He tossed her the Walther. "We've been authorized. Let's go get him back."

# CHAPTER SEVENTEEN

Jonathan Rutledge couldn't see, could hardly breathe, not just because he was on the verge of hyperventilating but because his captors had forced a black hood over his head. The inside of it smelled musty and damp—or maybe that was the smell outside of it, he couldn't tell.

Angry, urgent voices surrounded him. Coarse hands prodded him along unpleasantly. His hands were cuffed behind his back. His feet moved as if of their own volition, seemingly the only part of his body that knew that if he stopped, he might die too. His legs felt like jelly. Every step threatened to send him toppling over.

Nitzani was dead. That had become clear in that single, agonizingly terrifying moment on the dais. One moment Rutledge stood tall, prouder than he'd ever been in his career, feeling light of heart and foot, as if he'd somehow shed ten years. They were about to make history.

Then—well, then Dawoud *had* made history, though not in a way that anyone would have wanted or hoped.

*Why?* That was the only thought that distracted him from his own seemingly imminent assassination. *Why?* Why coordinate peace talks and visits just to murder the prime minister? Dawoud could have sent an assassin. Instead he did it himself. A leader, murdering a leader, on international television. In front of the world.

*Good lord. The world.* What was happening out there right now?

The voices around him whispered harshly to each other in a language he didn't understand as they moved. The ground beneath his feet felt uneven. Or maybe it was just his unsteady gait making him feel that way.

Despite his situation, he had a notion to call out to Dawoud. To attempt diplomacy. To speak with him, make him see that this was not the way…

"Move!" a harsh voice growled in English. Something thin and unyielding struck his ribs. The barrel of a gun. Rutledge yelped and picked up his pace.

There would be no diplomacy. He knew that. Dawoud had shot Nitzani with a smile on his face. Then he had turned to the US president and held the gun to his temple. Rutledge had, in that moment, been certain it was his last. But no. Dawoud had dragged him back, through the door behind the curtain. His men had followed.

*After slaughtering mine.*

Then came the hood, and then a series of disorienting turns, twists, and curves. At one point he had been lifted, and then lowered, and then manhandled by at least two others…

*Underground*, he realized. *We've gone underground.*

But he had no way to get a message out. No way to contact his people. Still, they would come for him. The Secret Service would work tirelessly to locate him. Barkley would be given emergency executive powers, and she was fully capable of leading the charge. And others. He had brought others into this.

"Rhubarb," he whispered to himself.

*

The Double was pleased. Someone like the American president might even say that he was "pleased as punch." He did not understand the saying, and frankly thought it ridiculous, but it came to him now. Ironic that he had first heard it from Ashraf Dawoud, on the return flight from New York after a visit to the United Nations.

The Double had had a bizarre fascination with New York City, if for no other reason than to witness the odd spectacle of it for himself. But no, he was there merely as an instrument of Dawoud's paranoia, and had spent the two-day trip on standby, hidden on the plane.

The pilot of that plane was dead now. He was a keeper of sensitive information, one of a very small circle that needed to be eliminated because they knew. Dawoud had kept the secret of his double very well guarded—he had to, or else people might have thought him paranoid. Another irony. Thirteen people had to take the secret to the grave, including the doctor who had, on more than one occasion, surgically altered the Double when necessary.

Here in the tunnels, the Double was pleased as punch. Yes, they had suffered losses. That was to be expected. Only he and three armed men in the garb of Presidential Guardsmen hastily escorted the US president as they made their way through the tunnel now, a haphazard string of battery-powered lights dimly guiding their path.

It had not been difficult to switch out the security detail. Dawoud's paranoia was well documented by those in his inner circle, so it came as little surprise when he declared he would be swapping men out for freshly vetted ones. But the Double had to be careful; he could not replace the entire detail or risk raising suspicions. The remainder became the first targets when the shooting began.

It had begun with him. He had never killed before, and hoped that by Allah's will he would only have to kill once more. But still there had been a certain glee in taking Nitzani's life. Not for the literal act of murder, but what it represented.

Peace. The notion was laughable. Arabs and Jews were destined for this, to fight until a clear victor became evident. Those of his group knew that. And yet the politicians prattled about peace. They talked about peace. They spoke empty sentiments, like this American president quoting the German physicist Einstein.

The irony of quoting a man who had an intimate association with the atomic bomb was not lost on the Double.

His group, and their members, they had no name. That was important. Names made them real. Names gave them meaning in the eyes of others. Names became whispers, and rumors, and then targets.

Hamas had begun as a political party. ISIS, as a liberation movement. And now those names were dangerous, spoken with vitriol and hatred. Excuses to commit murder and drop bombs were made out of those names.

It was fitting they had no name, for the Double had given up his own a long time ago. His associates, they had aliases, but they too had given up their names. The only name they went by now was a liberated Palestine, a self-governing and pure-Arab nation free from outside influence, one that could grow into a global power under all the grace and power of Allah.

Peace? Peace only lasted until the next war.

He wondered if there had been any declarations of war yet out there, out in the world. It was mere minutes after the attack, but condemnations would be as swift as the desire for retribution.

Peace. They spoke of peace only until the violence began again.

He wondered what people would be saying about President Ashraf Dawoud. Had he lost his mind? Was he secretly an Arab fanatic? Had he been manipulated, brainwashed, blackmailed, terrorized, hypnotized, or otherwise persuaded?

None of the above. Dawoud was dead, and in his place was the inscrutable Double. He had fooled the cabinet, the Parliament, the Guardsmen, and now the world.

Strange, fooling them all had been the easy part. It was his job, after all. Even executing Nitzani and making their escape had been relatively simple—but only because they had prepared so thoroughly. The difficult part had been the coordination.

The first step had been introducing black mold to the ventilation system of the Generali Building, several weeks prior. Just enough to get it shut down temporarily to be cleaned and scrubbed with UV light. While shut down, members of their faction entered the building under the guise of a maintenance crew and, under the cover of night, drilled down through the floor until they tapped into a vein, one of the myriad ancient tunnels weaving and crisscrossing beneath Jerusalem.

Of that network of centuries-old subterranean tunnels, the Western Wall Tunnel was arguably the most famous. But there were more, many more—Judaean tunnels, Roman quarry tunnels, Canaanite water channels, a grid so complex that no map existed that charted them all. Many had collapsed, others were dangerously unstable. The Double's group had worked meticulously to trace a single route as their escape path, lacing it with lights, among other things, from the Generali Building to just beyond the edge of the city, where their trail would end at the breakaway floor of an unmarked panel van.

But the Double could not underestimate those that would be in pursuit of the president. It was only a matter of time before someone discovered they were no longer in the building. It was time to enact the next phase of the plan.

As he moved at a half-jog, he nodded to the man nearest him and said in Arabic, "Radio the drivers. It is time."

# CHAPTER EIGHTEEN

Zero moved through the door first, the Glock in both hands and aimed at center-mass level. The door behind the curtain of the auditorium emptied onto a corridor, a few doors lining it before it turned to the left.

"Clear," he said quietly.

"Chip, Alan, clear these rooms one at a time," Maria told them. "Zero, Strickland, you two move on ahead, make sure we're not walking into any surprises. I'm going to try to catch up to the Secret Service and—"

A sudden cacophony of footfalls caught their attention. Zero snapped the pistol up at the ready as four black-suited men rounded the corner at a run.

Zero lowered the gun quickly. "What's going on?"

"We're mobilizing," one of the Secret Service agents told him quickly. "A vehicle rammed down a barricade just north of here trying to get out of the city."

"Finish clearing the building!" the lead agent shouted over his shoulder at them as they passed.

"Sure," Alan grunted. "*Now* we're all friends."

"What do you make of it?" Maria asked.

Zero shook his head. The people who did this planned it carefully. They must have known that the building and the city would be locked down. To make such a risky maneuver as ramming through a barricade seemed... well, foolish, considering all they'd done so far.

"A distraction," Zero told her. He looked around. "Either they're still here somewhere, or they found another way out."

Maria nodded. "All right, new plan. Alan and Chip, take the second floor. I'll go to the third. Zero and Todd, this one. We don't have radios, so if you see something you're going to have to handle it."

"I should go with you," he volunteered.

"Please. If anyone's the damsel in distress, it's usually *you*." She winked and added, "Take care of him, Todd," before hurrying toward

122

the stairs. Alan and Chip followed suit, leaving him and Strickland in the hall.

"Let's clear the corridors first," Zero told him, "and then double back room by room." He led the way, turning left at the junction and continuing on past administrative offices, conference rooms, a small cafeteria. Some of the doors had small reinforced-glass windows; they peered in each one for signs of movement, though with each room they passed Zero felt it less and less likely that the president and his captors were still there.

"What's this about?" Strickland gestured to a strip of yellow tape affixed to the nearest door and stuck fast to the jamb, just above the knob. Every door they'd passed so far had a similar strip, including the restrooms.

"Vinyl tape," Zero said knowingly. "Before the ceremony, after the Secret Service did their sweeps and cleared each room, they put a piece of that tape on the door. Broken tape means someone was in there, obviously. And the stuff is impossible to peel off without tearing."

The satellite phone chimed in his pocket. "What have you got, Penny?" he answered.

"A black SUV just rammed down a barricade leaving the city," she told him.

"I heard." He motioned for Todd to take point ahead of him.

"No, I mean *another* one," Penny said. "Four total so far, crashing right into police cars and through sawhorses. Two pedestrians struck."

Zero groaned. "And not one of them contained the president."

"The only thing they contained was a dead driver. Shot themselves in the head before police could get to them."

He was right. A distraction, a concerted effort to pull resources in several directions.

"Thanks, Penny. We're clearing the Generali Building right now. If there's anything more, let me know—"

"There is one more thing. Mossad agents are en route to your location. And I think we both know they're not going to be terribly pleasant to deal with, all things considered."

A blessing and a curse, Zero thought. The full name of the Israeli organization responsible for covert operations and counterterrorism was *HaMossad leModi'in uleTafkidim Meyuḥadim*, which translated to "the Institute for Intelligence and Special Operations." Known to most of the world simply as Mossad, its own members frequently referred to their group as "the Institute." It was one of the most clandestine agencies in the world, allegedly responsible for a number of successful assassination campaigns and anti-terrorist operations.

And while they would be none too happy with the assassination of their prime minister, Zero had a friend there.

"Penny, keep an ear on the chatter and let me know if you hear the name Talia Mendel," Zero told her.

"Ex-girlfriend?" Penny quipped.

"Something like it," he muttered. "Check in again when there's news." He ended the call and trotted to catch up to Todd, who had meandered far down the corridor and stood before an open door. "What have you got?"

"Broken tape," Todd told him. "But it's just a... closet."

Zero peered inside. It was a maintenance closet, wide enough for four men to stand in, the walls lined with shelves that held various cleaning supplies, a bulk supply of paper towels and toilet paper, and hand soap. On the floor was a mop and wheeled bucket, a vacuum cleaner that looked like it was as old as Sara, and a floor buffer.

"What do you make of it?" Strickland asked.

He wasn't sure. He stepped into the cleared space on the floor behind the door and looked up. There was no hatch in the ceiling, just smooth white drywall. He tugged at the steel shelves; they were firmly screwed into the walls. There was no indication that the screws had been removed recently, no dust of any kind...

*No dust of any kind.*

"Let's move on," Strickland suggested. "There's nothing here. Probably another distraction." He moved on down the corridor, but Zero didn't.

He was staring at the floor.

"Zero? What are you thinking?"

"I'm thinking..." He was thinking that the closet was just too clean. Too organized. And that space on the floor, just behind the door, was cleared of anything at all. An almost perfect thirty-by-thirty inch square...

*I know how they got out.* The thought struck him suddenly, almost violently, and he was ashamed he hadn't thought of it earlier.

He dropped to his knees as he practically shouted, "Tunnels!" His fingertips ran over the smooth concrete there, searching for a seam. "Goddammit, I should have thought of it earlier. Tunnels, below

Jerusalem. Ancient ones, a whole network of them. From a number of civilizations. Romans. Canaanites. Like the catacombs under Paris, but bigger." He was ranting now, but he didn't care. His fingers found nothing, no seams, no edges. He pressed down on the concrete with his palms, even slapped at it in frustration, but to no avail.

"Zero…" Strickland said behind him. "You know that sounds…"

"I know how it sounds!" It sounded crazy. It sounded just as crazy as a body double standing in for the Palestinian president to murder the Israeli prime minister on a global platform.

He stood on the empty space and jumped with all his body weight, bunny-hopping around the square. He didn't care if it looked crazy. He didn't care, as long as it meant…

A corner of the slab shifted, only slightly, revealing the razor-thin seam.

"There!" Todd grabbed a broom and dropped to his knees. "Do it again!"

Zero jumped in the same spot, the far right corner, and the opposite corner nearest the door bounced just a bit, just enough for Todd to jam the tip of the broom's handle beneath it. Zero breathed hard, not from exertion but from nervous excitement as the two of them pried up the perfect square, a slab of concrete two inches thick that had been meticulously crafted to fit the closet's floor.

And below it was a round hole, barely more than two feet wide at Zero's best guess. The hole appeared to go straight down for a short distance and then angled. A dim yellow light was visible somewhere down there.

"You were right," Todd breathed. "Remind me to never call you crazy again…"

"I'll save the 'I told you so' for later." Zero sat himself at the edge of the hole and put his feet in.

"Wait! What about the rest of the team?"

"Todd," Zero said quickly but somberly. "We have no radios. Dawoud and his people have a lead of several minutes on us. If you want to run and find the rest of the team, go now. But I'm going down there."

"Then I'm with you," Strickland said without hesitation.

Zero lowered himself into the hole. He had nothing to hold onto and had no choice but to let himself fall. The drop was only about eight feet, and from there the tunnel sloped downward, the ceiling low enough that he had to crouch as he carefully traversed an angle of about fifty-five degrees. A few yards later it opened wider, high enough for him to stand comfortably.

*They dug through the maintenance closet and into this tunnel*, he realized. It must have taken a week, if not more.

Todd joined him a few seconds later. "Whoa," he whispered.

"Looks like an old quarry tunnel," Zero told him. The ceiling overhead was vaulted, bolstered by weathered brick and wooden posts long grayed with age.

Strickland reached out to touch one but Zero grabbed his hand. "Don't," he warned. "These tunnels are extremely old. Touch nothing." He looked down the length of it. Wan yellow lights had been stuck on the walls, round touch-lights by the looks of them. "We follow the light, and we move fast. Let's go."

They broke into an immediate sprint. Zero noticed the scuffled footprints in the dirt just ahead of them—Rutledge's, he imagined, being forced to move through this musty old tunnel—but he didn't stop to examine them. They were on the right track, he knew it.

Not two hundred yards down the tunnel his knee began to ache, an old injury flaring up at a horribly inopportune time. Strickland, on the other hand, was young and seemingly tireless. He slowed his pace a bit to accommodate Zero's.

"Where do you think these lead?" Todd's voice wasn't even strained.

"Not… sure," Zero told him. "But wherever the lights stop… that's where we go." He had to pick up the pace. They had to be fast enough to catch up. The captors were only as fast as their slowest person, and Rutledge wouldn't be sprinting. Which meant they had to.

*This is why they cut the power*, he realized. They must have had someone on the outside with the ability to shut off the electricity to the Generali Building, maybe even the whole city block, for just long enough that they could make their escape through the maintenance closet unseen.

"What do you think these lights are wired to?" Todd asked suddenly.

"Huh?"

"These lights. They're wired together, see? Which means they're drawing power from somewhere. If we knew where, that might give us an indication of where they're going… Zero, you okay?"

126

Zero slowed to a trot, and then to a halt, panting. He saw what Todd was suggesting; each of the lights had a thin silver line of filament connecting one to the next. He reached out for one, and gently tugged it from the tunnel wall. It came off easily; the adhesive on the back of the round light wasn't strong and the plastic fixture only weighed a few ounces.

But the filament wasn't attached to the battery-powered light. It was attached to the small device *behind* the light.

Panic surged in Zero's chest and threatened to push bile up into his throat.

"Are those *explosives*?" Strickland took a step back.

"We have to go back. Now!" He took off anew, back the way they came. The captors had wired the tunnel with plastic explosives. Small charges. But more than enough to take down the ancient tunnel. And if they reached their destination before Zero and Strickland did…

From far down in the distance, farther than the dim yellow lights reached, a boom like thunder echoed to them.

Then another.

And another.

"Go!" Zero shouted. He didn't have to say it twice. Strickland turned on the speed and outpaced Zero by ten yards in seconds. Then twenty. Zero ignored the searing pain in his knee as the chain reaction boomed behind them like peals of thunder in his chest.

*We can make it,* his brain told him, and he wanted to believe it, because in that moment there was not a thought more terrifying than dying under tons of rock and rubble in a collapsed tunnel beneath Jerusalem.

"Zero, let's go!" Strickland shouted behind him. As if words of encouragement could make him go faster.

*We can make it.*

The booms were closer, spanned only a couple seconds apart from one another. Zero didn't want to look back—but he did, and he saw the dark cloud of dust and death less than fifty yards behind him.

The tunnel creaked and groaned, threatening to come apart around them at any moment.

*He can make it,* Zero realized.

*I'm not going to make it.*

Strickland reached the incline and bounded up it with the speed and grace of an Olympian. Just like that, he was gone, on the surface, and

Zero was alone, racing against an explosion that was, literally, hot on his heels.

He could feel increased heat behind him. A resonant boom that he felt far more than he heard. His feet hit the incline and he leapt up in a crouch, one step, two steps. There was Strickland's hand, outstretched, reaching down.

He leapt up. His fingers wrapped around Strickland's. The final charge exploded behind him as he was lifted up, only slightly, and then thrown forward, and then he lost all sense of direction entirely. His hand lost its grip. Dust choked him. Darkness enveloped him. Something solid pressed against him. There was no pain, and as he lost consciousness he was dimly aware that there might not ever be any pain again.

# CHAPTER NINETEEN

Sara awoke with a groan to the blaring sound of the alarm on her cell phone. She cursed at it, turned it off, and saw that she had a notification. A text from her friend Camilla, who was in rehab on the shore.

The text said: *Omg, did you see the news? The Israel thing?*

Sara tossed the offending device on the carpet. She was decidedly not a political person, and even less a morning person. Never had been. There was a sanctity to sleep, one that she understood even though her father and sister didn't seem to see it. They were often up before the sun. Heathens.

For a moment she entertained the notion of rolling over and going right back to bed—there was only one window in the basement, and she'd covered it with thick curtains so that it could feel like any time of day that she wanted it to down there. But then she remembered why she had set the alarm in the first place, and with another groan, and another curse, she forced herself to stand.

She had made a promise to her dad to look after the girl. More importantly, she had made an arrangement to get paid, the sum of which would put her more than halfway to her goal of a brand-new electric bicycle, the motorized kind that didn't require pedaling if she didn't feel like it.

Sara trudged up the stairs, intent on visiting the bathroom for her morning ritual of teeth-brushing, yanking a comb through her tangled blonde hair, and washing off the eye makeup that she perpetually forgot she had on the night before. But this morning she paused at the top of the basement stairs.

Mischa looked up at her from the sofa, a book open on her lap. The girl looked fresh as a daisy, fully dressed, her hair combed and parted.

"Hello."

"Uh, good morning," Sara said. "Been up long?"

Mischa looked at the wall clock. "One hour and forty-three minutes."

129

"Yup. Maya will just love you," Sara muttered as she headed to the kitchen to put on some coffee. "What are you reading?"

"A history of the Magyars. I found it on a shelf in the… that other room…"

"The den," Sara told her. "And that's interesting to you?"

Mischa nodded.

"You know, you could have turned on the TV or something. The remote's right there on the table," Sara offered.

"American television is propaganda," Mischa said simply.

Sara snorted. She was about to say that suggesting American television was propaganda sounded, in itself, like propaganda. But that reminded her too much of her older sister. So instead she said, "Sure. What isn't, these days?"

She fixed herself a cup of coffee—two sugars, no milk—and joined Mischa in the living room, sitting in an armchair opposite her. "I've got the car. What do you want to do today?"

"I would like to read this book," Mischa said simply. To anyone else it might have sounded like a passive-aggressive brush-off, and in fact at first it did to Sara, but something about the girl's tone made her think twice. It was just a fact; she wanted to read that book.

"Sure. Okay." Sara tapped a finger against the cup. She supposed she could just leave the girl there to read and go about her own business. Maybe do some painting. Watch TV down in the basement on the little flat-screen.

She glanced at the clock. There was a Common Bonds meeting that morning, in less than an hour. She would have very much liked to attend it. Mostly to hear if Lisa had had any further difficulties with the Mustang owner. Or if he had said anything to her about the crazy girl who had busted his windows out and threatened him with a hammer.

But she had promised her dad to keep an eye on Mischa. Not to leave her alone. What was it her dad had said?

*Don't take her anywhere I wouldn't take you.*

"Hey," Sara said. "I have somewhere to be this morning. Would you like to come along? You can bring the book."

*

Sara drove her dad's SUV to the community center, only a twelve-minute drive away from home rather than the forty-five minute bike

130

ride it often took. Mischa sat in the passenger seat, staring out the window, her expression as impassive as ever but occasionally asking questions.

The sort of questions that *really* made Sara wonder about this girl.

"That man." Mischa pointed while they were stopped at a red light. "What is he doing?"

"Uh… he's putting out decorations for St. Patrick's Day," Sara told her.

The girl frowned.

"You know. Leprechauns? Green beer? Luck o' the Irish?" Sara was starting to worry about having to explain things like this to her.

"Leprechauns are not real," Mischa said softly.

"Well, no. Neither is Santa Claus or the Easter Bunny, but that doesn't stop us." She winced immediately. Did this girl still believe in Santa Claus? If so, Sara had just gone and blown that lid for her. "You… sorry, do you believe in Santa Claus?"

"Of course not. Santa Claus is a fiction of Western Christian culture based on a combination of the Dutch *Sinterklaas* and the Germanic god Wodan, who led the Wild Hunt at Yuletide."

Sara turned slightly to face the driver's side window so that Mischa would not see her mouth the word *wow*. For everything this girl knew that she shouldn't know there seemed to be a counterpart that she didn't know but should. It was as if… well, it was as if she'd been terribly sheltered for most of her life with nothing but books. And as soon as she had the thought, it suddenly made a lot of sense.

"Mischa," she asked, "what was it like? In the…." She stopped herself from saying "loony bin," or "nut ward," but even "psychiatric hospital" didn't seem appropriate for some reason. "In the place, where you were?"

The girl sighed as she stared out the window. "It was quiet. And lonely. There was only one man there that would take care of me, and he did not speak to me often. Maria was the only one who would visit me. I did not trust her at first. But I grew to like her. I suppose it made sense, in a way, that I would come to live with her. It didn't seem like it at first. It does now, though."

It was Sara's turn to sigh. "Wow," she said aloud this time. "That sounds… well, I'm sorry that happened to you."

They drove the rest of the way in silence. When they arrived at the community center, Mischa took it all in with the curiosity of an animal

131

being introduced to a new habitat. The rest of the group was already present when they entered, including Maddie, who looked as irritatingly perfect as usual despite the hour.

"Good morning, Sara!" she said in a way that made the teen want to wince. "And who is this charming young lady?"

"This is Mischa," Sara introduced. "My…"

*Hell, might as well get used to it.*

"My stepsister."

"It's very nice to meet you, Mischa. I'm Madelyn, but everyone calls me Maddie." She shook hands with the girl. "And how old are you?"

"I am twelve, ma'am."

"I see. So polite!" The smile never left Maddie's face as she lowered her voice and said, "Sara, are we sure that Mischa should be here? She's quite young, and some of the subject matter here can be… well, I don't need to tell you."

"She's very mature for her age," Sara insisted. And she wasn't lying, not really. "Besides, she brought a book. She won't even be paying attention."

A flicker of doubt crossed Maddie's face, even though the smile remained. Sara could see that she wanted to argue it further, but it was starting time and the rest of the women had already arranged their seats in a circle. "All right," Maddie said at last. "Mischa, why don't you grab a seat over there, sweetie."

Sara led her to a spot near the corner and set up a chair for her. "Just sit here, okay? This won't take long."

"What is 'sweetie'?" Mischa asked quietly. "Is this a term of endearment?"

"Good grief," Sara muttered. "Yes, it is. Just sit here and read your book, okay?"

She joined the rest of the women in the circle of chairs, shooting a glance over at Lisa as she did. The young woman was noticeably different. She still wasn't wearing much makeup, but there was more color in her cheeks today. More of a shine to her hair. And if Sara didn't know any better, she was sitting up straighter in the chair, more attentive.

"Welcome, everyone," Maddie greeted. "We have a new member visiting today. Group, this is Stephanie." She gestured to a young woman seated beside her. Stephanie was strikingly pretty, with

132

strawberry-blonde hair and a puffy white winter vest. She couldn't have been more than a couple years older than Sara, if that. "Now Stephanie, I want to thank you for joining us. The way this works is very simple. Whoever holds the seashell gets to speak. We try our very best not to interrupt while they're relating their experiences to the group."

Sara tried hard not to roll her eyes at the comment that was clearly meant for her.

"When the speaker is done, we'll ask the group if anyone has shared experiences, hurdles they've overcome, that are similar to theirs," Maddie explained. "In this way, we form common bonds through our shared traumas. It's our tradition that new visitors get the opportunity to speak first, but it's entirely up to you."

*She won't.* First-timers never spoke. They sat and they listened and if they came back, they eventually shared. But not the first time. Herself included.

"Sure, what the hell." Stephanie shrugged. "I'll talk." Maddie handed her the scalloped seashell, and the girl crossed her legs. "Uh, okay. I'm Stephanie, hi. I'll be twenty next month. I, uh… I guess I'm here because I can't afford a therapist." She let out a small nervous laugh, though no one else did. "Okay. So I guess I'm here because I was seeing this guy for a while. Until pretty recently, actually. And he's older, like twice my age. But he liked me. And he had money. Bought me stuff. Treated me good… mostly."

Her voice lowered in pitch as the young woman shifted uneasily in her seat. "The thing was that when he wanted… you know, 'it'… he would get it." Stephanie stared at the floor and added, "One way or another." She cleared her throat. "I was still in high school when we met. I thought that it was… normal. For it to be that way. So I always kind of gave in. But not so long ago I met some new friends, and they helped me see that it wasn't. Normal, that is. And, uh, I broke it off with him. He threatened me and my family. Cut me off completely. I've got nothing now."

Stephanie fell silent for a long moment. "I wish I could say I was rid of him. But he still calls. DMs me on my socials. My mom says he's parked outside their house before. I just… I don't know how to get rid of him." She shook her head, and then she hastily pushed the seashell back into Maddie's hands. "I think that's enough sharing for now."

"Thank you, Stephanie. Thank you for sharing your experience." Maddie had a way about her of always seeming genuine, no matter

133

what the story or occasion. "Now I know that there are a few women here who have had very similar experiences, and even overcome them. So I invite them to share now, so that we can forge those common bonds..."

Maddie's voice became distant in Sara's head as the familiar yet fresh sensation of rage built in her stomach, warming her, rising, making her ears burn.

These men.

Like Lisa's Mustang-driving ex-boyfriend.

They were animals.

Like Stephanie's older man who saw her as his possession. His plaything.

These men, they objectified. They broke down these women into the basest version of what they thought they should be. They saw only what they could take from them.

Like the traffickers that had taken her and Maya. Intent on selling them into a child prostitution ring.

They deserved everything that was coming to them and more.

Sara saw something in her periphery. It was Mischa. She wasn't reading her book; it sat in her lap, her index finger holding her place between the pages.

*Had she been listening? Did she hear that story?*

She wasn't sure. But Mischa wasn't staring at Stephanie, or Maddie, or the woman currently holding the seashell and speaking.

She was staring at her. Right at Sara. And her expression was unreadable.

\*

"Why do you go to that place?"

The question took Sara completely by surprise. The ride home had been quiet so far, and she had just been about to suggest they grab a burger or something when Mischa asked it.

"I guess I go because I hope that one of these days, I can help someone who has a problem like ones that I've had."

Mischa shook her head. "I don't think that is it." She paused a moment before saying, "You wanted to hurt that man from the story."

"Sorry, *what?*"

*How could she possibly know that?*

134

"I saw it in your eyes," Mischa explained, as simply as if she was relating a news story or a chocolate chip cookie recipe. "I've seen it before, that anger. You want to inflict harm on him for what he's done."

Sara felt anger now suddenly, though she couldn't tell if it was because Mischa was making her sound so simple or if it was because she'd let herself be read so easily. "What would you know? You're twelve."

"I may not know as much as you about this life and this world, but I know that look. I've seen it on the faces of people that I was forced to hurt because they would have hurt me."

"God," Sara breathed. "Where did you *come* from?"

"I don't know. But you should. Hurt him, that is."

"Why? Because I'm angry?" Sara scoffed. "People get angry over stupid reasons all the time."

"No. Not because you're angry. Because of who he is and what he's done. What he could do to others. There is a quote by the statesman and philosopher Edmund Burke that says: 'The greater the power, the more dangerous the abuse.' Of course that quote pertained to politicians and a particular election in Middlesex. But it's still relevant." She looked over at Sara with something that almost looked like compassion, almost made her robotic little face look human.

Almost.

"I may only be twelve. But I know about abuse and abusers. They do not just wake up one morning and decide to no longer abuse. Sometimes they need to be persuaded. So maybe you should be the one to persuade him."

"This is the real world," Sara murmured. "It doesn't work like that."

But in her mind she was thinking something else. *Maybe it should.*

# CHAPTER TWENTY

"Zero?" the voice called to him.

*Kate?* He wanted to say it, but he couldn't. His mouth wasn't working. His vocal cords refused to make the sound. His body felt like it was in a box that had been designed just for him, tight against him everywhere. And dark. Just dark.

"Zero?"

*Kate! Where are you?* Was she here with him in this compressing darkness? It would not be the first time his late wife, the mother of his children, the great lost love of his life, had tried to beckon him to the other side. It had to be her, here somewhere in this Stygian hell, waiting for him to reach out and take her hand. But his hand couldn't move...

"Zero! Jesus, he's there, get him out!"

No. Not Kate. She had never known him as Zero; he had kept that part of his life hidden from her, and she had died for it...

His dark coffin shifted. There was light then, above him, a tunnel of it opening, beckoning. Strong hands grabbed him under the shoulders, stronger hands than his. A grunt of effort. He was moving. There was pain. Pain in his arms and back and in his head.

Then there was an explosion of light, not just above him but all around, and fuzzy shapes in his vision, voices shouting at him, asking if they could hear him and was anything broken, and he tried to say yes and then no but he only coughed and coughed.

"He's inhaled a lot of dust." That was Todd's voice, he was sure of it. "Get him on a stretcher and outside. Hurry up, this ground isn't stable."

The tunnel. He'd been in the tunnel when it exploded. How long ago was that? An hour? A week?

Then he was on his back but moving, bobbing, though all he wanted was to stand and take a damned minute and drink some water.

But they didn't have a minute. The president had been taken. Was he still alive? Was he too in the tunnel when it exploded?

His vision darkened at the edges, threatening the loss of consciousness. Part of him wished Kate would come, finally, and take him there. They could be together again. The girls would be okay. They were strong young women. They'd know he was happy and with her...

He sat up. He coughed violently into his hand and spat black in his palm as an EMT shouted at him in Hebrew and tried to force him to lie down. He shoved the man away.

"Zero!" Maria scolded. "Calm down!" She was there too, in the back of an ambulance. The rear doors were open and facing the Generali Building.

Smoke rose from the building. And behind it. And beyond it.

"Water," he croaked. His mouth felt gritty.

Then there was a chilled bottle in his hand. He drank too much too quickly and choked on it, spitting it into his lap. He tried again, slower, and it went down. He cupped a hand and poured some in and rubbed it on his face. His palm came back pink because his face was bleeding again.

"What—" Another violent cough erupted. "Happened?"

"Just        lie        back        for        one        damn        minute..."
"Maria." He coughed again.

She sighed and touched his face. "They blew the tunnel, Zero. Three miles of it. Jerusalem is... the streets are in ruins. Buildings collapsed. The vehicles that tried to run, to ram the barricades, were decoys."

*They got away.* Three miles of tunnels was long enough for them to be out of the city proper, beyond the barricades and checkpoints.

"The only reason you're alive is because the closest charge was placed far enough from the tunnel entrance that it didn't completely collapse it," Maria told him. "Todd almost pulled you out, but the explosion sucked you back down. We had to dig you out. You were covered with dirt and small rocks."

"Yeah," was all he could manage. He drank more water and then tried to say "Rutledge?" But it came out sounding more like "Relish?"

Luckily Maria picked up on it. Unluckily, she shook her head. "Known tunnel exits have been searched and are being guarded. But no sign of him."

He knew what that translated into: the captors and their hostage were long gone. He'd suspected as much; they wouldn't have blown the tunnels unless they were free of them. If it was his plan, he would have had transportation waiting on the other side for a quick getaway, and blown the tunnels at the last possible moment as a diversion.

137

"Help." He held up a hand and Maria hoisted him to his feet. Holding his arm, she helped him out of the back of the ambulance and into the daylight of the blocked-off street. It was only then that his senses seemed to fully register the scene around him. Cries of injured civilians caught in the collapse of streets and structures. Gunshot victims from the attack on the treaty signing. Crowds threatening to topple sawhorses, angry over the lack of answers from the myriad emergency vehicles, cops and ambulances and fire trucks that formed the two-block perimeter around the Generali Building.

He didn't want to think that it was his fault. It wasn't. He knew that. But it was the only feeling that came in the moment, other than the pain.

Someone handed him another bottle of water. It was Alan, and his other hand rested on Zero's shoulder. "You look terrible."

"Look who's—" He erupted into another coughing fit, less violent than before but his mouth felt gritty again. He shuddered to think what he had breathed into his lungs.

Chip and Todd were there too, nearby, helping to gather the injured. Noble. But their priorities needed to be elsewhere.

*But where?* Where were they going to take Rutledge?

The satellite phone chirped in his pocket.

"Give me," Maria ordered. He handed it over and she put it on speaker. "Penny, it's Maria. Talk to us."

"Is Zero alive?" she asked quickly.

"He's alive," Maria confirmed, "just not in a talkative mood. What's going on?"

"Can you get on the internet? There's something you need to see." The urgency with which Penny said it, the undertone of fear in her voice, was cause enough for alarm. Penny wasn't easily rattled.

The satellite phone didn't have a browser on it. None of them were carrying personal cells, and Maria had left the tablet behind at the hotel. Zero turned to the Hebrew EMT in the back of the open ambulance. "Phone?"

"Phone," the man repeated in English. "Phone. Yes." He pulled a cell out of his pocket and tossed it to Zero.

"Thanks." One-syllable words were easy enough to get out.

"Penny, what are we looking for?" Maria asked.

"The news," she said simply. "*Any* news."

Zero felt a knot of panic as he opened the browser and navigated to CNN. There it was, the top headline—and to his surprise, it was not the assassination of Prime Minister Nitzani.

"A website appeared," Penny explained, as Zero simultaneously scanned the article. "In the same moment the tunnels blew, a website activated. One minute later, the URL was shared to every major news network in the developed world. Hundreds of bot accounts on social media shared it to political influencers' pages."

"A countdown," Zero managed. He touched the link in the article and was taken to the site Penny was talking about. The URL address was an incomprehensible string of numbers and letters ending in a .cy instead of a .com.

The page was simple enough. A white background with the flag of Palestine at the top. Dominating the screen was a countdown of bold red letters, ticking down from 23:35:12.

23:35:11...

23:35:10...

23:35:09...

"Counting down to what?" Alan asked, peering over Zero's shoulder.

"Watch the video," Penny said somberly.

Zero scrolled down slightly with a finger and saw the embedded video. He pressed play.

On the screen, Dawoud sat behind a desk, his hands folded neatly upon it. If it was really Dawoud at all.

"I am President Ashraf Dawoud of the Palestinian National Authority," the man declared. "I have killed Prime Minister Jacob Nitzani. We have taken the American President Jonathan Rutledge as our hostage."

Zero frowned. This video was obviously prerecorded; Dawoud (as he was referring to the man in his head, Dawoud or not) was undoubtedly on the move at that very moment, not sitting behind a desk somewhere. This had not only been carefully planned, but they had been confident enough that it would work to make this video, touting their success.

"Peace is not and was never an option," Dawoud announced. "Israel deserves this, and everything else to come. America deserves this for its hubris. We make no demands for the president's life. We ask no ransom and we will not negotiate. Our terms are simple: at the end of this twenty-four-hour countdown, President Rutledge will be executed, and the video will be distributed. This is unavoidable. If anyone attempts to intervene before the twenty-four hours are ended, the president will be summarily executed. If any declaration of war is made before the twenty-four hours are ended, the president will be summarily executed. If any retribution is taken against my nation or my people before the twenty-four hours are ended, the president will be summarily executed. This is unavoidable. It is inevitable. It is the will of Allah, praise be unto him."

# CHAPTER TWENTY ONE

Maria stared at the screen for several moments after the video ended.

Rutledge was alive, at least. Of that much she was certain; her entire career had been built upon dealing with men like this, and they rarely bluffed. They made good on the promises they made, no matter how harrowing.

But they were intent on killing Rutledge, one way or another. And they wanted it to be a spectacle.

*But why the countdown?* Why wait? They must be buying time for something. What was it?

She looked up at the faces of Zero and Alan. Their frowns were almost identical, Zero's more soot-streaked, and she could imagine they were wondering the same as her.

"Penny, are you still there?"

"I am, boss. You should know that Director Shaw has asked me to take the website down immediately."

"No," Maria said forcefully. "Sync a timer with it but don't take it down. Find out whatever you can about it…"

"Already on it," said the tech. "The site is being actively monitored and updated from a server in Nicosia, the capital of Cyprus in the Mediterranean. But I also traced a few of the bot accounts, and they share an IP. They were activated from a mobile device in Sofia, Bulgaria."

"Sounds like a goose chase," Alan muttered.

"They're the only leads we have." Maria thought for a moment. "We're going to need transport. Alan and I will go to Sofia and track the device. There's a person behind it, and they know something. Strickland and Foxworth will go to Cyprus and investigate whoever is monitoring the site."

"And me?" Zero asked.

She sighed. "You're hurt. You're staying here."

"Like hell—" He coughed again and spat into the dirt. "Like hell I am."

She knew arguing with him was a losing battle. But it was one she'd still fight anyway, in the hopes that one of these days he'd actually listen instead of running full-speed into the burning building...

"Hey!" a stern voice shouted from behind her. "You!"

Maria turned to see four Secret Service agents headed her way. The lead agent looked irate, his tie loosened at his throat and dirt streaking his black jacket. His eyes were hard-set and looked like they were that way often, given the crow's feet bunched around them, but otherwise his features were oddly boyish. His face was round (and currently a shade of red), and his dark hair was no longer neatly combed but ruffled like an unctuous uncle had just rubbed a hand through it.

"You're the Executive Operations Team?" he demanded.

"We are."

He gestured to the billowing smoke in the city behind him. "What the *hell* did you do?"

Zero stepped forward, getting between the agent and Maria. "We didn't do a damn—" But he broke into another coughing fit, nearly doubling over.

"I'm told they blew the tunnels because your people chased them down," the agent said angrily. "How do we know these people weren't suicidal? How do we know POTUS isn't down there right now?"

*He doesn't know.* These agents must have been too busy chasing down the diversion cars that broke through the barricades to have seen the countdown and the video yet.

"What's your name?" Maria asked.

The man bristled. "I'm Deputy Special Agent in Charge Mick Chubb..."

Alan snorted behind her. She shot him a glare.

"And this is officially *my* investigation," this Agent Chubb added. "If you're going to be a part of it, you're going to report to me, and do as I order—"

Maria halted him with a dismissive wave of her hand. "There are two people that I report to. You're not one of them, Chubb. Here." She pushed the EMT's phone into his hand. "You're going to want to see this."

She turned on a heel and strode a few yards away before addressing the satellite phone again. "Penny, put me through to the DNI."

"On it."

"And you," she pointed to Zero. Her stubborn-as-all-hell future husband. "See if that ambulance has a couple of Tramadol shots. Looks like you're going to need them."

The satellite phone clicked, and a moment later a familiar voice said, "Barren."

She winced at the way he announced his name like that. It reminded her far too much of the way he'd scold her as a child.

"It's me. It's Maria. I've seen the countdown. We have a direction."

There was a short but pregnant pause before he asked, "What have you got?"

"We've got a mobile device in Bulgaria. A server in Cyprus. And a DSAC Chubb with a massive superiority complex. What we don't have is a spare plane."

"Maria, the government is in full-on crisis mode," he told her, with that same sternness in his voice that made her feel small again. "Interagency cooperation has never been more important. I can't make every decision for you. I have my hands full as it is. I need your best judgment here. If you can't do that, then defer to Agent Chubb's best judgment. Am I clear?"

She clenched her jaw but said, "Clear, sir."

"Good. Handle it. *Now*." He hung up.

*He needs my best judgment? Okay. I can do that.*

"So?" Zero asked behind her. He held two plastic-wrapped syringes in his fist.

"We've just been authorized to operate independent of the DNI and federal government due to emergency protocol," she told him.

"Really," he said flatly, clearly not believing it for a second.

She shrugged. "That was my interpretation. We have the Gulfstream, but we need another jet. Any ideas?"

"This might be a bad time," the phone said.

"Penny!" Maria exclaimed. "You're still on the line?"

"I am. And a certain Mossad agent has just arrived on the scene."

Maria frowned. "A certain Mossad agent...?" She spun to face Zero, who shrugged once sheepishly.

*Of course*, she thought peevishly. *Mendel.*

*

"You want an airplane?" Talia Mendel's English was flawless and only lightly accented. It was, annoyingly, only one of several things about her that seemed flawless.

"Yes," Maria told her. They stood two blocks behind the Generali Building, where she had found Mendel examining the veritable fault line in the broken street that had been caused by the collapsed tunnel. "If you can."

"Oh, I can." Mendel had sharp features, a strong jaw, black hair cut short that swept across her forehead. She was fiercely intelligent, good in a fight, and had, on more than one occasion, made passes at Maria's now-fiancé. "Where will you go?"

"We have a lead," Maria said simply. The rest of the team stood behind them, at a short distance, as Maria negotiated with the Israeli spy.

"And will you take your Secret Service friends with you?"

"I think they're going to miss the flight," Maria said simply. "They'll know what we know soon enough. And too many cooks in the kitchen can spoil the broth."

Talia Mendel grinned at that, but it faded quickly. "My country is furious. Already speaking of war. They are being emotional; declaring war would give cause for the American president to be executed early, and would put Israel at odds with America."

Maria nodded, but in her head she was dismayed that she hadn't yet worked that out for herself. Dawoud wasn't just out for Israel; he was actively trying to undo what Rutledge had accomplished thus far.

*Is that what the countdown is actually for?* she wondered. *To give just enough time for someone to get desperate, make a brash decision?*

"All the more reason to help us," Maria offered. "We can get him back. You've worked with us before; you know we can do this."

Mendel nodded. "But you forget, Ms. Johansson, that the times I've worked with you before, I was there too."

Maria's nostrils flared. She knew what was coming next.

"I will provide you your plane. And weapons. Equipment. But I am coming."

"No," Maria said instantly. Chubb was an ass; if she let him in, he'd try to take over and there'd be infighting. She'd worked with enough men like him to know that she and her team would be better off on their own. The Secret Service would likely soon know what Penny had already discovered anyway.

144

Mendel, on the other hand, would be an asset. Maria just didn't like her very much.

"That is the deal," Talia said. "I do not want war. I will help you find your president. Either I come, or you get no aid from me."

"Fine," Maria said tightly. They needed a plane. They needed weapons. And they were on a literal ticking clock.

"Ben Gurion, one hour. That is the best I can do." Mendel turned to leave, but not before flashing Zero a coy smile. "It will be a pleasure to work with you again, Agent Zero."

"Oh no." Maria flashed a vindictive smile of her own. She brought up one hand and pretended to smooth her hair, making sure that Talia Mendel saw the diamond ring on her finger. "Agent Mendel, you'll be coming with *me*."

# CHAPTER TWENTY TWO

"So, you go to the academy?" the Uber driver asked. He was a stout man, likely thirties, wearing a New York Giants ball cap and cursing under his breath every couple of minutes as he headed toward Poughkeepsie.

"That's right," Maya told him from the backseat. She wasn't in uniform, but she'd had him pick her up just outside of campus.

"Didn't think they let you cadets leave whenever you wanted. You're not... what do they call it... going AWOL, are you?" He chuckled to himself.

"No. I was suspended." Dean Hunt had agreed to the two-day suspension that Maya had suggested, allowing her to get off of campus for a bit—but not back onto it, if she needed.

"Huh," said the driver. "What'd you do?"

"I'd rather not talk about it," Maya said curtly.

"Sure, sure."

*817 Butler Street.* That was the address that Jimmy Bradley had given her. After Hunt had declared her suspension, Maya packed a backpack, retrieved her phone (cadets weren't allowed to keep their phones while on campus), and called an Uber. According to Google Maps, the address was two blocks from a pizza joint, so she gave that as her destination to the driver.

"So, you seen the news lately?" he asked. "Crazy, right?"

"I haven't been paying attention to the news. Been busy."

He let out a low whistle. "Well, you've missed some stuff, let me tell you—"

Maya leaned forward in her seat. "Look, I'm not one of those passengers you need to talk to. Silence is just fine. Preferable, even."

The guy shrugged. "Suit yourself."

They drove on in silence. Outside the window it was already dark, but it wouldn't be a very long ride. The lights of Poughkeepsie soon came into view, the city itself relatively small but sprawling. Despite its relative proximity to the New York metropolitan area, it was a rather rural-looking place, favoring trees and colorful facades over skyscrapers and cement.

"Here we are," said the driver as he pulled into a small parking lot behind a one-story beige building. "Fiesta Pizza."

"Thanks." Maya got out of the car and took her time meandering around to the front of the building, where wide, bright windows showcased a number of people inside eating. The smell made her mouth water, and reminded her of home, oddly. Pizza was always her dad's go-to when he was stressed out.

She waited until the Uber driver had pulled away before turning away from the small restaurant and heading west for two blocks down Butler Street.

Then she arrived at her destination, the house numbered 817, and cursed aloud at Jimmy Bradley.

It was a house, or had been at one point, a narrow two-story structure squeezed in between larger homes. But it had been renovated at some point into two separate apartments. The bottom level appeared to be 817A, and the upper level, 817B.

Jimmy Bradley had gotten his five hundred bucks, Maya had gotten suspended, and it wasn't like she had his number or he even had his phone on him at the academy.

*Great. Guess I'll have to do some spying.*

She hid in the shadows alongside the house, where a concrete walkway led to a tiny backyard, spanning only a few feet between the two buildings. There were no outside lights on, thankfully, so she crept window to window until she found one with the curtains drawn.

She peered inside. It was a small dining room, the lights off. But from her angle she could see partially into the adjacent room, a living room it seemed, where a woman who must have been pushing sixty was seated on a sofa, a television screen flickering colors across her face.

Maya frowned, immediately doubtful that this old woman was the forger, yet not entirely willing to discount it. Whoever it was had gotten this far, hadn't they? It would make sense if it was someone who seemed beyond suspicion.

A man entered the dark dining room and Maya ducked quickly. He hadn't seen her. When she dared to look again, he had passed through the dining room and into the next—a kitchen, she guessed—and then she heard the telltale popping of microwave popcorn.

147

Maya maneuvered to the rear of the house. The curtain over the back door's window was sheer, and through it she could see that the man was older as well, likely the woman's husband, and was watching the popcorn bag inflate inside the microwave.

*Him, maybe?* A forger of this caliber would have to be experienced.

She thought about knocking on the door—after all, Jimmy had sent her here—but first decided to see what was behind door number two. Behind the house was a set of wooden stairs that led to a back door on the upper level. She took them carefully, holding her breath each time one of them creaked under her weight.

She found a window with the blinds slightly open and peered inside. There was a young man in there—a boy, practically, no older than her, sitting in a bean bag chair in a sparsely furnished apartment and fiddling with a video game controller. He kept his hair short but had a wispy beard on his chin. He wore gym shorts and a tank top over his skinny frame and had a tattoo on his left shoulder, some sort of tribal design, and—

And he glanced up, just for a moment, right at the window.

Maya ducked down quickly. Had he seen her? No. Of course not. The lights were on inside and it was dark out. He would have seen a reflection off the glass, nothing more. At least she told herself.

She counted to thirty, crouched under the window and shivering despite her jacket, and then took another look. The young guy had gone back to his video game.

*He didn't see me.*

This kid did not look like the forger to her either. In fact, she would have put her money on the older man downstairs well before this boy. Her best bet would be to go knock on the door to 817A and tell them, "JB sent me."

But if they reacted with confusion, what then? Not only would she have picked the wrong door, but then the forger's downstairs neighbors might think their upstairs neighbor was up to something. Dealing drugs or whatever it was that older people usually suspected of younger people.

Inside the apartment, the young guy stood slowly from his beanbag chair and stretched. He padded in socks across the room and flicked on a light. A bathroom. Then he closed the door behind him.

148

*I'll just wait here a little longer,* she resolved. *Watch for a bit.* Maybe the boy would get a phone call that would tip her off, or something…

*Click-click.*

Maya froze. She knew that sound all too well. The cocking of a pistol, behind her and to the left. It wasn't the first time, but still an electric tingle of fear ran up her spine.

"Don't move," he warned quietly.

She obliged, remaining frozen. She really did not want her life to end at the hands of someone in gym shorts.

The outdoor landing, she realized, wrapped most of the way around the house. He'd slipped right out the bathroom window and around to her.

"JB sent me," she said quickly, her voice an octave higher than she would've liked.

"That so? Then why are you sneaking around, spying on me?"

"I was trying to make sure," she started to explain, but realized how lame it was going to sound. And what was this boy going to do—shoot her just outside his own apartment? No.

Instead she raised her hands and slowly turned to face him. His eyes were narrowed at her, and he was still wearing just the tank top, shorts, and socks she'd seen him in.

"Must be cold," she said.

"I don't mind. What do you want?"

She kept her cool despite the gun. "I need a letter. Signed, from my doctor. One that claims I'm on antipsychotics and ran out."

He looked her up and down, and then shook his head. "I don't think so. Get out of here."

"Please," she said adamantly. "I *need* that letter—"

"Get!" He shook the gun in her face and she winced.

But she also noticed something. The guy's finger was on the trigger. She remembered something her dad once told her: *Never, ever put your finger on the trigger unless you plan on pulling it.*

This young guy, he knew he could pull it. And Maya understood.

She threw herself to the right, a quick sidestep, while at the same time bringing up her left hand and forcing his arm, and the gun, with it. With the barrel pointed away she stepped in, toward him, and drove a knee into his sternum—not hard, not to injure, but to knock the breath from him. He grunted and doubled over, and Maya fell with him, all the way to the deck, bringing his shoulder along for the ride. He bent at the waist and didn't stop as she forced his own momentum into a head-over-heels throw.

The guy landed on his back with a heavy thud, and she quickly relieved him of the gun. It was a hammerless .38, snub-nosed and silver, and—she checked the cylinder—not loaded.

She tossed the gun aside. "I'm not going anywhere. I *need* that letter, or I'm going to be expelled."

The boy sat up with a grunt and rubbed his shoulder. "Yeah. I guess you do." He looked up at her and grinned. "You want a beer?"

"Water is fine."

The inside of the guy's apartment smelled like cheap body spray and gym socks. He led her into the small kitchen and gave her a bottle of water from the fridge.

"Name's Max," he told her. "But my friends call me Busboy."

She frowned. "Why do they call you Busboy?"

"Because I'm the busboy down at Fiesta Pizza."

"...Oh." She glanced around the narrow kitchen. There was a bulletin board on the wall, a slab of cork with a cracked wooden frame. On it were various stickers, pins, a calendar, and a couple of photos.

One of which showed that same boy, without the wispy beard, in a cadet uniform.

*Dammit.*

"You're not the guy I'm looking for," she said aloud.

Busboy bristled. "I could be."

She shook her head. "No, you're not. You're a former cadet." She gestured to the photograph. "I'm guessing the real guy uses more than one layer of protection. He's got Jimmy Bradley on the inside, giving desperate cadets this address. Then they come see you, they tell you what they need. But you're not the guy. You go to the guy, he makes what they need, and you pass it off like you did it." She stared Busboy right in the eye. "How am I doing?"

He blinked first. "What are they trying to expel you for? Being a smartass?"

"No. I like to beat up boys. And I spat in a lieutenant's face."

Busboy grinned at that. "Yeah. That'll do it. I wasn't even there for a whole year, myself. I was a perfect cadet. Almost top of my class. Except that my high school transcript was fake." He shook his head.

"You know, nine times out of ten they don't even follow up on things like that. And the *one* freakin' time they do…"

"I'm not worried about that," Maya said candidly. "They're going to give me the boot anyway. This is a Hail Mary on my part."

"It's not cheap," he warned.

"I have money. But I don't deal with middlemen. I can't get any assurances of quality or delivery from you if you're not the one doing it. This is my *life* we're talking about. I want to see the guy, the real deal, or there's no deal."

"Then there's no deal," Busboy said simply.

Maya's throat flexed. She resisted the urge to grab the skinny boy by the throat and force her to tell him where the forger was.

*No. Be smart about this.*

"Fine," she said instead. She took two steps out of the kitchen, into the shabby living room, and glanced around meaningfully. "Might be nice if you could afford some bullets for that gun, though. Among other things."

She headed toward the door, intentionally taking her time.

*Come on. Take the bait…*

"Wait." Busboy's voice was strained behind her. "Wait a sec."

She paused and turned, but said nothing.

"I… you're right. I could use the money." He sighed. "I'm gonna have to talk to him first, okay? You got somewhere to lay low for a bit?"

"I'll find a place."

He handed her a pen. "Leave me your number. I'll contact you. If he's okay with meeting up, we'll do it. If not, you don't come around here again. Yeah?"

Maya nodded as she wrote down her cell number.

"And it's going to cost extra," he added. "A premium on my end for sticking my neck out like this."

"Fine." Maya dropped the pen and headed toward the door again. "Just make it happen and we'll both be happy."

She headed out of the apartment and back down the wooden steps without looking back. She was going to have to find a place to kill some time. Maybe a motel nearby. And money could quickly become a problem, especially if cash was expected to trade hands tomorrow. The credit card her dad had given her had a two-thousand-dollar cash advance limit, and she'd already given Jimmy Bradley five hundred.

But she was closer. A step closer, another piece of the puzzle in place.

Her cell phone chimed from the front pouch of her backpack. It was a private number. Her dad, maybe, calling from some burner?

"Hello," she answered cautiously.

"Lawson. It's Dean Hunt. I'm looking for an update."

Maya almost groaned aloud. It had been mere hours since her suspension; what did Hunt expect of her? "I'm closer. I should have this wrapped by tomorrow—"

"See that you do," Hunt warned. "Many on my staff are unhappy with the suspension and are calling for your expulsion. The only remedy I can see is you finding the forger so that I can reveal it was me who put you up to all this. If you don't find them, I can't do that, or we risk losing the perpetrator."

Maya's face flushed. "I'll find them," she promised.

"Good. Because otherwise my hands will be tied. And I don't think I need to remind you that an official expulsion from West Point is viewed the same as a dishonorable discharge. The CIA will never accept you on those grounds."

"But ma'am—" Maya tried to protest.

"Figure it out. I have to make a decision tomorrow. Goodbye, Lawson."

The dean ended the call, and Maya kicked over a garbage can.

"Fuck!" she shouted at the night.

Why had she even taken this on? She had been doing fine on her own, catching up on her work, fast-tracking back to the top. And now she was playing make-believe secret agent, hunting down this forger— for what? For Dean Hunt to look good? To do the MPs' jobs for them?

She took a deep breath. It was too late to go back. She was in this mess now, and the only thing she could do was see it through. Find the forger. Bring him in. And get her life back.

# CHAPTER TWENTY THREE

"Zero? You feeling okay?" Strickland frowned at him from the opposite seat of the Gulfstream.

"Yeah, Todd. I'm good." He forced a smile. "Good" was a general answer. "Good" was noncommittal.

The truth was, he hurt all over. That was nothing new. He'd given himself a shot of Tramadol, a relatively mild painkiller that he had enough of a tolerance for that it took the edge off without making him drowsy. Still, his body would be mostly purple tomorrow, he was sure of it. The coughing fits had ceased; it seemed that most of the dust had been expelled from his lungs. He had hoped he might catch a catnap on the short flight from Ben Gurion to the island of Cyprus, but closing his eyes offered no respite from his churning mind.

Rutledge was a hostage in the hands of known killers. The clock ticked down with every passing microsecond. Just being in the air, the very act of needing to travel from one place to another, felt wasteful and inactive.

Chip Foxworth was at the helm. They had politely relieved their former pilot of his duties, sending him back to the US on a commercial flight as they commandeered the jet. They now hurtled over the Mediterranean at close to six hundred miles an hour. And considering that Cyprus was only about two hundred forty miles northwest of Tel Aviv, it would be a short flight.

"For what it's worth," Strickland said, "I'm sorry."

Zero frowned. "For what?"

"For leaving you behind in the tunnel." Todd chuckled nervously at himself, looking far more vulnerable than Zero could ever remember seeing him. "I just… ran right ahead of you. Even despite the Rangers' code."

*No man left behind.* Zero knew it. He didn't necessarily agree with it, at least not all the time. "Todd, if you hadn't gotten ahead of me and tried to pull me out—if you had tried to wait for me—we both would have died down there."

153

The younger man shrugged one shoulder but said nothing. It was clear that this had been wearing on him ever since the tunnel's collapse. And even though Zero couldn't quite understand it, it reminded him of a quote that he often repeated to his daughters: *Everyone you meet is fighting a battle you know nothing about.*

Todd was struggling with this, reconciling the necessity of the situation with the blatant disregard for a rule that he had lived much of his life by.

"You think we'll get him back?" he asked.

"Yeah." Zero nodded. "We're going to get him back."

The PA crackled, and Chip's Texan drawl boomed loud in the small cabin. "Ladies and gentlemen, we are about ten minutes out from our descent into Nicosia, capital of Cyprus. Please fasten your seatbelts and lock your tray tables in their upright position."

Almost there already. It would take another ninety minutes at least before Maria, Alan, and Talia reached Sofia, Bulgaria. Ninety minutes that ticked off the clock, ever running.

Back at Ben Gurion, Talia had procured a Learjet for her team. Funny, in an odd way; an American-made plane owned by the Israelis on loan to American forces. She'd also given them clean and secure phones, radios, weapons, clothes. All inside an hour.

Before leaving, Maria had cleaned some dirt from his face with her sleeve and kissed him and wished him good luck.

"See you soon," they had told each other. Not goodbye. Never goodbye.

And then Talia Mendel had winked at him, but he tried not to let it ruin the moment.

His graphene-infused clothes were ruined from the tunnel collapse, so he'd changed out of those in favor of a black tac vest, a gray sweater, and a beige jacket that hid the vest well beneath it. It wouldn't afford him the same protection, but it would have to suffice.

"Penny locked onto a location that the site is being monitored from." Todd turned the phone in his hand to show the GPS map of Cyprus's capital and the blue dot that represented their destination. "She said it's been continuously and manually monitored since…"

"Since the countdown began," Zero finished for him. Men like these would not want to leave anything to chance or machines. He had no doubt that some thugs, or a group thereof, would be waiting for them, carefully ensuring that nothing went wrong with the countdown.

154

He buckled his seatbelt as the plane began to descend. "Let's go see who's watching."

*

Nicosia International Airport was mostly unused these days, having been largely abandoned in favor of the three other airports on Cyprus. Since 2013 there had been attempts to turn it into an industrial zone, though no major developments had happened on that front.

But there were still functional runways, and Chip was able to set the Gulfstream down without incident or interference from the empty tower. They disembarked with their gear and hurried toward the main terminal, which would be empty save for a skeleton crew of maintenance people who kept the place from crumbling and being overrun by nature.

Zero silently apologized to whoever's Fiat they hotwired from the parking lot. There were only five cars in the lot and there wasn't exactly an Enterprise nearby.

Chip drove, and Zero rode shotgun as they headed the five miles east toward the city proper.

"Man," said Foxworth as he glanced out the window, "I know where I'm taking my next vacation."

"Let's stay focused," Zero reminded him. Though he had to admit, the city was beautiful. Nicosia had been continuously inhabited for more than four thousand years. It had seen the Assyrians, the Byzantines, the Ottomans, and the Romans. Palm trees lined streets that bore both modern homes and historic ruins. Castles shared avenues with steel and glass architecture. Nicosia looked as if someone had torn a hole in time and space and melded thousands of years of civilization into one city, and the way in which the blue sky met the calm sea in an almost seamless manner made it feel like it could actually be true.

Traffic was light, even in the city, since it was early afternoon local time. They reached the location only twenty-six minutes after leaving the airport, and rolled past it slowly.

"You sure that's it?" Foxworth asked.

"I'm sure," Strickland confirmed. "What do you make of it, Zero?"

The location was a sandstone-colored villa that looked like it should be a California vacation home, two stories and flat-roofed. From that rooftop one would probably have a good view of the glittering sea.

155

It looked… not ordinary, but not like any place Zero would have expected. Typically he would be bursting into an abandoned warehouse, or a gangland garage fronting as a repair shop, or an underground facility. Not a villa on a Mediterranean island.

"Zero?"

"Keep going," he instructed. "Park at the next block."

"Aye aye," Chip confirmed. A minute later he parked the stolen Fiat in front of a Cypriot café.

"Sidearms only," Zero told them. "Concealable. We don't want to sound any alarms if this is another diversion."

*Could this be a trap? Could Penny have been wrong? Could the president's captors be toying with us?* There were a thousand thoughts running through his mind, and not one of them was that this was actually the location of the mystery monitor.

They exited the car and hastily hiked the block back to the villa. "Act like you belong here," Zero told them as he slipped around the side of the building and toward the rear. In the back was a paved patio and a low fence that gave way to the adjacent villa behind it.

The windows were curtained, but there was a door. Zero gingerly jiggled the handle; locked. He positioned himself on one side of the door and pulled the Glock 19 from his jacket. Chip stood to one side, a Sig Sauer from Mendel in both hands.

He nodded to Strickland, who took a breath, brought up one foot, and kicked in the door. It flew open, splinters from the jamb flying, and Zero was inside in an instant, Chip covering him.

He stood in a kitchen. It was empty. The lights were out.

"CIA!" he called out, since their arrival had been announced already. "If anyone is here, come out slowly and with your hands raised!"

"Do they ever actually do that?" Chip whispered.

"Hush. Cover me." Zero pushed further into the villa. The entire first floor was empty, the lights out, no sign of life.

But above him, he heard a faint humming. He gestured to the other two and started up the stairs.

*A trap,* his instincts told him. *This is a trap.* But it wasn't the first time he'd walked into one. Besides, he had little choice but to hope it wasn't—or to attempt to outmaneuver it before it sprung on him.

He reached the top of the stairs and cleared the corridor. The hum was louder now, most definitely electronic equipment. He passed an empty bathroom. A small guest room, the bed made perfectly.

At the end of the hall. One more room. The door only partially ajar.

Chip was at his shoulder, Strickland behind him. He nodded to them and pushed into the room.

"CIA!" he shouted.

The man inside the room did not turn, did not react. He sat at a desk, a dual-monitor setup before him. On one of the screens, Zero saw the countdown. It read 20:51:19.

20:51:18…

20:51:17…

On the other screen, long green-texted strands of computer code that he could not begin to decipher.

Zero spun, clearing the rest of the room. There was no one else here that he could see. The desk was flanked with tall shelves of blinking electronics that Zero had only ever seen down in R&D at Langley. Server banks, he guessed. There was no bed in the room or any other furniture at all, besides the desk, the chair, and the computer equipment.

"Please leave," the man asked meekly in English, his voice accented.

"Are you alone?" he demanded.

"Yes."

"Stand up. Hands on your head."

"I cannot, sir." The man's voice trembled, as if he was apologetic, but still he sat in the tall-backed black chair.

Zero circled him cautiously, keeping the gun trained on him. The man was bald, wearing silver eyeglasses that made his frightened eyes look huge, sweat shining on his olive-skinned forehead. The accent, if Zero wasn't mistaken, was Turkish.

"Please just go." His voice was almost a whisper. "You do not know what this is…"

"Explain it then," said Foxworth behind him. "Because as I see it, we've got the guns and you don't."

"Pipe down, Chip." Zero pointed his gun at the floor, away from the man, but did not put it away. "What's your name?"

"Omer," the man said. "Omer Sarrafi."

"Okay, Omer. I want you to tell me what's going on here."

"I have a job to do." Omer looked as if he was holding back tears. "I must monitor the countdown. Keep it from being shut down. Monitor for attempted security breaches. I… I must keep it active. Or…"

"Or what, Omer?" Zero pressed.

"Or they will kill me," Omer said in a near-whisper.

"They're nowhere near here," Zero tried to assure him.

"They don't need to be." A thick bead of sweat rolled down Omer's forehead. "Please… just leave. It is too dangerous for you to be here."

*This man isn't with them,* he realized. He was a hostage. But what had they done to put such fear in him?

"Zero!"

He spun to see Strickland on his hands and knees, inspecting something low.

"Don't freak out or anything… but this man is sitting on enough C4 to blow this whole building. Maybe half the block."

Zero's chest tightened as he dropped immediately to his hands and knees. Todd was right; the underside of Omer's padded desk chair was wired, the leads trailing to a stack of yellow blocks of plastic explosive set beside the farthest server.

"I've seen this sort of setup before," Todd said, his voice strained with some dark memory. "In Afghanistan. I'm betting Omer here is sitting on a pressure plate, and if he moves, this blows."

The terrified man in the chair nodded, the color drained from his face.

"Go," Zero told them immediately. "Both of you, out."

"Like hell," Chip said.

"I have more experience in this than you do," Strickland argued.

*Stubborn asses.*

"Omer," he said calmly. "I need you to not move."

"You need not worry about that, sir," the man said quietly. "But you should know that if the countdown is interrupted, it will blow."

Zero recalled suddenly what Penny had said, that the CIA wanted the site shut down. He wondered if she had been forced to try yet, if she had been blocked by Omer's counter-attempts.

"Okay." He tried to ignore his rapidly thumping heartbeat as he holstered his gun. "Chip, get on the line with Penny—tell her that under no circumstances should she try to stop the countdown. Strickland, I want you over here with me. Omer." He looked the man in the eye and

158

tried to make it a reassuring one. "We're going to try to defuse this bomb from under you."

# CHAPTER TWENTY FOUR

Zero lay on his back, examining the underside of Omer's chair and the tangle of wires there. "Todd? Are you seeing what I'm seeing?"

Strickland blew out a frustrated breath. "Yeah." He knelt beside the small stack of C4 obscured behind the server array. "Either this was a hasty job, or…"

"Or they did it to make it more difficult." The wiring layout seemed like it should have been simple enough—but there were three more wires than there should have been, soldered to silver leads on a small circuit board that would send a signal to the detonator and the explosives.

In the movies, there was always a color to cut. In reality, the wire color was meaningless. Red, blue, yellow—those were just the plastic coatings on the lines. The only thing that mattered was which one sent the signal to the detonator. But there were multiple leads trailing into the box. Which could have meant multiple signals. Or could have meant a failsafe, designed to blow if the wrong wire was cut.

Omer squirmed a bit. Zero winced.

"Hey, Omer." He tried to sound calm as Strickland attempted to map the wiring. "Why don't you tell us how you got here?"

"No offense meant, sir, but this hardly seems the time for small talk." The man's voice was breathless, as if he was on the verge of a panic attack. And justifiably so.

*At least it'll be quick if we're wrong,* Zero told himself. The bomb was enough to incinerate them all in a heartbeat, and likely take out the villas adjacent to it. Which meant not just Omer, but other innocent lives lost.

"Humor me," Zero prodded.

"Penny," Chip said into the phone behind him. "It's Foxworth. Do *not* stop the countdown. You hear me? We've got a bomb situation here…"

Omer took a deep breath in an effort to calm himself. "I am… I suppose I am what you would call a 'hacker.' I hail from Turkey. I

160

worked in cybersecurity for Istanbul *Bankasi*. In my spare time, I would…"

"Steal?" Zero offered.

"Well, yes," Omer admitted. "It was, admittedly, more of a test of my own skill. But I would hack security systems of known syndicate banks. Targeting mostly the Cayman Islands."

"And you stole from the wrong guy," Zero guessed.

"Narrowed it down to two lines," Strickland announced.

"That is correct," said Omer. "He found me. Or rather, he had his people find me. They beat me, drugged me, and brought me to him…"

"Where?" Zero asked. He hoped the man in question was Dawoud, or the fake Dawoud.

"Cairo," Omer told him. "A white businessman in Cairo. I do not believe he was Egyptian. He sounded like something else. Armenian, perhaps? He called himself by a name. 'Mr. Shade.'"

"Doesn't sound ominous at all," Chip muttered.

"He told me he would kill me unless I came here, did what they asked. There was a man here who had a gun. He forced me to sit. I did not know about the bomb until then."

*Mr. Shade. A "businessman" in Cairo.*

"Okay," said Todd. "Okay… I think I got this."

"You *think*?" Zero asked.

Todd ignored him. "The striped blue line, and the green line," he said. "We're going to cut them both at the same time."

"How?" Zero didn't have wire cutters, let alone two pairs.

"This is fifty-gauge wire. It's very thin. You should be able to tug it loose with your fingers."

"Good lord," Chip murmured behind them.

But Zero nodded. What choice did they have? He reached up carefully and pinched the two wires between the thumb and forefinger of each hand, ready to give both a solid tug on Todd's say-so.

"On three," Strickland said. "One… two…"

"No!" Omer shouted suddenly.

Zero looked up. So did Strickland.

The countdown had ceased, at 20:43:51.

Zero closed his eyes, waiting for the bomb to ignite.

The circuit board, inches from his face, popped with yellow sparks.

"Ouch!" He rubbed his cheek. It smelled like burnt plastic.

Strickland laughed. "A dud. It's a dud. The wiring was faulty."

Foxworth let out a whoop of triumph—despite having done nothing to help, Zero noted wryly—and he couldn't help but chuckle himself.

"A dud," he repeated. It was troubling enough that someone had circumvented Penny and shut down the countdown. But the bomb was a dud.

Zero rolled out from under the chair. "You're sure, Todd?"

"I'm sure. That circuit board just fried itself. One of the wires must have doubled back on its own loop. Omer—you can stand up."

The man shook his head slightly, still fearful, but Zero held out a hand. Omer took it, and though Zero trusted Todd he still found himself holding his breath as the man slowly lifted himself from the seat.

Nothing happened. No bomb exploded. Omer smiled wide and breathed an intense sigh of relief, as if he'd been holding it for hours.

"Let's get out of here," Zero told the team. "Omer, we can get you to a..." He trailed off as his eyes met the computer monitor.

The countdown had started up again, skipping ahead to its current position.

20:43:36...

20:43:35...

20:43:34...

"What the hell?" Strickland whispered.

Realization struck Zero like a brick to the head. Someone had turned off the countdown—because that same someone knew that the bomb was supposed to go off when it ceased. But the bomb was faulty. Which meant...

*We're being watched.*

But how? Were there cameras? Or maybe through a—

The window to Zero's left exploded suddenly, sending glass shrapnel bouncing off of him. The bullet entered Omer's skull, and the man crumpled to the ground in an instant.

162

# CHAPTER TWENTY FIVE

"Sniper!" Zero shouted. But it was drowned out by a second shot, this one spinning Foxworth and sending him to the floor. "Chip!"

Strickland was on one knee, gun out in an instant, aimed out the window. Zero pulled the Glock 19 and saw it—a man with a rifle, on the flat rooftop of the adjacent villa.

The wiring of the bomb, the cessation of the countdown, a sniper watching. A failsafe to the failsafe to the failsafe.

Strickland fired several rounds as the sniper rolled away and out of sight.

"Did you hit him?" Zero shouted.

"I don't think so. Omer?"

"Dead." He spun toward Chip. "Foxworth?"

"I'm hit." Chip sat up with a groan, holding his shoulder. "That hurt. I'm bleeding, but not bad."

Zero frowned. A bullet strong enough to penetrate the graphene Chip wore was high caliber—a fact that he already knew based on the state of Omer's skull.

"Stay with him!" he ordered Strickland. They needed to get to that man. They needed to know what he knew.

Zero holstered the Glock as he kicked away shards of broken glass from the shattered window frame and stood on it, bracing himself against the edges. He looked up; the lip of the flat roof was just out of reach. He was going to have to jump for it.

He looked down. If he missed, it was only an eighteen-foot drop or so. Right onto concrete. Still high enough to shatter both legs.

He took a breath, ejected mangled limbs from his mind, and jumped, reaching—his fingertips grazed and then grabbed the lip of the roof. For a moment he just dangled there, legs kicking, pulse pounding in his strained fingers.

With a grunt and a herculean effort, he pulled himself up and rolled onto the flat roof of the villa. The gun was out in an instant, aiming— but he didn't see the sniper on the adjacent roof.

No, the man was already two villas away, running.

163

The span was eight feet at most. Not impossible, but an above average long jump for a human. And he wasn't in the best shape he could have been.

"Screw it." He quickly backed up several strides, got a running start, and leaped.

His heart was in his throat as the toes of his boots hit the adjacent rooftops. His arms windmilled for a moment, and then he forced his weight forward—first his hips, then torso, until his shoulders propelled him forward into a roll.

Then he was on his feet again, running. Another leap. Another opportunity to congratulate himself later on being forty and capable of a rooftop chase.

But the sniper had a lead on him, and seemed faster on his feet. Zero raised the Glock, took careful aim. He was just over fifty yards away.

He squeezed the trigger. Once. Then twice. The shots cracked in his eardrums. The sniper cried out and fell forward on the second shot.

The next rooftop, thankfully, was closer than the others, practically touching, and it took Zero only seconds to catch up to the fallen man. He was young, twenty-five if he was a day, with a black curling beard a sneer on his lips.

"Don't," Zero had the gun trained on him as the young man clearly thought about going for the rifle that had fallen a few feet from him. "I have questions for you, and they're going to be difficult to answer with two bullets in you."

The young sniper grunted in pain as he got slowly to his feet. "I will tell you nothing," he said in Arabic.

"I think you're going to surprise yourself… hey! Stop!"

The young man backed up a few feet, getting dangerously close to the edge.

Zero edged closer, both hands around the pistol. "Don't…"

Without another word, the sniper turned and leapt from the rooftop, headfirst, in a swan-dive.

The sound of the impact made Zero's stomach turn. He didn't want to look, but he had to, and when he did there was absolutely no doubt that the man was dead. He heard shrieks and cries of pedestrians, some shouting in English and others in Greek, and knew the police would be called any moment. No time to search the sniper or to get himself involved in politics with local authorities.

164

Two minutes later he returned to the Fiat to find Strickland and Foxworth waiting for him inside. They pulled away immediately, putting distance between them and the screaming sirens behind them.

"Dead," Zero told them before they could ask. "Jumped from the roof before I could get any answers. But the perpetrators must have been in touch with him. Someone was—someone stopped that countdown in the hopes the bomb would go off."

"Why?" Strickland asked. "Just to kill whoever found Omer?"

Zero shook his head. *Why indeed?* Because...

*Because they don't care if the countdown is stopped, or the website is taken down.*

It was another diversion. They knew that the first way to track them would be to find the source of the site and whoever was behind it. Omer was a patsy. The world had already seen the countdown; it was likely being tracked in real time by a thousand websites and media outlets. Even if the original countdown was stopped, it would continue elsewhere.

*All of this was so that we would hit a dead end.*

But they hadn't. Not entirely.

"Where to?" Chip asked.

"Back to the plane," Zero told him. "How's the shoulder?"

"I'll live. Barely penetrated."

Zero pulled out the satellite phone. "Did you try to contact Maria and her team?"

"Tried and failed," said Todd. "They should be in Sofia by now. Likely went silent."

He shook his head. If their experience was anything like the one in Nicosia, his friends might be walking into a similar trap.

He called Penny.

"I'm seeing emergency services near your location," she answered by way of greeting. "You guys all right?"

"We're fine enough. But Maria, Alan, and Mendel might not be. I want you to get a message to them, let them know to be aware for traps. Especially bombs."

"Sure thing. Where are you headed?"

"Cairo," Zero told her. "What's the update on our friend Chubb and the Secret Service?"

"They're en route to Nicosia as we speak," Penny replied. "Should I presume they'll find themselves cleaning up a mess?"

165

"Two messes. And a thoroughly dead end—for them, at least." For a moment he had a pang of doubt. To have more hands on deck could be beneficial. But those were men he didn't know, hadn't worked with before, and after the episode on Air Force One with the Ayatollah of Iran and a rogue agent, he wasn't ready to let unknowns in on his plans. Besides, he'd worked with guys like Chubb before. They were tough, and thorough, and believed in justice—which meant they were the type who would waltz in with handcuffs, throw around threats, and demand answers.

What he had planned required a little more subterfuge than that.

"Penny, I need everything you can find on an underground businessman that goes by the name 'Mr. Shade' in Cairo. It seems he has some holdings in the Caymans."

"I'll start digging ASAP," Penny confirmed. "What's he got to do with this?"

"Not sure yet," Zero told her. "But I have a hunch he might be bankrolling this operation."

*And we're going to go pay him a visit.*

# CHAPTER TWENTY SIX

Maria couldn't help herself. She glanced at the phone's screen for what must have been the fourth time inside a minute.

She had synced the website's countdown with the timer app on the phone Mendel had provided. She knew she should but she wished she hadn't. Every second ticking by was another grain of sand in a vast hourglass that would never be flipped.

20:19:22…

20:19:21…

20:19:20…

She tore her gaze from it and darkened the screen. Ahead of her, Talia Mendel drove the black sedan, a loaner from a contact of her passenger, Alan Reidigger.

One of these days Maria would sit down with Alan and have a long chat about how he had forged relationships with half the world's underbelly during his two years of being dark. For now, she was thankful for it. He had a car waiting for them before the wheels of the Learjet had touched down.

Sofia was a gorgeous city. Funny, to her, that so many Americans seemed to think of this part of the globe, Eastern Europe, as being third-world. There was so much history and culture here, from still-standing Roman amphitheaters to a rich museum scene. The Cathedral Saint Aleksandar Nevski was particularly striking, layered sea-green domes rising above one another into the sky.

*Zero would love it here.*

She hoped they were okay, and that Nicosia had provided a lead on the president's whereabouts. No one had tried to contact her yet. She'd call them after this was done.

She found herself wondering too if Mischa would like it here. And then, had the girl ever been on a vacation before? On a beach? Had she ever walked through a museum, or dined at a restaurant?

*Focus, Johansson.*

"Alan?" she asked. "Location?"

"Still static," he reported. He was monitoring a GPS blip on a smartphone in his hand. It was the mobile device from which the bot accounts had launched when the countdown began. Since then, several more posts had gone out, in seemingly mechanical intervals, every half hour according to Penny. But the location of the device hadn't changed. Whoever was behind it had stayed put for the last... what was it? Three hours and forty-two minutes?

*Don't look at it again,* she told herself.

There was still time. Lots of time.

Mendel slowed the car as they arrived near their location. Even through the trees Maria could see the bell tower and the dome of the central cathedral.

"We're sure this is the place?" she asked.

"We're sure," Alan confirmed.

*Sveta Troitsa,* this place was called. A nineteenth-century Bulgarian Orthodox monastery turned church turned museum turned historic landmark.

And whoever they were looking for was inside.

"What do you think they're playing at, hiding in an old church?" she wondered aloud.

"If I had to guess?" Alan turned in his seat with a slight grin. "I'm guessing they don't think we'll do what we're about to do in such a holy place."

Mendel got out first and popped the trunk. Maria joined her just in time to see the Mossad agent hefting an Israeli-made IWI Tavor-21, a reliable bullpup assault rifle that was standard issue for Israel Defense Forces.

"Hey," Maria told her, "we're here to get information, not fight off a battalion."

"It is better to have it and not need it, yes?" Mendel gestured toward the long black case before her. "I have two, if you'd like."

"No. Thanks." She had a Sig Sauer holstered under her jacket, and hoped she wouldn't even need that. They were looking for one man with a mobile device. And though he might be armed, their goal was to interrogate, not blast him full of holes.

They approached the church from the west. The architecture might have been beautiful had it not been for their reason for visiting, but now wasn't the time to stop and admire. Maria wasn't expecting to encounter anyone other than their perp and any friends of his; the

168

church was waiting on government funding for a restoration project and had been for three years.

"Mendel," she said. "Around back. Alan, with me."

Talia split off, the Tavor cradled in her arms, while Maria and Alan approached the wide main entrance. She positioned herself alongside the door and pulled the Sig Sauer, and then nodded to Alan.

He reached for the door. To their surprise, it pulled open easily. Unlocked.

A tingle went up her spine. Unlocked meant welcoming, and welcoming—in these situations—often spelled trouble.

Still she spun and entered the atrium, pistol up, tracking quickly left to right. "Clear."

Alan followed, passing her, taking point to the second set of doors. They repeated the process, again finding them unlocked, and Maria clearing the lengthy nave.

It appeared empty.

Still she stepped forward slowly on the carpet of the central aisle, checking the left rows of pews while Alan stepped in time with her, checking the right.

Stained glass windows depicted saints and angels. The ceiling was an ornate mural of various biblical figures. The front altar and apse bore a life-sized statue of Jesus on the cross. But they heard nothing, saw no one in the cavernous cathedral.

Maria got down on one knee and checked beneath the pews, in case someone was hiding. No one there.

She heard footsteps and whirled around, the gun up. Mendel appeared from a door off the north transept.

"Clear." The Israeli said it quietly but still it echoed in the room.

"Over here," Alan announced. The two women hurried to his position, staring down at a pew about two-thirds to the front altar.

Lying there was a cell phone.

Maria spun quickly. "Whoever it was already ran. Or he's hiding. I'll check the exits. Alan, you check the—"

"Hold on one moment." Talia picked up the cell phone and tapped the screen.

"We don't have time for this," Maria argued.

"Just... wait." Mendel scrolled, frowning. "Aha," she said after a moment. "Very clever."

"What is?!" Maria demanded. "He could be getting away—"

"There is no 'he.' Social media apps are open on this phone. The posts that have been traced to this place were prewritten and set to go live on timed intervals." She turned the screen to show them a list of composed but not-yet-transmitted posts.

Maria shook her head. She didn't want to admit that she wasn't exactly up to date on social media, and had no idea that was something someone could do. "Then that means..."

"Yes. Dead end."

"They wanted us to come here," Alan grunted. "To waste time chasing nobody."

Maria wanted to kick something, a pew perhaps, but it didn't feel right. "At least shut it down."

"Already have," said Mendel.

"Let's take it with us. We can see what else might be on it." She pulled out her phone to try to contact Zero and his team, hoping that Nicosia had panned out better than Sofia had. She dialed his phone and hit the green send button. But all she got was a warning.

"Airplane mode?" She scoffed loudly and waved the phone in Mendel's face. "You gave me a phone that's been on *airplane* mode?"

Mendel merely shrugged. "You did not check first?"

Maria cursed under her breath as she turned it off. And then balked as several new voicemails rolled in. "Christ, they've been trying to call me..."

Alan tensed suddenly beside her like a bloodhound with the scent of a fox. She did too, trusting his instincts, and an instant later she heard the screech of tires just outside the church.

Then car doors slammed, and shadows fell over the stained glass windows. The shadows of hasty men with weapons in their hands.

"You turned off the media accounts," Maria whispered.

"Yes." Mendel's grip on the Tavor tightened.

"And that turned them on to us."

"It would seem."

They'd been nearby. Waiting for someone to come after the phone.

"Alan, flank left! Mendel, cover the entrance—"

The stained glass window closest to them exploded inward. Maria dropped instantly to the pew, turning as she did, and fired the Sig Sauer twice into the chest of the man climbing through it.

Even as she did, another window exploded. The doors to the nave were kicked in. Talia's Tavor shrieked in a rapid burst.

170

Maria rolled to the floor and crawled quickly to the aisle. Across from her, another window was shot in, and a man leapt through it—right into the path of Alan Reidigger. He fired twice into the assailant, grabbed him by the black vest, and tossed him back out the window.

*How many?* She didn't know. But there had been a back entrance, and someone needed to cover it...

Too late. As Maria stood, she saw herself face to face with three men who had crashed through the transept door, raising their guns in her direction.

"Down!" Mendel shouted, and before Maria had even hit the carpet the Tavor screamed again as the Mossad agent emptied the clip into the trio.

Shells rattled against the floor and pews, and then fell silent.

"Clear?" Maria asked.

"Clear," Alan huffed.

"Clear," said Mendel. She propped the Tavor on one shoulder. "I saved your life just now, you know this."

Maria rolled her eyes. "I had it under control..."

A man grunted in pain somewhere in the nave.

"Oh look, one lives," Talia mentioned casually. She glanced down at the man as he tried, with much difficulty, to crawl on his elbows toward the atrium.

"Alan, keep an eye out." Maria stepped up to the man, even as he continued to struggle forward. She turned him onto his back with a foot, and then planted it on his chest.

He cried out in pain. It looked like he was the one who had crashed through the window, the one she'd shot twice. His vest hadn't stopped both rounds, it seemed.

"Arabic?" she asked him in what she presumed was his native tongue, assuming he was with the group that had taken Rutledge.

"Go to hell, dog!" he spat at her in the same language.

Maria shook her head. They didn't have time for usual interrogation tactics. "I have questions." She turned slightly and shot him in the right kneecap. He screamed, thrashing against the foot on his chest, but most of the strength had left his body. "You have answers. Give them to me, and you might live. Yes?"

His breath came in hisses between gritted, bloody teeth. But then—he laughed. It was a pained laugh, half a grimace and half a grin, but unmistakably a laugh.

171

"I know nothing of value to you," he panted. "I am but a servant…" He groaned, eyes clenched shut. The shot that got through his vest must have penetrated vital organs. He was dying.

"You have to know something!" Maria leaned over him, shouting in his contorted face. "You have to!"

He murmured something then, something that at first sounded unintelligible—but she made out the words. It was scripture, from the Quran.

*Is he praying?* It wasn't like any prayer she'd heard before.

And then his chest stopped heaving, and the muscles of his face relaxed. He was dead.

"We should go," said Alan. "Time is ticking, Maria."

She nodded, still as intrigued as she was confused by the man's choice of final words.

"I did not make out what he said," Mendel admitted. "Did you?"

Maria shook her head. "Something about a curse. A dying man's gibberish. Nothing more." She looked up at the Israeli. "Thanks. For… helping me. Let's move."

The three of them hurried out of the church, away from its broken windows and bullet-pocked pews, and back to the car.

Bulgaria had been a dead end. They'd stopped the social media transmissions, but that was hardly a victory. And time kept ticking. Ticking. Ticking.

19:58:41…

19:58:40…

19:58:39…

She needed to call Penny, find out where Zero and his team were, what they had found. But as they sped away from *Sveta Troitsa*, she couldn't seem to get the man's last words out of her head.

*Their curse*, he had said. *The nation made to wander for forty years, until the generation of men had died.*

172

# CHAPTER TWENTY SEVEN

"We do not negotiate with terrorists," Secretary of Defense Colin Kressley insisted. "Engaging in negotiations legitimizes them—"

"This is not a negotiation," Joanna Barkley interrupted. She sat at the head of the conference table in the Situation Room of the White House. For the time being, until Rutledge was recovered—she refused to let herself think of any other outcome—her title was Acting President Barkley. "There is a difference between a demand and a condition, General Kressley, and we would be keen to recognize it."

If men like Kressley had their way, Palestine would already be a crater on the map. He was leading the charge to declare war. And Jonathan would be…

*No. Don't even think it.*

She knew that Jerusalem was a bad idea, had felt it from the beginning. But the time for that acknowledgment was past. Here and now, in the Situation Room of the White House with key cabinet members assembled, including the Secretary of Defense, the DNI, Chief of Staff Halpern, and several others, she was expected to act in Jonathan's absence.

But she wasn't Jonathan. Nor would she pretend to be.

Tabitha Halpern cleared her throat. "Ms. Vice President, intelligence out of Israel suggests they are organizing a coordinated missile strike on key Palestinian locations as we speak, including the PNA's seat in Ramallah."

"Despite the fact that President Dawoud is not there," Barkley interjected.

"And," Tabby continued, "they are requesting that the US joins them in condemning Palestine's actions and ask that we sanction 'retaliatory measures' they may take…"

"A missile strike is an act of war," Barkley said calmly. "We will not sanction it. Especially since this attack was carried out by a handful of men—"

"This is the action of a man that represents a country!" Kressley cut in. "Ma'am, these men are holding us hostage as much as they are the

173

president with their ridiculous concessions. We need to show our strength—"

Joanna eyed him carefully. "By showing what you think is strength, General, we risk President Rutledge's life unnecessarily."

"His life is already at unnecessary risk!" the Secretary of Defense all but shouted. "We have no guarantee they will hold true to their 'conditions.' Damn their countdown! They have him, and at any moment, regardless of our actions, they could put a bullet in his—"

"General Kressley." Barkley stood. She was not a loud woman by nature, but the Senate floor had taught her that some moments required learning to control one's diaphragm to their advantage. "You are dismissed."

He blinked at her, his face rapidly turning pink. "What?"

"Dismissed, I said. Please leave this room."

"Y-you can't…"

"I can. I am. To be clear, you are dismissed from this meeting. If this untoward conduct continues, then next will be your position. Am I clear?"

All eyes were on Kressley as his throat flexed in an inaudible gulp. "Yes," he muttered. "Ma'am." He stood forcefully from his seat, shoved his hat under one arm, and marched briskly from the Situation Room.

Barkley slowly lowered herself back into her seat. Kressley was not a bad man, not an evil one, nor a bully. He simply had a myopic perspective. He was here to offer it when others wouldn't or couldn't, but pushing an agenda onto her was simply not acceptable.

"We can condemn the actions of President Dawoud without condemning a nation," she told the room. "And we can do so without a declaration of war. It is my personal belief that this attack was planned and carried out by a small group. If it wasn't, we would see Palestinian troops mobilized. We would see attacks at borders. And until I am proven wrong, this is our position. We will not endanger innocent lives, civilian or military, American or Palestinian, because of the actions of a few men. Instead we will focus our efforts on finding those few men."

She paused for effect before adding: "If anyone present disagrees, or shares General Kressley's point of view, or is willing to sacrifice the one life that is on the line at the moment in favor of a formal declaration, please speak up now."

No one spoke. She knew they wouldn't. It wasn't a matter of arrogance or superiority; she simply knew she was surrounded by people who were loyal to Rutledge, and by extension to her, and wanted to see him returned home safely.

"Ms. Halpern." She turned to the Chief of Staff, the primary liaison to the Secret Service field agents in this emergency. "Who do we have on the ground right now?"

"Several teams have been dispatched," Tabby reported, "but gaining little ground. However, we have been in contact with one team, led by the Deputy Special Agent in Charge of the president's security detail in Jerusalem. Agent Chubb was on the scene when Jon was— excuse me, when the hostage crisis unfolded. They had a lead on the countdown website's source in Cyprus, but..." She sighed. "But it yielded nothing. They came onto the scene of an active murder-suicide situation. Our best guess is an attack by a rival faction. Though we're not certain. All we know is it was a dead end."

Barkley mulled that over for a moment. A murder-suicide that involved this renegade faction, mere moments before the Secret Service showed up? It didn't sound entirely plausible.

"Director Barren," she said suddenly, turning to the DNI. "What about the Executive Operations Team? They were on the scene as well."

"Yes. They were, ma'am." Barren shifted in his seat. "We were in contact briefly after the attack. I instructed them to join the Secret Service in their efforts, and to assist in whatever capacity they were able—"

"And where are they now?" Barkley asked.

"I, uh..." Barren glanced over at Tabby Halpern for help, but she only shrugged slightly.

Clearly EOT was *not* with the Secret Service.

"I'll find out, ma'am," Director Barren said quickly. "As soon as possible—"

"No," Barkley said simply.

She wasn't Jon Rutledge. Nor would she try or pretend to be. But he believed in the EOT, spoke highly of them—almost to the point of irritation at times, the way a boy might talk about a comic-book superhero.

But that's not why she told DNI Barren no. She recalled last month, when the South Korean ship bearing a plasma railgun had been stolen, and no one had any idea where it was. At the same time, no one had any idea where the CIA team that later became EOT was either.

And Jon had said something then, something that Joanna Barkley found herself repeating now: "If we're not hearing from them, hopefully it's because they're doing their jobs."

They'd done their jobs then. They were somewhere now. And the less Barkley and Barren knew about their operations, or tried to interfere, the likely the better.

Barren nodded. "Yes ma'am."

A long silence stretched across the room.

At last, a young aide standing in the back cleared his throat and stepped forward. "Ms., uh… President, I have some information that I believe we should review. There's been a lot of media chatter since the transfer of executive power, and I think we should address portrayal and general opinion—"

Barkley waved a hand and he fell silent. "That's not important right now."

"Right." He cleared his throat again. "Of course not."

"Ms. Halpern, where is the countdown currently?"

The Chief of Staff addressed her phone briefly. "Eighteen hours, fifty-seven minutes."

Joanna sighed. It felt like they had time.

But they did not. Israel would continue to put the pressure on. Palestine had been entirely silent so far. It was possible they were as baffled as anyone, and trying desperately to locate Dawoud. Or torn in parliament. And if missiles flew…

"Let's recess briefly," she announced. "Ten minutes. Stretch your legs."

Seats shuffled and quiet chatter broke out as people exited the Situation Room. But Tabby Halpern remained, seated to Barkley's right.

"You should try to get some rest, Joanna." She put her hand over Barkley's.

But she shook her head. "I'll be here. Please keep me abreast of all new developments."

She wasn't moving. She would sit there, in the seat that belonged to Jonathan Rutledge, until he returned to sit in it himself.

And she hoped she would not hear from EOT.

# CHAPTER TWENTY EIGHT

Zero resisted the urge to jab himself in the thigh with another shot of Tramadol. Barely five hours and already it was wearing off. Aches, in his head and neck and shoulders and... well, everywhere, down to his ankles.

*It's just because you're at rest*, he told himself. Once he was off the jet and moving again, he'd feel better. Get the blood flowing. But even being seated on the plane offered no rest; he fidgeted. He drummed his fingers against the armrest. His left knee bounced rapidly of its own volition.

Cairo was three hundred seventy-three miles from Cyprus, as the crow flew. Even in a jet as fast as the G650, their travel time was an hour and five minutes, including the hastiest takeoff and landing Chip Foxworth could manage.

Nearly four hundred miles to travel. Another sixty-five minutes off the timer.

18:55:17...

18:55:16...

Where was Rutledge now? With five hours they could have taken him to countless locations. A search would be useless. They needed solid information. Leads.

He couldn't just sit there anymore. He got up, knees popping and his lower back protesting, and made his way to the cockpit.

"Chip, how we doing?"

Foxworth glanced over his shoulder briefly. "We'll be landing shortly. You really should really up."

"All right." Zero lowered himself into the empty copilot chair and strapped the buckle over his chest. Through the windshield beyond him, wispy clouds parted and the glittering blue sea gave way to the coast of Egypt. "How's the shoulder?"

"Slapped a Band-Aid on it, good as new." Chip grinned. "I've had worse. But hey, first time being shot on this job. There must be some kind of ribbon or medal for that kind of thing, right?"

Zero snickered. "We'll get you a cake when we get home."

Foxworth frowned then, and cocked his head slightly; he was hearing something through his headset. Zero reached for a spare and slipped it over his ears in time to hear an accented voice say in English, "…identify, please."

"Cairo, this is November-seven-niner-eight-Charlie-Alpha, American general aviation, carrying a goodwill ambassador to Riyadh." Foxworth rattled off the lie as easily as ordering off a menu. "We've got a minor mechanical issue here with our heading indicator. With your permission we'd like to put her down, check it out, and maybe grab some lunch."

He winked, and Zero stifled a chuckle.

There was a lengthy pause, and then the voice came back, instructing them toward a minor runway outside of the commercial lanes, and even comped a vehicle for their brief stay.

"Now that's hospitality," Foxworth quipped.

"Good thing they were speaking English," Zero noted. He didn't think he could have pulled that off, and Chip's Arabic was rusty.

The former pilot shrugged. "English is the international language of aviation."

"Is that so?"

He nodded. "All countries under the International Civil Aviation Organization require their pilots and air traffic controllers to speak it."

"Huh." Zero pulled off the headset and tried to enjoy the front-row seat as they made their descent into Cairo International Airport.

As soon as wheels were on the ground, Zero was out of his seat and on the phone with Penny. "I hope you have good news."

"It's not as if I had a lot of time," she began, and his shoulders slumped. He'd charged her with finding anything she could about this mystery financer, Mr. Shade, and his whereabouts. "But… I think I have something."

"You think…?" Zero started to say they didn't have time for conjecture, but he held back. She was under the same pressure that he and his team were. "What is it?"

"First off, Mr. Shade is obviously an alias, so tracking accounts in the Caymans was a nonstarter. His digital footprint is almost nil— almost. I did a dark-web deep-dive and found a mention to an event happening today in relation to a 'Shade.' The description was coded, but it looks like some sort of auction. It's going down in the penthouse of the Nile Ritz, about three hours from now."

178

*Three hours?* That would put them at six p.m. local time. "No way. We can't waste three hours on a hunch."

"It's all I've got, Zero. I'm sorry. If you think you can do more the old-fashioned way, have at it."

"The old-fashioned way would be to kick in the penthouse door right now," he admitted.

"I would advise against that," Penny warned. "I could be wrong, but I have a feeling the nature of this auction might be... people."

*People.* Traffickers. Auctioning people. Girls, most likely. A flare of rage lit like a match head inside him at the very notion. He'd dealt with those types before, when they had tried to take his daughters. No, they *had* taken his daughters, and it took a race across Eastern Europe and fighting an entire train to get them back.

"If I'm right," Penny continued, "security is going to be tight. That place will be like a fortress. But you could get into the auction. With three hours I could get you fake credentials, decent clothes, and a cover story. A good reason to get close to him. And then the heroics are up to you."

Zero sighed as the Gulfstream came to a stop on the tarmac. They had no other leads. Nowhere else to go. They weren't the only ones looking for the president. He didn't like it, but this was their best bet.

"All right," he told her. "We'll get the clothes. You handle the rest."

# CHAPTER TWENTY NINE

Jonathan Rutledge sweated under the hood as he bounced in his seat with every rut in the pitted road. If they were even on a road. Beads of sweat rolled down his cheeks, over his dry lips, soaked through his shirt and into his socks. Wherever they were was hot, and the hood made it hotter. They had offered him no water, and dehydration was setting in. They had not removed the hood at all, not once, since first putting it over his head.

How long had it been? Hours, certainly. A day by now? He couldn't tell. Time was lost to him under the hood.

The vehicle bounced again, and he yelped. Or he tried to; barely a sound came out of his parched throat. With each bounce, the steel of the handcuffs binding his sore wrists behind him bit into his flesh.

They had been traveling nonstop. First he was forced through that musty space, on his feet. Then there was a vehicle, the strong smell of leather, a piney air freshener, and gun oil. Then there was a plane, a small one, which rattled alarmingly with turbulence. Then there was another vehicle, this vehicle. It had no top, but the wind that whipped at the hood offered little respite against the heat. Even with the hood on he could tell the sun was beating down directly onto him.

At least the wind drowned out the voices. Not one word of English had been exchanged between his captors; they spoke entirely in Arabic to each other, and Rutledge knew only a few phrases of salutations and well wishes. The only time English was spoken was harsh words directed at him, threats when he made a noise or did not move fast enough from one vehicle to the next.

The terror and panic had not left him, but it had dulled a bit, like a sharp pain waning to an ache. Perhaps he was just getting used to it, he wondered. Desensitized to the notion of being kidnapped, carried off to some corner of the world, and inevitably killed.

That was obviously the endgame of these men. There could be no other. The American government did not engage in negotiations with terrorists, and he would not expect them to barter for his life. He could

180

not help but wonder, however, what demands had these men made in return for him.

At the same time, he was glad to not know. The last thing he wanted was to know the value that had been put on his head.

At long last the vehicle rolled to a stop, and he was dragged out of his seat. He complied, as much for the reason of having such little strength in his limbs as a fear of physical reprisal. Two men had a brief foreign exchange, and then he was grabbed by two pairs of hands.

His first instinct was to struggle, to cry out as they grabbed him roughly, their grips like iron. This was it. This was the moment when—

But then he found himself behind lifted, and set down again on a surface. It was soft under him, and… and moving. There was an odor, one he had smelled before, and then a deep snort.

*A horse. They've put me on a horse. Or perhaps a camel?*

Was this dehydration delirium setting in? Had he lost his mind? Was he in the throes of a fever dream? Had he already died, and this was some bizarre afterlife episode?

It was all of that and none of that at the same time under the hood. Time did not pass, but a man barked an order and the animal below him began to trudge forward. His body rocked rhythmically with it, swaying slightly. Nothing made sense anymore, and nothing needed to.

*This is what I get. I flew too close to the sun. I wanted too much.*

He felt deeply ashamed of the thought as soon as he had it. This was not his fault. He had tried to make a difference, to enact real change in the world. And evil men had resisted that change. They demonstrated their opposition with hatred and horrible violence.

Were they not both products of the same world? The ones wishing for peace and the ones defying it?

It was then he understood. At least he thought he did. An example was being made of him. These men, they wanted to show the world what happened to those who might be inspired to follow in Rutledge's footsteps. They had obviously taken great pains to gain access to the American president—and if they could get to him, who could they not get to?

He would not become a martyr; he would become a warning. Like a hanged man at a crossroads to ward off scheming highwaymen. Like heads on pikes of medieval fortifications.

And that thought was far more harrowing than any other he'd had so far, because it meant that his captors may not have demanded anything. There would be no negotiations for his release. If he was right, his situation was truly hopeless.

Outside the hood, time must have passed because eventually the animal stopped. It snorted again, but Rutledge remained on its back even while stationary. There were sounds then, not just dialogue exchanges but the sounds of work, grunts of effort and clangs of metal. Time passed outside the hood, and Rutledge sweated, swayed, and willed himself to not fall over.

Hands grabbed at him. They lowered him from the beast's back. Fingers around his throat. He recoiled in fear. Then there was air, as suddenly as a heartbeat there was fresh air, and the heat of the sun was so much more, and the light blinded him.

Time passed again, the hood torn from over his head, and for a full minute he could make nothing out but the whitest white light. Slowly things began to focus. First the stern, scowling face of a black-uniformed man in front of him. A gun in his hands. Two others, dressed the same.

And Dawoud. Dawoud was there, but he did not scowl. He smiled.

"You will not speak," he said in English. "You will not try to run. You will not move unless you are told to move. If you do, you will be hurt. Do you understand?"

Rutledge could not have answered yes if he wanted to, and he did not want to, since he had been warned against it, so he simply nodded.

Dawoud said something to the man in front of him. Something glinted in the man's hand. A weapon? No. A bottle.

The man lifted a bottle of water to Rutledge's lips and tipped it back slightly. Cool, wonderful, delicious water splashed over his lips, tingled on his tongue, flooded his throat.

All too quickly it was pulled away. Not enough. Not nearly enough.

He was forced down then, into a chair behind him, his hands still cuffed uncomfortably behind him, the flesh of his wrists chafed and probably bleeding.

And he noticed now where they were.

They were nowhere.

There was nothing around them, nothing at all, for as far as the eye could see. The landscape was drab, beige, rock and sand.

They had brought him to the middle of a desert.

The animal that had carried him there was indeed a horse, one of three that grazed some sagebrush nearby. And the sounds of work that

182

he had heard were the establishing of a small encampment. A tarp overhead, held aloft by poles. Two domed tents, the tops beige to nearly match the sand. Under the tarp, a gas-powered generator.

A camera.

A table with computer equipment.

Fresh panic gripped his chest, a familiar yet new sensation. They had brought him to the middle of nowhere. He was going to die. And these men were going to film it.

# CHAPTER THIRTY

Zero knotted the tie at his throat into a double Windsor knot and thought again of how little he liked this plan. The suit was black, slim fit, double-breasted, a little tight around the midsection, but there was no time for tailoring. It offered no protection, no graphene or Kevlar, and no place to hide a weapon that wouldn't be found by Shade's guards. He was certain there would be security wands and armed men.

He still had the boots, at least, clashing terribly with the suit but affording him at least one minor measure of defense. It wasn't much. But it would have to do.

"You look like a million bucks," Chip chided from the hotel room's bed. They were situated on the fourth floor of the Nile Ritz-Carlton, fourteen floors below where Shade's auction was set to go down shortly. They had procured suits for himself and Todd; Chip would be staying behind, on standby, not only because of his injury but because it would be foolhardy to send them all into an unknown situation like this. If needed, Chip would kick in the door with an Israeli submachine gun blazing.

He just hoped it wouldn't come to that. Things could get messy fast.

Penny had reserved the room in the name of a Rod Iverson, an American expat who owned three exclusive storefronts in Amsterdam's Red Light District and was here in Cairo to explore some "aggressive expansion." That was also his cover for a personal tête-a-tête with Mr. Shade, to introduce the potential for a deal to have his "wares" shipped directly to Mr. Iverson without needing to travel to Egypt first.

If Shade was interested, he would invite him for a private conversation. And then…

*And then we'll have to improvise.* Beyond that he had no intel going into the auction. He couldn't be sure that Shade would tell him what he wanted to know, or if he even knew anything at all. All the while the timer kept ticking.

15:37:01…

15:37:00…

15:36:59…

"Time to go," he told Strickland, who emerged from the adjoining bathroom in a dark blue coat and powder-blue shirt, the collar open and tie-less. "Chip, stand by."

"Will do. Good luck, gents." Chip flashed a thumbs-up and set about loading a Mendel-supplied Tavor machine gun.

*We won't need it,* he told himself again.

He and Strickland rode the elevator up to the penthouse level. Ordinarily it would only be accessible by a keycard, but a tip from Penny proved correct—the feature had been disabled for this evening and Mr. Shade's high-profile guests.

"Let me do the talking," Zero said. It wasn't personal, but everything about Todd's demeanor shouted "all-American" and not at all "trafficker auction guest."

The doors opened and he sucked in a breath. He'd been in penthouse suites before, had seen and even experienced the ridiculous level of luxury these sorts of places afforded, but the top floor of the Nile Ritz-Carlton was outright stunning.

As they stepped off the elevator they were met by a receiving room that looked like a living room in Hollywood. The dark hardwood floors underfoot were met on two sides by floor-to-ceiling windows affording a generous view of the Egyptian city below. The furniture was pure white, spotless, modern. Opposite them was a small oak mini bar, a few people milling about it while a man in a white tuxedo mixed drinks. The guests here sported garb that made Zero feel like he'd come in sweatpants. The nearest woman's diamond earrings were no doubt worth more than his car.

Zero led the way as they headed across the room toward a pair of double doors that led into the suite proper. Three men guarded the entrance, all wearing black turtlenecks under gray blazers under stern expressions.

One held up a hand to pause them. "Purpose?" he asked, though his thick accent made it sound like, "*Porpoise?*"

Zero flashed a smile, channeling his cover, and—

And it was gone. In that instant, he forgot who he was supposed to be, why he was there. Not the real reason, but the cover story that Penny had fabricated for him.

*Not now. Christ, not now.*

The smile never left his lips, even as he opened his mouth, hoping that the identity would come surging back. But it didn't, and he just stood there, open-mouthed, as the guard in front of him raised an eyebrow in suspicion.

"Ex*cuse* me." Strickland stepped forward, between Zero and the guard. "My employer is not in the habit of explaining himself or his motives to those he doesn't know. Especially not the *help*."

Zero blinked, taken aback by Todd's sudden takeover of the situation.

"I'm Mr. Malone," he told them, "and this is Mr. Iverson." He gestured to Zero.

*Iverson. Of course. Rod Iverson, from Amsterdam.*

"We all know why we're here," Todd continued, dangerously close to the guard's face. "And I don't think your boss is the kind of man that would require us to say it aloud. So why don't you wave your little wand, open those doors, and let my boss spend some money, which will make your boss very happy. *Capiche?*"

The guard's frown deepened. But he stepped aside wordlessly as a second man stepped forward. They each raised their arms as he passed the metal-detecting wand over them, all the while Zero staying passive and keeping the incredulity off his face.

The wand guy nodded once, and the third man opened the double doors and admitted them into the sanctum beyond.

"What was that?" Todd asked quietly as they stepped inside.

"I'm sorry. I forgot the name, and then I froze…"

"You never forget the name," Todd challenged.

"I know. It won't happen again," Zero said dismissively. "By the way, that was nicely handled. Maybe you're spending too much time around Foxworth."

"Yeah. Maybe." Todd glanced around. "Man. Look at this place."

He did. The penthouse suite was nothing short of magnificent, contemporary design in a high-ceilinged space. The main chamber was enormous, open-concept from entrance to the far end of tall windows, taking up the entire top floor of the hotel. A man at a baby Steinway played light classical music for the guests, of which there must have been twenty-five that Zero could see, elegantly dressed and clustered in small groups. Men in white tuxedos passed around champagne and hors d'oeuvres, and there were at least four more armed guards like the ones outside the doors—again, that Zero could see. There were several doors and other rooms off of the main one.

"This doesn't look like an auction," Todd noted. "Looks like a party."

"Yeah." He had just been thinking the same thing. Were they in the right place? Had Penny been off the mark? He doubted it; she hadn't been wrong yet. "Split up. See if you can't locate this Mr. Shade. Discreetly."

"Got it." Todd peeled off to the left, toward the suite's kitchen, while Zero meandered forward. He grabbed a champagne flute from a nearby footman without breaking his stride. It took some effort for him to walk casually and hide the increasing pain in his left knee, and he wished he'd had the foresight to take the second Tramadol shot before this.

*But hindsight's twenty-twenty.*

He pushed further into the suite, catching snippets of conversation in French, English, Farsi, Arabic, among others, from women in lamé and chiffon and men in pressed, bespoke suits. Strickland was right; this didn't look like any sort of auction he'd ever seen.

He noticed, though, that most of the patrons were sticking to the perimeter of the wide room… and seemingly circling it. It only took a moment to see why; there were art pieces hung on the walls, small ones that required a close inspection. He stepped up to the nearest one, which currently had the attention of four guests, and took a look for himself.

It was a photograph, a simple one but an artistic one. An austere eight-by-ten print of a young woman—a girl, really, no older than his own daughters. She was strikingly pretty, standing at profile with her head turned toward the camera. She wore a plain yellow dress, which looked all the brighter against her blonde hair and the stark black background.

But what made the photo truly beautiful, truly haunting even, was the look in her eye. It was a doleful look, possibly soulful, but more indicative to him of a deep sorrow, a veritable well of it behind her eyes…

*Oh.*

*Oh, no.*

There it was, the familiar knot of dread in his stomach as he came to a horrible realization.

Beside the photograph was a small white card. If this was an art piece, this was where the artist's name would be printed, the name of the piece, the year it was produced. A price, perhaps.

But no. The card read:

*Lot 12241*
*170 cm.*
*48 kg.*
*Swedish*
*No visible scars*

The knot of dread inside him burst into furious flames. This *was* an auction—but Shade wasn't stupid enough to bring his wares here in person. This was an auction sight unseen, and these people—all of them, every single one here—they were window-shopping.

Four guards inside that he could see. Between him and Todd, they could take two of them out. Get their weapon. Kill the other two. And the rest would just be guests. Unarmed, and Zero would still be able to sleep soundly at night if any of these monsters were hit in fray...

An arm linked into his. He tensed, ready for a fight, when a familiar voice purred in his ear. "Heinous. Is it not?"

He glanced over in shock.

"But remember why we are here. It is not for them," she reminded him.

It was Talia Mendel.

# CHAPTER THIRTY ONE

"Come," Talia said, her arm still linked in his. "Walk this way. Wipe that look from your face." She led him away from the wall, and away from the photograph, away from the blonde Swedish girl with the haunted look that desperately needed his help, anyone's help...

But Talia was right. That's not why they had come. Blowing their cover now could mean Rutledge's death. Yet there was such a thing as two birds with one stone, and he'd find a way.

"How are you here?" Zero asked her in a low voice.

"Your friend from work," she said simply.

*Penny.* Of course Penny had told them where to find Zero and his team, and hadn't told him they'd be there. A contingency, in case they screwed it up. He wanted to be irritated about it, but then reminded himself that he *had* in fact almost screwed it up at the doors.

Talia wore a strapless black dress, her equally dark hair styled in stout curls atop her head. "Your bearded friend is one floor below us," she told him quietly. "He has liaised with the other, the one with the silly name."

"Chip."

"That would be him, yes." She let out a laugh, fake and tittering but not unpleasant, as if Zero had just told a joke. She was, admittedly, a much better actor than he was.

"And Maria?" he asked.

"See for yourself."

He glanced around the room. It took only a half second to locate her, the blonde bombshell in the red gown, a high slit up one leg, champagne in her left hand, the diamond there sparkling.

She was undercover, yet hadn't taken off the engagement ring.

"I'm assuming you have a better plan than I do," Zero asked.

"Indeed. See those doors over there?" She directed him with her gaze. "There is a bedroom behind it. I will cause a distraction. You go there, and make yourself unseen. Then wait."

Zero nodded as Talia unhooked her arm from his. "See you soon."

189

Then she tripped, or pretended to, lurching forward and colliding with a white-tuxedoed man carrying a full tray of champagne. The tray tipped; glasses flew and shattered. And Talia threw out her arms and shrieked, covered in champagne.

"You insipid, clumsy, *stupid* man!" she shouted. "How dare you!"

All eyes turned suddenly at the outburst and sound of broken glass. Guests gathered for a closer look while Zero stepped back, toward the closed door and the room beyond.

\*

"You clumsy, halfwit imbecile!" Mendel shouted over the party guests. "This dress is worth more than your miserable life!"

Maria sipped casually from her own glass, stifling a smile as best she could. Not only because Mendel was playing her part well, but also because she was drenched in champagne, which was thoroughly satisfying.

"I'm s-sorry, ma'am," the poor waiter stammered. "It was an accident…"

"Accident?! *You'll* have an accident when I throw you from the balcony!" She wiped champagne from her eyes. "Who is responsible for this oaf?"

Maria didn't move. She didn't react. But her eyes followed the man who stepped forward. He was in a white tuxedo, just like the wait staff, but the eighteen-carat Rolex Cellini on his wrist suggested otherwise.

*Clever.* Mr. Shade had come incognito to his own party.

The man looked rather unremarkable, and Maria couldn't help but think it was by design. He was easily mid-forties, but thin, his dark hair greased back, and otherwise not at all striking. A chameleon in his own lofty world.

"Madame," he said, his voice accented in French, "my sincere apologies. This behavior is simply not tolerated, and there will be swift consequence." Shade snapped his fingers at the nearest guard. "You. Please. Get *rid* of him."

"S-sir," the waiter protested, "please…"

Maria bit her lip. She couldn't make a move, not yet. But Talia's diversion was supposed to only identify Shade, not get a man killed.

190

"Wait." Mendel raised her hand, rolling her eyes as if it caused her great indignation to admit, "I... may have overreacted. It is *possible* that I tripped into him."

Shade examined her for a moment, and then a smile broke across his face. "I see. I appreciate your honesty, madame. Good help is very hard to find." He turned to the waiter. "Clean this up."

"Yes sir."

To Talia he asked, "Is there anything I can offer you, as my esteemed guest?"

She waved a hand. "No. I have a room here; I will just have to change." She stepped toward the door in her heels, head held high.

Shade watched her go as the rest of the party guests appeared to return to business as usual. But as Maria watched, the Frenchman sidled up to one of his guards, leaning in...

*To have her followed. He's suspicious.*

She made her move, striding across the floor and putting a hand gently on Shade's shoulder. "Pardon me, sir."

He turned, seemingly irked for a moment, but his frown quickly turned to a smile as he looked her up and down wolfishly. "Yes, madame? Or is it mademoiselle?"

"You may call me Jane. May we speak privately?"

"On what matter?" he asked directly.

This time she smiled, and leaned in to whisper in his ear. "I represent a prominent member of European royalty who is interested in partnering with a broker like yourself. One who can discreetly procure certain..." She glanced over at the photographs for effect, feeling her stomach churn as she did. "...items."

She took a step back and raised an eyebrow.

"What country?" he asked her.

"If I wanted you to know, I would have said." She turned then. "I'll be waiting." Without another word, she headed toward the closed door that led to the master bedroom, hoping she was pulling off an effective and alluring sashay. Surprising, and a little amusing, that in all her undercover work she rarely used sexuality as a tactic. It just made her feel... gross.

She pushed into the room and closed the door quickly behind her. Was Zero in place already? If he was, he made no indication, no sound. The room was wide, with a vaulted ceiling, a California king bed, a curved white chaise lounge, and French doors that led to a stone balcony.

But no Zero. Should she call to him? Ask for a signal?

Before she could make up her mind, the door opened behind her and Shade slipped in.

"You have piqued my curiosity," he admitted. "You have five minutes of my time."

She sat slowly on the edge of the bed and crossed her legs, the slit in the dress riding high up her thigh.

"Perhaps ten minutes." Shade smiled.

Maria felt nauseous. This man was a trafficker. The worst of the worst. Ogling her. No doubt mentally valuing her. She'd break his neck herself if they didn't need what he knew. If Rutledge's life didn't depend on it.

He sat beside her, closer than she would have liked. "So. What country, my dear?"

*Where the hell are you, Zero?*

"Would it surprise you if I said France?" she teased.

"*Non*," he said with a laugh.

"It is not." She laughed as well, forcing one, hoping it sounded genuine.

*Really taking your time here…*

"Before I tell you," Maria grasped at straws, "I need your word that we will still have your utmost discretion if we decide not to move forward with an arrangement."

Shade put a hand over his heart. "Discretion is my middle name— *ack!*"

In an instant, something passed in front of Shade's face, slipped around his neck, and tightened. Zero was there, behind him, his untied tie around the Frenchman's throat as he pulled it with both hands.

"Don't move," Zero said quietly. "Don't make a sound or I'll kill you faster than your men can get in here."

Shade's face turned red, but still he smiled at Maria as she stood from the bed.

"Is something funny?" she demanded.

He wanted to say something but pointed at his throat. Zero loosened the tie by a fraction of an inch.

"Who are you?" he asked. "Interpol? CIA?"

*Son of a bitch. He's American.* The French accent was gone. Nothing about Shade seemed genuine.

"Do you think this is the first time people like you have threatened me?" He scoffed. "It's all political theater. You'll bring me in, I'll give them four or five names far more important than mine, and I'll be back here by this time tomorrow." He shrugged and grinned wider. "I am a nobody who deals with everybody. No one wants the minnow when they can reel in the bass."

"You're bankrolling the faction that kidnapped President Rutledge," Zero said behind him, tightening the tie a little more.

"Sure I am," Shade admitted, his voice strained. "Them and several others. War is profitable. If they are successful, they'll need guns. If they're not, another faction will rise in their place, inspired by their failure. In the long run, my investment will return ten-fold." He again looked right at Maria. "It's all a *numbers* game."

She exchanged a quick glance with Zero, who also noted the strange emphasis. But Shade was just a creep. She shook the thought from her head. "Here's the thing. We're not taking you in, Shade. You're going to tell us where they took him, or we're going to kill you right here."

He shook his head. "No, you're not." He seemed troublingly untroubled by the threat to his life, and Maria fully believed that he had been in this situation before, possibly more than once. "I have information that you need. Even if I tell you that I know nothing, and that they would not share the details of their plan with me, you won't believe me. You'll take me out of here, and then… well, I already told you that part." He chuckled lightly. "You won't like it, but your superiors will. They'll get bigger fish. It will make them look good."

"This is the President of the United States we're talking about," Zero hissed in his ear. "There is no bigger fish. If you don't tell us what you know, we're going to send you to a place worse than hell…"

Shade laughed again, though it ended in a choking sound. "Is that… so?"

*He's stalling.*

Maria looked down sharply. His hands were in his lap, left over right.

His left hand was fidgeting. Covering something. She slapped it away.

The Rolex Cellini. A small red dot blinked on the watch face.

193

It wasn't just a watch, she realized. It was a panic button.

# CHAPTER THIRTY TWO

Zero held the tie taut around Shade's neck and watched in confusion as Maria vaulted to the bedroom door. She twisted the lock and then shoved a chair under the knob.

"What is it?" he asked urgently.

"The watch. It's a panic button. Quick, the balcony doors!"

As much as Zero wanted to continue strangling the trafficker, he released the grip on the man's neck and threw open the French doors to the balcony.

"What am I…" *Looking for*, he was about to say, when a shout floated up to him from above.

"Zero!"

He looked down. One floor below the penthouse was another balcony, smaller, and leaning out over seventeen stories of nothing was the face of Chip Foxworth. "Catch!"

Chip heaved something straight up into the air with both hands. Zero reached out for it, further than he would have liked, his full weight leaning against the railing.

But he caught the gun deftly. An Israeli Tavor submachine gun, loaded, cocked, and ready.

*Now how the hell do we get out of here? Shoot through the guards? Fight off the guests? All with Shade in tow?*

He stepped back into the room to find Maria tearing the sheets from the bed. "Any moment, I'm sure they'll be—"

A thunderous boom rattled the door in its frame. Zero whipped the Israeli submachine gun to his shoulder, finger on the trigger, and waited.

Maria tied the ends of two sheets together and pulled firmly. "Egyptian cotton. Hope it holds."

"What are you planning on…?"

The door boomed again. The jamb splintered but the chair held it. For now.

"You! Come here." Maria grabbed Shade by the collar and dragged him toward the French doors. He struggled against her and she jabbed him in the face with a quick elbow—once, then twice. The man reeled, bleeding from the lips, and looked as if he might pass out.

Gunshots blasted then, into the door and the lock. Screams from the other side accompanied the dull stampede of feet. Guests fleeing, he could imagine.

Still he waited.

As far as the guards knew, he was unarmed, and their boss was in trouble.

One final kick from the other side and the chair toppled. The broken door flew open, hanging from only one hinge. Three men were on the other side, armed, ready to burst in.

And met with a fully-automatic blast from the Tavor.

Blood spouted. None of them had a chance. Bodies crumpled in the doorway. But he knew there were more.

He turned, for just a second, to see Maria securing the end of the bed sheet around Shade's ankle.

"What are you doing?" he shouted, though he didn't like the guess he'd already formed in his head.

Shade's terrified expression suggested he was wondering the same.

"Just cover me!" Maria told him.

Zero spun back to the door and fired another burst. There were more screams out there, panicked shouts, yelps of pain as party guests fled, running each other over in their fancy clothes and flashy jewelry. If any of them had been hit by ricochet or errant shots, they deserved it by virtue of being there.

He saw a flash of dark jacket as one of the guards took a position behind the wall, waiting for an opportunity to fire into the room.

The man would have it, eventually. Zero didn't have a spare magazine. How many rounds had he fired? He wasn't sure.

He switched to semi-auto and fired off two more, just to keep the man hidden in place, and hazarded another glance behind him. Maria had secured the other end of her bed sheet rope to the balcony's railing.

And then Zero knew. "Hang on, will that hold—?"

Maria shoved Shade over the railing. Zero heard his high-pitched shriek of terror for a half-second, which was cut off just as quickly as the sheets went taut.

*Crazy. This is crazy.* The logical voice in the back of his head told him this should be the last place on Earth he wanted to be, but it was muted, far away. This was what he lived for. There was no pain now. Instinct and adrenaline had taken over.

He fired three more rounds, intentionally hitting the wood of the door jamb, sending splinters flying.

"Come on!" she shouted behind him. He backed out to the balcony as Maria, in heels, climbed over the railing. She gripped the bed sheets, and in the next instant she vanished, sliding down it like a rappel line.

Zero backed up to the railing, the Tavor still stock to shoulder.

He switched it back to full-auto. He emptied the magazine, a burst through the open doorway.

Then he tossed the Tavor down and scrambled over the railing as quickly as he could.

*Just don't look down.*

He looked down. There was almost two hundred feet between him and the street below, the lights of cars as tiny as insects visible from his height. If he fell straight from the railing, the wind would probably blow him into the side of the hotel at least once on his way down.

It wasn't a pleasant thought.

He gripped the bed sheet in both hands. *Here goes.*

His feet left the railing. He was sliding. But through the open doorway came a guard. Pistol raised. A shot fired.

Pain seared through Zero's left shoulder as the guard and the gun and the suite fell away from view, and then the balcony flew past him. He was sliding down, holding on with just his right hand, his left hanging at his side. His grip wasn't strong enough to stop him. The sheet kept sliding, and soon it would run out.

One foot touched the railing of the balcony below him but it wasn't enough to stop him. His right hand ran out of sheet. His left windmilled in the open air as if he could somehow swim against the darkness. He was falling backward...

And then his torso hit the railing. He was upside-down, staring down at the emptiness yawning between him and the street—but not falling. Why wasn't he falling?

Zero looked up. Alan Reidigger held his leg with both arms, in a tight bear hug. He'd caught Zero's leg, the leg that had hit the railing.

"Got you," he grunted. "Little help here?"

Strickland was there, grabbing another leg. Foxworth reached for a hand. Mendel watched in amusement as Maria held a white-as-a-sheet Shade by the collar.

Above him, the guard leaned over the balcony and aimed down. Zero threw himself forward, onto the balcony, as shots rained down from above. The four of them collapsed in a heap.

There was no time for thanks or to even acknowledge that he was alive. No one had to shout encouragement or a reminder to get the hell out of there. They were on their feet in an instant, out of the room, down the hall, on the stairs. Strickland led, then Maria with Shade, forcing him along, and Mendel brought up the rear, covering them with a Sig Sauer in both hands, checking her six every few seconds.

It had been less than two minutes since the shooting started. He didn't know what the response time was like in Cairo, but he hoped it was long enough.

By the time they reached the seventh floor they had caught up with Shade's guests, those fleeing for their lives who had opted for the stairs, and despite the tuxedoed host trying twice to shout for help before Maria silenced him with a sharp jab to his ribs, his cries were lost among the panicked shrieks and gasps for air.

Then they were in the lobby, amid the small escaping crowd, more coming from the elevators, other guests in the lobby frozen in confusion and alarm. They didn't stop, hurrying out onto the street as sirens wailed from a short distance, Shade in tow as they escaped the hotel and the scene the police would soon find at its peak.

# CHAPTER THIRTY THREE

Down in the windowless Research & Development sublevel of Langley, Virginia, Dr. Penelope León paced anxiously.

She was not alone down there, under the bright lights and sheer white walls intended to simulate some measure of daylight. She rarely was. Teams of techs and engineers scurried about, coordinating with other CIA field teams and developing projects. That was the term they used, "project," whether it was a weapon or communications or a viral culture or changing the light bulbs in the restrooms. Always a project.

Someone brought her a clipboard and a pen for a sign-off on some permission and she scribbled her name without reading it. Whatever it was wasn't important right now.

Penny paced, because she'd done all she could. For all the information she could provide and threads she could tug at and gadgets she could supply, she'd reached the terminus of her usefulness, at least for the moment. EOT was in the lion's den, and she had no way to track them or tell what was going on in the top floor of the Nile Ritz-Carlton.

*Almost* no way to track them. Open on the workstation in front of her were two laptop computers in durable clamshell cases. Displayed on one was the countdown website, ticking onward.

15:14:41…
15:14:40…
15:14:39…

She tore her gaze from it. Watching the seconds go by was useless. Just as useless, she noted, as pacing.

The second laptop screen was actively monitoring 1-2-2 in Cairo, the emergency equivalent of 9-1-1, specifically looking for calls to the Ritz. It was the only way she had at the moment of keeping an eye on things as Zero and his team infiltrated Mr. Shade's auction. So far, there had been no activity to the hotel.

So she paced. There were a hundred other things she could have been doing, other duties to tend to, but their importance paled in comparison to this, even if "this" was waiting. The president's life was on the line, and she would make herself available for whatever was needed, when it was needed.

She thought briefly of Bixby, her former mentor, the man who had taught, prepped, and vetted her for this very position, to take over the lab that he had built and cultivated. She wondered if he was ever in her shoes, pacing and worrying about Zero's team while they were out in the field. It didn't seem likely; Bixby wasn't a worrier. Never had been.

But she pushed the thought from her head. Bixby was gone, hiding somewhere out there in the world. He'd never step foot in this lab again…

An alert flashed across the laptop screen. Penny nearly tripped over her own feet lurching for it, leaning close to it.

*Shots fired at the Nile Ritz-Carlton. Police, fire, and EMTs dispatched.*

Penny's hand instinctively went to the satellite phone in her pocket. No; wait for them to call. But the alert was distressing. Zero and his team had gone in unarmed. So who fired the shots?

"Dr. León," a voice boomed behind her.

Penny quickly slapped the laptop closed, the one displaying the emergency service alert, as Director Shaw approached her workstation. She put on a fake smile despite the worry knotting her insides. She knew Shaw's appearance down here could not be a good sign. He'd only ever stepped foot in R&D once since she'd began, and that was on her first day, to welcome her.

"Director Shaw. To what do we owe the pleasure?"

The smile he returned was just as painfully false as her own. "I wanted to come down here to personally deliver a communiqué. The official order has been handed down to shut down the website."

Penny did not take her gaze from the director, but his eyes glanced briefly over her shoulder, where the open laptop displayed the countdown.

"I don't think that's advisable, sir. Right now it is the only link we have to these men and the president." More importantly, it was the only direct link that *she* had, and despite two dead ends coming of it so far, she still wanted to believe that some clue could be gleaned from it.

"Doctor, I wish I could agree with you," he said, his tone wheedling, "but this order doesn't come from me, or even the DNI. The acting president believes that it would be a symbolic gesture, however small, in the face of active war or further endangering the president's life."

An order from the White House. She could defy Shaw, or at least buy herself some time, but not the Oval Office.

"And," Shaw continued, "given that you enjoy a certain level of impunity when it comes to disobeying direct orders, I am going to stand here and watch you do it." The smile on his face was no longer fake.

Penny's jaw clenched so hard her teeth ached, but there was no arguing it. She nodded once, and then turned to the open laptop. She pulled up a chair, making sure to do it slowly, sat, and set her fingers to the keys.

"Anytime you're ready," Shaw prodded behind her.

"Wait." Penny frowned at the screen. "Wait, look—"

"No theatrics, please, Doctor…"

Penny ignored him. Beneath the countdown was the embedded video of Dawoud seated behind the desk, the one that had launched with the countdown. But now there was a second rectangular video box, side by side with the first.

A new video. They had uploaded a new video, mere seconds ago.

Shaw saw it too. He leaned over her shoulder. "Well? Play it."

She did. And she immediately sucked in a breath as it began.

The video showed President Rutledge, seated on a wooden chair, his hands behind his back. He looked exhausted, weary, but alive. Unharmed, even, for the most part. He did not look at the camera, but rather at a spot on the ground in front of it, as if he refused to give his captors the satisfaction of seeing the look in his eye.

They were outside somewhere, it seemed, at dusk. Or perhaps in a dark room. No, outside; the president's chair was against a simple beige backdrop, a sheet or a tarp, and it ruffled slightly with a gentle breeze.

There were sounds in the background. Quiet, but there. Something rustling? Or low voices? She couldn't tell.

A man stepped into frame. His face was unmistakable. Ashraf Dawoud—or someone who looked exactly like him, if Zero was to be believed.

"There are fifteen hours and nine minutes remaining," he said in accented English.

Penny glanced at the countdown. It was at 15:09:17.

"The American president still lives," Dawoud continued, his tone sepulchral and flat. "But he will die when zero reaches."

The video went black.

That was it; just fifteen seconds and a reiteration of the pending threat.

"Proof of life," Shaw said quietly, a deep frown etched in his features. "They gave us proof of life. Why?"

Penny didn't know. She didn't want to say it aloud, but this could have been prerecorded and then launched at the same time-stamp that Dawoud mentioned in the video. But it looked like night was falling wherever they were, and in the part of the world where the president was taken, it would be dusk.

Penny didn't know whether to fully believe it or not, but she did know one thing.

"Sir, I cannot in good conscience take down this website until I'm certain the acting president has seen this video, and reissues the order."

Shaw cleared his throat and straightened. "I… I suppose that is advisable." The director no doubt knew that he would be in scalding water if this new development wasn't brought to the attention of the administration. "I will… make them aware, and follow up." He turned on a heel without another word and strode out of the lab.

Penny got to work immediately. She copied the video, made a backup, grabbed a pair of headphones, and then played it twice more at full volume blaring in her ears.

There were other sounds. Voices, in the background.

She would do a full analysis. Isolate every background sound into separate audio tracks, amplify them as best she could. Analyze the video every which way.

Zero and his team would have to work through whatever was going on in Cairo. She couldn't help them at the moment. But this, the video, was something she could do. She was back in the game.

# CHAPTER THIRTY FOUR

"You're bleeding."

Zero looked at his left shoulder. The bullet that had nearly sent him plummeting to his death from the hotel balcony had torn the shoulder of his jacket and the flesh beneath it, but it hadn't hit bone.

"Just a graze," he assured Maria. He smiled; she still wore the red dress and heels, though her hair was windblown and wild.

They hadn't stopped until they reached the runway at Cairo where the Gulfstream sat. The Learjet that had carried Maria and her team wasn't far. The four of them—him, Maria, Strickland, and Foxworth—milled about on the tarmac outside the jet while Alan and Talia Mendel were inside the plane's cabin with Mr. Shade.

He half expected a cavalcade of cops to come screaming down the runway at any moment. But at the same time he had a feeling that none of Shade's guests would care much about his disappearance, or admit any knowledge of him to the police at the Ritz.

"What are we at?" Zero asked.

Maria showed him the phone screen. The timer app was at 14:42:23.

14:42:22…

14:42:21…

There was a grunt behind him as Alan Reidigger emerged from the plane, scowling. Mendel followed. She'd changed out of her champagne-drenched dress, and now wore jeans and a motorcycle jacket that somehow suited her far better than the strapless black affair.

"Well?" Zero asked impatiently.

"Well nothing." Alan wrung his hands, and Zero noticed that there was no blood on them. Apparently the interrogation had not gotten as creative as he'd expected. "As soon as the guy realized we weren't handing him over to anyone he could bargain with, he pissed himself. Gave up every name at his little party and then some." Alan shook his head. "But he doesn't know anything about where they took Rutledge."

Zero shook his head. He couldn't accept that. "Mendel, you're an expert at reading people. You believe him?"

She nodded somberly. "I do."

"Shit." Almost ten hours had run off the clock and they were back at square one. They'd wasted hours in Egypt for nothing.

Well… not entirely nothing. Just not what they'd come for.

"As much as I'd like to put a bullet in that guy's head, he knows plenty more about other things," Zero said. "We can't hand him over to anyone he can negotiate with. He's too dangerous. He knows where those trafficking victims are, and he's probably got hands in lots of other dirty laundry too."

"What do you suggest?" Strickland asked.

"We have six people and two jets. I think one of us should take him to H-6."

H-6 was the designation of a CIA black site in Morocco, a completely off-the-grid operation that looked like a small military outpost but was really a prison, where holes in the desert became new homes for the worst of the worst. Hell-Six, as it was called by those familiar with it, was run by Sergeant Jack Flagg and a crew of retired Special Forces members who didn't quite fit with civilian life.

Flagg wouldn't negotiate. He'd squeeze Mr. Shade until he gave his whole life story.

"We shouldn't give up a plane," Maria countered. "We might need to split up again—"

"We have no leads," Zero argued. "Not even one, let alone two." He took her hand in his. "Maria, those girls."

She closed her eyes and nodded. "Yeah. I know." All eyes were on her; as team leader, it would be her call of whom to send. "I don't suppose there are any volunteers."

"It would have to be me or Foxworth," said Reidigger. "No one else can fly."

"I fly," Mendel offered.

"But Flagg doesn't know you," Zero objected. "Chip is injured, so maybe he should—"

"Hey now." Foxworth put up a hand. "I'm no more 'injured' than you are."

"I'll do it," Alan offered.

Zero turned to him sharply. It was nothing personal against Chip, but if he had to choose between keeping one and sending one, Alan would stay by his side.

"If anyone is going to get information out of him, it's me," Reidigger said. "Foxworth doesn't have the stomach for it and you know it. Besides—he might not be better in a fight, but he definitely has more zeal for this than I do." He winked. "I'll take him, and I'll stick around long enough to make him sing. If I get anything useful, you'll be the first to know."

Zero looked to Maria for her approval, hoping he didn't get it. But she nodded.

"All right. Alan, take Mr. Shade in the Learjet. Chip, you'll fly us in the Gulfstream."

*As soon as we have somewhere to fly to*, Zero thought.

Talia Mendel retrieved the trembling Mr. Shade from the Gulfstream and practically dragged him down the steps as he yammered in protest.

"Wait, wait, I have money, I can pay you... or something else? Anything. Weapons? Property? You could retire tomorrow, no one would need to know..."

"Shut up." Mendel shoved him roughly toward Alan, who caught the smaller man by the nape of his neck.

Alan nodded once to Zero. "Be safe. See you soon."

"Yeah. See you."

"Wait!" Shade yelped as Alan dragged him away toward the waiting Learjet. "Where are we going? Don't leave me with him... wait!"

"Scum," Maria muttered. "I'm going to change. I feel ridiculous in this." With that, she stepped onto the Gulfstream.

"Let me look at that." Talia gestured to his wounded shoulder.

"It's fine—"

"Let me *look*," she insisted.

Zero made a show of rolling his eyes, but he removed the suit jacket, unbuttoned the shirt beneath it, and slid it down off his shoulder. It had bled amply, soaking half the sleeve, but it didn't hurt much. Those types of superficial wounds tended to bleed a lot.

Talia retrieved a med kit from the plane, along with a bottle of water, and she cleaned the wound. *Then* it stung, and Zero sucked a breath through his teeth at the touch.

The Learjet's engines rumbled from the adjacent runway as she pressed a bandage over it. Maria rejoined them, now in a black sweater and jacket, and it was not lost on him that she narrowed her eyes at the sight of Talia cleaning his shoulder. If Mendel noticed she didn't say anything, though he thought he saw the hint of a smirk playing on her lips.

With that done, Zero buttoned his shirt again and the five of them watched silently as the plane carrying Alan and his prisoner roared into the sky and vanished from sight. Zero wondered if the rest of them were silent because they were thinking the same thing he was.

*What the hell do we do now? Where do we go?*

There was still time, though that window was closing with every passing moment they milled about on the runway. But what use was doing anything, going anywhere without a direction? What was the Secret Service doing at that same moment? Where was Rutledge, and what had become of him?

"Chip," he said suddenly. "Do you have the sat phone?" He'd left it behind in the hotel room when he and Strickland had headed up to the penthouse level.

Foxworth pulled it from his pocket and tossed it to Zero. He had a text waiting for him: *Call ASAP.*

It was Penny.

"Zero!" she shouted into the phone as soon as the call connected. "Where are you? What happened? Are you okay?"

"Cairo. We got Shade. We're all okay. But Penny—it was a dead end. He's the financer, but he doesn't know anything useful."

"Good," she said quickly. Zero frowned at that. "Now listen. There was a new video, about twenty-five minutes ago, and I've traced its origins to the South of France, or the upload of it at least, but I think we can safely say that's—"

"Whoa, hang on, Penny," Zero interjected, dizzy at the sudden flood of words. "What video?"

"A second video was uploaded to the countdown site!" she said in exasperation. "Do try to keep up. I traced its upload to the South of France but that's most likely another diversion. However, the Secret Service isn't listening and Agent Chubb's team is heading there as we speak…"

"There's a second video," Zero told the team. Maria immediately pulled out her tablet to locate it. "Penny, can we skip to the part where Shade being a dead end is a good thing?"

"Right. So the video shows that Rutledge is alive, or was at the time it was uploaded. Now I've been analyzing this video every which way, separating audio tracks, and I found a few different layers. One is most certainly a humming motor, and the pitch of it suggests it's most likely a generator, which means they're somewhere without power, likely remote..."

While Penny spoke, Maria played the video on the tablet. He watched, listening to the phone while trying to pay attention to the video as well. He felt an odd flood of relief at seeing Rutledge alive, though bound and looking worse for wear. Even so—it meant they still had time.

"You see the way the backdrop is slightly rustling?" Penny continued. "That suggests a breeze, one that by my best guess is an easterly wind, and that they're outdoors in an open area, rather than a forest, or underground, or some such thing." She spoke quickly and excitedly, like she was onto something big, but so far Zero failed to see the significance of what she'd found. It could be ten thousand different places.

"And finally," Penny said, "there are voices in the background. Speaking very quietly and in Arabic, it seems. Most of the words are unintelligible, even amplified. However, there was one word that I managed to isolate. Behind the camera, someone says the word 'Sinai.'"

"Sinai?" Zero repeated. "Are you sure?"

"Am *I* sure? Not entirely. But my voice recognition software is ninety-two percent sure, so that's the best I can give you."

"Sinai," he said again, his mind churning. The first thing that came to mind was the Sinai Peninsula, located in the very country that he and his team were in currently. The Egyptian stretch of Sinai was not only close at hand, but its northeastern border touched on Israel. It was, in fact, once the property of Israel, and then contested territory until an agreement in 1989 definitively made it Egypt's.

It was also vast, more than twenty-three thousand square miles in area.

"Do you think it could mean Sinai in Egypt?" he asked.

"Could be," Penny conceded. "Which is why I've already got satellites directed overhead and scanning the area. It'll take a bit of time, of course..."

Something nagged at him about that. Every thread they'd pulled at so far had resulted in traps, hazards, and dead ends. Now they were here, in Egypt, and a final clue had fallen into their laps that suggested they were close. It felt… well, too closed. Too convenient. To search the entire Sinai Peninsula would already be a needle in a haystack, but it would be made completely fruitless if there was no needle there at all.

"I'll call you back," he said shortly, and ended the call.

He paced as he quickly broke down the news to his team. "Penny is certain she caught the word 'Sinai' spoken on the video. We need ideas. Let's hear them."

"There are a lot of hospitals named after Sinai," Todd offered. "Could they be on a rooftop somewhere, maybe?"

"Possible," Zero admitted. "But unlikely they'd want to be that visible."

"There's Mount Sinai," said Foxworth.

"True—but no one actually knows where the biblical Mount Sinai is," Zero said. "Though the general belief is that it's the Egyptian mountain called Jabal Musa." Which was, of course, located in the Sinai Peninsula, and he had little doubt it was among the first places Penny had satellites search.

"Sinai means 'hatred,'" Talia Mendel proposed with a shrug.

Zero ceased his pacing. "What?"

"Yes. In Rabbinic tradition, Sinai derives from the Hebrew word *sin-ah*, which means 'hatred,'" Talia explained. "More specifically it was in reference to the hatred for Jews, as they were the people who received the word of God." Then she yawned.

Zero blinked at her, impressed. *But what does it mean?* Likely nothing; they were grasping for answers and closing fists around empty air. There was no reason a native Arabic speaker would use a Hebrew word for anything other than a location.

*Sinai Peninsula.* It had to be, didn't it? It made the most sense. But that was also the problem with it…

He glanced over at Maria, who hadn't yet said anything, and noticed her arms folded over her chest, a thousand-yard stare on her face.

"Maria? What are you thinking?"

"I'm thinking…" Something was turning in her brain, he could tell. "I'm thinking about Bulgaria." She looked up at him. "One of the men who attacked us as *Sveta Troitsa* said something strange before he died. I thought it was meaningless. But now…"

"What did he say?" Zero prodded.

208

"Something about a curse." She shook her head. "He said, 'The nation made to wander for forty years, until the generation of men had died.'"

Zero frowned so hard that a tension headache threatened to storm in his skull. It sounded like a quote—no, it sounded like a *verse*, specifically referencing the Israelites wandering the desert.

*Forty years.*

Meanwhile the countdown ticked along. 14:21:12…

14:21:11…

14:21:10…

*Numbers. Endless numbers.*

*It's all a* numbers *game.*

That's what Shade had said. In the moment it had seemed odd that he'd put such emphasis on the word "numbers." And it still did.

*Numbers.*

"Son of a bitch." Shade had played them. He knew where the men were going, where they were holding the president. Yet he'd pretended to be terrified, had even peed himself to avoid torturous interrogation tactics. Just like he'd dressed as part of the wait staff and feigned the French accent. The man was a master manipulator, and he'd manipulated them.

But he didn't need Shade now. The man had gotten caught up in his own game, and had given them a necessary clue.

*Numbers.*

The phone was to his ear in an instant.

"Go for Penny," she answered.

"There's a Bible verse from the book of Numbers that references Sinai and the Israelites," he said quickly as he put her on speaker. "I need you to look it up. Verbatim."

"Sorry, *what?*"

"Penny, please…"

"All right, give me a moment." He heard fingers rapidly tapping keys in the background, and seven seconds later she told him, "Got it. Numbers 10:12 says: 'Then the Israelites set out from the Desert of Sinai and traveled from place to place until the cloud came to rest in the Desert of Paran.'"

*And they wandered for forty years, until an entire generation of men had died.*

Zero's heart pounded despite standing still.

"The biblical 'Desert of Sinai' is believed to be the Sinai Peninsula," Maria suggested. "Which means we have the right spot. Doesn't it?"

"I don't think so." Sinai was too easy. He just *felt* it. "I think they're in the Desert of Paran."

"…Which is also in Egypt," Talia pointed out.

"Where the hell did y'all go to Sunday school?" Foxworth asked, incredulous.

Zero ignored him and turned to Mendel. "Yes—in Christian and Judaic faiths." And therein lay the problem.

*Sinai. Hatred. Cursed.*

They couldn't approach this from a Christian or Judaic perspective, because their perpetrators wouldn't be.

"In Islam," Zero told them, "the Desert of Paran is believed to be in Libya." This was a wild goose chase, intended to throw them off at every turn—as long as they thought like themselves and not the people they were after.

*But that's it. I've figured it out.* It had to be. It made sense, especially for the bigger reason that he hadn't yet addressed.

Penny was the one who said it aloud, through the phone's speaker. "You think they're in the Sahara Desert."

"I do," he confirmed. But it wasn't his call to make.

Maria met his gaze and held it for a long moment. He hoped that she saw conviction there and not the doubt that he'd started to feel ever since saying it aloud.

"Penny," she said at last. "Put every available resource you can into a search. If Zero is right, they needed a signal to upload that video. Let's find it. Chip—fire up the jet. We're going to Libya."

He nodded to her as the others quickly boarded the Gulfstream. If he was right, they would be on the right track for the first time since the tunnel explosion.

But if he was wrong, they were pulling resources from what seemed a likelier location to search in entirely the wrong part of the world.

# CHAPTER THIRTY FIVE

It wasn't hard for Sara to find him.

The new girl from Common Bonds, Stephanie, had an impressive social media presence. All of her posts were positive, rife with hashtags, and talked about "living your best life," whatever that meant. Sara just had to scroll through for about a minute before she found a post with the ex tagged in it. She jumped over to his profile, which was far less active and only seemed used to celebrate milestones. A change in career, a new car… She scrolled back further, almost two years, and found a post of him posing in front of a large home he had just bought.

A reverse-image search of the house gave her a listing on a real estate marketplace site, and *voila*. She had an address. It wasn't far, and she had her dad's car at her disposal.

It wasn't terribly late but it had long since fallen dark. Sara tiptoed to Mischa's doorway and peered inside. The girl was lying on her back, on the bed, eyes closed, her index finger holding her place in the history book—which she'd nearly finished.

Sara could have laughed aloud. The girl read herself into exhaustion. She flicked off the light and padded to the foyer.

Yes, she had promised her dad that she wouldn't leave Mischa alone. But the girl was fast asleep. And even if she woke, what was she going to do? She'd probably assume Sara was sleeping down in her basement room and would go right back to bed. She wasn't going to leave the house and start wandering the neighborhood in the middle of the night.

Besides, despite her youth, Mischa was right. Abusers would not just wake up one morning and decide to no longer abuse. They needed to be persuaded. And Sara would be the one to do it.

She slipped on her shoes and a jacket as quietly as she could. She grabbed her phone and her keys and her hammer and, as stealthily as possible, pulled the front door open. She winced as the alarm beeped twice in stay mode. But after hearing no movement or sound from Mischa's room, Sara locked the door again behind her and hurried down to the car.

This would be quick, she told herself. Get there, scare the hell out of the guy, and get back home. Just the drive over there gave her the tingle of fear mixed with excitement, just like she'd felt the last time when she'd busted the hell out of the red Mustang. What would it be this time? He seemed like the kind of guy who kept his cars in a garage. So maybe the windows of his home then?

Fifteen minutes later she parked the SUV two blocks from the address. As she walked, the head of the hammer in her hand and her hands in her coat pockets, she tried to map an alternate route back to the car, looking for yards without fences or ones easy to leap if she needed a faster and more direct getaway.

And then, there it was. The home wasn't all *that* impressive, all things considered. It was big, bigger than one person needed. Three stories tall with a stone façade and a tall front door, at least eight feet. Sara remembered seeing one of those dumb home renovation shows during her long period of malaise after rehab, that said a good front door adds a lot of value to the house.

*Maybe I should break it?* She wasn't sure she could with just a claw hammer.

Her general plan was to make noise, break something, get him outside. Then threaten. And then run for it. Just like last time. Easy.

She went around the right side of the house. There was no fence; that was a good thing. There were no lights on inside; also good. On that side of the home she spotted two tall, narrow windows in frames that had been cut on an angle to be parallel with the slope of the roof.

Custom windows. Those were expensive to replace.

*Here we go.* An electrified thrill chilled her slightly as she reared back with the hammer, and then swung it forward.

The sound of shattered glass was, to her, as euphonious as someone running a finger down the length of a piano. She could have laughed aloud, but there was work to do. She hurried to the next window and sent the hammer through that one, too.

She ran then, dashing around to the back of the house, where she would hide and wait for the guy to come stumbling out in his pajamas, blinking through a fog of sleep and confusion—

A bright light suddenly clicked on, so bright it blinded her for a moment. Sara threw one hand over her eyes to shield her face but there were already spots filling her vision.

*A motion sensor. Son of a bitch!* She had to hide. She was standing in plain view on the guy's rear patio. But she couldn't see, and when she took a step forward she tripped over a chair, her feet tangled, and fell forward onto her hands and knees.

A door opened. Feet pounded against the patio.

"Who the hell are you?!" a male voice demanded.

The hammer. Where was the hammer? It was there, had fallen just a few feet away, but out of reach. Sara turned over, on her elbows, facing the guy. And the electric tingle of delight soured instantly into one of terror.

The guy's face was obscured in shadow by the bright floodlight behind him, but his arm was outstretched toward her, and the revolver in his hand was plain as day, glinting as if it was gloating at her.

"Well, well," the guy said, obvious pleasure in his voice. "What's this? Just a girl. You come alone?"

He quickly looked left and right on the patio, the gun tracking his movement. As soon as the barrel was off of her, Sara tried to squirm backward, to put some distance between them—but he snapped around with the revolver back on her.

"No, no," he said. "You stay right there. Now, why are you coming around smashing my windows? You know what those cost? What was this, a dare?"

Sara said nothing. Her throat was dry. All she could see was the gun, the barrel of it like a dark mouth leering at her. It wasn't her first time facing down a gun. But she'd been stupid to let it possibly be her last.

"Oh," the guy said slowly. His lips curled into a wolfish grin. "Oh, I think I know what this is. You're one of Steph's new friends, aren't you? You look like the type. One of those liberal college bitches that convinced her I was the bad guy." He leaned over her. "Tell me something. Did Steph ever tell you what I do?"

Sara still said nothing, just staring back, her heart pounding in her chest.

*You were stupid to come here. You got sloppy.*

"See, I'm a lawyer," the man said. "And let me tell you, it doesn't look very good, you skulking around my house, smashing up my windows and…" He gestured toward the hammer on the ground behind Sara. "Possibly trying to assault me. So tell you what. Why don't you come on into the house, and maybe we can work this out. Just between us."

Terror mixed with panic at that notion. There was no way in hell she was going into his house. She'd be trapped worse than she was now.

Finally she spoke. "No."

"No?" He chuckled. "Okay. That's fine. Way I see it, I can just as easily shoot you now. See, someone was trespassing on my property, smashing my windows. I went outside to check it out. It was dark. All I saw was a person with a hammer. What's a guy to do? It'll be self-defense, darling. Trust me on that."

Sara closed her eyes. She wished her dad was there. Or Maya. Anyone at all.

"So unless you can give me a damn good reason not to, I don't see why I shouldn't—"

There was a sound then, a flat, slapping sound like beating the dust out of a pillow.

"*Ooph!*" she heard.

She opened her eyes to see the man doubled over. The gun was pointed at the ground. A shape, a small shadow, circled him quickly, like a predatory animal. Not an animal, though; a foot came up, kicked the gun away. It skittered across the patio.

*What the hell?*

The blazing floodlight caught the shadow's face, and Sara's mouth fell open.

It was Mischa.

The girl jumped, higher than should have been possible, and wrapped both legs around the man's neck. Her body twisted in the air, and then she was upside-down, her palms on the ground, like doing a handstand. She folded herself, legs coming down to earth—and the man's head came with them. His body left the ground, tumbling end over end, and landing with a startling thump.

Mischa grabbed one of his arms and forced it straight, arching her back with her legs still wound tightly around his neck, twisting him into a painful-looking lock.

Sara just sat there in stunned silence, uncertain that what she was seeing was really happening. But it was; the small girl held the man, his neck and limbs locked, with a passive expression on her face that suggested it was taking very little effort to hold him.

214

Suddenly Sara was on her feet, and the hammer was in her hand. She didn't even realize she'd grabbed it but was glad she did, needing to feel like she had some measure of security in this insane situation.

"Go ahead," Mischa told her. The man tried to say something but only sputtered, his face turning red. "Do what you came here to do."

She had a thousand questions on her mind. But only one made sense in the moment.

*What* did *I come here to do?*

To break windows? To threaten? No. More than that. Put a stop to this, to him and his ways. She looked down at the hammer in her hand. That wasn't the way.

"I have a better idea," she said aloud as she pulled her phone from her pocket.

Mischa tightened the grip on the man's neck between her thighs. His head slumped, and he lost consciousness as Sara dialed 9-1-1.

*

When the police arrived, they found a man unconscious, a loaded revolver, and two terrified girls on the front lawn. Sara was just as impressed with Mischa's acting ability as the way she'd taken the guy down; somehow the girl was able to instantly summon thick, brimming tears, streaming down both cheeks, and for added measure she ran to the first responding officer and flung her arms around his waist.

Their report would say that the two stepsisters were walking back to their car from a friend's house when they heard a cry for help. Thinking someone was in trouble, they investigated the patio and found the man waiting for them with a gun. He tried to lure them inside. But Sara found a hammer and fought back, knocking the man unconscious, and called the cops.

The man coughed hoarsely as he came around, and found himself being handcuffed. "Wait one damn minute!" he tried to protest. "That girl broke my windows! And the little one, the little one, she…"

"She what?" challenged the arresting officer, a stern-looking woman.

"Well, she… she beat me up," he said lamely, and coughed again.

"Uh-huh. You can tell us more about it down at the station." She pulled him away by an elbow, even as he struggled and swore at her.

"You two need a ride home?" the male officer on the scene asked.

Sara wiped her own crocodile tears from her cheeks. "No. Thank you. Our car is parked two blocks away. We'll be okay. Thank you," she said again. "I don't know what would have happened if... if..."

"Hey. It's okay. It didn't happen, and you two are safe." He shook his head. "This isn't the first time we've gotten a report on this guy. You two just caught him in the act. Believe it or not, this is a good thing, in the long run. We'll make sure he can't hurt you. But I'll need your phone number and address, so we can follow up tomorrow. Okay?"

"Okay. Thank you, sir." Sara sniffled, gave him her information—mentally noting that she was going to have some serious explaining to do when her dad got home—and then put her arm around Mischa as they walked back to the car.

They were silent until they were both seated inside the SUV. But Sara didn't start it just yet. She had a thousand questions on her mind. But only one made sense in the moment.

"Okay, just who the *hell* are you?" she demanded.

"I'm not supposed to say," Mischa replied simply.

"How did you know where to find me?"

"I hid in the trunk."

"You *what*? How? You were asleep—"

"I was pretending to sleep when you checked on me," Mischa explained calmly. "I had a suspicion you would try something tonight. While you were putting on your shoes and jacket, I slipped out the back and climbed down the balcony. You left the car unlocked earlier, but I said nothing so I could sneak into the trunk before you got there."

"Jesus," Sara murmured. How could she be that fast? That quiet? And those moves... "So that brings me back to my original question: who are you? And don't give me that 'I can't say' crap. We're going to be sisters. Family trusts each other."

She was fully well aware how hypocritical that sounded, given how many secrets they'd kept from each other over the years. But Mischa just stared ahead.

"Family," she repeated. "Fine. I will tell you. But only if you tell me about you, and why you go to those meetings. Why you wanted to hurt that man."

Sara nodded. "Deal."

"I do not know where I was born," the girl said. "I do not know who my mother was, or even what country I came from. I was raised

216

and trained by a former Russian spy who defected to the Chinese. Together we smuggled an ultrasonic weapon into the United States and attempted to melt down the Culvert Cliffs nuclear reactor. Your father and Maria stopped us. I was held by the CIA for three months until Maria formally adopted me."

Sara blinked. It was a *lot* to process, and the girl said it plainly, as if she was reciting a well-rehearsed poem.

"Okay," was all she managed. "Wow."

Most families just brought home a stray dog or cat. *Leave it to mine to bring home a deadly spy kid.*

Mischa looked over at her. "I understand if you don't want to be sisters anymore."

Sara chucked. Despite herself, and despite the abject lunacy of the situation, she laughed. "Mischa, your story is wild, but trust me when I say that in this family, it's the tip of the weirdness iceberg." Then she fell silent; she had made a deal, and though she didn't much like to talk about it, she wasn't about to go back on her word.

"I was taken," she told Mischa. "A couple of years back. Before I knew what my dad was—*who* he was. A guy who was after him came and kidnapped me and Maya. He… sold us to traffickers. To get back at my dad. There were other girls. They killed one of them, right in front of us. They put us on a train, where there were men, who paid to…"

*No.* Not that part.

"Anyway. My dad came for us. He got us back. And there was other stuff, after that, but that was the big life-altering moment. It took something horrible like that for him to admit to us what he did, what his job was." Sara sighed. "I don't go to those meetings to talk about it, because I don't like to talk about it. I go to those meetings because I can't get back at those traffickers. I can't do anything to them. But there are others out there, and… I don't know. Maybe I can make a difference in other ways."

"I am… sorry that happened to you," Mischa said quietly.

"Yeah. Me too." She started the car. "Anyway. Let's go home and get our story straight." But she didn't pull away just yet. "Hey. One more question. Can you teach me to fight like that?"

"No," Mischa said. "I started learning when I was two years old. The training ingrained in me has been there since before my earliest memories."

"Oh…"

"But I can teach you some things. So that a situation like this one does not happen again." She paused for a moment before adding, "I assume you might find yourself in a situation like this one again."

"Yeah," Sara agreed quietly as she put the car in drive. "I think I might."

She still had work to do.

# CHAPTER THIRTY SIX

Maya felt herself drifting. Her eyelids felt so heavy, as if being pulled down like a shade. Once they were closed it felt remarkably good. So good that she couldn't open them again no matter how many times her brain told her to.

It had been hours since she'd left Busboy's place and the empty promise that he would see if the forger would meet her in person. She had found a cheap motel, less than a ten-minute drive from the guy's apartment, and taken an Uber there.

That was so long ago it could be considered yesterday at this point. Though it was still dark out, morning would be blossoming in about an hour, give or take. Maya had insisted on staying awake in case Busboy called, under the fear that her ringtone would fail to wake her.

But he hadn't called, and now she sat on a yellow bedspread facing an old boxy television that didn't work in a motel room that cost thirty-nine dollars for a night and smelled like mildew. As dawn approached it occurred to her that he'd never said it would be that night. Or even tomorrow. Just a vague promise of "soon," if ever.

She sighed in frustration. There was nothing she would have liked more in the moment than to drift off to sleep. Through the day and into the evening. But if she did, she'd be expelled by the time she woke. Dean Hunt was expected to make a decision about her future today, and she had already made it clear that she would not hesitate to actually boot Maya from the academy if she failed at this task, all in the name of saving face…

Her phone rang. She jumped. Her eyes sprang open and a wave of irritability washed over her before she grabbed for the device. The number was listed as "unknown" but it wasn't, not really, not when she was waiting for the call.

"Yeah," she answered.

"You're awake," Busboy said, as if surprised. "I wasn't sure."

"I am. And?"

"And… he agreed. He'll meet."

"When?"

219

"Now. If you can."

"I can." Maya stood from the bed. "Where?"

"The address is 23 Cottontail Drive. Don't write it down."

"I'll remember it," she assured him. "Tell him I'll be there soon." She hung up, opened her GPS, and looked it up. The address was about a half hour north, at the edge of what was considered the Poughkeepsie city limits but in a decidedly more rural area.

*What did you expect? That a professional forger would be living in a loft downtown or something?* No. It made sense that someone like that would want to be at least somewhat off the beaten path, out in the sticks.

She called herself an Uber—no easy feat at that time of the night, or morning, depending on how one looked at it. It was going to cost her a premium but she didn't care. Onto the credit card it went. Then she gathered her belongings into her backpack and waited outside for the car to arrive. She had paid in advance for one night and wouldn't be returning.

*

Thirty-six minutes later Maya stood next to a dirty white mailbox, off-kilter on its post, sitting at the end of a long, dark driveway surrounded by trees. She waited until the car that had delivered her had driven away, and then she waited a bit longer. It was still dark out, and felt even darker since there were no streetlights here to illuminate the road.

At last her eyes adjusted enough to make out shapes, and she started up the driveway, toward the small house and the single light that was on inside, guiding her like a beacon.

She checked her surroundings as she approached. It looked like this place was on a decent plot of land, mostly trees. The driveway was just packed dirt underfoot. The home, when she got closer, was little more than a one-story ranch-style modular, as if someone had bought the property and dropped a house on it.

It seemed—well, normal, if she was being honest, but something felt off to her. Perhaps it was being out in the middle of the woods this late at night. Maybe it was the criminal she was about to face. After all, what did she expect—that the forger would be living in a downtown loft or something? No, being out here in the sticks made more sense.

The blinds were closed over the windows, but she could see a dim light on behind one. She held her breath, with little choice but to knock on the door, and hoped this was the right place.

"Hello? This is Maya Lawson. We have a… meeting."

A pause. She raised her fist to knock again when a gruff voice came from within: "It's open."

*Here goes.* She turned the knob and pushed into the small house, finding herself in a dark living room. The single light on was coming from down a hall, toward the rear of the home.

"Hello?" she called out.

"One sec," the gruff voice called back.

The place looked rustic, cozy even, and smelled pleasant, like lavender potpourri.

But there was something else. Another scent, like… cologne?

Suddenly arms wrapped around her from behind, holding her fast. Her first instinct was to struggle against them, but her assailant was taller, stronger than she was.

"Hi, Lawson," hissed a voice in her ear.

Another shape moved toward her in the darkness. She went limp, letting the arms hold her up, and kicked out with both feet. She caught the boy in the chest and sent him sprawling. Then she planted her feet and swung her head backward. The back of her skull connected and there was a cry of pain as the grip around her softened.

She whirled around.

It was Chad Something-or-other, the boy whose nose she'd broken with her physics book. By the looks of it, she'd just broken it again.

*This was a setup.*

More hands on her, from behind. A pair of them grabbed an arm. Another pair grabbed her other arm and wrenched it upward at an angle.

"Make a move and I'll break it!" a harsh voice told her.

Maya knew that voice, and she believed him. She stopped struggling, breathing hard through her nose as she looked at the face of the boy holding her. It was Greg Calloway, her sort-of ex, the one she had beaten academically and physically, and had made a fool of in front of the entire student body of West Point.

Greg. Chad. And by the looks of it, three other Firsties had been here, waiting for her.

A sixth boy came from the back room. He flicked on the living room light. The gruff voice was a ruse. All of this had been a ruse.

"You *ass*hole," she hissed at Busboy. "You cheated me…"

"I cheated *you*?" he scoffed. "I knew something wasn't right about you. Demanding a meeting with him like that. Funny, he was right under your nose…" Busboy laughed.

*Right under my…?*

*Son of a bitch.*

She knew who the forger was. But there was little she could do about it right now.

"See, I called our mutual friend Jimmy and asked about you." Busboy grinned. "He put me in touch with these fellas, and it turns out they were willing to pay a lot more to get you alone than I was going to ask from you. So I took the better deal." He glanced over at Chad and shook his head. "Come on, man. My parents will kill me if they find blood on the carpet next time they're up here."

"She broke my goddamn nose again!" Chad said nasally through tears. He lurched for the kitchen, blood dripping through his palm as he held it to his face.

*So five now.* She couldn't win this fight, not with Greg twisting her arm.

"What do you want from me?" she demanded.

"Well," Greg sneered, "for starters, we want you gone. And a little birdie told me that Hunt is under pressure to expel you today. We all know you're her little pet, so we don't want you getting the chance to make an appeal.

"Which brings me to the second item: we just want to hurt you." He leaned in close enough for his sour breath to invade her nostrils. "Remember Randolph? Doug? Tim? Those three you put in the hospital? Our friends that got expelled because of you?" He clucked his tongue. "I heard Tim has permanent damage in the arm you broke. Can't even hold a pen right."

Maya shook her head in disgust at the mention of their names. "They assaulted me in a locker room. They deserved everything they got and more—*ow!*"

She cried out as Greg twisted her arm farther, the muscles screaming in pain. An inch more and it would break.

"What do you think, Maya? An arm for an arm?"

222

"Nah," said one of the other boys. "We don't want her getting back to campus. We should break a leg."

"Both legs," said another boy she didn't recognize.

"You." Greg snapped his fingers and pointed at Busboy. "What do you have around here that'll do the trick?"

"Um… got a shovel out back. Maybe a crowbar?"

"Good. Bring both."

Busboy scurried off, and panic tightened in Maya's chest. They were really going to do this. They were going to break her legs and leave her here, in this cabin in the woods with no one around, a phone with no signal, all so she could be expelled and out of their lives. She didn't even know two of them. Did they really know her? Or were these pathetic, fragile boys just following their leader unquestioningly? Believing that this was what they had to do to maintain their porcelain masculinity?

But now Busboy was gone to fetch their implements. Chad was tending to his nose.

*And then there were four.*

"Get her phone," Greg demanded. One of the boys dumped her backpack out on the floor.

Still too many to fight off. Greg alone was tough enough to worry her.

The boy located the phone and stomped it under his foot.

She looked around quickly. There was a television mounted to the wall. A sofa and an armchair. A coffee table, bearing—as she had guessed—a bowl of lavender potpourri. A floor lamp in the corner, its bulb the only light in the room.

She had an idea. A crazy one, but the only way she could see out of this.

Maya twisted slightly, just enough to face Greg. His square jaw, his movie-star looks. Not a hair out of place. And she laughed right in his face.

It was a fake laugh, a forced laugh, a strained one. But it was still enough for his admittedly handsome features to contort to an ugly scowl.

"Something funny about all this, Lawson?"

"Yeah," she said. "There is. I mean, you guys are only doing this because I beat you. I beat you so badly, in *every* way that matters…"

"Shut up," he warned her through gritted teeth.

223

"And you're just so used to being the golden boy, with your rich parents and your sheltered little existence, that you don't know how to handle being beaten by a girl—"

"I said shut up!" Greg reared back, and he punched her in the abdomen.

The breath rushed from her lungs. For a long moment she couldn't breathe as pain spider-webbed from the point of impact and out, radiating, burning.

But—he'd let go of her arm to hit her.

She stood there, doubled over, coughing, as Greg bent too. "Give me another reason," he whispered. "Next time it'll be your face—"

Maya straightened quickly, and as she did she brought her freed fist up, straight up, and connected just under Greg's chin. His teeth clacked together like a nutcracker. His head snapped back.

The boy holding her other arm pulled at her, and instead of struggling against him she stepped toward him, folding her arm, and her elbow smashed into his windpipe. She drove him against the wall as a wet choking sound emitted from his throat.

The two other boys leapt toward her, but Maya was already vaulting over the coffee table, putting it between them. She grabbed the edge of it and flipped it over, scattering potpourri across the floor.

"Found the shovel!" Busboy called from the rear of the house. "Hope this works."

Maya grabbed the floor lamp and batted the shade away, wielding it in front of her like a spear, the bulb forward, as the boys rallied. Greg cradled his chin, seething at her. The boy in the corner clutched at his throat. The other two kept a distance, looking for an opening. Busboy came around the corner and froze, baffled.

*Now. Do it now.*

"Just grab her!" Greg shouted.

Maya swung the floor lamp. The two boys jumped back. Then she brought it down, smashing the bulb against the carpet.

The bulb broke. The filament popped and sizzled in a brilliant white flash.

And the lavender oil–soaked chips that were scattered across the floor caught fire.

"Shit!" Busboy screeched. The shovel fell from his hands. "Put it out!"

Maya flung herself forward, shoving a boy into Greg, kneeling, scooping up the lockback knife that had tumbled from her backpack. She snapped it open and put her back to the door.

Two of the boys ran for the back door. She heard Chad's voice shouting for them to wait up as he followed. Busboy scurried to the sofa and grabbed a knitted blanket. He threw it over the burning potpourri, and it instantly caught fire. He yelped and jumped back.

"Guys, help me put this out!" he pleaded.

Greg ignored the fire, and Busboy, as he glanced between her and the knife. Fear flickered in his eyes as he deliberated.

"Try it," she threatened. "You know I'll do it."

He took a step back. "This isn't over!" Then he too turned tail and ran for the back door, his last crony on his heels.

"Help me, please!" Busboy begged her. He looked as if he was about to burst into tears. "There's no signal out here, I can't call anyone!"

"Give me your keys! I'll go get help!" Maya told him.

The idiot actually dug into his pocket and tossed her his car keys.

"Where are you parked?"

"Left at the end of the driveway!" he told her as he tried to stomp out the flames with a sneaker. "Hurry... hey! Wait a second!"

But Maya was already out the door. She sprinted down the driveway, the knife still in her fist in case anyone was waiting for her in the darkness.

"Don't leave me here!" Busboy shouted behind her. "Wait..."

She found the car, a beat-up old coupe, and slid behind the wheel. The engine rolled over as Busboy caught up with her, slapping against the passenger-side window.

"Let me in! Please?"

She gave him the finger and then stomped on the accelerator, leaving him to deal with the burning house.

*

Dawn broke as Maya drove back to downtown Poughkeepsie. She passed the pizza joint, drove for two more blocks, and double-parked outside of 817 Butler Street.

The upstairs apartment, 817B, that was Busboy's place. But that's not where she was going.

225

She walked up to the door of 817A and banged on it with a fist as hard as she could and didn't stop until the older woman pulled the door open, wearing a robe, looking tired and quite angry.

"What is this?" she snapped. "Who are you?"

Maya shoved past her and into the apartment.

"Excuse me!" the woman sputtered. "Who do you think you are?!"

Maya ignored her and strode across their living room. The old man, the one she had spied making popcorn the night before, emerged from a bedroom while tightening the knot on a blue robe. He froze in the doorway when he saw her.

"Can we help you?" he asked cautiously.

*He was right under your nose.*

"Are you the forger?" she asked flatly.

"Sorry? What?" He feigned confusion. But his eyes flitted slightly to the left as he said it.

"The forger," Maya repeated. She showed him the knife. She didn't hold it up, or wave it around, or make any threatening gesture at all. She merely showed it to him.

His eyes widened and he held up his hands. "Now hang on, we don't want any trouble…"

"I'm calling the police!" the woman screeched behind her.

"Martha, wait." The man took a deep breath. "Yes. I am," he told Maya. "Do you need something? We can come to an arrangem—hey!"

Maya grabbed him by the collar of his robe and yanked. She half-dragged the man toward the door, shoved the screeching woman out of her way, whose words had become unintelligible. Or maybe Maya was just beyond listening at that point. She was going to put him in the car, drive him straight to West Point, and drag him into the dean's office…

Out on the sidewalk, the woman continued to scream behind her even as the cars pulled up. First, a black sedan pulled up behind Busboy's car. Then an SUV, boxing her in.

From the SUV climbed two men in black suits. Maya froze.

*The Feds?*

"Ms. Lawson," one of them said. "Please put the knife away."

They didn't have guns. Or at least they didn't take them out if they did.

"We'll take it from here," said the other.

Maya let go of the forger, who just stood there, his hands up and trembling. One of the agents took him by an arm as the other handcuffed him.

*What the hell is going on?*

No one got out of the black sedan. But the rear window rolled down, and the familiar face behind it said, "Get in, Lawson."

Maya was tired. Too tired to protest. While the FBI agents took away the forger, Maya got into the car beside Dean Hunt.

"Nicely done," said the dean as the car pulled away from the house.

"You knew. You knew who he was."

"Admittedly, no. We've been following you. We lost you for a little while there, but we had a hunch you'd come back here."

"We," Maya repeated. "Who's we?"

But Dean Hunt ignored her question. "There's a house on fire about thirty minutes north of here. We sent the fire department."

"Great," Maya said flatly, throwing honorifics and courtesy to the wind. "Look, you don't know what I've been through tonight. I'd really just like to sleep for a while. So are we done here? Can I get back to work?"

"No," said Dean Hunt. "I'm afraid that your time at West Point is done, Ms. Lawson. Effective immediately."

Maya stared at her, jaw agape. She couldn't believe she'd just heard the dean right. "I did what you asked. I found the forger. In less than twenty-four hours. You told me I had time. You told me—"

"I know what I told you," the dean said sharply. "But the fact of the matter is that West Point is a place where we make officers. Simply put, you are not officer material, Lawson."

Maya scoffed aloud at that. All she had gone through, all she had done, not just to catch the forger but to catch up when she was behind, to excel while doing so, it was all for naught. Her future was spiraling down the drain, all because she wasn't "officer material"?

"You're agent material," Dean Hunt said.

Maya opened her mouth to respond, but then shut it. Had she heard the dean correctly? What did that mean? Hunt's face was impassive, but there seemed to be just a hint of a smile in her eyes. "Sorry... what?"

"Your transcript will reflect that you caught up on the work you missed and were able to test out of your fourth year at West Point," Dean Hunt told her.

Maya shook her head. "I wasn't aware that was an option…"

"It's not. You'll be the first, and only on paper. Not that anyone will ever need to see it. There's simply no point to you continuing your education at the academy when the skills you'd be acquiring aren't suited to your abilities. DNI Barren and I are starting a new program. A junior agent program. You'll be among our first recruits."

Maya blinked in shock. "A junior agent program? You mean with the…"

"Yes, Ms. Lawson. With the CIA."

"So… this was a test." All a test. And she had passed. "So I'm in?"

"In the agency? Lord, no." Hunt chuckled. "This is a training program. Pass it, and you'll be in."

*This was all a test.* She had spat in a lieutenant's face, nearly gotten herself expelled, almost had her limbs broken, and set fire to a house.

Was it worth it?

Of course it was.

*A junior agent.* This was it, this was her shot at making the dream come true. One step closer.

"I can't help but notice," said Hunt, "that you haven't said a word about Greg Calloway and his friends sneaking off academy grounds."

"Oh, did they?" Maya asked casually.

"Mm," Hunt confirmed. "I think the fire department is going to find evidence of arson at that house today. A fire marshal will investigate, and I'm fairly certain he will find evidence of their presence there."

"Well. You know how boys are. They just love playing with fire." Suddenly Maya remembered the news she had seen the night before, and she sat bolt upright. "Wait, the president. Is he still… Have they…?"

Dean Hunt shook her head. "He is believed to be alive. But no, he has not yet been recovered."

Maya shook her head. "Do we know who's out there? Looking for him?"

"Lots of people," Hunt said cryptically. "Lots of organizations. Lots of authorities." The dean knew what Maya was asking, and was being purposely coy. "You know, when I lost you for a little while there, I wasn't terribly concerned. I had a feeling you would pop up again, and when you did, you'd have the solution. And you came through." She glanced over at Maya. "I suppose now we all need to have faith that it runs in the family."

# CHAPTER THIRTY SEVEN

"Goddammit!" Zero flung his pen against the far wall of the crumbling structure. He was quickly losing faith.

Not in his theory; no, that had proven sound. Reidigger had arrived at H-6 with Mr. Shade in tow and quickly employed some creative interrogation tactics. As promised, Shade sang like a bird; he was aware that the plan was to bring Rutledge to the Libyan Desert, but a specific place had not been determined. Like the Israelites, Dawoud and his party had wandered out there, aimless but for their faith, and set up shop somewhere in a country of nearly seven hundred thousand square miles.

The theory was sound. But finding them was like a needle in a cornfield.

"We need to stay positive," Maria said, but her voice was tight. She'd repeated that phrase no less than a dozen times during the night, and clearly she was struggling to abide by it herself.

"We're wasting time," Zero argued.

"It won't be a waste if we find him—"

"And a *complete* waste if we don't!" Zero stood forcefully and paced. He was tired, his eyes hurt, his body hurt. He was irritable, and all the more so because he knew the rest of the team was too and wasn't showing it the way he was.

The night prior, they had flown across the border from Egypt, the plane's lights off to avoid being shot out of the sky by the Libyan government. Chip had put the Gulfstream down on an abandoned airstrip that had been unused since the Libyan Civil War in 2011. They set up shop in an old building beside the airstrip, a one-room boxy structure that still held a few rusting desks and creaking chairs, all of it covered in a fine coating of sand blown in through broken windows.

They'd set to work instantly. Penny had digitally parceled sections of the Libyan Desert and carefully scanned with live satellite images for signs of life. There were dozens of hits, either creatures or nomads or even people living out there, each one carefully reviewed by Maria and Strickland via the tablet. Zero marked off the grids on a physical map with the pen, which now was across the room in his frustration.

It was morning. Dawn had come and gone. The minutes ticked by.

05: 41: 17…

05: 41: 16…

05: 41: 15…

Possibly their only saving grace, the one thing that had kept them going, was that their search wasn't completely random. For one, they knew that the location would be within what was considered to be the fabled Desert of Paran in the Islamic faith, which hugged the Egyptian border. They also knew that the second video had been uploaded less than nine hours after Rutledge's capture. Including necessary travel time, they could surmise that the location was no more than seven hours' distance, by vehicle, from an airstrip.

That still left tens of thousands of square miles to painstakingly and manually check.

A needle in a cornfield.

*The American president still lives.* That's what Dawoud had said on the second video. *But he will die when zero reaches.*

Zero had watched the video at least five more times, searching for any sort of additional clue, something that Penny had missed, and had found nothing. Now they had less than six hours remaining on the clock, and absolutely no assurance that even if they found him that they could reach him in time.

To make matters worse, Foxworth and Mendel weren't back yet. The two of them had gone on foot to an oasis town about fifteen miles northeast to procure a vehicle. Whether that meant stealing, bartering, or paying for it, Zero didn't know and hadn't asked. All he knew was that even if they located the place where Rutledge was being held, they had no way to get there.

*Hopeless*, he thought. *This is hopeless.*

The Secret Service team led by Agent Chubb had hit another dead end in France, as expected. No more videos had been posted. No signals from the desert to track. They were sentenced to satellite images, Penny's motion-detecting software, and bleary, naked eyes.

"Look, guys," said Penny through the satellite phone. The battery was dying; she'd been up all night with them, periodically checking in as she sent them parcels of desert and updates. "I know you don't want to hear this, but maybe it's time to let someone know what we know. Bring in others on this."

Zero shook his head. He'd thought the same thing before, on other ops, only to have things fall all to hell when some hothead like Chubb decided to try to take charge or do something foolish.

"We can't do that," he said, trying to keep the irritation and exhaustion out of his voice. "Any official channels we go through will alert the Libyan government. One way or another, they'll want to get involved—and that's a recipe for disaster. Our own people will want to put drones in the air, if not choppers or planes. They'll send whoever they can. And at the first sign of trouble, that countdown... well, it'll mean nothing."

He had little doubt that the people behind this would be true to their word and end Rutledge's life before zero reached if they thought there was a chance their plan could be thwarted.

"I suppose you're right," Penny said quietly. "Another motion detection incoming."

"Received." Maria rubbed her red-rimmed eyes.

*Am I wrong?* Zero wondered. Were they withholding information that could prove vital to rescuing the president? Or were they safeguarding it from those who would put Rutledge's life at unnecessary risk?

"Silver lining," said Penny. "Looks like Barkley has successfully negotiated with the Israelis to hold off on a missile strike until the end of the countdown."

"So it'll be retaliation for two dead leaders," Maria muttered.

Zero and Strickland both looked up at her in shock.

"Sorry, I'm sorry." She pinched the bridge of her nose. "That was uncalled for. I'm just running on empty." She passed the tablet to Strickland. "Check this one out. I can't look at these anymore right now."

Zero heard a sound then, a rumbling that grew louder. He ceased his pacing and watched through a broken window as a half-rusted, clattering Jeep rolled to a squealing stop outside.

"You've gotta be kidding me." He stepped out to meet them as Chip and Talia climbed out. "This was the best you could get?"

Foxworth held up a hand. He had a thin trickle of blood on his temple. Mendel had streaks of soot on her face.

"You do *not* know what we had to do to get this," he said shortly.

"Any luck?" Mendel asked. She winced with each step, favoring her left hip.

Zero shook his head as the three of them headed back inside.

*Hopeless. This is hopeless.*

At least they couldn't say they didn't give it their best shot. Cyprus, Bulgaria, Egypt, Libya; they'd trotted hundreds of miles to get this far, and even if it wasn't far enough, they could still save those trafficking victims from Shade. They could still end the financing of a dozen insurgent groups. They had no idea if Rutledge was even still alive right now…

*My god. I'm resigning myself already. There's still time on the clock and I've thrown in the towel.*

His face warmed with shame at the thought.

Strickland dropped the tablet onto the pockmarked desktop. "It's nothing. Just another patch of sand and rock."

Zero picked it up and examined the image. Todd was right; it looked like another barren stretch of desert. He put two fingers against the screen and spread them, enhancing it, but still saw nothing of note.

"Penny, what zone is this?" He couldn't give up. There was still time on the clock. "I'll mark it off."

"That would be… E-17 on the map."

He checked the map he'd printed on the Gulfstream, showing the easternmost stretch of Libyan Desert. Then he frowned. "E-17 was already marked off."

"It must have set off the motion detection again," Penny replied through the phone with a yawn.

"Maybe some animal's territory," Strickland suggested. "I don't see anything. No vehicles, no people, no setup."

"Me neither," Zero murmured. "Penny, check when E-17 was set off before, would you?"

"Sure. One moment." She paused and then said, "It was set off twice before, actually. Once during the night. Three seventeen a.m. Libya time. Then again just after dawn. But nothing was spotted. No lights in the night, no shapes in the day."

"Probably an animal," Foxworth agreed.

*But what animal?* Something nocturnal wouldn't be active now. Something not nocturnal wouldn't have been active in the night. "Penny, can you pinpoint where the motion was captured?"

"Sure can. Incoming... now." A new dialogue opened on the tablet screen. Zero clicked it and the same image appeared, now with a small red circle showing the point of motion.

Zero magnified it as much as he could. Was there something there? It was hard to tell; the image lost resolution the further he zoomed. But he could have sworn he saw something there. It just couldn't be what he thought it was...

Then Talia was at his side, one hand on his shoulder as she too leaned over and examined the image. "This may sound crazy," she said. "But that looks to me like a horse's head."

"Yeah," Zero agreed. "Me too."

Suddenly all five of them were crowded around the desk, staring at the magnified image, the gray oblong mass that looked remarkably like a head on a long neck.

*Like a horse. Stretching its neck to eat...*

"From under a canopy," he murmured aloud. "Son of a bitch. They're under a canopy! They set up a sand-colored canopy!"

It was visible then, like a Magic Eye puzzle shaping into a 3D image. A roughly square patch, just barely a shade off from the surrounding desert. The horse beneath it giving them their final clue as it was trying to reach some breakfast.

"Penny!" Zero was already reaching for the nearest bag of gear. "Where is that?"

"E-17," she said quickly, "is fifty-seven miles southeast of your location!"

"Chip, there'd be better be gas in that bucket," he said breathlessly.

"The bigger concern is it making fifty-seven miles," Chip admitted.

"Grab the gear. Let's go!"

The five of them rushed out of the crumbling old airstrip station and piled into the Jeep. It clattered to life with Chip behind the wheel, kicking up sand and small rocks as it lurched forward.

They had them.

They *had* them.

Now they just had to get there in time, form a plan, and take them out, all without any harm coming to Rutledge.

If he was still alive.

05: 31: 57...

05: 31: 56...

05: 31: 55...

# CHAPTER THIRTY EIGHT

The old Jeep's shocks protested with every rut in the sand. Every small rock sent them bouncing in their seats. The engine clattered; the brakes squealed terribly with every light touch.

With every minute that ticked by, Zero worried that the Jeep wouldn't make it. As it was, Chip could barely top forty-five miles an hour without the thing shaking terribly, threatening to come apart at the seams.

With every rut in the desert, he was afraid that *he* wouldn't make it, his body aching in protest. He dug in his pocket for the plastic pouch there. The second Tramadol shot from the ambulance in Jerusalem. *No time like the present.* He jabbed himself in the thigh with it.

They needed to go faster. But faster might mean a breakdown, and they couldn't afford that. They had no water. The sun was dangerously blazing overhead. They would be stuck out in the desert with miles to go and many more to return.

04: 09: 15…

Zero sat in the passenger seat, holding the roll bar since there was no seat belt to be had. Behind him, Strickland was squeezed between Maria and Mendel, the latter doing a weapons check. He wasn't even sure what they had available to them, but a glance over his shoulder told him that Mendel had brought along a collapsible rifle, which she was currently assembling.

"Penny!" he said into the sat phone, practically shouting over the desert wind that whipped over the windshield. "When we arrive I want you to give us a ten-minute lead time, and then call it in!"

"To whom?"

"To Barkley. Directly to Barkley. No one else!"

"Got it. You're only about two miles—"

Penny's voice fell away. "Hello? Penny?" The satellite phone was dead in his hand. "Damn it! I lost her. We're dark. But she said about two miles—"

A gunshot went off, and Zero instinctively covered his head. He felt the Jeep slowing as Chip swore loudly.

It wasn't a gunshot. White smoke eked from beneath the hood of the Jeep.

"That was our head gasket, if I had to guess," said Foxworth.

"Can you still drive it?" Maria asked from behind them.

"Technically? Yes, but there's no coolant going to the engine. And considering we're in the freakin' desert, it'll probably be about a minute before the engine overheats completely." Chip shifted and eased down on the accelerator. "Come on, baby. Just a little further…"

But he was right. Not even another full minute passed, another half mile at best, before the Jeep slowed to a crawl, then stopped, refusing to go any further.

"It's fine." Zero leapt out. "We don't want to get too close anyway. For all we know they heard that pop." Sounds traveled over a place like this, much in the way that visibility was far clearer in the dry heat than it was in humidity. In some of the flattest places, one could see ten miles away with the naked eye, though actually making out details would be impossible.

"Talia," Zero said. "The rifle." She passed it along.

"What are you doing?" Maria asked in alarm.

He tapped the scope Mendel had affixed to the top. "Just taking a look. Stay here." He climbed to the peak of a nearby sand mound, hardly tall enough to be considered a dune, and lay on his stomach, slowly bringing the rifle to his shoulder and the scope to his eye. If there were lookouts, and there certainly would be, he didn't want anyone seeing a would-be sniper in the distance—even if a shot from a mile and a half out was absolutely impossible for him.

Zero scanned slowly, from left to right. The Libyan Sahara Desert was vast swaths of sand, mostly flat but rising and falling in small mounds and dunes here and there, shaped by winds and dotted with small, rocky brown plateaus.

He spotted movement.

*There you are.*

The shapes weren't easy to discern through the heat ripples in the air and the sweat in his eye, but he definitely saw movement. There— he made out a figure. Then two. At least three total. One of them seated…

*Rutledge.*

He saw a horse. Definitely a horse. No, two of them. And something stout and domed. A tent? The longer he stared, the more he

236

could make out. One of the men stood right next to Rutledge. The shape in his arms was unmistakably a rifle. And another, holding something up to his face, turning slowly, just as Zero had been…

*Binoculars.*

He dropped quickly to the sand, hugging the rifle close.

*Did he see me?*

No. He couldn't have. Because if he had, it would all be over before it started.

Zero slid down the sand mound and rejoined his team. "I saw them. They're out there. There's at least one scout with binoculars. Three armed that I saw."

"Dawoud?" Maria asked.

"I didn't see him. But there was a tent."

"So how we gonna play this?" Foxworth asked.

Maria nodded to Zero, deferring to him. "Okay," he said as he dropped to one knee. He drew a small circle in the sand. "Here's them. Here's us. Rutledge is there, facing this direction. Who's the best shot here?"

"I am," said both Strickland and Mendel at the same time.

"That plateau," Zero pointed, "should put someone within about four hundred fifty to five hundred yards of the targets. And at an angle that may or may not be slightly obscured by their canopy."

Strickland put his hands up in surrender. "That's all you then. I can't make that shot."

Zero passed the rifle off to Talia, though she too looked doubtful. "Take a position on the plateau. You three—take the other guns and fan out." He drew directions in the sand, wide semicircles around the encampment. "Use the dunes and plateaus as cover. Stay low, but move fast. Find a position as close as you can get and be ready."

"And what are you going to do?" Maria asked uneasily.

He didn't want to tell her. He wished they would just go, get into positions, be ready.

But that wasn't going to happen. So he pulled the Glock 19 and handed it to her. "I'm going to walk into their camp unarmed and hope they don't just shoot me."

"Or the president," Strickland added.

"That's utterly insane," Mendel noted.

"Not happening," Maria agreed.

Zero threw up his hands in exasperation. "What choice do we have?"

"There's just under four hours on the clock," Maria said. "Penny was told to give us ten minutes and then call in the cavalry—"

"Right," Zero argued. "And what do you think they'll do? How long will it take for them to plan and get here? *Maybe* they'll get here in time. *Maybe* they'll send the right people, whoever that might be that's not us. *Maybe* they won't send drones and helicopters and planes. Hell, *maybe* we'll even get a crack shot or two that could easily make a five-hundred-yard target. You want to sit and wait, and take that chance? We're here, right now—"

"It's better than taking the chance of them shooting you, and then him!" Maria countered.

He took her hand in both of his. "They won't."

"How do you *know*?"

"Because… I think they want an audience. Think about it. Do you really think they came all the way out here just to wait for zero, pop the president, and then pack up and go home? No. They gave us time for a reason. To figure it out. To get here."

"To send in a bunch of guns," Strickland said, picking up what Zero was suggesting. "To make it look like we forced their hand."

"Like there could not be a peaceful resolution," Mendel added with a nod.

"Exactly. Now one guy comes walking out of the desert, unarmed, with his hands up?" Zero shook his head. "It's not what they want. With any luck, it'll confuse the hell out of them. I'll get as close as I can to Rutledge. And while I'm distracting them, you four—you find a position, and you find a way."

"I don't like it," Maria said quietly.

"That's never been a job requirement."

She scoffed. Then she grabbed the back of his neck and kissed him. When she pulled away her expression was tight, and he thought he saw the slightest of glisten in her eye. "You come back," she told him. Not a request, but a demand, her voice choked.

"I'll see you soon," he told her. "Promise." To the rest of the team he said, "I'll walk slow. You move fast."

He turned, and he started up the sand mound behind them.

*This is crazy. This is absolutely crazy.*

But it was too late to turn back now. He'd reached the top of the mound and stood to full height, putting his hands up slightly, at elbow level, in case the scout with the binoculars was watching.

He took a step forward…

And so did someone else.

"Foxworth! What the hell are you doing?"

Chip stood beside him, hands slightly raised as well, facing the encampment in the distance. "Not letting you walk in there alone, that's what I'm doing."

Zero huffed. "Now's not the time to be noble—"

"Yeah, well, if they can see you, they can see me. Too late now."

"Son of a…" *Stubborn Texan mistake of a hire.* "Well. Come on, now."

They started forward, keeping their hands up. "Hey, look," Chip said. "With one of us, they'll know you didn't come alone. With two of us though, they might think it's just you and me out here."

"They are *not* going to think that."

"Then we can pull their focus in two directions…"

"We're standing next to each other," Zero countered.

"Okay. Then if they gun us down, you're not going to die alone."

Zero sighed. "Yeah. I guess there's that."

They walked on in silence, their pace slow, the sweat dripping into their eyes, the encampment growing larger as they approached.

If they shot him dead before he had a chance to do anything, at least he had found them. There was some small solace in that. He had his team with him. His brain was going to kill him eventually anyway; dying in the field seemed oddly preferable than a slow end by atrophy.

*But what if my memory slips again?* Suddenly he was glad to have Chip at his side. His backup. Foxworth didn't deserve this sort of end, if it came to that, but he knew what he was signing up for when he'd taken that first step.

*Besides. Wouldn't you have done the same if you were in his shoes?*

Soon they could see that the man with the binoculars was watching them, occasionally scanning left and right. The other two held assault rifles, bringing the stock up to their shoulder and taking aim.

*We're in their range.* Any moment now they could pull the triggers and end two lives in an instant. He would never see his wedding to Maria. He would never see either of his girls blossom into adulthood, have weddings of their own someday. But he could see *her* again.

Somehow he just knew who was waiting for him, to bring him to the other side. Patiently waiting, always there.

"You know," said Chip, "I'm beginning to think this was a bad idea." His collar and underarms were soaked.

Zero barely felt the heat now, his heart jackhammering in his chest. Behind the armed men was Rutledge, in a chair against the beige backdrop, his hands behind him. His head lolled, chin against his chest.

He didn't look alive.

*He's alive. He has to be.*

There was no sign of Dawoud.

"Stop!" one of the men shouted in Arabic. They did, about twenty yards from the edge of the encampment. Close enough to recognize the men as the fake Presidential Guard from the treaty signing. Close enough to see the video camera, on a tripod, and the computer array beside it atop two overturned crates.

The two men with guns aimed at them. The two agents stood there with their hands up. An easterly breeze blew gently. The man with the binoculars scanned the horizon for a long moment. Then he said something, over his shoulder, that Zero couldn't quite make out.

The domed beige tent rustled. Its flap opened, and the ersatz Ashraf Dawoud stepped out. He made sure to keep his body obscured behind his two guards with guns. But that was fine; at the moment there wasn't a gun on Rutledge.

Dawoud smiled broadly. "Gentlemen," he said in English. "Welcome. Please—come join me in the shade."

# CHAPTER THIRTY NINE

Maria stayed low, crouching as she ran, glad for the regiment of a hundred squats per day. She dashed behind a small rock formation, about twice her height and just wide enough to hide her, and held the position for a three-count.

Then she peeked from behind it.

She was about a hundred yards from the encampment. Maybe a little more. And by the looks of things, there was no more cover to be had. It was open sand between her and them. The bodies were too close together to fire indiscriminately, and even careful aim with the Glock or the Sig Sauer could result in friendly fire.

She was going to have to get closer. And she couldn't do that until there was an opening for her to make a mad dash forward.

*Be ready.* That's what Zero had told her. So she sat, and she waited, and she would be.

*

*Stupid plateau.* Talia Mendel pulled herself up onto the flat, rocky peak, the rifle slung over one shoulder. *Why did I insist on volunteering for this?*

Her hip still ached terribly from the brief fight with the Libyan nomads who had first agreed to sell them the Jeep and then tried to rob her and Foxworth. He had proven himself useful in a fight. Attractive, even. At least more so after that shared encounter. She hoped he did not die today.

*Focus, Mendel.*

She lay flat on her stomach and shimmied, slowly and carefully, to a position at the edge of the stone tabletop, facing the encampment. Then she wiped sweat from under her eye, brought the rifle to her shoulder, and peered through the scope.

Zero and Foxworth had made it to the camp. They were being ushered forward, under the canopy. Heat rippled the air; shapes became hazy. She did not have as good an angle from up here as Zero had thought. She could not even see the American president from there.

The shot, it seemed, would be an impossible one.

*

"You're not Ashraf Dawoud," Zero said coldly as the man in the binoculars patted them down beneath the canopy. The other two kept their rifles trained on each of their heads, point-blank. "Is he dead?"

Not-Dawoud smiled again. He still wore the suit, Zero noted, that he'd worn at the peace treaty, though now it was dirty and rumpled. "Dead," the man said. "Or reborn. Does it matter?"

They weren't dead yet, somehow. Zero was right; they wanted an audience.

"You must have gone through great pains to find us," said Not-Dawoud. "Tell me, are we surrounded?" He laughed then.

"Yes," Zero lied. Was it a lie? Not if three people could constitute surrounding four others. "We have snipers on the plateaus capable of a thousand-yard shot. You and your men could be dead in a heartbeat."

Dawoud seemed to be enjoying this. "Of course you do! And were that the case and you had this opportunity, you certainly would not have taken it by now, and instead sent two men to... to do what? To have a nice chat?"

"That's right," said Zero. "A chat about peaceful resolution."

"There will not be one!" Dawoud snarled suddenly. "Not for Israel, not for your president, and not for either of you!" The man took a calming breath and smiled again. "Now. I have a hunch of why you are here. I think you are here because zero has reached. Hmm? Am I correct?"

Zero and Foxworth exchanged a glance. "No," said Chip. "No, there's still at least three hours on the countdown."

*Has he not even been paying attention to his countdown?* Zero wondered. Was this all a ploy? If so, to what end?

"Oh," said Dawoud, as he paced slowly behind his two guards. "I see. You misunderstand. Let me explain: me and my people, we have been paying attention. President Rutledge is a threat, but one that many see as a harbinger of peace. What they do not see is that the path to his goal is paved in blood. The Saudis know this. The Russians know this. The Hamas factions in the West Bank know this. They whisper the

242

name. They speak it in their final moments. The harbinger of death. The… how would you say? The yin to Rutledge's yang. The one who quietly eliminates those who oppose his offerings of 'peace.'"

*Oh.*

*No.*

He realized all too late that he had just walked into a trap.

"We left all the clues…"

He thought he had figured it out. But it was yet another trap.

"Hoping no one but he would find the breadcrumbs."

A trap invented for *him*.

*The American president still lives.* That's what Dawoud had said in the video. *But he will die when zero reaches.*

Not zero. Not when the countdown ended. When *Zero* reaches.

The countdown was a distraction. To make him rush, to make him panic, to get him there faster than anyone else.

"Am I correct?" Dawoud asked gleefully. "If so, please tell me. Which of you is the great Agent Zero?"

Had he actually figured anything out? Did they know that his own hubris would keep others out of the loop, keep help from coming, inspire him to be the one to charge in here, unarmed and assuming he knew the score?

"I am."

Before Zero knew what was happening, Foxworth stepped forward, a cocky grin on his face. "I'm Agent Zero."

"Chip, what the hell are you—"

"This guy," he said loudly, pointing at Zero, "is just a partner. Old guy could barely keep up. But I followed your clues. I figured you out. I'm Agent Zero, I'm here, and now I'm going to kick your doppelgangin' ass all the way back to—"

Dawoud casually raised an arm. Too late Zero saw the flash of silver. Too late he recognized the stout pistol in his hand. The same one that killed Nitzani.

And with a quick pull of the trigger, he sent a bullet through Chip Foxworth's head.

# CHAPTER FORTY

In movies there is what is commonly referred to as a "reaction shot," a moment after a big event that seems to freeze in time to give actors the chance to emote, to show their terror or shock or resolve. In reality, that moment rarely existed. Terror fueled adrenaline, and few things provoked genuine, knee-quaking terror like the impossibly loud sound of a gun fired in close quarters. Like watching a man die in front of you.

But, in reality, rare as it might be, sometimes that moment did exist. It existed now, as Zero found himself frozen in shock, watching Chip Foxworth's body fall backward. Dead instantly. Blood staining the sand.

*For me. Because of me. Claiming to be me.*

He couldn't breathe, couldn't move.

But this wasn't a movie. Those who treated it like it was often found themselves sorely disappointed at best and dead at worst.

He wanted to leap at the fake president. To strangle the life from him slowly and watch the light die in his eyes.

"Kill that one," he heard Dawoud say in Arabic, "and then start the camera—"

A rifle crack split the air. A plume of sand exploded near Dawoud's feet.

Two of the guards snapped up their rifles and fired bursts in the plateau's direction as Zero hit the deck, sand in his mouth. More shots now, from his left, as Maria sprinted across open desert with a pistol in each hand.

Two of her shots hit one of the guards in the back. He grunted and fell forward.

*But he's wearing a vest.*

The man groaned as he staggered to his feet again. Zero leapt at him, throwing his whole body weight against him. They went tumbling back into the sand as another loud, single crack echoed.

Sand plumed; Dawoud yelped and fell. A ricochet to the leg.

244

Zero tried to wrestle the assault rifle from the guard, but he bucked and threw him off. Zero hit the sand on his back.

Automatic gunfire ripped from a distance. Strickland, somewhere, with the Tavor. He shredded the guard in an instant.

Dawoud was on his side in the sand, the silver pistol firing at Maria. She threw herself down. The two remaining guards were shooting at something, and the Tavor was silent.

On his elbows and knees, Zero scrambled to Dawoud. The fake president tried to turn the pistol on him but Zero got there first. He caught the arm, reared back, and smashed him across the face with a fist. And then again.

He yanked the silver gun away and turned it on him, pressing it to his head.

"*I'm* Agent Zero," he said, "and you just killed my friend."

He pulled the trigger.

*Click.*

The gun was empty.

Another metallic flash. A sear of pain. Dawoud held a knife and slashed at Zero's arm. He grimaced and fell back as Dawoud hobbled toward Rutledge.

*No.* He hadn't come this far to fail now. He ignored his bleeding arm, his friends who he didn't know were on their feet or down, and lurched for Dawoud. He grabbed a foot, the pant leg torn and bleeding where Talia's ricocheted shot had hit him.

He pulled. Dawoud howled. He swung again with the knife but Zero slid backward in the sand. A rifle cracked. Automatic weapons rattled. Zero stayed low and wrestled with Dawoud for the knife, twisting it out of his grip.

He heard a cry of pain. *Maria.*

He turned to look. Just for a second. She was in the sand, on her side, still firing with one pistol.

Dawoud swung his head forward and caught Zero in the forehead with a vicious headbutt.

He reeled. Bright stars swam in his vision. He saw double, Dawoud and an identical Dawoud. Another one, a second. A Double.

Zero saw two arms, each holding a knife. Two knives, flashing in the sun. He swayed with dizziness. He didn't know which one to try to stop, if he could even stop one.

*Plunk!*

An odd sound. A sharp yelp of pain from Dawoud.

Zero shook the fog from his head as best he could as the sound came again.

*Plunk!*

One of the guards fell. The remaining one was firing upward, on an angle...

*Toward the sky?*

Zero glanced upward and saw a small, dark shape flitting like a hummingbird against the blue sky.

The drone. Penny's drone. Maria must have deployed it from the Jeep.

Dr. Penelope León was currently five thousand two hundred and twenty-eight miles away from their current position—but with them in more than just spirit.

*Plunk!* The small electronic cannon on the underside of the drone fired, and the guard shielded his face as sand plumed from the missed shot. He took aim then, and emptied his magazine into the air.

At least one round found home, striking one of the drone's propellers. It wobbled in the air, flying in lazy circles, the cannon trying to track its target.

The guard turned and tossed his assault rifle to the ground. Zero was on his knees. His head throbbed. His limbs didn't want to respond.

*Get up, old man.*

The guard drew a curved knife from his belt and took a step toward him.

*Get up.*

*You've come too far for it to end now.*

One foot planted in the sand. With a groan he stood. The guard reared back with the knife.

The rifle cracked. The guard's head jerked, and his body fell sideways in the sand.

Zero let himself fall to his hands and knees. "Thanks, Talia," he muttered. She'd made the shot.

For a long moment, he closed his eyes and just breathed. He needed to check on Maria. He needed to check on Rutledge and Strickland. And get some damned water.

But it was done. The guards were dead. Penny had taken out Dawoud with the drone.

He opened his eyes and frowned. There was something in the sand there. He reached for it; a tiny, perfectly round steel ball. Like a ball bearing, or a marble.

Right—the rounds that the drone fired. He remembered Penny showing him in her lab, before Jerusalem.

*Nonlethal?* he'd asked her.

*Depends on how close it is. And where it hits.*

He spun suddenly. This round had bounced off of something. Or someone.

Rutledge's chair was empty.

Zero staggered to his feet and lurched forward, nearly falling again. He rounded the domed tent to see Dawoud, breathing hard but still on his feet, grunting with effort as he tried to mount one of the horses.

*He's alive.*

He had the limp, handcuffed president flung over the horse's back as he mounted behind Rutledge. Zero surged forward, arms outstretched.

"*Addhab!*" Dawoud cried, and the horse shot forward.

Zero stumbled and fell into the sand where the horse and two presidents had just been.

*Get up.*

He hauled himself to his feet and, with no small effort, flung a leg over the back of the nearest horse, a gray and black brindle stallion with a black mane.

It had no saddle. Zero had never ridden bareback—he couldn't remember the last time he'd ridden a horse at all—but still he grabbed two fistfuls of mane and dug a heel into its flank.

"Yah!"

The horse didn't move.

"Go! Run! Giddy-up!"

The beast snorted at him. Dawoud gained ground across the sand ahead of him.

*Arabic horse*, he reminded himself.

"*Addhab!*" he shouted as he kicked at its flank again. The horse shot forward with the Arabic command to go, and Zero teetered precariously for a moment before throwing his body weight forward, almost lying flat against its back.

He bounced dangerously, every stride threatening to throw him off, but he held fast with his thighs and ankles and a firm grip with both hands on its mane.

There was less weight on his horse. He was gaining. But he had no idea what to do when he caught up.

"*Addhab!*" he shouted again, and the horse broke into a full gallop.

Zero had leapt out of helicopters onto moving trains. He'd jumped off of bridges into rivers. He'd dived headfirst into firefights and hornets' nests and lion's dens, but nothing had been quite as terrifying as riding a horse bareback at full speed. His knuckles were white against the horse's black mane, and his breaths came quick and panicked.

Dawoud was mere yards ahead and the distance was closing as the two horses sprinted across open desert toward the shadow of a tall spire of a plateau.

*Where is he going?* Where would he want to take Rutledge when he could have just killed him quickly?

*He's not taking him anywhere*, Zero realized. *He's drawing me away.* Dawoud's plan wasn't just to eliminate Rutledge, but him as well. And it seemed he was still intent on doing it.

His horse's head was level with the other horse's flank then. Another few feet and he'd be able to reach out, to grab Dawoud and yank him off...

Something silver flashed. Not a gun; Dawoud still had the knife. He slashed out, not close enough for Zero. Aiming for the horse.

The beast shied away and the blade missed by inches.

Zero tugged the mane, trying to direct the horse to get closer again. Dawoud held the knife with one hand and the mane with the other, daring them closer again, as Rutledge bounced, still not looking conscious.

"Come on!" Zero demanded, as if the horse would listen to frustration.

He heard a high-pitched buzz behind him and hazarded a glance over his shoulder. It was the drone, flying unevenly with three propellers and struggling to keep up.

*Plunk!*

A plume of sand popped behind Dawoud's horse.

*Plunk!*

248

Another miss, by a wider margin. The damaged propeller was throwing off Penny's aim.

The drone flew wide then, not behind them but at an angle.

*Is she out of ammo? Is she peeling off?*

He had to get closer. Stop Dawoud and get the knife away. If he slashed at the horse and Zero was thrown, that was all he'd need to take them both out quickly.

*"Addhab!"* he commanded, digging in his right heel. The horse seemed to understand, drawing nearer to Dawoud as they ran nearly side by side.

He snarled at Zero. The knife was ready. Zero wasn't sure he could let go with even one hand and still stay on the animal's back. But he had little choice...

A shadow passed over Dawoud's face. Zero looked up to see the drone arcing, coming in at an angle from the east. Too far for an effective shot. It wobbled once, and then—

*Plunk!*

Sand sprayed as the hooves of Dawoud's horse skidded. The beast whinnied in pain and shook its great head as the steel ball bounced off its neck.

*Nonlethal, at that distance.*

Its front legs came up, just slightly—and then it bucked, throwing its rear quarters high.

Dawoud vaulted forward, right over the horse's head, tumbling through the air. Rutledge, his body limp, rolled over onto the sand several times.

"Stop!" Zero pulled at his horse's mane. "Stop! *Qaf!*"

The horse slowed quickly, and Zero jumped off. His legs were like jelly and gave out, sending him to his knees in the shadow of the tall plateau.

*Get up.*

He swayed on his feet but stayed upright as he teetered toward Rutledge.

*Please be alive.*

The wobbly drone buzzed nearby, the cannon hanging limply at its underside. Out of ammunition, he guessed. At least that last shot had counted.

But then he saw him. Dawoud rose from the desert like a beast from the sea, not twenty yards from Zero, Rutledge's unconscious body

249

between them. Sand stuck to the blood on the Double's face and one arm hung loosely at his side.

But the other still held the knife.

Dawoud staggered forward, toward Rutledge, just as unsteady on his feet as Zero was. He stumbled, fell to his knees, and crawled as quickly as he could with one good arm.

Zero tried to run, but his foot hit a soft mound of sand and sank, giving way beneath his weight. He had no traction, even in these boots.

*These boots.*

He didn't have to run. He just had to aim.

Zero brought his left heel up and smacked it with the back of his hand. The blade slid out from the toe. The last of the three that Penny had loaded.

Dawoud crawled closer, loping along with his useless arm swinging.

With his foot pointed toward the fake president, Zero lifted the boot—and then stomped it down.

Nothing happened. The blade stayed there, jutting from the toe. The sand was too soft.

He tried again, stomping harder, but the sand gave way, the surface tension breaking. His knee gave out and he fell to his side.

Dawoud was mere feet from Rutledge, his face a sandy, bloody, leering mask of madness.

Zero wrenched the boot from his foot. He flipped it around in his hand, heel-up. He aimed it like a gun.

Dawoud reached the prostrate US president and huddled over him. But he stared ahead, right at Zero, his eyes furious but his mouth contorted in a grin.

He raised the knife.

Zero hammered down onto the heel with a fist, as hard as he could muster.

The ballistic knife shot out and caught Dawoud in the throat, about an inch above the sternal notch, and stuck there. His mouth fell open, but no sound came forth. Blood arced across the sand. Then the Double fell backward, the knife still raised in his one good arm.

Zero tossed the boot aside and crawled the rest of the way to Rutledge. He hauled the president onto his back. His eyes were closed, his face red from heat exhaustion, his skin puffy from dehydration.

But he had a pulse. It was weak, but it was there and steady.

"Mr. President?" With a groan, Zero sat him upright and held him there. "Jon?"

His eyelids fluttered open. He coughed twice.

"Zero?" It was barely more than a croaking whisper.

"Yeah. It's me."

Rutledge glanced left and right, his eyes glassy and bloodshot. "This real?" he managed.

Zero grinned despite himself. "Yes. This is real. You're alive."

"Never…" Rutledge coughed, a deep, lung-rattling hack. "Never doubted. For a second."

There was a sound then, a familiar one in the distance, growing louder. Zero stood and shielded his eyes against the horizon to see shapes—first two, and then four, and then ten dotting the sky as they flew over the desert in formation.

*Helicopters.*

The cavalry was here.

And somehow he just knew they'd send helicopters.

# CHAPTER FORTY ONE

Jonathan Rutledge had never been happier to step foot again on American soil.

He was helped down the flight stairs by Agent Chubb, and at the bottom he waved and smiled to the crowd that had gathered behind barricades to see the American president returned safely to Joint Base Andrews.

He made no attempt to hide the bandages around his wrists from where the handcuffs had bitten into his skin. His face and neck were still quite red, despite being given IV fluids and treated for heat stroke on Air Force One.

He was exhausted, aching, hurt, and his ego had taken quite the blow. But he was alive.

*And EOT deserves one hell of a raise.*

Rutledge didn't stop for any comments, despite the amount of press present. Speaking was still somewhat difficult, and he wasn't sure he wanted those types of sound bites circulating in the media.

The helicopters had taken him and EOT back to Egypt, and from there to Jerusalem, where Air Force One was waiting. He had offered to give Zero and his team a lift home in style, but apparently they'd had a jet of their own waiting that they would have been remiss not to return.

Unfortunately, they did need to borrow a pilot, due to a loss on the team out there in the desert. There would be posthumous accolades for Charles John Foxworth, and Rutledge vowed to personally see to it that his loved ones were taken care of.

He waved once more to the crowd as the Secret Service ushered him into the back of a fortified SUV in a motorcade. He was glad, but not all that surprised, to see who was waiting for him inside.

"Mr. President." Joanna Barkley smiled as he climbed in opposite her in the rear-facing seat. "Forgive me if it would be unbecoming, but I'd like to give you a hug."

"Just be gentle." She hugged him briefly, punctuating it with a slight squeeze, and then settled back in her seat and smoothed her lapels. "I understand…" He cleared his throat, his voice still quite hoarse. "I understand you got to enjoy… being president for a day."

"'Enjoy' might be a strong word," she admitted. "Perhaps someday. Maybe in a few years. Until then, it would be appreciated if you'd stick around."

He smiled. Joanna deserved a lot more praise than that, and eventually she would get it—when he was able to give it. He had been fully briefed on the flight back to D.C., and he knew that she had singlehandedly talked Israel down from a missile strike that would have undoubtedly sparked a new war. She ignored the media, kept her cool under pressure, stood up to Kressley and others who would have favored conflict, and led by her morals.

One day she would be a great president. He was just very glad it wasn't today.

"So tell me," he said.

She nodded. "First and foremost, a DNA and blood test have conclusively determined that the man who took you hostage was not Ashraf Dawoud. There is currently a large-scale manhunt in Palestine for the real Dawoud, but unfortunately, he is presumed dead. Thirteen others close to him, including a chauffeur and a pilot, had also been murdered, and the running theory is that the double killed anyone who knew about him."

Rutledge nodded. Rumors of Dawoud's paranoia had been rampant, but he had no idea they had been that extensive. To have a body double, and one that looked and spoke and acted exactly like him, it was unthinkable.

"No one from the group responsible has been identified outside of those that were killed in the operation," Barkley continued. "If they're out there, they're hiding."

"Rightly so," Rutledge said. "They know now…" He put a hand to his mouth and coughed. They know now, he thought, that whatever lengths they might be willing to go to try to stop peace, there were others willing to go further to stop *them*.

"Prime Minister-Designate Levi has assured me that Israel has stood down with the knowledge of the double," Joanna told him. "And he is amenable to continuing the discussion of a treaty…"

"In Washington, D.C."

She smiled. "That's right, sir. And to that end, the Palestinian Parliament has put forth a proposal. A joint task force between the three

253

nations with the specific goal of finding and eliminating militant factions that threaten the peace."

Rutledge nodded. And he already had someone in mind to run it—a certain Mossad agent who had proved invaluable to EOT.

*Peace cannot be made by force; it can only be achieved by understanding.* He realized now that he had gotten Einstein's quote wrong in his address. Einstein said, "Peace cannot be *kept* by force."

Although, maybe he hadn't gotten it so wrong after all. Force alone did not make peace. But sometimes force was the only thing that some people could understand, and applying force against resisting force showed strength.

And he would have to be stronger.

*

The man had no name. He did, once, but he had given it up for the cause.

Was there still a cause? One could argue there was. As long as the hope of a true, pure Arab nation beat in one man's heart, it was still a cause.

But what good was it when that man had no name? His group, they had no name either. Names made them real. Names gave them meaning in the eyes of others. Names became whispers, and rumors, and then targets.

But what was a group of one man? He did not know if any others had survived. He knew only that the Double and the rest involved in capturing the US president were dead. He knew that he was alive. He knew he was in Cairo International Airport with fake documentation and about to board a plane to Ankara, in Turkey, where they had established a safe house for this type of situation.

He would have to go underground. For how long? Until he was certain *he* wasn't looking for him. The phantom. The bloodhound. The one they called Zero.

The Double had gotten overzealous. He could have killed the American president and made history. He could have dashed the hopes and empty promises of false peace in front of the world. But no; the Double wanted the president's executioner too. He had lured a cold, quiet killer and had been killed for it.

The man glanced over his shoulder at the very thought of it. The tall white man in the business suit sipping coffee, he could have been Agent Zero. The too-tan man sitting three seats away at the departure gate, he could have been Zero.

Or perhaps he would never even see Zero, and his throat would be cut in his sleep…

The man jumped a little at the sudden ringing of a phone. He frowned in irritation that whoever it belonged to was not answering—and then realized it was *his* phone, ringing from his bag.

The burner? He had only ever made calls from it, never received one. Who could this be? A survivor, perhaps. Another who could join him, and rebuild.

"*Alo*," he answered cautiously.

"English?" the man asked. "It is nothing personal, I just prefer it."

He frowned deeply, panic knotting in his chest at how this number had been acquired. But he switched to English all the same. "Who is this?"

"I could ask the same question," the man said. His accent was European. German, it sounded. "And you would tell me 'no one.' Though in another life, you were Al Najjar, were you not?"

*Hang up. End the call. No good can come of this.*

But his curiosity won out over his panic. "What do you want?"

"Money," the German said simply. "I know that your organization was funded by a businessman who called himself Mr. Shade. My resources indicate that Shade is now incarcerated—which is putting it mildly. But I *also* know that you still have access to the funds he had allocated to you and your… former partners. May they rest in peace."

The man who used to be Al Najjar hesitated. How did this European know about Shade, or the money?

"Are you still there, née Al Najjar?"

"I am. Go on."

"I want twenty-five million euros," said the German. "And for this price, I will kill Agent Zero for you."

Al Najjar laughed. He could not help himself; the notion itself was abject lunacy, and the seriousness with which the German stated it only made it more laughable.

"You are laughing," the German noted.

"You are insane. And I am hanging up—"

"Krauss," he said quickly. "You have heard this name?"

255

The man paused. "...I have," he admitted.

"I am him," said the German.

*Krauss.* He had heard the name mentioned in some circles, in relation to certain deaths, ones that remained unsolved as far as any governments or authorities were concerned. Deaths that had toppled regimes and built empires.

But he had assumed that Krauss was the name of an organization, not a single man.

"How do I know you are telling the truth?" he asked the German.

"You have only my word. But I have your telephone number, do I not? Your former name. The name of your financer. His location. The names he has given up. And—I know the name that haunts your dreams at night."

The man shook his head. "None of that matters. Even if I did believe you, I do not have twenty-five million. Nowhere near that."

"No, you do not. But as I said, I have names. Mr. Shade financed several groups like yours. And like yours, they too are afraid of the American bogeyman. Find them. Pool your resources."

"How?"

"Go to Beirut. There is a Kiwi there named Dutchman—"

"A Kiwi?"

"A New Zealander," said the German. "Named Dutchman. He will put you on the path. I will be in touch. And when you have my twenty-five million, I will hunt and kill Agent Zero. Godspeed."

The German ended the call.

The man who used to be Al Najjar sat there for a long moment, the phone still in his hands. He knew he should ignore it, forget the call ever happened. Continue on to Ankara. Hide.

But what if the clerk at the duty-free was Agent Zero? What if the passenger behind him on the plane was Zero? What if he was already there, in Ankara, lying in wait?

He felt no shame in feeling fear, but great shame in living in fear. So he rose, and he headed toward the ticket agent to change his flight to Beirut.

# EPILOGUE

"Well. This is just sad," Maria said with a sigh.

"What's that?" Zero asked, but he didn't look up from the kitchen counter. He was carefully stuffing bell peppers with a blend of tomato sauce and sausage, intent on getting the recipe right this time. Last time he'd just used ground beef and they'd come out too bland. Italian sausage, he had decided, was the way to go.

He'd taken over most of the cooking, with occasional help from Sara, since Maria's left arm was in a sling where a bullet had winged her three days prior in the Libyan Desert.

The memory of it was already like a dream. Rutledge was home, and safe; the plot had been thwarted. War had been averted. And they had settled right back into domestic life as easily as changing clothes. Strange, how simple it was. Though it helped a lot that he had Maria there, and Sara, and even Mischa to come home to.

"Our guest list." Maria sat at the island with a pad of paper before her and a pen touching her bottom lip. Since she was limited physically, she had taken to wedding planning in the meantime. "It's eighteen people long and I'm hard-pressed to think of anyone else."

Zero shrugged. "Eighteen sounds nice. Small and intimate."

"That's including plus-ones."

He laughed. "Okay. Maybe that is a little sad. Did you put the girls' Aunt Linda down—"

A dull crash from below them interrupted him. Zero sighed, pulled open the basement door, and shouted down the stairs. "What's going on down there?"

"We're painting," Sara called back.

"Yes," Mischa agreed. "Painting."

"Then what was that crash just now?" he asked.

"…We're aggressively painting," Sara called back, obviously holding in a laugh.

He closed the door again. "You know what? I don't want to know." It seemed like the two had bonded during their time alone. He wasn't about to question it, unless one of them got hurt.

"There's still the big question of where," Maria said.

"A beach in the Bahamas," Zero said right away.

She laughed at him. "We can't get married on a beach in the Bahamas."

"Why not?"

"Because..." She tapped the pen against her lip again. "You know, I actually don't know why not."

His cell phone rang then, displaying his eldest daughter's name. "One minute," he told Maria. "Hey, sweetheart. How are you?"

"I'm good," Maya answered, her voice sounding a little more chipper than normal.

"How's school?"

"School is... great. Hey, Dad, has the dean called you?"

He frowned. "No. Why? Should she have? Is everything okay?"

"Oh yeah. Everything is great. There's just... um, there was an opportunity," she told him. "Remember when I was able to test out of my senior year of high school? Well, they offered me the same chance to do that here. At the academy. And I did... and I passed."

Zero's frown deepened. He was starting to get lines around his eyes. "You're telling me that you tested out of your final year of West Point?" From the island, Maria smirked a little and shook her head. "I didn't know that was a thing they allowed."

"It's brand new," Maya said. "They just started. But anyway, Dean Hunt and I had a meeting, and she had another opportunity for me. Advanced training, down in D.C. So... I'll be coming home, as soon as next week."

Zero blinked. "Advanced training," he repeated. "Uh-huh."

He didn't believe it for a second.

*But you know what? As long as no one's hurt, I don't need to know.*

"So you need me to come get you?" he asked.

"Nope. It's all taken care of. I'll call you when I'm heading back—"

"Just one quick question," he interjected. "Does this have anything to do with you taking a two-thousand-dollar cash advance on your credit card?"

"...Testing fees," she told him.

"Testing fees."

*Nope. Don't want to know.*

"Okay then. We'll see you next week."

"Love you, bye!" Maya hung up.

Zero frowned at the phone.

"Secrets?" Maria asked.

"Secrets," he confirmed. "And speaking of, I have a lunch date tomorrow."

Maria raised an eyebrow. "One that I'm not allowed to know about?"

He smiled. "Just visiting a friend." It wasn't a lie. He had made a promise, and he intended on keeping it.

"Okay. Just don't forget, we have the…" Maria trailed off. "The other thing, tomorrow afternoon."

"I won't forget."

They both fell silent. Chip's funeral was tomorrow.

His body had been recovered from the scene, cremated, and sent to his sister and nephew in Austin. As far as they were concerned, Chip had died in a plane crash. An engine malfunction in a small commuter jet. He had been the only one aboard. The manufacturer was settling with the family for a hefty sum, which Zero knew was not actually coming from any airplane manufacturer but the federal government.

"I should…" He gestured back to the unfinished tray of stuffed peppers behind him.

A moment later he felt Maria's good arm wrap around his waist and her head rest on his back. "You know," she told him, "it wasn't your—"

"Don't." He said it quietly, not forcefully, but still didn't want to hear it. "Please. Don't say it."

She had already told him that it wasn't his fault, probably a dozen times now. Strickland had said it. Reidigger had said it. Even the president had said it.

And he knew it wasn't. He hadn't asked Chip to come with him that day. He hadn't asked him to step forward and claim to be Agent Zero.

But the simple fact was that Zero was alive, and Chip wasn't. It hadn't been his fault, not directly, but it was *because* of him.

And he would have to live with that.

\*

The next day Zero dressed in a dark suit and stuffed a tie in his pocket so that he could go directly to the funeral afterward. It would be a token ceremony, in a church but without a casket or body. People who knew him would say nice things about him. Zero would not. Maria would not. Todd and Alan would not, because as far as anyone was aware, they had not worked together on a covert operation to rescue the President of the United States.

If anyone asked how they'd known Chip, he had been their pilot a few times. A charming fellow. Always pleasant. Always joking. Doing great impressions and making up wild stories.

But first, he had a promise to keep.

It took him twenty-eight minutes to get to the cul-de-sac and the two-story colonial where Seth Connors was staying—or being kept, was more appropriate. Zero had texted yesterday morning about the visit and Seth had responded with a simple message: *Looking forward to it.*

He knocked on the door and waited.

He knocked a second time.

After the third knock without a response he tried the knob and found it locked, so he circled around to the rear, to the patio where they had talked once before. Not there, either.

He gave the sliding patio door a tug and found it opened easily.

*Maybe he's in the shower or something*, Zero thought, already knowing that wasn't true.

He found Connors in the living room. He wasn't sure where he had gotten the gun, but guns weren't hard to come by in their line of work. There was a suppressor on the end of it to stifle the sound. A single shot, to his own temple. Seth had laid down plastic, on the floor and on the sofa, where he had fallen in such a way that he could have been lounging if his eyes weren't still open.

Zero sighed and shook his head. This was no way for anyone to go—though he couldn't fully relate to how haunted Seth had been by the fragmented memories of a past life he knew almost nothing about.

"I'm sorry," Zero whispered. "I know it was hard."

He knew he had to call this in, but he didn't want to be here when he did. There was a mini-mart up the road a bit with a working pay phone; he could be anonymous from there…

He paused. On the coffee table was a sticky note, just a small yellow square stuck to the glass.

It was short.

*I'm sorry.*

*More came back. Couldn't do it anymore.*
*Thanks for being there when you could. Dillard.*

He read it again, and then a third time. It felt like it was meant for him, but that final word, "Dillard," was unfamiliar. It looked like a sign-off. A CIA alias that had come back to his mind? Had Connors been too confused to remember who he was? Or was there an intended recipient other than Zero?

He wasn't sure. He stuffed the note in his pocket and gently closed Seth's eyes with two fingertips. He wiped the doorknobs clean of his prints, and then he got back in his car. For a moment he just sat there. He had to report a suicide and go to a funeral.

He was alive.

Seth wasn't.

Chip wasn't.

He slammed a fist on the steering wheel. Then again, and again, until the knuckle of his middle finger split. He grabbed the wheel with both hands and, with the windows up, he screamed as long and loud as he could, at no one and nothing but everything. It fell into the void, his scream, along with every other thing he'd ever done that meant nothing as long as lives kept ending around him.

Then he took a deep breath, in through his mouth and out through his nose. He wiped his knuckle clean with a tissue from the glove box. He took the crumpled note from his pocket and read it once more.

*Thanks for being there when you could.*

*Dillard.*

The name meant nothing to him.

But… maybe that was the point.

Had Seth Connors remembered something more, something that could help Zero? Was this his way of leaving a clue, but cryptically, just in case someone other than Zero had found him first?

Zero was alive.

Seth wasn't.

Chip wasn't.

Was Dillard? He didn't know. But as he started the car and pulled away from the colonial house on the cul-de-sac, he vowed to find out.

# NOW AVAILABLE!

## VENGEANCE ZERO
### (An Agent Zero Spy Thriller—Book #10)

"You will not sleep until you are finished with AGENT ZERO. A superb job creating a set of characters who are fully developed and very much enjoyable. The description of the action scenes transport us into a reality that is almost like sitting in a movie theater with surround sound and 3D (it would make an incredible Hollywood movie). I can hardly wait for the sequel."
--Roberto Mattos, Books and Movie Reviews

VENGEANCE ZERO is book #10 in the #1 bestselling AGENT ZERO series, which begins with AGENT ZERO (Book #1), a free download with nearly 300 five-star reviews.

**When a minor terrorist group, looking to make its mark, aims to take out a "soft target" in the United States—one relatively unguarded yet which can be hugely damaging to the U.S.—the race is on for Agent Zero to discover their object and stop them before it's too late.**

**Yet Zero faces his own battles: when he is targeted for assassination and someone close to him ends up the victim instead, it sends his life into a downspin, and allows him only course of action: vengeance.**

**Will Zero be able to save the target—and himself—before he spirals out of control?**

VENGEANCE ZERO (Book #10) is an un-putdownable espionage thriller that will keep you turning pages late into the night.

Book #11 (ZERO ZERO) is also available.

**"Thriller writing at its best."**

--Midwest Book Review (re *Any Means Necessary*)

"One of the best thrillers I have read this year."
--Books and Movie Reviews (*re Any Means Necessary*)

Also available is Jack Mars' #1 bestselling LUKE STONE THRILLER series (7 books), which begins with Any Means Necessary (Book #1), a free download with over 800 five star reviews!

VENGEANCE ZERO
(An Agent Zero Spy Thriller—Book #10)

## Jack Mars

Jack Mars is the USA Today bestselling author of the LUKE STONE thriller series, which includes seven books. He is also the author of the new FORGING OF LUKE STONE prequel series, comprising six books; and of the AGENT ZERO spy thriller series, comprising ten books (and counting).

Jack loves to hear from you, so please feel free to visit www.Jackmarsauthor.com to join the email list, receive a free book, receive free giveaways, connect on Facebook and Twitter, and stay in touch!

# BOOKS BY JACK MARS

## LUKE STONE THRILLER SERIES
ANY MEANS NECESSARY (Book #1)
OATH OF OFFICE (Book #2)
SITUATION ROOM (Book #3)
OPPOSE ANY FOE (Book #4)
PRESIDENT ELECT (Book #5)
OUR SACRED HONOR (Book #6)
HOUSE DIVIDED (Book #7)

## FORGING OF LUKE STONE PREQUEL SERIES
PRIMARY TARGET (Book #1)
PRIMARY COMMAND (Book #2)
PRIMARY THREAT (Book #3)
PRIMARY GLORY (Book #4)
PRIMARY VALOR (Book #5)
PRIMARY DUTY (Book #6)

## AN AGENT ZERO SPY THRILLER SERIES
AGENT ZERO (Book #1)
TARGET ZERO (Book #2)
HUNTING ZERO (Book #3)
TRAPPING ZERO (Book #4)
FILE ZERO (Book #5)
RECALL ZERO (Book #6)
ASSASSIN ZERO (Book #7)
DECOY ZERO (Book #8)
CHASING ZERO (Book #9)
VENGEANCE ZERO (Book #10)
ZERO ZERO (Book #11)